ARTICLE 5

TOR BOOKS BY KRISTEN SIMMONS

ARTICLE 5

BREAKING POINT

ARTICLE 5
KRISTEN SIMMONS

TOR®
TEEN

A TOM DOHERTY ASSOCIATES BOOK
NEW YORK

ARTICLE 5

A Tor Teen Book
Published by Tom Doherty Associates, LLC
175 Fifth Avenue
New York, NY 10010

www.tor-forge.com

Tor® is a registered trademark of Tom Doherty Associates, LLC.

ISBN 978-0-7653-2961-5

First Edition: January 2012
First Trade Paperback Edition: January 2013

Printed in the United States of America

0 9 8 7

FOR JASON.

Thanks for today.

ARTICLE 5

CHAPTER
1

BETH and Ryan were holding hands. It was enough to risk a formal citation for indecency, and they knew better, but I didn't say anything. Curfew rounds wouldn't begin for another two hours, and freedom was stolen in moments like these.

"Slow down, Ember," Ryan called.

Instead I walked faster, pulling away from our pack.

"Leave her alone," I heard Beth whisper. My face heated as I realized how I must look: not like a conscientious friend who was minding her own business, but like a bitter third wheel who couldn't stand seeing other couples happy. Which wasn't true—mostly.

Sheepishly, I fell into step beside Beth.

My best friend was tall for a girl, with an explosion of dark freckles centered at her nose and a cap of squiggly red hair that was untamable on chilly days like this one. She traded Ryan's arm for mine—which, if I was honest, *did* make me feel a little safer—and without a word, we danced on our tiptoes around the massive cracks in the sidewalk, just like we'd done since the fourth grade.

When the concrete path succumbed to gravel, I raised the front of my too-long khaki skirt so the hem didn't drag in the dust. I hated this skirt. The matching button-up top was so boxy and stiff that it made even busty Beth look flat as an ironing board. School uniforms were part of President Scarboro's new Moral Statute—one of many that had taken effect after the War—mandating that appearances comply with gender roles. I didn't know what gender they'd been aiming for with this outfit. Clearly it wasn't female.

We stopped at the gas station on the corner out of habit. Though it was the only one in the county still open, the lot was empty. Not many people could afford cars anymore.

We never went inside. There would be snacks and candy bars on the racks, all priced ten times higher than they'd been last year, and we didn't have any money. We stayed where we were welcome—on the outside. Three feet removed from the hundreds of tiny faces imprisoned behind the tinted glass. The board read:

MISSING! IF SIGHTED, CONTACT THE FEDERAL
BUREAU OF REFORMATION IMMEDIATELY!

Silently, we scanned the photographs of the foster-care runaways and escaped criminals for anyone we might know, checking for one picture in particular. Katelyn Meadows. A girl with auburn hair and a perky smile, who'd been in my junior history class last year. Mrs. Matthews had just told her she'd gotten the highest grade in the class on her midterm when the soldiers had arrived to take her to trial. "Article 1 violation," they'd said. Noncompliance with the national religion. It wasn't as if she'd been caught worshipping the devil; she'd missed school for Passover, and it had gone on to the school board as an unauthorized absence.

That was the last time anyone had seen her.

The next week Mrs. Matthews had been forced to take the Bill of Rights out of the curriculum. There was no discussion permitted on the topic. The soldiers posted at the door and at the recruiting table in the cafeteria made sure of that.

Two months after Katelyn's trial, her family had moved away. Her phone number had been disconnected. It was as if she'd never existed.

Katelyn and I hadn't been friends. It wasn't that I didn't like her; I thought she was all right, actually. We always said hi, if not much more. But since her sudden disappearance, something dark had kindled inside of me. I'd been more on guard. As compliant with the Statutes as possible. I didn't like to sit in the front row of class anymore, and I never walked home from school alone.

I couldn't be taken. I had to look out for my mother.

I finished my review. No Katelyn Meadows. Not this week.

"Did you hear about Mary What's-her-name?" Beth asked as we resumed our walk to my house. "She's a sophomore I think."

"Let's see, Mary What's-her-name," said Ryan pensively, pushing the glasses up his sharp nose. His uniform jacket made him look studious, whereas the other guys at school always looked like their mothers had dressed them up for Easter Sunday.

"No. What happened to her?" A chill tickled my skin.

"Same thing as Katelyn. Moral Militia came to take her to trial, and no one's seen her in a week." Beth's voice lowered, as it did when she suspected someone might be listening.

My stomach sank. They weren't actually called the Moral Militia, but they might as well have been. The uniformed soldiers actually belonged to the Federal Bureau of Reformation—the branch of the military the president had created at the end of the War three years ago. Their purpose was to enforce compliance with the Moral Statutes, to halt the chaos that had reigned during the five years that America had been mercilessly attacked. The hammer had come down hard: Any violation against the Statutes led to a citation, and in the worst cases, resulted in a trial before the FBR Board. People who went to trial—like Katelyn—didn't usually come back.

There were all sorts of theories. Prison. Deportation. A few months ago I'd heard a crazy homeless man spouting off about mass executions, before he'd been carted away. Regardless of the rumors, reality was bleak. With each new Statute issued, the MM became more powerful, more self-righteous. Hence the nickname.

"They took a freshman from gym, too," said Ryan soberly. "I heard they didn't even let him change back into his uniform."

First Katelyn Meadows, now Mary Something and another boy. And Mary and the boy within the last two weeks. I remembered when school had been safe—the only place we didn't have to think about the War. Now kids never ditched. There weren't any fights. People even turned in their homework on time. Everyone was scared their teacher would report them to the MM.

As we turned up my empty driveway, I glanced next door. The boxy house's white paneling was stained by dust and rain. The bushes had overgrown so much that they connected over the concrete steps. Long, fragile cobwebs sagged from the overhang. It looked haunted. In a way, it was.

That had been *his* house. The house of the boy I loved.

Deliberately, I looked away and climbed our front porch stairs to let my friends inside.

My mother was sitting on the couch. She had at least four too many clips in her hair and was wearing a shirt that she'd stolen from my closet. I didn't mind. The truth was I wasn't much into clothes. Sorting through a collection of worn hand-me-downs at a donation center hadn't exactly cultivated my desire to shop.

What I *did* mind was that she was reading a paperback with a half-naked pirate on the cover. That stuff was illegal now. She'd probably gotten it from someone she volunteered with at the soup kitchen. The place was chock-full of unemployed women spreading their passive-aggressive contraband beneath the Moral Militia's nose.

"Hi, baby. Hi, kids," my mother said, hardly moving. She didn't look up until she finished reading her page, then she jammed a bookmark in place and stood. I kept my mouth shut about the book, even though I probably should have told her not to bring that stuff home. It obviously made her happy, and it was better than her reading it on the porch, like she sometimes did when feeling particularly mutinous.

"Hi, Mom."

She kissed me noisily on the cheek, then hugged my friends at the same time before releasing us to our homework.

We pulled out our big heavy books and began deciphering the mechanical world of precalculus. It was horrid work—I detested math—but Beth and I had made a pact not to drop. Rumor was, next year, girls weren't even going to be able to take math anymore, so we suffered through in silent rebellion.

Smiling sympathetically at my expression, my mother patted my head and offered to make us all hot chocolate. After a few minutes of frustration, I followed her into the kitchen. She'd forgotten to water her ficus plant again, and it drooped pitifully. I filled a glass from the sink and poured it into the pot.

"Bad day?" she ventured. She spooned the chocolate powder into four mugs from a blue canister with a picture of a sunrise on the front. Horizons brand food was government owned, and all we could get with our meal rations.

I leaned against the counter and scuffed my heel against the floor, still thinking about the two new abductees, the contraband. The empty house next door.

"I'm fine," I lied. I didn't want to scare her by telling her about Mary Something, and I still didn't want to rag her about the book. She hated when I got on her back about the rules. She could be sort of reactive sometimes.

"How was work?" I changed the subject. She didn't get paid at the soup kitchen, but we still called it work. It made her feel better.

She didn't miss my obvious avoidance, but she let it drop and launched into a full story about Misty Something dating Kelly Something's boyfriend from high school, and . . . I didn't bother keeping up. I just nodded and soon was smiling. Her enthusiasm was infectious. By the time the teakettle whistled, I felt much better.

She was reaching for the mugs when someone knocked on the door. I went to answer it, thinking that it was probably Mrs. Crowley from across the street, stopping by to visit my mother like she did every day.

"Ember, wait—" The fear in Beth's voice made me stop and turn back toward the living room. She was kneeling on the couch, her hand on the curtain. The color had drained from her already-fair complexion.

But it was too late. My mom unlatched the dead bolt and opened the door.

Two Moral Militia soldiers stood on our front steps.

They were in full uniform: navy blue flak jackets with large wooden buttons, and matching pants that bloused into shiny boots. The most recognized insignia in the country, the American flag flying over a cross, was painted on their breast pockets, just above the initials FBR. Each of them had a standard-issue black baton, a radio, and a gun on his belt.

One of the soldiers had short brown hair that grayed around his temples, and wrinkles around the corners of his mouth that made him appear too old for his age. His narrow companion brushed at his tawny mustache impatiently.

I sagged in disappointment. Somewhere in the back of my

mind, I had hoped that one of them was *him*. It was a fleeting moment of weakness whenever I saw a uniform, and I kicked myself for it.

"Ms. Lori Whittman?" The first soldier asked, without looking her in the face.

"Yes," my mother replied slowly.

"I need to see some ID." He didn't bother to introduce himself, but his name tag read BATEMAN. The other was CONNER.

"Is there a problem?" There was a snarky tinge to her tone, one I hoped they didn't pick up on. Beth came up close behind me, and I could feel Ryan beside her.

"Just get your ID, ma'am," Bateman said irritably.

My mother pulled away from the door without inviting them in. I blocked the threshold, trying not to look as small as I felt. I could not let them search the house; we had too much contraband out to avoid a citation. I tilted my head subtly to Beth, and she meandered back to the couch, stuffing the romance novel my mother had been reading beneath the cushions. My mind raced through the other things she had: more *inappropriate* paperbacks, old magazines from before the War, a home manicure kit. I'd even heard that my favorite book, Mary Shelley's *Frankenstein*, had made the list, and I knew that was right on top of my nightstand. We weren't scheduled for an inspection tonight; we'd just had one last month. Everything had been left out.

A burning ignited in my chest, like the flicker of a lighter. And then I could hear my heart, thudding against my ribs. It startled me. A long time had passed since I'd been aware of that feeling.

Bateman tried to look past me, but I blocked his view. His brow lifted in judgment, and my blood boiled. Over the past year the MM's presence in Louisville—and all the remaining U.S. cities—had increased tenfold. It seemed there wasn't enough for them to do; harassing citizens appeared to be a high priority. I stuffed down the resentment and tried to stay composed. It was unwise to be impolite to the MM.

There were two cars parked on the street, a blue van and a smaller car that looked like an old police cruiser. On the side of each was the FBR emblem. I didn't need to read the motto below to know what it said: One Whole Country, One Whole Family. It always gave me a little jolt of inadequacy, like my little two-person family wasn't *whole* enough.

There was someone in the driver's seat of the van, and another soldier outside on the sidewalk in front of our house. As I watched, the back of the van opened and two more soldiers hopped out onto the street.

Something was wrong. There were too many soldiers here just to fine us for violating a Statute.

My mom returned to the door, digging through her purse. Her face was flushed. I stepped shoulder to shoulder with her and forced my breath to steady.

She found her wallet and pulled out her ID. Bateman checked it quickly before stuffing it into the front pocket of his shirt. Conner lifted a paper I hadn't seen him holding, ripped off the sticky backing, and slapped it against our front door.

The Moral Statutes.

"Hey," I heard myself say. "What are you—"

"Lori Whittman, you are under arrest for violation of the

Moral Statutes, Section 2, Article 5, Part A revised, pertaining to children conceived out of wedlock."

"*Arrest?*" My mom's voice hitched. "What do you mean?"

My mind flashed through the rumors I'd heard about sending people to prison for Statute violations, and I realized with a sick sense of dread that these weren't rumors at all. It was Katelyn Meadows all over again.

"Article 5!" Ryan blurted from behind us. "How could that apply to *them?*"

"The current version was revised on February twenty-fourth. It includes all dependent children under the age of eighteen."

"February twenty-fourth? That was only Monday!" Beth said sharply.

Conner reached across the threshold of our home and grabbed my mother's shoulder, pulling her forward. Instinctively, I wrapped both hands around his forearm.

"Let go, miss," he said curtly. He looked at me for the first time, but his eyes were strange, as if they didn't register that I was present. I loosened my hold but did not release his arm.

"What do you mean '*arrest*'?" My mother was still trying to process.

"It's quite clear, Ms. Whittman." Bateman's tone was condescending. "You are out of compliance with the Moral Statutes and will be tried by a senior officer of the Federal Bureau of Reformation."

I struggled against Conner's firm hold on her shoulder. He was pulling us outside. I asked him to stop, but he ignored me.

Bateman restrained my mother's opposite shoulder, dragging her down the steps. Conner released her arm for a moment to jerk me aside, and with a stunted cry, I fell. The grass was cold and damp and soaked through my skirt at the hip, but the blood burned in my face and neck. Beth ran to my side.

"What's going on here?" I glanced up and saw Mrs. Crowley, our neighbor, wrapped in a shawl and wearing sweatpants. "Lori! Are you all right, Lori? Ember!"

I sprang to my feet. My eyes shot to the soldier who had been waiting outside. He had an athletic build and gelled blond hair, neatly parted on the side. His tongue slid over his teeth beneath pursed lips, reminding me of the way sand shifts when a snake slithers beneath it.

He was walking straight toward me.

No! The breath scraped my throat. I fought the urge to run.

"Don't touch me!" my mother shrieked at Bateman.

"Ms. Whittman, don't make this harder than it has to be," responded Bateman. My stomach pitched at the apathy in his voice.

"Get the hell off my property," my mother demanded, fury stabbing through her fear. "We're not animals; we're people! We have rights! You're old enough to remember——"

"Mom!" I interrupted. She was just going to make it worse. "Officer, this isn't right. This is a mistake." My voice sounded far away.

"There's no mistake, Ms. Miller. Your records have already been reviewed for noncompliance," said Morris, the soldier before me. His green eyes flashed. He was getting too close.

In a split second, his vicelike fists shot out and trapped both my wrists. I bucked against him, retracting my arms in an attempt to shake him loose. He was stronger and jerked me close, so that our bodies slapped together. The breath was squashed from my lungs.

For a second I saw the hint of a smirk cross his face. His hands, cuffing my fists, slipped behind my lower back and drew me in tighter. Every part of me went rigid.

A warning screamed in my head. I tried to get away, but this seemed to drive new excitement into him. He was actually *enjoying* this. His hard grip was making my hands prickle with numbness.

Somewhere in the street I heard a car door slam.

"Stop," I managed.

"Let go!" Beth shouted at him.

Conner and Bateman pulled my mother away. Morris's hands were still on my wrists. I heard nothing over the ringing in my ears.

And then I saw him.

His hair was black and gleaming in the last splinters of sunlight. It was short now, cleanly cut like the other soldiers', and his eyes, sharp as a wolf's, were so dark I could barely see the pupils. JENNINGS was spelled out in perfect gold letters over the breast of his pressed uniform. I had never in my life seen him look so grave. He was nearly unrecognizable.

My heart was beating quickly, fearfully, but beating all the same. Just because he was near. My body had sensed him before my mind had.

"Chase?" I asked.

I thought of many things all at the same time. I wanted to run to him despite everything. I wanted him to hold me as he had the night before he'd left. But the pain of his absence returned fast, and reality sliced at my insides.

He'd chosen *this* over me.

I grasped on to the hope that maybe he could help us.

Chase said nothing. His jaw was bulging, as though he was grinding his teeth, but otherwise his face revealed no emotion, no indication that the home he'd been raised in was twenty feet away. He stood between where Morris held me and the van. It occurred to me that he was the driver.

"Don't forget why you're here," Bateman snapped at him.

"Chase, tell them they're wrong." I looked straight at him. He didn't look at me. He didn't even move.

"Enough. Get back in the van, Jennings!" ordered Bateman.

"Chase!" I shouted. I felt my face twist with confusion. Was he really going to ignore me?

"Don't speak to him," Bateman snapped at me. "Will someone *please* do something with this girl?"

My terror grew, closing off the world around me. Chase's presence didn't soothe me as it had in the past. The mouth that had once curved into a smile and softened against my lips was a hard, grim line. There was no warmth in him now. This was not the Chase I remembered. This wasn't *my* Chase.

I couldn't take my eyes off of his face. The pain in my chest nearly doubled me over.

Morris jerked me up, and instinct tore through me. I reared back, breaking free from his grasp, and wrapped my arms around my mother's shoulders. Someone yanked me back. My grip was slipping. They were pulling her away from me.

"NO!" I screamed.

"Let go of her!" I heard a soldier bark. "Or we'll take you, too, Red."

Beth's fists, which had knotted in my school uniform, were torn from my clothing. Through tear-filled eyes I saw that Ryan had restrained her, his face contorted with guilt. Beth was crying, reaching out for me. I didn't let go of my mother.

"Okay, okay," I heard my mother say. Her words came out very fast. "Please, officer, *please* let us go. We can talk right here."

A sob broke from my throat. I couldn't stand the obedience in her tone. She was so afraid. They were trying to separate us again, and I knew, more than anything else, that I could not let them do that.

"Be gentle with them, please! *Please!*" Mrs. Crowley begged.

In one heave, Morris ripped me from my mother. Enraged, I swiped at his face. My nails caught the thin skin of his neck, and he swore loudly.

I saw the world through a crimson veil. I wanted him to attack me just so I could lash out at him again.

His green eyes were beady in anger, and he snarled as he jerked the nightstick from his hip. In a flash it was swinging back above his head.

I braced my arms defensively over my face.

"STOP!" My mother's pitch was strident. I could hear it above the screaming adrenaline in my ears.

Someone pushed me, and I was flung hard to the ground, my hair covering my face, blocking my vision. There was a stinging in my chest that stole the breath from my lungs. I crawled back to my knees.

"Jennings!" I heard Bateman shout. "Your CO will hear about this!"

Chase was standing in front of me, blocking my view.

"Don't hurt him!" I panted. Morris's weapon was still ready to strike, though now it was aimed at Chase.

"You don't need that." Chase's voice was very low. Morris lowered the stick.

"You said you'd be cool," he hissed, glaring at Chase.

Had Chase told this soldier—*Morris*—about me? Were they friends? How could he be friends with someone like that?

Chase said nothing. He didn't move.

"Stand down, Jennings," Bateman commanded.

I scrambled up and glared at the man in charge. "Who the hell do you think you are?"

"Watch your mouth," snapped Bateman. "You've already struck a soldier. How much deeper a hole are you looking to dig?"

I could hear my mother arguing through her hiccuping sobs. When they began to move her toward the van again, I lunged forward, my hands tangling in Chase's uniform. Desperation blanketed me. They were going to take her away.

"Chase, please," I begged. "Please tell them this is a mistake. Tell them we're good people. You know us. You know *me*."

He shook me off as though some disgusting thing had touched him. That stung more than anything could in this moment. I stared at him in shock.

The defeat was devastating.

My arms were pulled behind me and latched into place by Morris's strong grip. I didn't care. I couldn't even feel them.

Chase stepped away from me. Bateman and Conner ushered my mother to the van. She looked over her shoulder at me with scared eyes.

"It's okay, baby," she called, trying to sound confident. "I'll find out who's responsible for this, and we'll have a nice long chat."

My gut twisted at the prospect.

"She doesn't even have her shoes on!" I shouted at the soldiers.

There were no more words as they loaded my mother in the back of the van. When she disappeared inside, I felt something tear within me, loosing what felt like acid into my chest. It scalded my insides. It made my breath come faster, made my throat burn and my lungs clench.

"Walk to the car," Morris ordered.

"What? No!" Beth cried. "You can't take her!"

"What are you doing?" Ryan demanded.

"Ms. Miller is being taken into custody by the federal government in accordance with Article 5 of the Moral Statutes. She's going into rehabilitation."

I was getting very tired all of a sudden. My thoughts weren't making sense. Blurry lines formed around my vision, but I couldn't blink them back. I gulped down air, but there wasn't enough.

"Don't fight me, Ember," Chase ordered quietly. My heart broke to hear him say my name.

"Why are you doing this?" The sound of my voice was distant and weak. He didn't answer me. I didn't expect an answer anyway.

They led me to the car, parked behind the van. Chase

opened the door to the backseat and sat me down roughly. I fell to my side, feeling the leather dampen from my tears.

Then Chase was gone. And though my heart quieted, the pain in my chest remained. It stole my breath and swallowed me whole, and I tumbled into darkness.

CHAPTER
2

"MOM, I'm home!" I kicked off my flats at the front door and proceeded straight down the hallway to the kitchen, where I heard her laughing.

"Ember, there you are! Look who's back!" My mother was standing at the stove, beaming like she'd just gotten me a shiny new toy. Skeptical, I rounded the corner and stopped cold.

Chase Jennings was in my kitchen.

Chase Jennings, who I'd played tag with and raced bikes with and had a crush on since before I knew what crushes were.

Chase Jennings, who had grown into a rough-around-the-edges kind of handsome; tall and built and so much more dangerous than the scrawny fourteen-year-old I'd last seen. He was leaning back casually in his chair, hands in his denim pockets, a mess of black hair stuffed beneath an old baseball cap.

I was staring. I looked away quickly, feeling the flush rise in my cheeks.

"Um . . . hi."

"Hey, Ember," he said easily. "You grew up."

MY eyes blinked open as the FBR cruiser shuddered to a stop. Slowly, I sat up, head heavy and clouded, and pushed the hair from my face.

Where was I?

Night had descended, and the darkness aided my disorientation. I rubbed my eyes, catching a glimpse of the blond soldier's profile through the thick glass partition between the front seats and the back. *Morris.* I remembered his name badge. I looked out the front windshield, distorted by the barricade. With a jolt of panic, I realized I was searching for a van. One that was no longer in front of us.

Then I remembered.

The MM. The arrest. *Chase.*

Where was my mother? I should have been watching! I banged on the glass divider, but Morris and the driver didn't even flinch. It was soundproof. Frightened now, I crossed my arms over my chest and eased back into the leather seat, trying to gain a lock on my bearings.

Without a car or a television, we'd been isolated in our neighborhood. The FBR had shut down the local newspaper on account of the scarcity of resources, and had blocked the Internet to stifle rebellion, so we couldn't even see pictures of how our town had changed. We knew Louisville had been relatively lucky during the War. No bombed buildings. No evacuated areas. But even if it didn't look damaged, it did look *different.*

We passed the lighted convention center, now a distribution plant for Horizons brand food. Then the airport, which had been converted to FBR Weapons Manufacturing when commercial air travel had been prohibited. There had been an influx of soldiers in this area when they'd changed Fort Knox and Fort Campbell into FBR stations. Row after row of blue cruisers were now parked in the lot at the old fairgrounds.

We were the only car on the freeway. Knowing I was out with the MM when *only* the MM could be out, surrounded by the flags and crosses and sunrise logos, chilled me to the bone. I felt like Dorothy in some twisted *Wizard of Oz*.

An exit ramp led us into downtown Louisville, and at the bottom of the curve, we rolled through an empty four-way stop. The driver aimed toward a monstrous brick high-rise, which spread out on the bottom floors like the tentacles of an octopus. Its yellow eyes—windows, lit by a team of generators—peered out in all directions. We were at the city hospital.

I couldn't see the van anywhere. Where had they taken my mother?

Chase Jennings. I tried to swallow, but his name on my tongue felt like boiling water that I couldn't push down.

How could he? I'd trusted him. I'd even thought that I loved him, and not just that, but that he'd genuinely cared for me, too.

He'd changed. Completely.

The driver parked the cruiser close to the building in a shadowed lot. A moment later Morris opened the back door and yanked me out by the forearm. The three red lines where my fingernails had raked his skin were bright against his white neck.

The hum of the generators filled the night, a sharp contrast to the soundproof containment of the cruiser. He led me toward the building, where, in the gleam of the sliding glass doors beneath the Emergency Department sign, I caught my reflection. Pale face. Swollen eyes. My boxy uniform shirt drooped on one side where Beth had stretched it trying to save me, and my knotted braid hung down my ribs.

We didn't go inside.

"I always pictured you blond," said Morris. His tone, though bland, held a hint of disappointment. I worried again what sort of things Chase had told him.

"Is my mother here?" I asked.

"Keep your mouth shut."

So he could talk, but I couldn't? I scowled at him, focusing on the place where my fingernails had drawn blood. Knowing I was capable of defending myself made me feel a little braver. He jerked me across the driveway, where floodlights washed over a navy school bus that cast a looming shadow into the parking lot. Several girls were lined up there, guards posted on either side.

As we neared, a chill ran through me. The soldier had used the word *rehabilitation* earlier, but I didn't know what that entailed or where this facility—if it even was a facility—was located. I pictured one of the massive temporary foster homes erected during the War, or worse, the state penitentiary. They couldn't possibly be taking me there; I hadn't done anything wrong myself. Being born wasn't a crime, even if they were treating me like a criminal.

But what if they were taking my mother to jail?

I remembered the kids who had disappeared from school. Katelyn Meadows and Mary Something and that freshman boy I didn't know. They'd been involved with trials for Article violations, for benign things like missing school for a non-approved religious holiday. It wasn't like they'd killed anybody. And yet Katelyn hadn't come back, and Mary and the boy had been gone a week or two already.

I tried to remember what Beth had said about Katelyn, but I was shaking so hard my brain seemed to rattle. *Her phone number was disconnected. She isn't on the Missing Persons boards. Her family moved away after the trial.*

Moved away, I thought. Or they'd all gotten on a bus and disappeared.

I fell in line behind a heavyset girl with a short blond bob. She was crying so hard she began to choke. Another was rocking back and forth with her arms wrapped around her stomach. They all looked around my age or younger. One dark-haired girl couldn't have been more than ten.

Morris loosened his hold around my bruised arm as we approached two guards. One had a black eye. The other flipped through a list of names on a clipboard.

"Ember Miller," Morris reported. "How many left until they transport, Jones?"

My knees weakened. I wondered again where they were taking us. Somewhere distant, otherwise I would have heard about it at school or from the gossip tree at the soup kitchen. It struck me that *no one* but these soldiers knew our destination. Not even my mother. Beth would look for us, but she'd get a citation or worse if she asked the MM too many questions.

I had a terrible feeling that I was about to disappear. That I was about to become the next Katelyn Meadows.

"Three more. They just radioed in. We should be heading out within the hour," the soldier responded to Morris.

"Thank God," said Morris. "These little bastards are vicious."

The soldier with the black eye grunted. "Don't I know it."

"If you're going to give us a citation, I'll get you the money," I blurted.

In truth, we didn't have the money. We'd already used up nearly all of our government assistance check this month, but they didn't need to know that. I could hock some of our stuff. I'd done it before.

"Who said anything about a citation?" Morris asked.

"What do you want then? I'll get it. Just tell me where my mother is."

"It's an offense to bribe a soldier," he warned, smirking as if this were a game.

There had to be something. I couldn't get on that bus.

He saw my eyes dart behind him and anticipated my flight before I took the first step. In a flash his rough grip locked around my waist.

"*No!*" I struggled, but he was much stronger and had already trapped my arms against my sides. He chuckled—a sound that plagued me with fear—and shoved me forcefully up the steps with the assistance of the other soldiers.

It's happening, I realized with morbid clarity. *I'm about to disappear.*

The soldier with the black eye had climbed up the stairs behind me and was now tapping his baton in one hand.

"Sit down," he ordered.

I had no choice but to do what he said.

Never before had I felt so heavy. I trudged down the long

rubber mat to an open seat in the middle and crumpled onto the bench, vaguely registering the sobs of the girls around me. A trickle of numbness inched down my spine, anesthetizing my fear and worry. I felt nothing.

The girl next to me had long, wavy black hair and mocha skin. She glanced my way then continued to bite her nails, irritated but not scared. Her legs were crossed at the knees, and she wore a tight T-shirt and pajama pants.

"Forgot your shoes." She pointed at my feet. My socks were muddy and grass stained. I hadn't noticed.

"What did they get you for?" she asked, without looking up from her hand.

I didn't say anything.

"*Hello?*" she said. "Ember, right? I'm talking to you."

"Sorry. How do you know . . ." I looked at her face and did recognize her faintly.

"I went to Western last year. Rosa Montoya? We had English together. Thanks for remembering."

"We did?" I felt my nose scrunch up. I was usually better with faces.

She rolled her eyes. "Don't worry. I was only there for a couple months. Between placements, you know."

"Placements?"

"Group homes. Foster care, *princesa*. So what are you in for?" She spelled the words out slowly. I did remember her now. She had sat in the back of the classroom, biting her nails, looking bored, much as she did today. She'd come in mid-semester and had left before finals. We'd never said a word to each other.

I wondered if there were other girls from my school on this bus. No one else looked familiar when I glanced around.

"The soldier said an Article 5," I answered.

"Ooh. You got hauled into rehab because your mom's the village bicycle."

"The . . . what?"

A girl in the back began sobbing louder. Someone shouted for her to shut up.

"The village bicycle. Everyone's had a ride," she said sarcastically. Then she rolled her eyes. "Ay. Don't look so innocent. Soldiers? They'll eat that up. Look, *princesa*, if it makes you feel any better, I *wish* I didn't know my dad. Consider yourself lucky."

I didn't like her assuming I didn't know who my father was, even if it was the truth. Most of the men attracted to my mom's free spirit tended to beat it for the same reason.

Most, but not all. Her last—and worst—boyfriend, Roy, had thought he could control it, but even he had been wrong.

I was glad Rosa and I hadn't spoken before at school. I nearly wished we weren't talking now, but she did seem to have some idea about what was happening.

The bus lurched out of the ER circle, and as it did I felt a physical pain tear through me, as though my limbs were being pulled in all different directions. My mother and I had always been together, through everything. Now I'd lost her, and who knew what she was going to say, what she was going to *do*, to try to get home.

Anger rose above the grief. Anger at myself. I didn't fight hard enough. I didn't play nice enough. I had let her go.

The bus climbed back onto the highway. Garbage was piled up against the line of broken-down vehicles that lined the slow lane. I recognized the old houses and the painted silos in front of the old University of Louisville. The Red Cross had turned the campus into a housing colony for people displaced by the War. I could see dim candlelight still burning in a few of the higher dorm-room windows.

"Where are they taking us?" I asked Rosa.

"They won't say," she said. Then she smiled. There was a gap between her two front teeth. "I already asked the guard back there. The one with the shiner."

I could picture this girl punching someone in the face. I thought of Morris and the scratches on his neck, and it seemed surreal that I had done that. Attacking a soldier—that was *insane*.

"Will my mother be there?"

The girl looked at me as if I were a full idiot.

"Kiss that dream good-bye, *chica*," she told me. "An Article 5 means that she's not even your mom anymore. You're property of the government now."

I pinched my eyes closed, trying to ignore her words, but they echoed in my head.

She's wrong, I told myself. *And we were wrong, too.* I forced myself to picture Katelyn Meadows walking up the driveway of her two-story house in . . . Indiana. Or Tennessee. She'd moved there because her dad's job had been relocated. It had happened fast. Jobs *were* scarce these days. That's why even her friends didn't know. She was probably acing her history tests at some new high school. *Believe it*, I thought desperately; *it could happen*. But my imagination was too brightly colored to fit reality. It was a lie and I knew it.

My mind turned to Chase, and there was such a harsh burn within me that I nearly gasped. *How could he?* I pressed my cheek against the cold window as the countryside grew black as the night.

"TRUTH *or dare?*"

I smiled at his question. We'd played this game a thousand times when we were kids. The dares always got us in trouble.

"Truth," I said, soaking in this world he'd brought me to. The woods ablaze, the trees defining every graduating degree of red and yellow. The sun, warm on my face, and the chatter of the birds. It was so different here than the noise and asphalt of the city. The perfect place for secrets.

"Have you ever liked someone you shouldn't?"

"Like someone with a girlfriend?" I asked, weaving around a tall tree in our path

"Yeah. Or a friend."

His question caught me off guard, and I missed a step.

"Yes," I answered, trying not to read too much into his smile. "Truth or dare?"

"Truth." He reached for my hand, and I tried not to be stiff and awkward, but I was, because this was Chase; we'd grown up together, and so what? Maybe I'd loved him for my entire life, but he didn't think about me that way because . . . well . . . we were friends.

Oh.

"Do you like . . . pb and j? Because you used to, and that's what I packed for lunch." I finished lamely.

"Yes. Truth?" His thumb skimmed along the inside of my wrist, and my whole body reacted as if I'd been shocked. It scared me how much I liked it, how much I wanted more.

"Sure."

"*Would it be weird if I kissed you?*"

We'd stopped walking. I hadn't even noticed until he shifted his weight, the leaves crunching loudly beneath his feet. He laughed, then cleared his throat. I couldn't look up. I felt like glass, like he could look inside me and see the truth: that I'd waited half my life to kiss him. That no boy I'd ever met compared to him.

He leaned down, so close that I could feel the air warm between us.

"*Do you dare me?*" *he whispered in my ear.*

I nodded, my pulse flying.

He lifted my face gently. When his lips touched mine everything within me slowed and melted. The tightness in my throat disappeared, the nervous tingle in my chest eased. Everything faded. Everything but him.

Something changed between us then, a spark of light, of heat. His lips pressed mine open, teasing first, then tasting. One of his hands pulled me nearer, the other slid under my hair, pressing beneath the band of my loosened ponytail. My fingers longed for his skin and found his face, traced the strong lines of his neck.

He pulled away suddenly, breath uneven, gaze piercing mine. His arms stayed locked around me, though, and I was glad, because my legs were weak.

"*Truth?*" *I whispered.*

He smiled, and my heart soared. "*Truth.*"

"EVERYBODY up!"

I snapped alert at the man's voice booming off the bus's elongated compartment.

Morning light glared in through the windows, and I sheltered my face—swollen from my earlier crying jag—from its cheerful mocking. I wasn't sure if I'd slept or just drifted in and out of consciousness. Since we'd left Louisville, I'd relived Chase taking my mother at least a hundred times.

Rosa and I had talked some more. She'd been charged with an Article 3—her cousin had claimed her as a dependent on her tax forms, which didn't exactly fit the whole one-man-plus-one-woman-equals-kids thing—but since the West Virginia state line we'd been silent. Cool as she was, Rosa couldn't fake shock. We were a long way from home.

The bus hissed and slowed to a stop outside a large brick building. Implanted in the dying grass alongside the drive was a green metal sign with glowing white letters:

GIRLS' REFORMATORY
AND REHABILITATION CENTER.

I looked around anxiously, wondering, *hoping*, that there was a separate building for my mother. That maybe they'd brought her here to rehabilitation, too. At least that way we'd be close and could straighten out this mess together. But my dismal intuition was right. There were no buses following ours.

We filed out of the seats one at a time. My back and neck ached from spending hours confined to the same position. As we exited the bus, soldiers holding batons flanked us on either side, as though we were running the gauntlet. Rosa blew a kiss to the man with the black eye, and his face reddened.

From outside the bus, I had a better view. We stood before an old building, like the kind you see in history books surrounded by men wearing ruffled shirts and curly wigs. It was red brick, but some of the bricks had faded to gray, giving the illusion that its flat face was potholed. The front doors were tall and freshly painted white and bordered on both sides by stout columns supporting a triangular overhang. My eyes wandered up six floors, squinting in the fresh morning sun. A copper bell hung dormant in a tower on the roof.

Across the street behind me was a clover-patched knoll, and on it a long set of stairs that descended to an open pavilion and a more modern, glass-plated building. Another set of stairs disappeared below this level down the hill. It looked like one of the old college campuses that had been shut down during the War.

When I turned back toward the main building, a woman had materialized at the top of the stairs. Next to the soldiers she was petite but even more severe. Her shoulders arched back beneath her snow-white hair. Her whole countenance seemed to withdraw into each orifice, making her eyes look overly large and sunken and her mouth appear toothless when closed.

She wore a white buttoned-up blouse and a navy pleated skirt, thin enough to show the bones of her pelvis jutting forward through it. A baby blue handkerchief hung in a sailor's knot around her neck. The MM appeared to be apprising her of the situation and awaiting orders, which seemed odd to me. I'd never seen a woman in the FBR's chain of command. As the woman glared down the line of girls, all the things I didn't know, all the uncertainty, swelled within me. Things may not have been perfect at home, but at least I'd known what to expect—at least until yesterday. Now nothing felt familiar. Nowhere felt safe. I hunched, grasping my hands together to keep them from shaking.

"Great," Rosa said under her breath. "*Sisters.*"

"Is she a nun?" I whispered back, perplexed.

"Worse. Haven't you ever seen the Sisters of Salvation?" When I shook my head, she leaned closer. "They're the MM's answer to women's liberation."

I wanted to hear more—if the Sisters of Salvation were meant to counteract feminism, what was a woman doing in charge?—but just then her head snapped to the soldier beside her.

"Bring them in."

We were led into the main foyer of the brick building. Here, the floor was tiled and the walls were painted nursery-room peach. Beneath a staircase on the left, a hallway lined with doors extended to the end of the building.

One by one we were brought to a rectangular fold-out table where two check-in clerks, wearing the same white and navy uniforms, waited with files. After Rosa had identified herself in an overdone Latina accent, I stepped forward.

"Name?" a clerk with braces asked me without looking up.

"Ember Miller."

"Ember Miller. Yes, there she is. Another Article 5, Ms. Brock."

The frail but menacing woman behind her smiled an inauthentic welcome.

Article 5. That label was like a pin under my fingernail every time I heard it. I felt a rush of heat rise up my neck.

"Just call me Hester Prynne," I mumbled.

"Speak clearly, dear. What was that?" asked Ms. Brock.

"Nothing," I answered.

"If nothing is what you said, all the better to simply be silent."

I looked up, unable to hide the surprise from my face.

"She's a seventeen as well, Ms. Brock. She ages out in July."

My heart skipped a beat.

They can't possibly hold me until I'm eighteen. I'd considered the possibility of a couple days, or until we could arrange the citation money for bail, but July eighteenth was five months away! I'd done nothing wrong, and my mother, whose only crime had maybe been irresponsibility, needed me. I had to find her and get back home.

Katelyn Meadows never went home, a small, frightened voice in my brain said. A citation suddenly seemed too easy. An unrealistic punishment. Why would they waste money hauling me here if just to send us a bill? My throat tightened.

"Ms. Miller, I have record that you attacked a member of the Federal Bureau of Reformation yesterday," said Ms. Brock. I automatically glanced back for Rosa. She'd given a guard a black eye; why didn't she get in trouble?

"They were taking my mother!" I defended, but my mouth snapped shut at her glare.

"You will address me respectfully, as Ms. Brock, do you understand?"

"Um . . . sure. Yes."

"*Yes, Ms. Brock,*" she corrected.

"Yes. Ms. Brock." My skin felt very hot. I quickly understood what Rosa meant; Ms. Brock was almost worse than the soldiers.

She sighed with infinite patience. "Ms. Miller, I can make this time here very difficult for you or very easy. This is your last warning."

Her words put an instant chill on my humiliation.

"You are fortunate," continued Ms. Brock. "You'll be rooming with the Student Assistant. She has been with us for three years and will be able to answer any of your questions."

Three years? I didn't know places like this existed three days ago, much less three years ago. What had she done that had been so terrible that she'd been stuck here that long?

"Over with your cohorts, and remember what I said." Ms. Brock raised a withered hand to where Rosa and several other girls my age were standing. She had a skeptical gleam in her eyes, as though my birthday was hardly a deciding factor in my discharge.

On my way there I was stopped against the wall, where a stout, droopy-faced woman took my picture in front of a blue screen. I didn't smile. The cold reality of my situation was sinking in, filling me with dread.

Sisters. Cohorts. Ms. Brock's superior grin. This was not a temporary setup.

Bright blotches from the camera flash were still blocking my vision when I joined the others.

"I think the nut job is going to try to make us stay until we're eighteen," I whispered to Rosa.

"I'm not staying here until I'm eighteen," she said convincingly. When I spun toward her, she grinned, showing her gapped teeth. "Relax. Group homes like this, they always say that. Screw up enough, and you can get out on early release."

"How?" I demanded.

She opened her mouth to answer, but we were interrupted by two guards who entered through the main doors, escorting a girl in a hospital gown. They led her past the sign-in table and down a hallway to our right, holding her elbows as though she might fall without their support. The few seconds I saw her were enough to make my skin crawl. Her eyes stayed pinned to the floor, and the black, messy hair made her pallid face and exhaustion-bruised eyes stand out in sharp contrast. She looked like an overmedicated mental patient, but worse. She looked *empty*.

"What do you think happened to her?" I asked Rosa, disturbed.

"Maybe she's sick," she speculated weakly. Clearly she was contemplating her early release theory. Then she shrugged. I wished that I could be so dismissive, but I could not deny the impression the girl had left on me. She did look physically ill, but something told me a virus had not been the cause of her symptoms. What had she done? What had *they* done to her?

I wanted to ask, but just then we were corralled into a common room with chartreuse low-backed couches that smelled like moth balls. There were eight of us labeled for our age. Eight new seventeens. In a huddled mass across the room were at least a dozen others, probably sixteens or fifteens. I recognized at least two of them. Both underclassmen at Western. I was pretty sure one was named Jacquie, but she didn't meet my eyes when I glanced her way.

A group of residents had also arrived, all flashing eerily robotic smiles. They were dressed like clones of one another: Little black flats met long navy skirts, and matching long-sleeved tees topped them off. It was an utterly drab outfit, even for a fashion moron like me.

"Attention please, ladies," called Ms. Brock. The room silenced. "Welcome. I am Ms. Brock, the headmistress here at the Girls' Reformatory and Rehabilitation Center of West Virginia."

I shifted uncomfortably. Ms. Brock turned and seemed to stare straight at me.

"Section 2, Article 7 mandates that you become ladies, and until your eighteenth birthday you will be groomed to be nothing less than the very finest models of morality and chastity."

At the word *chastity,* Rosa snorted. Ms. Brock shot her a look of pure venom.

"The world has changed, my dears," she continued through her teeth, "and you are fortunate to be a part of that change. From today forward, it is my great hope that you press on with open minds and modest spirits. That you embrace your call to the Sisters of Salvation, and return to the dark world with one true mission: to spread the light.

"Now the hall monitors will show you to your dormitories."

I took a deep, quaking breath. No. I could *not* stay here five more months. I wasn't going to be a light-spreading messenger of crazy. I couldn't end up like that empty girl the soldiers had practically dragged down the hall. I had to get out of here and find my mother.

The crowd of androids parted, revealing a bright-faced girl with spirals of blond hair cascading down her shoulders. Pretty blue eyes matched a perky smile. All that was missing was the halo.

"Hi! I'm Rebecca Lansing, your roommate." Her annoyingly high-pitched voice sliced through the shuffle. "I'm *so* pleased to meet you, Ember." She motioned for me to follow her down the hallway beneath the stairs. I wondered how she knew who I was.

"I'll bet you are," I replied sourly, glancing around for Rosa. She'd already disappeared.

Rebecca frowned at my tone. "I know it's hard at first. But you'll get used to it. Pretty soon this will feel like home, but better. Like summer camp."

When I realized she wasn't joking, I swallowed hard.

Rebecca led me into a dorm room. Something about being around her made me feel grimy. My school uniform was still stained with grass and dirt from yesterday.

"This will be your side." She pointed to the twin bed nearest to the door. The mattress was thin as cardboard, covered by the thin pink blankets you see in hospitals, and flanked by matching furniture: a dresser on one side, a desk on the other. Atop the desk was a small aluminum reading light, a few thin notebooks, and a Bible. Rebecca's bed was pressed against the far wall under the window. Just as mine had been at home.

Tears stung my eyes, and I turned toward the wall so that Rebecca wouldn't see.

"I went ahead and got your uniform," Rebecca told me helpfully. She handed me a neatly folded blue ensemble and a gray wool sweater. "And I brought you up some breakfast. We're not supposed to have food in our rooms, but they made an exception because I'm the SA."

Whether Rebecca was human or not, I was grateful for the food.

"You've really been here three years?" I said between ravenous bites of granola.

"Oh, yes," she said in a sugary voice. "I love it here."

I felt as if I were in a science fiction story. The kind where they make you take pills that control your mind.

Rebecca had been dropped off by her parents before President Scarboro had instituted the Moral Statutes. They were missionaries and had gone to serve God overseas before international travel had been banned.

As Rebecca told me more, my shock wore off and turned into pity. Her parents hadn't contacted her since leaving the country, and though she adamantly defended that they were alive, I was doubtful. There was a lot of anti-American sentiment abroad during the War.

I couldn't help thinking what terrible parents they were to abandon their child, especially in a place like this. I questioned again if I had tried hard enough to reason with the soldiers who'd taken me, but though I swallowed the guilt, it weighed down my stomach like a rock.

Rebecca sat on the end of my bed and braided her yellow hair over her shoulder while I changed. She prattled on about how excited she was to have a new roommate and how we were going to be best friends, which put a halt to any questions I'd been thinking I might ask her about Ms. Brock and the Sisters of Salvation. Because the conversation seemed so superficial it had to be fake, and because I was pretty sure it *wasn't* fake, I blocked out her voice and checked my reflection in the mirror.

I'd never been conventionally pretty: My eyes were big and brown and I had long black lashes, but my eyebrows didn't arch right and my nose was slightly crooked. Now my complexion was ghoulish—not entirely unlike the girl the soldiers had escorted back into the building—and my cheekbones appeared too prominent, like the last hours had added ten hungry years to my life. The navy uniform was even worse than my school uniform, probably because I resented it a hundred times more.

I forced a deep breath. My hair smelled like the synthetic seat of a school bus. I quickly combed out the kinks with my fingers and tied it back into a ragged knot.

"Time for class," Rebecca chimed, catching my attention.

My brain began flipping through my options. I needed to find a phone. I'd try home first, just in case the MM had released my mother. If not, I'd call Beth to see if she'd heard anything about where they'd taken the Article violators.

When I glanced down at Rebecca, I found her overly excited at the prospect of showing me around. She had a position of some power here as a Student Assistant and could potentially tell on me if I got out of line. She looked like the type.

I was going to have to be covert.

A few minutes later we were walking to the pavilion, just across from the cafeteria, where nearly a hundred girls milled about. It could have been high school—the whispered gossip that preceded all new kids was here, too—but the mood was too somber. Instead of being curious or petty, they were afraid of us. As though we might do something crazy. It was a strange reaction considering I was thinking the same of them.

When the bell tolled, all conversation ceased. Girls darted away to their classes, where they fell into cookie-cutter lines. Rebecca pulled my arm, and I complied like a rag doll, allowing her to set me in place. Silence reigned over the pavilion.

Within moments, soldiers appeared to lead, follow, and flank each line. A young man with pockmarked cheeks and the build of a weasel passed me on his way to the back. His uniform read RANDOLPH. Another, at the front of the line, had an almost glowing complexion by comparison. He had a neatly shaved jaw and sandy-colored hair and would have been handsome had his blue eyes not been so vacant.

What does the MM do to suck out a person's soul like that? I banished the automatic conjuring of Chase from my mind.

"Ms. Lansing," acknowledged the almost-handsome guard.

"Good morning, Mr. Banks," she said sweetly. He gave her a quick, emotionless nod, as if to approve of her line formation. The whole interaction seemed awkward and forced.

"*Hola, princesa,*" whispered a girl behind me. I turned to see Rosa, noticing how she'd refused to tuck in her navy blouse. The redheaded girl behind her—the roommate, I guessed—had a look of disapproval on her face. Clearly, she wasn't pleased with the new living arrangements.

Her red hair reminded me of how much I already missed Beth.

It was comforting having Rosa nearby. Even if she was rude, at least she was real, and when the bell tolled and the heads of the lines dispersed, we stayed close, bound by our mistrust of the others.

We followed Rebecca down the stairs, past the laundry facility, medical clinic, and a squat brick office with a fire hydrant out front. There, the seventeens separated from the other lines and marched over a plot of grass connecting to a path that led us between two tall stone buildings. I hungrily surveyed the grounds, trying to form a mental map in my mind. It appeared there was only one way in and out: the main gate.

When Rosa spoke again, it was barely above a breath.

"Watch and learn."

I turned back, but she was already gone.

CHAPTER
3

WITH her skirt hitched up around her thighs, Rosa disappeared between the two buildings. The guards shouted things, words I couldn't make out because the adrenaline was already roaring through my body. One immediately tore after her. Another picked up his radio and gave a few clipped orders before following. The girls whispered feverishly, but no one moved.

The blood pounded through my temples. Where was she going? Had she seen an exit I hadn't?

The thought hit me that I should run the other direction. Rosa had distracted the guards and the rest of the seventeens; they might not notice if I slipped away. I could race back up the stairs toward the front gate and . . . and then what? Hide in the bushes until a car came through and sneak out behind it? *Right.* No one would notice that. The bus ride hadn't revealed any signs of civilization since before dawn, and it wasn't like I could walk down the highway wearing a reform-school uniform without someone reporting me.

Think!

A telephone. There had to be one in the dormitory. Or maybe in the medical clinic. *Yes!* The staff would need one in case someone was seriously injured. The clinic was close; we'd passed it just minutes ago. It was right beside that brick building with the fire hydrant.

All eyes were still trained on the alley between the buildings where Rosa had disappeared. Even the guards that remained close by were looking that way. The air prickled. I took a slow step back, the grass crunching beneath my newly issued black flats. It was now or never.

Then a hand clamped down hard on my arm. When I spun right, Rebecca's blue eyes were sending ice cold darts through me. Her fury was surprising. I hadn't thought she'd had it in her.

No, she mouthed to me. I tried to shake her off, but she grasped me harder. I could feel her nails digging into my skin. Her skin had whitened in reflection of the morning sun.

"Let go," I said in a low voice.

"They got her!" someone cried.

All the girls, Rebecca and myself included, inched curiously toward the break between the buildings. I'd managed to rid myself of my roommate's grip, but it hardly mattered now. The moment had passed. The guards were watching us now that Rosa had been captured. If any of us felt inspired to follow in her footsteps, they were ready. Rebecca had ruined my chances.

I pushed between two girls and saw Rosa, twenty feet in front of me, cornered inside the dead end of the alleyway, trapped. Our two line guards were trying to box her in. They held their arms out wide and low, like they were herding a chicken. Rosa shrieked as she burst through them up the middle, back toward the wide-eyed group of seventeens. The ugly soldier beat her there. He rammed into her from the side and sent her sprawling to the ground.

"No!" I shouted, struggling to reach her. A new guard blocked my way. The skin was tightly stretched across his face, and his insidious glare gave me chills.

Try it, he seemed to say, *and you'll be next.*

Everyone watched as the jeering, pock-faced Randolph contained the flailing Rosa with a knee, harshly planted between her shoulder blades. After catching his breath, he hauled her body to a stand and locked her hands behind her back with a zip tie.

And then he hit her.

My belly filled with horror as blood spewed from Rosa's nose and painted her dark skin. I would have screamed if I'd had the breath. I'd never in my life seen a man hit a woman. I knew Roy had hit my mom. I'd seen the aftereffects. But never the actual act. It was more violent than anything I could have imagined.

And then it hit me, like a punch to *my* face. If this was what could happen to us, to the girls in rehab, what were they doing to the people who actually committed the so-called crimes? What had Chase done to us? The urgency to flee grew even stronger. I was more afraid for my mother than ever before.

"She's crazy," I heard one of the seventeens say.

"*She's* crazy?" I said in disbelief. "Did you not see that he just—"

The girls beside me parted silently as Ms. Brock pushed

her way through. She stared at Rosa, then at me. My blood turned to ice.

"That he just what, dear?" she asked me, brows raised in either cold curiosity or challenge, I couldn't tell.

"He . . . he hit her," I said, immediately wishing I hadn't spoken at all.

"And placated the beastly child, thank God," she spouted with feigned relief. I felt my mouth go very dry.

She assessed Rosa down her pointy little nose for several seconds, clicking her tongue inside her mouth. "Banks, take Ms. Montoya to lower campus please."

"Yes ma'am." The sandy-haired guard shoved Rosa past me, leaving her attacker behind smirking with satisfaction. I tried to meet Rosa's eyes, but she still appeared dazed. The ripe twinge of blood elicited a wave of bile up my throat.

And then Ms. Brock turned, humming, and walked away.

WE spent the next hours in silent meditation. *Class*, they called it. Where we sat on stiff-backed wooden chairs and read until our eyes crossed, while cow-eyed attendants occasionally interjected comments like "Heads down," and "Don't slouch."

I was afraid for Rosa. They hadn't brought her back. Whatever was happening to her was taking a long time.

The guard Banks had returned, and he and Scary Randolph patrolled the rows, deterring any notion of escape or misconduct. None of the other girls whispered now. They seemed shaken by the morning's events and were on their best behavior.

Because no one, not even Rebecca, would pass me a sidelong glance to validate the craziness of the situation, I read. Nothing fictional like Shelley's *Frankenstein,* or even the Shakespeare we'd been reading in English. Nothing that in some way might have transported me from this hell.

We read the Statutes. I'd read them only halfheartedly in school, but now, as my eyes tumbled over the words again and again, I knew they would be seared into my brain forever.

Article 1 denied individuals the right to practice or "display propaganda" associated with an alternative religion to Church of America. Apparently this included taking off school for Passover, like Katelyn Meadows had done.

Article 2 banned all immoral paraphernalia and 3 defined the "Whole Family" as one man, one woman, and children. Traditional male and female roles were outlined in Article 4. The importance of a woman's subservience. The necessity for her to respect her male partner while he, in turn, supported the family as the provider and spiritual leader.

I thought again of my mom's one-time boyfriend. Roy had been neither a provider nor a spiritual leader, and when I searched for some clause prohibiting domestic violence, I found no mention of it, not even in Article 6, which outlawed divorce, and gambling, and everything else from subversive speech to owning a firearm. *How pathetically predictable.*

Article 5 I memorized. *Children are considered valid citizens when conceived by a married husband and wife. All other children are to be removed from the home and subjected to rehabilitation procedures.*

All the Articles had one thing in common: Violation permitted full prosecution by the Federal Bureau of Reformation.

But what did that mean, *prosecution?* Rehab? I wondered if

my mother was in a room like I was in right now, reading the Statutes, or if she was awaiting trial, possibly even in jail. I wondered if Chase had let her go, and if she was already waiting at home for me to call her and tell her where I was.

I raised my hand.

The Sister at the front of the room rose from her desk and walked toward me. Up close, I could see that she was younger than I had originally suspected. Maybe in her mid-thirties. But her gray peppered hair and drooping eyelids made her appear much older.

A sick shudder passed through me. The Sisters did to women what the MM did to men: tore away the soul and brainwashed what was left.

"Yes?" she said, not quite meeting my eyes.

"I've got to go to the bathroom." Rebecca, who was seated in front of me, flinched but did not look back.

"All right. Randolph, please escort Ms. Miller to the restroom."

"I can find it on my own," I said quickly, blushing. *What am I, five years old?*

"It's procedure," she said, and returned to her desk.

I stood, nervously biting my lower lip. I didn't want to go anywhere with this soldier alone. Even if he hadn't punched Rosa, he was too creepy.

Silently, he led me from the building, taking care not to stand directly in front of me, but at a slight angle so I was always in his peripheral vision. As we walked, an image of Chase filled my mind—Chase the soldier, in a uniform like Randolph's, carrying the same baton, the same gun. What was he doing now? Was he with my mother? Was he willing to stand before Morris's raised weapon for her, the way he'd done for me? Because no one here had blocked Randolph's fists.

I shut him firmly from my mind.

We left the classroom and proceeded down a linoleum-floored hallway toward the main entrance. Sun filtered through the windows. It looked almost summery outside.

There was a women's restroom just inside the front doors. I ducked in, waiting for a moment to make sure that Randolph wasn't going to follow me in. When he didn't, I darted over to the toilet and removed the porcelain lid to the tank.

There's one thing I can say about living without a father: You learn to problem-solve a lot of home-repair jobs on your own. It only took a second for me to unhook the chain, allowing the water to refill the tank, and lightly replace the lid.

A moment later I was back in the hallway.

"The toilet's broken," I told him. As I expected, he pushed past me to check for himself.

Apparently Randolph had not grown up living month-to-month on government checks. His family probably could afford to call the plumber. Densely, he flicked the handle several times, and sure enough, the toilet did not flush. He didn't even bother lifting the lid to check the chain.

"Isn't there another one?" I whined.

He nodded, radioing in the problem as we headed outside. The fresh air prickling through the loosely woven sweater gave me a rush. We turned left outside of the building and followed the stone path back around toward where Rosa had run several hours ago.

"There!" I said, walking more quickly past the alleyway

where I could still see Randolph hitting her. "The clinic will have a restroom, won't it?"

We were only twenty yards away. A dubious look crossed his face, and for a moment I thought he would argue just so I wouldn't dictate our course. But then he seemed to realize the inconsequentiality of my request, and we veered toward the clinic.

The waiting room was small and sterile and smelled vaguely of cleaning products. My shoes squeaked across the shiny floor as he pushed past a counter where a brunette nurse was reading the Bible. She looked up but didn't ask any questions as I made my way across the short hallway.

I found what I was looking for on the counter of a blood-draw station, right between a mini fridge and a plastic box of alcohol swabs and plastic syringes. A telephone. My heart leapt in anticipation.

As nonchalantly as I could, I entered the bathroom and closed the door, racking my brain for ways to distract the nurse and my evil guard. I didn't have to think long. There was a noise outside, loud enough that I could hear it through both the bathroom and outer clinic walls. It was a screeching sound, like a car makes when someone hits the breaks too fast, originating from that building next door with the fire hydrant. But when I heard it again, I wasn't so sure that the sound wasn't *human.* My heart rate quickened. It felt like someone was gripping my spine. I forced myself to focus on the task at hand.

I cracked the door and saw that both Randolph and the nurse had gone into the waiting area. Seizing my chance, I sprinted around the restroom door and into the small booth where the nurses drew blood. A second later the phone was in my hand.

A scuffle on the floor startled me. I jumped, spinning around, and saw Randolph two feet behind me. Staring. The phone clattered against the countertop.

"Go ahead," he offered. He'd known exactly what I wanted to do.

I sensed this was a trick, but the offer was too tempting to refuse.

I snatched the phone and lifted it to my ear. There was a clicking noise, and then a man picked up.

"Main gate, this is Broadbent."

Randolph smirked. I turned away from him.

"Yes, can you connect me to Louisville?" I said urgently.

"Who is this?"

"Please, I need to dial out!"

There was a stretch of silence.

"There is no line out. The phones only connect within the facility. How did you get this number?"

My hands were trembling. Randolph snatched the telephone away and hung up, a self-righteous sneer on his face.

A veil of hopelessness fell over me.

THE hours passed. Randolph had decided to keep a closer watch on me based on my stunt in the clinic, and though I was allowed to go with the other seventeens to the cafeteria, I was permitted only water. No lunch. No dinner. Watching them eat was torturous, but I refused to show Randolph or Ms. Brock or even Rebecca that I was bothered.

I'd gone stretches like this without eating before. There

had been a few months during the War before the soup kitchen opened when the only meal I could count on was my government-issued school lunch. I'd always saved three-quarters of it: half for my mom, and what little there was left—an apple, a pack of peanut-butter crackers maybe—for dinner. The gnawing hunger I felt now reminded me of my days rib-counting in front of the bathroom sink.

With a sharp pang I wondered if my mother had eaten today. If it was a sandwich—she liked sandwiches—or something off the line at the soup kitchen. For my sanity, I banished this from my mind. But other forbidden thoughts surfaced.

Chase. The same question, over and over. *How could he?* He'd known us all his life. Had he honestly thought when he'd promised to return to me that it would be like this?

But that was the problem. He hadn't returned. Not really. That soldier at my doorstep had been a stranger.

In the evening I was permitted to go to the common room with the other seventeens, and was alarmed to learn that Rosa was still not back from her punishment. I wondered if she had a concussion, then I thought of the empty girl we'd seen this morning and worried that Rosa had been injured worse.

While I agonized over these thoughts, Rebecca recited with a sickening amount of enthusiasm the school rules for the new people. Then we prayed. At least, *they* prayed. I continued to ruminate anxiously.

Before we were excused, the guard announced that there was one final issue to attend to. I cannot say exactly why, but I knew from the moment Ms. Brock set foot into the room that she meant to harm me.

"Ladies," she began slowly.

"Good evening," several of them chimed, Rebecca included. I said nothing.

"There was another incident today. A breach in the rules. Those of you who have been with us some time will know how we handle these issues, yes?"

I concentrated on sitting tall, with my chin lifted and my eyes fixed on the witch that moved soundlessly before me. Apparently starvation had not been enough; she meant to humiliate me publicly for the telephone incident. She could do whatever she wanted. I refused to show her I was afraid. Someone needed to stand up to the school-yard bully.

The next thing I knew, Randolph was yanking me out of my chair. He dragged me over to a side table in the common room, testing my commitment to be brave.

"But Ember is new, Ms. Brock!"

Rebecca could not completely sugarcoat the defiance in her tone. Her face was streaked with red. I was shocked that she was defending me.

"She is entitled to a probation period while she learns the rules. *Ma'am*," she added as an afterthought.

Another guard placed himself between us. The girls were staring from their SA, to me, to Brock in quick succession. No one spoke.

Ms. Brock glared at my roommate for several seconds. I held my breath. I didn't want Rebecca's support, but I sensed it was better to keep my mouth shut.

Finally Ms. Brock exhaled loudly through her nostrils.

"You've worked quickly, Ms. Miller," she said. Her harsh stare traveled to Rebecca. "Like a *virus*, infecting our brightest.

But you see," she announced to the rest of the room, "Ms. Miller has already attacked a soldier, and her actions today cannot go unpunished." The other girls were watching, some in shock, several now in interest. It was sickening.

"Here, Ms. Miller."

Ms. Brock motioned to the table, sidling around to the opposite side. Randolph stepped behind me and removed the baton from his belt. He had an absent, almost dead look in his eyes. My breath quickened.

"Would you like to tell the other seventeens how you broke the rules today?"

I locked my jaw as tightly as I could.

"You have been asked to explain yourself, Ms. Miller."

"I'm sorry, Ms. Brock," I told her clearly. "You told me if I have nothing to say, better just to keep quiet."

I felt a wave of triumph speaking the words out loud and thought, with both pride and trepidation, that my mother would have approved. Several of the other girls gasped. I broke away for a moment to see Rebecca's expression grow grim.

Ms. Brock sighed. "It appears insubordination is a communicable disease amongst our new students."

"Speaking of, where is Rosa?" I asked.

"That was not the question," she said. "The question was if you would like to—"

"The answer is no. I feel no need to explain myself," I answered as assertively as I could. I was so mad my organs vibrated.

Ms. Brock's face pinched with fury, and her eyes lit with fire. She removed a long, slender stick from her belt that had waited beneath the folds of her skirt. It was thin like a chop-stick, only twice the length, and flexible. The end of it swung back and forth as she waved it before my face.

Who *was* this woman?

"Hands on the table," she commanded coldly.

I took a step back and nearly tripped over Randolph. A chill swept through me. This wasn't the Middle Ages. Human rights still existed, didn't they?

"You can't hit me with that," I found myself saying. "That's illegal. There are laws against that sort of thing."

"My dear Ms. Miller," Ms. Brock said, with patronizing warmth. "I *am* the law here."

My eyes shot to the door. Randolph read my intentions and raised his baton higher.

My mouth hung agape. Her beating. Or his.

"Hands on the table," Ms. Brock repeated. I looked at the other girls. Rebecca was the only one standing, and most of her was hidden behind a guard.

"Girls . . ." I started, but I couldn't remember their names. None of them moved.

"What's wrong with you?" I shouted. Randolph grabbed my wrists and slammed them down on the table. They burned and then went numb as I struggled. "Let go of me!"

He did not. With his free hand he brought the baton right in front of my face, so that I nearly went cross-eyed staring at it, and then he smacked me once, right in the throat.

I couldn't breathe. It felt like my windpipe had been crushed and what was left was on fire. A choking reflex took over, but the more I gasped, the more I panicked. No oxygen was getting through. He'd broken my neck. He'd broken my neck and I was going to suffocate. Bright, white streaks cut across my vision.

"Oh, for pity's sake, take a deep breath," chided Ms. Brock.

I tried to scratch at my neck, but Randolph held my hands down. His face was getting blurry. Finally, *finally*, a tiny bit of air siphoned through. The tears streamed down my face. Another breath, then another. God, it *hurt*.

I'd fallen to my knees, my tingling hands still pinned to the table. I tried to speak but no words came out. I gaped at the faces of the girls around the room, who refused to meet my eyes. Even Rebecca was now staring into her lap.

No one was going to help me. They were all too scared. I was going to have to do what Ms. Brock said or I would be hurt much worse. My body felt as if it were filled with lead. Eyes on Randolph, I flattened my quaking hands on the table.

And with that, Ms. Brock wheeled back and slammed the narrow rod across them while the other girls watched, paralyzed by fear. A silent scream broke through my constricted throat. Immediately red lines from the whip burst into welts over my knuckles.

The look on Ms. Brock's face was pure madness. Her eyes swelled until the irises were islands within a sea of white. A row of blunted teeth emerged beneath her retracted lips.

I jerked my hands away, but Randolph raised his baton again. He was a machine. Cold. Dead. Completely inhuman.

I snapped them back into place, swallowed a burning breath, and ground my teeth together.

Again and again, Ms. Brock struck the backs of my hands. I pressed them so hard against the table my fingers turned white. I forgot my audience. The pain was excruciating. I buckled again to my knees. Long welts criss-crossed over one another, until finally one cracked and bled. There was blood in my mouth, too, from where I had bitten the inside of my cheek. It was warm and coppery and made me want to vomit. Tears poured from my eyes, but still I made no sound. I didn't want to give her the satisfaction of hearing me crumble.

I despised Ms. Brock with a level of hatred I had never known. I hated her more than I hated the MM and the Statutes. More than I hated *him* for taking my mother. More than I hated myself for not being strong enough to fight back. I directed every fiber of hatred toward this woman until the pain and the anger became one.

Finally, she stopped, wiping away a line of sweat from her brow.

"Dear me," she said with a smile. "What a mess. Would you like a Band-Aid?"

HE'D *left a flower on my pillow. A white daisy, with clean, matching petals and a long green stem. The thought of him lifting the window, placing it delicately where I rested my head made something ache deep inside of me.*

My eyes were drawn to the windowsill, where he'd left another flower, this one smaller but no less perfect. It made me smile to picture him picking just the right ones. I pushed up the window and leaned out, half expecting him to be waiting, but he wasn't.

Another daisy lay evenly spaced between our houses, on the grass. Thrilled with the game, I climbed through the window then bent to add it to my growing bouquet. I glanced around and found another, a few yards down, near the back of the houses. It angled into his yard.

Giggling, I followed the trail, one daisy at a time. My anticipation grew, envisioning how he'd take me in his arms when I found him, how he'd touch my face just before he kissed me.

I climbed the deck and called his name as I pushed through his back door. The room was dark, and it took several seconds for my eyes to adjust.

Something was wrong. I felt it, tingling at the base of my neck, warning me to go no farther.

"Chase?"

He was wearing a uniform. The blue jacket was pulled back to reveal his belt. My insides went hollow when I saw the gun and the empty slot where his baton should have been.

"Ember, run!" I jumped at my mother's voice. She was kneeling on the far side of the room, her fingers spread over the coffee table. Ms. Brock was there, her whip raised high.

I looked down in horror to see the blood running freely over Mom's knuckles.

I dropped the daisies and tried to get to her, but Chase blocked my way. His eyes were cold and empty, his body only a shell of the boy I'd known. With a baton in one hand he backed me into the corner, crushing my flowers into the carpet beneath his boots.

"Don't fight me, Ember."

I BURST from the nightmare, sweating, even without the blankets. Moisture beaded on my forehead, my neck, and dampened my hair. My throat was hot and thick and bruised to the touch. My hands throbbed furiously, as if my skin were on fire.

The vision continued to poison my mind. Ms. Brock in the house next door, beating my mother's hands. Chase blocking me in the corner. *Don't fight me, Ember.*

I tried to focus on the real memory: My Chase had been waiting inside, ready with a smile and his open arms. But after everything he'd done, even the memory seemed false.

Slowly, the world became familiar. I was still at the reformatory. Still in my dorm room.

I heard something *click*, then rattle. It was coming from Rebecca's side of the room. From the window.

Someone's breaking in! My muscles coiled, ready to bolt out the door.

"Rebecca!" I croaked, forcing a painful swallow. My sock-clad feet were already on the floor. The skirt that had bunched at my hips untwisted around my legs.

She didn't move. I listened, but there was no sound.

No sound at all, actually. Not even Rebecca breathing.

I forced myself to steady. It was probably a gust of wind against the glass. A tree branch or dead leaves or something. It wasn't an intruder. No one was coming to get me. Not even if I wanted them to.

"Rebecca?" I asked, this time just above a whisper. She didn't stir.

I slid off the bed and padded toward the window, still watching the glass.

I said her name again. She lay absolutely still.

I put my hand on the mattress. The moon shone through the window and lit the bandages on my bloated knuckles a pale blue. My fingertips stretched farther, feeling the blanket.

And the pillow beneath it.

"What the hell?" I said out loud. My eyes shot up, through the glass, into the woods, where a figure in white crossed the tree line. My jaw hit the floor.

Rebecca was running, the fraud. She'd stopped me earlier from the same, while she'd been planning this all along. There was no time to focus on that, though. Rebecca had found some way to escape, something more planned than Rosa's impulsive flight, and I'd be damned if she was going to leave me behind.

I stuffed my feet into my shoes and threw the jacket on my chair across my back. I wasn't tired or hungry. The thrill of anticipation collided with the absolute terror of being caught. Defiance surged.

I didn't think twice about stepping onto Rebecca's bed in my dirty shoes; I would have relished more in the action if I had. I propped the window open. It made the same *click* and rattle that I had heard earlier, when I had thought someone was breaking *in*, not breaking *out*.

From our room on the bottom floor it was almost too easy to slide out the little frame and swing my legs to the ground. So easy, in fact, I wondered why everyone hadn't tried. Sudden doubt gave me pause—there had to be a reason the whole school hadn't disappeared after curfew—but if Brock's prized little Sister was out here, she had to know what she was doing.

I forced a slow, pained breath and continued. My skirt rode up around my hips, and the cold night bit into the skin at the tops of my thighs, but as soon as my feet hit the ground I was running.

The night was bright enough that I could partially see the

way. I sprinted across a narrow lane and into the woods where I had seen Rebecca disappear. The hum of a power generator masked the crunch of dead leaves under my footsteps, both a blessing and a curse. No one could hear me, but I couldn't hear them, either.

Though I worried about getting caught, my feet continued on. Rebecca had been here three years. She knew this system, this facility. She wouldn't be attempting an escape unless she was positive it was a sure thing.

The deeper I dove into the woods, the darker it became, even under the starlight. I wondered where we were going. To a broken fence maybe. The long shadows blended with the night sky, leaving only highlights of bare branches and textured tree trunks. I walked with my hands in front of me, feeling my way forward. I was getting anxious, fearing I'd lost her. The generator was getting louder.

Finally, I heard voices. One male, the other so bubbly it couldn't be anyone *but* Rebecca. I stopped dead in my tracks and ducked, hiding behind the broken tree trunk. I couldn't make out what they were saying. As stealthily as possible, I scooted closer.

"I can't believe Randolph smacked her," I heard Rebecca say.

"Yeah. He liked it, too, the sick bastard." The voice was familiar.

"Sean . . . what did you all do to her?"

"Brock said take her to the shack. Come on, you knew that was coming."

My muscles hardened. They weren't talking about me; they were talking about Rosa.

In my mind's eye I saw the unmarked brick building beside the clinic. Was that the "shack"? Brock had said to take Rosa to "lower campus"; maybe that was what she'd meant. My memory conjured the metallic screech I'd heard when I'd found the clinic's phone. Had that been Rosa's scream?

My head was spinning. I still couldn't place the other voice.

Rebecca was quiet for a moment. "I guess I did."

"What, you feel sorry for her? Aw, don't be sad, Becca. Hey, I bet I can cheer you up."

They were quiet, and I was gripped by the fear that they were moving on without me. In a panic, I lifted my head to see over the log.

My mouth fell open.

Rebecca Lansing was sitting on the generator, wearing a big blue canvas coat. Her bare legs were wrapped around a guard's hips—the soldier with the sandy hair. The nearly handsome guard who had approved of her line this morning. He had one hand shoved through her messed blond hair, the other on her bare thigh. Their lips were smashed against each other with a frenzied passion.

Part of me knew this was a dream. There was no possible way in the history of the human race that prude, holy Rebecca, my roommate, my *Student Assistant*, was getting it on with a soldier. On school grounds. In the middle of the night.

Anger scored through me. Rosa was in the shack being punished while Rebecca was screwing some guy on the generator. My hands balled into fists. My jaw clenched. And if reason hadn't completely abandoned me earlier, it did then.

Before I knew it, I was standing.

"What was—"

I wasn't surprised to be blinded by the flashlight. It caught me right in the face, blacking out the people behind it. I threw up a hand to guard my eyes and marched forward blindly around the log, over the branches and debris.

"Who is that?" I heard Rebecca say. And then, "Oh, my God."

The guard cursed. *Sean*, she had called him. He detached himself from Rebecca and lunged forward toward me. I almost wanted him to reach me. All I saw when I looked at him was his stony face as he'd dragged Rosa away.

"Stop it!" Rebecca hopped down off the generator and jumped in front of him. "Ember, what are you doing here?" I hated that perky little voice.

"You *liar*!" I growled.

"What? How long have you been here?"

"Long enough, *Becca*." My words, though raspy, flew out like water from a busted pipe.

"It's not what it looks like."

"Oh, *really*?"

"I thought you said she was asleep!" Banks nearly shouted.

"Shut up, Sean!" she snapped. When he didn't answer, she grabbed my sleeve and tried to jerk me toward the facility. "Come on, we're going back."

"I don't think so," I said. "I'm done listening to you."

"You have to come. The next guard will be coming through in a few minutes. You get caught, you're done for. Get it?"

"Just me? I don't think so," I said, in a voice that sounded like mine but far bolder. Everything about me seemed disconnected. My skin was ice cold, but the blood running beneath was hot. My organs all felt like separate fragmented pieces. It took great effort to breathe the frigid air. I did not feel like myself at all.

"You think they care that Sean and I are out here?" she said, waving her arms in frustration. "You think they haven't done the same thing? They watch each other's backs, okay? They'll punish you for telling on him."

"Maybe they will," I agreed, and felt my resentment kick up another notch. "And maybe the guards don't care, but I'm sure Ms. Brock would love to hear how her shining star is sneaking around with one of the soldiers."

Banks looked at her, his face twisting with panic—with *real* emotion. Then he stared at me, terror melting into desperation.

"She'll never believe you," he said to me.

"Maybe not. But they'll watch *her*, won't they? They'll have a guard by our room, making sure she doesn't try anything, and—" In all honesty, I didn't know what Ms. Brock would do, but Sean's darkening look told me I'd hit the mark.

"You can't tell her . . . Miller, right? Becca's out in three months. You have to give her that long."

"Let me handle this, Sean," she said.

I was taken aback by his burst of chivalry. Was he really trying to protect her? I crossed my arms over my chest. Maybe they weren't all as dead inside as they seemed.

Well, maybe some of them weren't, anyway.

"You . . . you can't tell, Ember. You *can't*."

"And what's stopping me?"

With an audible intake of breath, Sean flicked the strap off the gun at his waist. I could tell by his round, conflicted eyes that he didn't want to shoot me, but that didn't stifle my fear one bit. In that moment I remembered Randolph's baton on my throat, and Brock's whip on my hands, and wondered why I thought this soldier wouldn't be capable of the very same or worse.

I fought the urge to run.

"She said the next guard will be through in a few minutes!" I shouted. "How are you going to explain why Rebecca was here if you shoot me?" I was shaking now. I hoped neither of them could see it in the darkness. He wouldn't shoot me. Not for this. He couldn't. There was too much risk.

Please don't let him shoot me.

"Sean," Rebecca said softly. He lowered his hand, but I still didn't breathe.

"What do you want?" Sean asked. In exchange for my secrecy he was going to cut a deal.

"I need to get out of here. I need to find my mother," I said, my voice getting hoarser the more I talked.

"We have to go!" Rebecca's voice squeaked higher. She was looking over her shoulder, presumably for the next guard on rotation. Now that I said I'd tell Brock, she was afraid I would tell everyone.

Sean sucked in a sharp breath. "And if I help you, you swear you won't tell the headmistress." He wasn't asking. He'd taken another step forward, placing himself between me and his girlfriend. I was surprised at how lean he looked now, with his face drawn in fear. How large his eyes seemed. The thin lines of his mouth.

"*No.* Sean, no!" Rebecca was pulling on his arm like a child. When he continued to stare at me, she pushed past him, standing inches away from me. "If he's caught he'll get in trouble. *Serious* trouble. You don't—"

"Miller," Sean prompted, ignoring her.

"Yes. I swear. You get me out, and I won't tell Ms. Brock." I felt a piece of me break inside, suddenly remembering the horror in my mother's face when I'd told Roy to leave our home. I had been trying to do the right thing, but hurting someone else to accomplish that goal was almost unbearable. It was not so different now, even though I hardly knew these people.

"Okay," said Sean. "I'll . . . figure out something." He kicked the log I had been hiding behind.

"How? When?" The blood was rushing back through my body at his assent.

"Not now. She's right. The next guard will be rotating through soon. You have to let me think."

I was disappointed, but I knew it was the best I would get tonight.

"Thank you . . . Sean," I said. Saying his name made him feel infinitely more real, like a boy I could have known in school. His shoulder jerked. His face was full of contempt.

A moment later, Rebecca shrugged out of his jacket and tossed it over to him. They looked at each other for one long moment. Even in the dark, I saw her face soften.

"I'm sorry," she whispered. "It'll be okay. I promise."

One of his hands rested awkwardly at the base of his neck, as though his muscles were too tight. He shrugged into the jacket and disappeared into the darkness.

Rebecca's face was hard again when she stomped back toward our room. Reluctantly, I followed, mad that I was tripping and stumbling while she walked nearly effortlessly. I reminded myself that she had made this trip more than once.

When we got to the window three from the left, Rebecca shoved open the frame—much harder than she would have if I had been asleep inside, I'm sure—and nimbly hopped up, her hip resting on the sill. Then she ducked back and rolled onto her bed. I followed suit a lot less smoothly.

Once inside, we were engulfed by awkward, strained silence.

"How could you?" she finally blurted. In the muted moonlight from the window I could see that her face was flushed from the cold and anger. "I should have let you run, just like that Rosa girl. I knew you wanted to. I would have, had I known you'd blackmail me! How *could* you?"

All of the anger and fear and shock broke through in one hard stroke.

"*Me?* You are such a *hypocrite!* I asked you for help and you ignored me! Spewing that crap about summer camp and loving it here, sucking up to Brock. It's all lies! You're ten times meaner than her; you just hide it better."

"You're absolutely right. So what?" She put her hands on her hips.

My eyes widened. "You need to be medicated. Seriously. And I'm not an idiot because I believed you. You're just a damn good actress."

"Yes," she said. "I am."

I sat on my bed, facing her. She sat on her bed, facing me. It was like we were children again, having a staring contest. It was Rebecca who finally broke the silence.

"You're putting him in danger for no reason," she said. "No

one escapes. You either leave with your exit papers, or you leave in the back of an FBR van."

"What do you mean?" I choked. My fingers drew to the bruise on my neck.

She made a small wincing noise. "The guards have orders to shoot anyone that makes it off the property."

My sore hands grasped each other atop my skirt. That was why Sean had reached for his gun. He could have pretended I was escaping. No one would have questioned him when they saw my dead body so far from the dorms. I felt an instant surge of affection for Rebecca. Had she not been present, and had Sean *wanted* me dead, I'd be bleeding out in the West Virginia woods right now.

But then again, I wouldn't have been out there in the first place if she hadn't snuck out.

"Do you think they'd really do it?" I asked, without much question. I'd seen the cold, dead looks in the soldiers' eyes. I could picture several I'd run across—Morris, Chase's friend from the arrest, and Randolph, the guard here—killing a girl.

"I know they would. The last one they . . ." she hesitated, looking back toward the window, wondering, I knew, where Sean was. "She was Stephanie's old roommate."

Rosa was now Stephanie's roommate, I realized with a pang.

Rebecca swallowed. "Her name was Katelyn. Katelyn Meadows."

CHAPTER
4

"KATELYN Meadows," I repeated, dazed. *She isn't on the Missing Persons boards. Her family moved away after the trial.*

She wasn't on the Missing Persons board because she wasn't a Missing Person. She was dead. I was glad the bed was behind me, because my knees promptly gave way.

"She was a nice girl," Rebecca said. "I try not to like anybody here—they always get weird. But she was all right."

"I know," I said quietly. I remembered her picture clearly from the posters around school, and before that, from her smiling face in my junior history class.

"Did you know her?" Rebecca asked.

I nodded. "Not well, but yes. We went to school together."

"Oh." She bit her thumbnail, lost for words.

"When did it happen?"

"I guess about six months ago. She was just about to age out when Brock asked her to stay on as a teacher. And when Brock asks you to stay on, she's not really asking."

I am the law here, Ms. Brock had said when she'd whipped

my hands. No, I didn't imagine her invitation to become a teacher had sounded anything like a request.

Six months ago I'd been just starting my senior year at Western. It should have been Katelyn's senior year, too. I wasn't sure if the knowledge of her death made me sad; I didn't know her well enough to grieve. But I did fear what this meant for me and my chances at escape. I felt selfish, scared, and sick all at the same time.

I rubbed my hands over my eyes. They stung from the dried tears in my lashes.

"Did Sean . . ."

"No. No, it was someone else." She smiled weakly. "Sean's never killed anybody. He told me so. The FBR makes them practice on these human-shaped targets in training, and he could barely do that. That's why they sent him to a girls' rehab and kept him out of the cities."

I pictured the soldiers lining up at the shooting ranges, and shivered. Chase hadn't been detailed to a girls' rehab, which could only mean he was a better shot than the guards here. I wondered if he'd killed anyone, but the thought made me so uncomfortable, I locked it from my mind.

"Apparently not everyone has the same conscience as Sean," I said bitterly.

"Right," she agreed. "Obviously you've met Randolph."

I clutched my knees involuntarily. My knuckles hurt. "He's the one? Who did . . . *that* to Katelyn?"

It was dark, but I could still see her nod. "So you see, there's really no point in trying to escape."

"I have to try," I said. "If they're doing this kind of thing to us, what do you think they're doing to my mother?"

She hesitated. "Probably the same."

I stood up so quickly my head spun. "What has Sean told you? You have to tell me!" The weight of our deal hung in the air between us. There was no point in lying now that I knew her secret.

"He doesn't hear much," she said defensively.

The guards at the school were isolated; the rest of the soldiers had direct contact with their command, but a particular unit, the ones who had failed some aspect of their training like Sean, had been transferred under the authority of the Sisters of Salvation.

"Who are these Sisters, anyway?" I asked. "Is Ms. Brock in charge of all of them?"

"She wishes," said Rebecca. "Brock was appointed by the Board of Education during the Reformation Act. She's like, I don't know, the school superintendent of this region. There are other Brocks, in other regions, running other reformatories with the same iron bra." She giggled. "That's what Sean calls it—an 'iron bra.' Instead of an iron fist, you know?"

"I get it," I said flatly. More evil headmistresses. More reformatories. It was enough to make me weak all over again. Rebecca's brief smile faded.

"Brock says that the Sisters are taking over," she said. "Running charities and food lines and stuff. Of course, who knows if that's true."

My mom volunteered at our local soup kitchen. I could hardly picture her wearing a blue skirt and a stupid handkerchief around her neck.

"So Brock reports to the MM, but the soldiers here report to her?" I asked. Rebecca gave me a blank look, and I realized she'd never heard the nickname for the FBR. Having been here since she was fourteen, she was a little out of touch with mainstream culture.

"Moral Militia," Rebecca said wistfully, after I explained. "That's funny."

Apparently, tending to the miscreants of society didn't require the highest level of skill. The FBR was still technically in charge of the soldiers here, but Ms. Brock supervised their daily activities. Unfortunately, that meant that Sean had very little contact with the rest of the military.

"But there's a courier," Rebecca continued. "He comes weekly to deliver messages to Ms. Brock from the outside. Mandates from the head of education. Revisions to the Statutes. Things like that. Sean hears rumors sometimes. He knew that they were going to stop the trials for Article violators a while ago, and he was right. It's been over a month since a soldier came out here to pick up a witness."

"Stop the trials? What does that mean?" I asked, my voice rising.

"Shh!" She motioned for me to sit back down on the bed. "I don't know what it means. Maybe they're just letting your mom go. Or maybe they're sending her to rehab. Sean did say they need to 'complete' something in place of a trial. It's a new protocol, I guess. He gets training on it next month."

In my mind I pictured my mother in my place. Her small, manicured hands on the table while Brock slammed the whip down upon them, like in my dream. I could see the obstinacy melt into fear. Her folding into the floor, just as she'd done with Roy.

I couldn't let that happen. The thought of her suffering made me ill.

"My mom can't do *this*. I have to find her. There's got to be a way out somewhere. What was Katelyn doing? How did she get caught?" I asked.

"Sean said they got her out by the southern fence. She was trying to climb over."

Katelyn was lanky but by no means athletic. I couldn't picture her scaling a fence. But then again, people did all kinds of crazy things when they were desperate. I should know.

"There's no other way? No holes in the fence? No other exits?"

She shrugged helplessly. "The guards walk the perimeter every hour. The only way out is through the front gates. And there's a watch station there, and guards that search the vehicles."

"*No one* has ever escaped?" I asked in disbelief.

Rebecca curled in over her midsection. When she spoke again, her voice sounded small, as if she were years younger.

"One girl did, right after I got here. She made it over the fence and into the woods, but it was snowing so badly she died of hypothermia. Brock made the soldiers bring her body into the cafeteria to show us what would happen if we tried to run away. She was all black and blue and . . ." Rebecca shook her head as if to clear the memory. "That was when Brock okayed the orders for the guards to shoot anyone who got too close to the fence."

I flinched, thinking of how crushing it would feel to gain freedom only to lose it.

"Only three people have made a decent run for it since then, and they've all been killed. No one tries for a long time after something like that happens. If you're crazy enough, you'll be the first since Katelyn."

The realities of my intentions were rooting deep in my gut. If I ran, I had to face the possibility that I might not survive, and if I died, it would most likely be violently. But if I stayed, I wouldn't know if my mother was being beaten or thrown in prison or shot.

Entrapment. I had two choices. And both were bad.

"You know, if you age out, they don't legally have to look for you," she told me.

I couldn't wait until I turned eighteen, but something in her voice told me she wasn't talking about me.

"Is that why you and Sean haven't run?"

She nodded. "I'll be safe in three months. But if he ever decides to leave, the FBR could kill him."

So she was staying of her own choice. To protect a soldier.

I shook my head skeptically. "They wouldn't kill one of their own."

"You're wrong. The Board would give him a trial. If he goes AWOL and they catch him, they'll execute him. That's the way things are now. If you don't think they'd do it, re-member why you're here."

As the air stilled between us, my thoughts branched into a dangerous place. If Sean could be executed, could my mother? It seemed improbable, but not impossible.

I needed to get out. Soon.

· · ·

TWO nights passed before Sean figured out a plan.

We were in class, reading a handout entitled "A Lady's Dress Code" when he caught my eye. A slight nod of his head, and without hesitation I raised my hand to request an escort to the restroom. Before the Sister could ask Randolph take me, Sean had stepped forward and was holding the door open to usher me down the hall.

Once we were away from the others, he quickly told me that the headmistress had given him orders to cover for another soldier preparing to take leave, which meant a double shift of his normal perimeter sweep. When this happened, he would lead me to the fence and look the other way as I climbed over.

It sounded simple but was far from problem-free. First, it was still eight days away. Second, I was on my own after I got past the fence, which meant roughly four hours and fifteen miles of walking through the Appalachian wilderness alone. And third, once I got to the nearest gas station, I would have to hitch a ride home, which meant I'd have to find a willing civilian with a car who didn't care about gas money.

"You'd better book it," Sean advised. "Once they figure out you're gone, they'll come looking. I won't be able to do anything then."

I nodded, and though the swelling in my throat had gone down, I felt a new lump emerge. It was a terrible plan, but it was all I had. He looked at me for a long while, as though surprised that I was really considering this. I couldn't tell whether he thought I was brave or stupid. Probably the latter.

"It'll be better for everyone if you just wait until you age out, Miller."

"I can't wait," I told him firmly. "Not knowing she could be in a place like this."

His expression was bleak. I asked if he knew anything more about my mother, and he denied it. I wondered if there was more to this than he was letting on, but as we were already on a fine line, I let it go. I didn't have enough dirt on him to risk what he'd already offered. And ultimately, the guy with the gun calls the shots.

So I waited.

ROSA returned the following afternoon. She sat beside me in silence during Brock's session on social etiquette. There were no snide jokes, no cocky, gap-between-her-two-front-teeth grins. Her eyes, resting atop half-moon bruises from Randolph's fist, were no longer rebellious, but bland. Vacant. She was as empty as the girl we'd seen after we'd first arrived.

There was no question in my mind now that the scream I'd heard when I'd been in the clinic had been Rosa in the shack. When I asked Rebecca about it, she remained vague. *Spooky*, she called it. That's all. But I was frightened.

In the days that followed, I did what I could to be inconspicuous. I was polite when forced into awkward social interactions with the staff and the girls, and I followed the rules. I didn't show my frustration or pain when my clumsy, distended hands dropped things, or when I couldn't close my fist to hold a pencil. I didn't attract any attention, and in that way, I let Brock think that she'd won.

But right under her nose I gathered things, like I had when my mother and I were at our worst during the War. A cup from the cafeteria when no one saw. A washcloth from the bathroom. I began hoarding nonperishable food beneath my mattress in preparation for my departure.

And I found myself relying on Rebecca. Though she played the rehab queen whenever we were around others, she had obviously found a way to survive. Her deception recharged my hope.

At night, we talked, and she became surprisingly open. Almost as if I were a confidante rather than someone who could cause her a great deal of trouble by exposing her secret. Through her lens, I began to see Sean in a new light. I began to notice the way he diverted Randolph's attention from the girls and purposefully nodded his agreement when Brock lectured on something absurdly ridiculous, like appropriate ways for a Sister to talk to men.

To my shock, I opened up some, too. I told her some of the things I missed about my mother. The popcorn and old, pre-War magazine nights. The songs we used to sing together. How we'd never really been apart. Rebecca liked those stories. I think it helped her understand my drive to escape.

On the fifth night, I even told her about Chase.

I don't know why. Maybe because she loved a soldier, or maybe because I felt the need to reciprocate some private piece of my life to her. Maybe because not an hour passed without me asking myself why he did what he did. Whatever the reason, it slipped out of me. Not the details, not the depth of what I'd felt for him, but the basics of what had happened between us.

"They're not supposed to date. Not unless they're officers," she informed me when I said he hadn't written. "They have to dedicate their life to the *cause* or something. It's a form they sign when they enlist."

"Sean doesn't seem to care." I couldn't hide the pettiness in my voice.

She grinned, and it struck me how pretty she was. "Can you blame him?"

We both laughed then. It was the first and only time we would.

ELEVEN days had passed at the reformatory with no word from my mother or Beth.

On the eleventh night, I prepared to leave.

"I'll go out with you," Rebecca said for the tenth time. She was pacing around the room. It was after midnight, but she was still wearing her full uniform.

"No." We had already talked about this. "Sean wants you here."

"I don't care what he wants!" Her voice went impossibly higher. She was wringing her blouse between her fists. "I can't do *nothing* while he's risking his life for you!"

The tension between us had been building steadily over the last few days. The reality of the plan was finally sinking in. Unconsciously, I traced the still-swollen welts over the backs of my hands and made a tender fist. The wounds had finally closed but were now painted with purple and yellow blossoms. They ached terribly, especially on cold nights like this one.

"He's just going to point me toward the perimeter fence and then pretend like he doesn't see me," I assured her— again. "He won't be in danger."

Neither of us believed it.

The minutes ticked by. One. After another. After another.

I hadn't been able to eat dinner. I'd been too nervous. But I'd hidden a cold baked potato with the rest of my supplies in Rebecca's sweater, tied to my waist.

"Okay, I'm going," I finally said at twelve-thirty on the dot. She nodded, her face pale.

"I guess . . . it was nice knowing you," she said weakly. "Thanks for not telling Brock about me and Sean. And . . . don't get shot."

I attempted a smile, but it didn't work. I almost said that I hoped to see her again, or something similar, but I knew it wouldn't happen in a million years. When she aged out, she and Sean were going to have to hide from the MM, and so were my mother and I. Instead I grabbed her shoulders, gave her a quick, awkward hug, and slid out the window.

It was snowing outside, just like the night the girl had died of hypothermia, but I was prepared, layered in all the clothing they'd issued me: two skirts, a camisole, three long-sleeved T-shirts, and my gray sweater. And I had some food for fuel, close to my body.

The ground was solid as a rock, and the cold leaked through my flats to the soles of my feet. The brick dorm building was covered with a thin layer of white. Long icicles hung from the rain gutters like jagged teeth.

I glanced both ways across the lane before darting into the woods toward the generators. Sean would be there, ready to get this over with. I was ready, too.

By the time I heard the steady drone of the machines, my muscles were warm and limber and my heart was pounding steadily. My stomach didn't even hurt anymore; there was too much adrenaline building in my body to be bogged down by anxiety. I was glad. I needed whatever edge I could get.

My hearing was sharper than normal, and my head snapped toward the sound of crackling twigs nearby. I froze automatically, fingernails digging into my palms. It took every ounce of effort to push Katelyn Meadows from my mind.

Sean materialized from behind a wide tree made black by the night shadows. His winter FBR coat made him appear thicker through the chest; he was more intimidating than before. The scars on the backs of my hands from Brock's punishment burned.

He didn't say a word but turned past the enormous metal blocks emitting their low buzz and stalked deeper into the woods.

I led with my hands, swiping away the brambles and low branches that impeded our journey. The fence had to be close. How long had we been heading this way? Ten minutes? It was one mile from the dorm building. We should have been getting close.

"How tall is it? The fence," I whispered.

"Fifteen feet," he answered without turning around. I forced a deep breath.

"Sean, if I forget later—" I tripped over a branch, caught myself. "Thank you."

He didn't speak for a minute, maybe more.

"Hope you make it," he said finally.

I wasn't sure if he meant he hoped I found my mother, hoped I could climb the fence, or hoped I didn't get shot in the process, but his words were a small comfort.

"Hold it, Banks!"

I felt like a piece of wood at the moment the ax strikes. My whole body tried to tear in two different directions. One side tried to sprint toward the fence, the other back toward the dorms. The screaming fear was the only thing that locked me in place.

"Do *not* run," Sean ordered under his breath. In a flash, he'd swept the sweater holding my supplies into a bush and fisted a hand in my hair, knotting it all up. My eyes watered. I didn't struggle for long before he released me.

Footsteps were approaching. Someone was close. How had I not heard them? I'd been thinking too much about the fence, and saying thank you, and what I was going to do once I got outside. *Stupid!*

Did Sean know about this? Was this a trap? Of course he hadn't wanted Rebecca to come! He was planning the whole time on turning me in!

Pulse slamming through my veins, I wrapped my arms around my midsection, as though this shield could stop a bullet. The frenetic trail of a flashlight preceded the two soldiers who stepped through the night.

Randolph. And another lanky guard with thick eyebrows lifted in judgment.

Their light blinded me momentarily. I heard the rustle of leather and fabric. And then a metallic *click.*

"She running?" the lanky guard asked. The flashlight tore away, revealing both he and Randolph's raised guns, pointed directly at my chest.

I couldn't breathe.

"Looks like she's running to me," commented Randolph.

Sean grinned—a grin I'd never seen, not even with Rebecca—and my fears were validated. Then, to my shock, he lifted his hand, calmly now, and fixed my hair. I jerked away.

"Well," he said. "This is embarrassing."

Randolph snorted. Sean's hand trailed down to my lower back, and then shoved me almost playfully away. I stumbled before catching myself, and all three of them laughed.

"Go on back to your room now, sweetheart," Sean said. "And keep your mouth shut about this, just like we talked about."

It took me a minute to catch up.

"I wasn't expecting the next rotation for an hour or so," Sean continued casually, fixing his pants as though we'd been doing exactly what he did out here most nights with Rebecca.

Girls were executed for running, not for messing around with the guards. He was giving me a window. A chance to live. As much as I wanted to escape, I could not leave this place in a wooden box.

I tried to sprint back toward the dorms, but Randolph lurched in front of me. A second later his hands were pinching my hips and his knee was shoved intrusively between my legs. His sour breath clouded around my mouth.

"Stay a little while longer," he whispered, and at his words terror shot straight to my core. I struggled against him and was tossed back into Sean's arms.

"*Trash*," spat Randolph. "Reform-school trash." They were laughing again, laughing, and though it was against everything I believed, I was ashamed. I couldn't help it.

Sean's grin was not nearly as bold as before. I gripped onto him hard, not knowing where else to turn.

"You got sloppy, Banks," the skinny guard said. "The headmistress wanted us to watch you. But we thought it'd be the blonde, not this one."

"I said it was this one," said Randolph. "He's been staring at her."

Staring at me because he was afraid I'd tell Brock his secret, I realized.

It became clear what was happening. They had set up this trap for Sean, not for me. They suspected him because he had changed since I'd blackmailed him.

Do not run, Sean had whispered. Everything inside of me said to do the opposite. I could feel my heels already shifting inside of my shoes, ready to bolt at any second. But if I ran, they would most certainly shoot me.

Randolph laughed. "I could make it go away, Banks." He raised the weapon an inch higher. He wanted to shoot me.

I was going to die.

I didn't think of my mother, or if I'd been a good person or led a good life—any of those things you're supposed to think about when you die. I saw one face in my mind, and just for an instant. The one person who couldn't possibly give me any comfort.

Chase. Black shaggy hair, copper skin softened by the light rain. His dark eyes, peering straight into my soul. And that mouth, turned up at the corners in curiosity.

"Shut up, Randolph," groaned the other guard. "We're in a no-fire zone; perimeter's too far out. Besides, the headmistress already figured this is what we'd find."

My mouth dropped open. Time seemed to pause. Was I still alive? I felt the pressure of arms wrapped around my body. I was so numb, I barely noticed.

"Tell Becca I'm sorry," Sean whispered in my ear. A moment later, there was a shuffle and a sickening crack as Randolph hit him hard in the back of the head with his baton. I felt the reverberation through my body as though I'd been the one struck, and stared in horror at the ground where Sean lay.

Run, my feet said.

Run and they'll shoot you, my brain answered.

I didn't have a chance. The next moment, I had a gun to my back, and we were returning to the dorms.

I PACED the length of the common room for hours awaiting the headmistress's judgment. I thought about screaming for Rebecca, but I refused to put her in danger.

My good intentions didn't matter. As soon as curfew broke, I heard the slapping of feet against the hallway floor. This was part of the plan. She was to report me missing when she woke up.

Her hair was flattened, her cheeks pale, and there were dark circles under her bloodshot eyes. She'd been crying. Either out of fear for Sean or me. I found myself both touched at the prospect of her true friendship and torn by the betrayal I'd dealt her.

She caught my eyes, and a change came over her face.

"Don't," I mouthed to her. I was too late.

"Where is he, Ember?" she said shakily, approaching the lanky guard. He lifted his radio. With a lightning fast paw, she slapped it down to the floor, then kicked it aside. He laid a hand on his baton.

"Where is Banks?" The desperation was heavy in her voice.

"Rebecca!" I said sharply. She was going to ruin everything. Sean had already protected her—and me—by pretending he and I were together. If he'd agreed I was escaping, I'd be dead.

Other girls, seventeens and some of the sixteens that shared our hall, had come out of their rooms. Another guard was pushing them back as he passed.

I heard the light clicking of heels on the wooden floor and knew Brock had arrived. She entered the foyer wearing her traditional skirt and a navy sweater. There was an attendant with her, a short, plump woman who had fear strewn across her face.

"What did you do with him? Sean! Where is he?" Rebecca spouted before the headmistress could speak.

Another guard had reached us. There were three now, one beside me, two on either side of Brock. The breath was raking hard up my throat.

"She doesn't know what she's saying," I tried.

"Silence, Ms. Miller," Brock snapped. "I will deal with you in a moment. Genero, call for assistance." Her voice never faltered.

"Where. Is. *Sean?*" Rebecca demanded one final time. Her shoulders were heaving.

"He's gone," spat Brock. "And so are you."

"You—"

"Rebecca, no!" I shouted, just as she launched herself onto the old woman.

The next events happened very fast.

With the force of a cannonball, Rebecca took Brock to

the floor. I saw a nightstick rise high and land with a dull thud on my tiny roommate's back. The bones cracked, a sickening sound, and her scream halted prematurely.

I had been frozen up until then, but when Rebecca was hit, pure adrenaline scored through me. In a flash I saw my mother. I saw the blue uniforms pulling her toward the van. Taking her away.

My vision compressed behind narrow slits. With all my strength, I attacked the guard who had hit Rebecca. I kicked him, hit him, bit him. I felt skin gather and rip under my fingernails. Everything within me acted on instinct, as though my very survival depended on it. I saw fuzzy images, mostly blue, some gray, as Rebecca was thrown in front of me. Someone yelled. A girl screamed.

Steel arms clamped around my waist. I thrashed.

"Rebecca!" My eyes searched frantically for her. The snow was falling heavily from the thick, black sky. We were outside. One of the guards holding me slipped. I felt us plunge toward the cement steps before he righted himself. He swore loudly over the ringing in my ears. Then we were descending the steps backward, and my stomach was lurching as if I were diving into a bottomless pool. Warm blood filled my mouth. I'd bitten the inside of my cheek again.

"Let me go!" I hollered.

"Shut up!" barked one of the guards.

My shoulders hurt from where they pulled my arms. Out of the corner of my eye I saw the cafeteria pass on my left. More stairs. It took me some time to orient myself to lower campus, down by the infirmary. A metal door was pushed open. To my right I saw the fire hydrant in the gleam of the spotlights, defiantly red against the snow.

I was in the shack.

They dropped me unceremoniously on the dank cement floor. All my trembling extremities retracted into my chest. A soldier pointed his club in my face and I tucked my chin hard against my chest so that he couldn't hit my throat as Randolph had done.

"Keep your scrawny butt down," he commanded.

The room was small. A single overhead bulb hung from the center of the ceiling. There was a brightly lit space to my right, like a large shower, and to the left a dark closet with cement walls, but no racks or hangers. A confinement cell.

The fear was petrifying. I scooted into a corner, back to the wall, and waited.

LONG seconds stretched into torturous minutes. I saw their faces. Sean's as the soldiers found us. Rebecca's, torn with worry. What had I done to them? And worse, what *hadn't* I done? I should have been on the outside now, running back toward home and my mother. What had this cost her?

The door creaked open finally, and a woman slid inside. My gut twisted.

Brock.

She had changed into a fresh Sisters of Salvation uniform. There was a bandage on her right cheek. The single yellow bulb overhead made her skin appear jaundiced, but it couldn't hide the flush of rage still blanketing her severe features.

"Ms. Miller, I am very disappointed in you."

"What have you done to Rebecca?" I stood, my legs trembling with fear or anticipation, I didn't know. Tears burned my eyes, but I blinked them back, refusing to let her see me cry.

"You are a very bad girl. The worst kind. The wolf in sheep's clothing. We shall need to shed that cover and remold your interior. I see that now."

"What—" Even though I didn't know what she meant, I was terrified.

"Guard, take Ms. Miller to the clean room."

The clean room. The one that looked like a shower. One of the soldiers was already preparing the fire hose inside. Beside him, a pair of leather cuffs were chained to the floor beside his baton. He intended to strap me down and beat me, maybe even spray me with the hose. For a fraction of a second I saw Rosa, laid out across the floor, watching her blood twist down the drain while the force of the water pummeled her body.

My arms locked protectively over my body, fisting in my shirt.

"No," I whispered.

Two guards moved forward. Dead eyes. Reaching hands.

"NO!" I shouted at them.

I spun to the wall, trying to hide my body from them. I could not go into that room. I could not let them touch me. They gripped my shoulders. My thighs. I screamed.

Just then there was a knock at the door.

The guards waited for Brock's order. She flipped her head to the side, annoyed.

Randolph stuck his head in.

"What do you want?" she snapped.

"Sorry ma'am. I thought you'd want to know there's a Dispatch who just arrived from Illinois. He's come to collect her for trial."

Several beats passed before I realized he was talking about *me*.

Brock and I must have thought the same thing at the same time. There weren't trials for Article violations anymore. *It's been over a month since a soldier came out here to pick up a witness*, Rebecca had said. Could Sean have misheard?

My blood turned to ice. It seemed impossibly cruel for life to offer such an illusion. But if it was true there would only be one trial I'd be called to attend. My mother's. I tried to sort through the mixed emotions—joy that I might see her, fear, because this meant that she was still imprisoned, pure relief at the interruption.

"I thought they were doing away with those," said Brock, annoyed.

"They still do trials in certain cases, ma'am," said a low, familiar voice from outside. My mouth fell open. My heart thumped in my chest.

A moment later Chase Jennings entered the room.

CHAPTER
5

HE seemed taller than before, and bigger, even since he'd become a soldier. Maybe it was the low ceilings of the shack or the company I kept. Randolph was only a few inches above my five four, and Brock was just between our heights. Chase towered over us at six three.

His face was blank, his eyes unreadable. After I got over the shock of his presence, I found myself hoping more than anything that his words were true. He had come to take me to a trial, to get me out of those gates and deliver me to my mother.

Chase removed a folded piece of paper from his breast pocket and handed it to Brock. She snatched it away, reading for what felt like several minutes.

"When must you leave?" she asked sourly. My eyes darted to the guards before me, and my arms hugged tighter around my chest. I needed to leave now. I couldn't wait to see what they would do to me.

"Immediately. The trial is tomorrow morning, in Chicago," Chase said.

I turned away then, fearing that my face might betray me. Of all the soldiers, of course they had to send Chase Jennings. The reason I was here in the first place. And if I looked at him now, surely one of them would see the betrayal, the questions, written across my face. And what was worse, my eagerness to get in the car with him. To get out of here.

Brock sighed irritably. "As an Article 5, Ms. Miller's mere existence is enough to sentence the birth mother. Why the trial? Highly unusual for the offense."

I forced myself to breathe. Why *did* the MM need me? Would my presence become the evidence they needed to condemn her? I had no idea what this trial or the sentencing entailed, but I was feeling the pressure to get there as soon as possible.

"All I have is the summons and order to transport," Chase answered, his voice bland.

No one moved or spoke for a full minute. The only sound I heard was my heavy pulse, throbbing in my ears.

"Very well," said Brock reluctantly. "But I'm only approving one overnight pass on account of Ms. Miller's inability to stay where she belongs."

For the first time Chase's eyes floated over me. I still wasn't looking at him, but I felt his impartial stare. I straightened, trying not to show I was afraid. I needed to maintain a cool head from this point forward.

"Is that why she's here?" he asked, voice flat. "Her 'inability to stay where she belongs'? I'm sure the Board will be interested."

A ghost of a smirk passed over Randolph's face. "More like an inability to keep her legs closed," he said under his breath.

My teeth clenched. I remembered the way he'd grabbed me outside, ready to share in Sean's supposed fun, right before he planned on shooting me. Again, a hot, misdirected shame filled my gut, as though I were dirty and tainted. I hated him.

"Don't be crass," Brock snapped. "There is at least *one* lady present."

She grabbed a pen from Randolph and scribbled her signature on the bottom of the summons.

"Sergeant, I'm assuming you're new to this line of work, since I haven't seen you before, so I'll make this clear," she directed to Chase. "These girls are federal property and under my authority, even when temporarily removed from campus. Therefore, you must abide by my treatment recommendations, do you understand?"

"Yes, ma'am," Chase answered respectfully.

"Observed one-to-one contact at all times. No release from restraints except during restroom breaks. No extra rations, and do *not* speak to her under any conditions." She passed a threatening look down her nose at me.

"We'll continue this *conversation* when you return, Ms. Miller."

We would not. I knew that much. I wasn't coming back.

In a hurry, I was ushered outside and back up the stairs to the main hall. My stomach was pinching uncomfortably, but not from hunger. Soon I was standing beside a navy blue MM van with Chase and Randolph.

The morning was dreary and still. The snow had stopped, but the freeze still scraped my cheeks and iced my throat as I gulped down breath after breath.

Chase opened the door but blocked my entry, first removing a double circle of thin green plastic from his pocket. A zip tie.

"Hands," he ordered, holding the restraints out expectantly. I'd known this had been coming, but I still felt a wave of claustrophobia staring down at the cuffs. They immobilized my arms. I wouldn't be able to run, defend myself, or even go to the bathroom unless Chase released me. I was, for all general purposes, trapped. But I needed to be trapped in order to achieve freedom. The process seemed too twisted to be real.

I balled my hands into fists to prevent the soldiers from seeing them shake. Chase's eyes paused on the thin, crisscrossed welts that were now turning white in my exertion to hold still.

"Make sure they're nice and tight," Randolph said. I bit my lower lip hard to keep quiet.

Chase snorted, snatched my forearms, and jerked me closer so he didn't have to reach. My breath caught—I had never known his touch to be harsh—and I looked deliberately away. But as he secured the loops, Chase did something unexpected. Subtly, he slipped his first two fingers within the tie beneath my wrist, where my pulse beat like the wings of a hummingbird, while simultaneously tightening the strap with his other hand. The space didn't allow me to get out, but it impeded the tie from cutting off my circulation.

I felt a flutter of anger, deep in my stomach. He couldn't think this made up for everything he had done. But before I had too much time to think about it, he'd shoved me roughly up the two steps into the van's front seat, purposefully blocking Randolph's view of my noncompliant restraints.

A moment later the door was slammed shut, Chase was in the driver's seat, and the key brought the ignition to life.

MY fingers wove together on my lap, as they could do little else within the restraints. We pulled down the lane, passing the dorms on my right and the cafeteria below on my left. The van picked up speed, leaving the last of the main campus buildings.

I am never coming back, I promised myself. *Never.*

"It's her, isn't it? My mother. Is she okay?"

A dark expression spread across his face. "Quiet. We're coming to the gate."

I glared at him. No one was listening now, why couldn't he talk to me?

We slowed as the road turned to gravel, and a small check station came into view. It was a single brick cottage, nestled right against the side of the road. Beyond it, I saw the high steel fence, latched by a security gate. Its sinister embrace stretched into the woods around us.

Almost there. Almost free.

Chase slowed the van to a halt and rolled down the driver's side window. A guard leaned out the porthole on his elbows, scowling when he saw me. He disappeared for a moment and returned with a clipboard.

"Get the papers signed?" he asked Chase, flipping through the pages. He had a bald spot right on the top of his head. His name badge said BROADBENT.

My spine straightened. I recognized his name from my phone call in the infirmary. I looked ahead at the closed gate in front of the van as Chase handed Broadbent my summons. He scribbled something on the clipboard.

"Walters!" he called outside the station. "Sweep the van so they can get moving when I'm done. Damn, you'll be driving straight through, huh?"

"I guess so. Your headmistress didn't approve more than one night," said Chase. I remained silent.

Walters, clearly a merit-badge winner, opened my door and reached his hands beneath the seat. I tried to remain calm. He slammed my door and jerked open the slider, checking the empty body of the car.

"All clear," shouted Walters. He closed the trunk.

"Good luck with that," Broadbent said to Chase, nodding my way.

I nearly jumped out of my skin at the blaring buzzer that unlatched the front gate. With a lurch, it swung open.

Chase pressed the gas. And the Girls' Reformatory and Rehabilitation Center of West Virginia faded behind us.

I WAS out. Away from the shack and from Brock, from the terrifying guards and the Statute classes. Everything within me wanted to push Chase aside and slam my foot down on the accelerator, but I knew that couldn't happen.

I was out. But not free.

I glanced over to the driver. His face was set, like it had been in front of my mother's house. This was not the Chase I'd pictured in the woods, in those seconds before I'd thought Randolph would pull the trigger. This was the soldier, and I was still very much imprisoned. Unconsciously, my wrists jerked against the restraints, making my still-sore hands even more sensitive.

We left the winding road outside the facility and joined

the highway. The area was clean here. No stalled cars, no giant potholes in the asphalt. It was obviously a heavily traveled military route: The MM only paid for maintenance on the roads they used most.

As we continued, the frequency of military vehicles increased. A blue van sped past, then several more cruisers, then a bus filled with frightened new residents who had no idea what awaited them. Each sighting made my stomach lurch. If I had escaped last night, there would've been no way I could have snuck by all these soldiers. I'd be shot and bleeding in a ditch right now.

The radio squealed, making me jump. Irritated, Chase flicked it off. The van seemed very quiet without its consistent hum.

I glanced at the speedometer. A perfect sixty-five miles per hour. What a good soldier.

"How long will it take to get there?" I tried not to sound too impatient.

He didn't answer, completely focused on driving.

"I'm not going to tell anyone if you speak to me," I assured him.

Silence.

Why was he doing this? Continuing to punish me after all he'd done? I wanted to throttle him. He had seen my mother, and despite my aggravation, being near him made me feel closer to her than I had in days. I wanted to ask how she looked, if she'd been harmed, if they'd given her enough to eat. But he was adhering strictly to Brock's rules. Any slight hope that he'd come to rescue me slipped away.

"You don't know if she's been doing any kind of rehab, do

you?" I ventured, wondering if she had to "complete" something, like Rebecca had heard.

"Can't you just be quiet?" he snapped. "Right now? You're a prisoner. And I need to think."

I blinked, instantly livid.

"Ms. Brock didn't mean *absolute* silence." I tried to keep my voice even, still hoping that being congenial might earn me some information.

"It's not her rule; it's mine."

I knotted my restrained fists in my skirt. Another MM vehicle flew by. I watched Chase tense, and I felt my face heat up.

"How embarrassing it must be for you to cart around reform-school trash," I said quietly. His grinding jaw told me I'd hit the mark.

WE didn't talk for over an hour. The silence took on a physical presence, a hammer, that bruised me again and again with the reminder that, despite all my memories, I was nothing to him.

It pounded me with new fears, too. What had the last two weeks been like for my mother? And what was going to happen tomorrow morning? Images filled my mind: her dragged into a courtroom in shackles, with Rosa's empty eyes, while a bright, accusing spotlight pinned her in place. Her hands, marked with welts like mine. I shook my head, trying to rid myself of these thoughts, and glanced over at Chase.

What was wrong with him? Was he really going to pretend like I wasn't sitting three feet away? Like our histories hadn't

been braided together since we were children? He was a soldier now, I got that. But he'd been human once, too.

Switching between anxiety and anger was exhausting, and
yet I still found myself watching him, as if at any moment he'd
confess this whole thing was some sick, twisted game.

The clock on the dash said 8:16 A.M. when I felt the van
decrease in speed.

"Are we getting near Chicago?" I asked him, not expecting an answer. It seemed odd. I was poor at geography but
had enough sense to know our trip had been too short. Plus,
we'd taken a side road about twenty miles back and hadn't
passed any MM vehicles since that time. I would have thought
there should be an increase in soldiers as we neared the base.

Even so, I felt a flutter of panic anticipating that my mother
might be close; I still knew nothing of her trial.

The van curved off the highway down a single-lane ramp
and stopped completely before turning right onto an isolated
road. The weeds here had grown over the edges of the asphalt
during the summer and then died in their tracks with the
winter freeze. Dead branches littered our path. This area had
not been maintained by city workers in a long time.

As the van slowed, my heart rate doubled.

"We *are* going to the trial, right?"

He exhaled. "There's been a slight change of plans."

My shoulders, which had been hunched over my restraints,
jerked back sharply. "What do you mean?"

"There is no trial."

My mouth fell open. "But the summons . . ."

Chase bore right again on a narrow dirt road. With every
bump, the van jolted.

"It's a fake."

"You . . . faked an MM document?" I was baffled for only an instant before the floodgates opened. "Well, where is she then? She didn't have a trial? Did they put her in rehab? Oh, God, was she hurt?"

"Don't forget to breathe," he said under his breath.

"Chase! You have to tell me what's going on!"

There were dark shadows under his eyes that I did not understand. He looked to the side, as though the answer were hidden somewhere in the foliage, and then raked one hand through his black hair. I was getting a very bad feeling about all the things he wouldn't say.

"I promised her I would get you out of there."

"You promised—"

"My CO thinks I'm assisting with an overhaul in Richmond."

I didn't know what an overhaul was. I didn't immediately understand why Chase was here when he'd been ordered to be somewhere else. None of it made sense.

"Is she still in jail?" I felt as if I were standing on the edge of a cliff, anticipating a horrible fall.

"No."

The pieces came together too slowly in my impatient brain. My mother was free. *I* was free. Rebecca and Sean were right: There were no more trials. And as for Chase . . .

"You're not a soldier anymore. You're a runaway, too."

"It's called AWOL," he said flatly.

I stared at him, remembering what Rebecca had said about Sean running away, how the MM would punish him for defecting. Chase had condemned himself by bailing me out.

My mother had asked him to risk his life for me. I couldn't think of what this meant, if he might not be so terrible after all. I could only think of her and how we were free and whether we were in more or less danger than I'd previously anticipated.

Chase braked suddenly, and made a hard right down a hidden path that I never would have noticed had he not turned just then. After a curtain of low-hanging tree limbs, we came upon a clearing, where an ancient seventies-era Ford truck was parked. The maroon paint was peeling off in bubbles from the side paneling, and the step bar beneath the door was warped by orange rust.

I looked down at my bound wrists. If Chase had intended to reunite me with my mother, why was I still in restraints? Why were we parking in a deserted clearing miles off the main road? I became increasingly aware of how isolated we were. I'd trusted him once, but after what I'd seen at reform school, being alone with a soldier didn't seem like such a good idea.

"If she's free, why didn't you just tell me?"

He heard the tremor in my voice and looked over. His eyes held a depth of guarded emotions.

"That's a major FBR route we were on, in case you didn't notice. Any one of those soldiers could have stopped us if they'd been suspicious."

I thought of how focused he'd been while driving, watching each MM vehicle that passed, demanding silence. He'd been fearful. If we were caught, his life would be at risk.

A moment later he reached into his hip pocket and retrieved a large folded knife. I siphoned in a tight breath, and for an instant I forgot that it was Chase. I saw a weapon and a uniform, and before I could process anything else, my bundled fingers were jerking at the door handle. It didn't open. A small cry let loose from my strangled throat.

"Hey! *Easy.* I'm just going to cut the restraints," he said. "Jesus, who do you think I am?"

Who *did* I think he was? Not Randolph, preparing to murder me in the woods. But not my friend. Not my love. Not a soldier, either, apparently.

"I have no idea," I answered honestly.

He scowled but didn't respond. The knife flipped open, and adeptly he cut the straps off. The second the task was done he jerked his hands away and unlocked my door from his side. I rubbed my wrists, willing my breath to come more steadily.

An instant later he was out of the van, leaving me in a haze of confusion.

I tore out of the seat after him, toward the truck. My feet splashed through cold puddles of mud.

"So where is she?"

Chase jerked open the rusted door, threw his shoulder into the seat, and popped it forward. A stuffed canvas backpack was revealed, along with a large box of matches, bottled water, a steel pot, and a knitted blanket. He emerged with a screwdriver and returned to the MM transport.

"Not here."

He pushed aside the utility box in the back of the van, ripping away a section of loose carpet covering the floorboards. There waited a slender metal rectangle, which he removed before slamming the trunk closed. A license plate.

"Did you . . . steal that truck?" I asked after a moment. My mouth was hanging open.

"Borrowed it."

"Oh my God." Was he crazy? The MM was probably looking for us right now, and he had stolen a car? I felt a jolt of panic echo through me.

What else would you have him do? a small voice inside my head asked.

He began screwing the license plate in place beneath the tailgate of the truck. "Minnesota" was written in blue letters over an image of a fish jumping from the river to snag a fly.

"Don't freak out," he said without looking up. "It was abandoned." He placed the screwdriver handle between his teeth and rattled the plate with both hands to make sure it was secure.

Clearly my abduction had not been on impulse; Chase had already packed a getaway car with supplies. I began to feel the urgency ripping through my veins. He had gone AWOL and forged documents to get me out of rehab. It wouldn't be long before Brock and the MM figured out what he had done.

"What happened?" I asked.

I blocked his path back to the van. He shoved past.

"There's no time to explain, trust me. We've got to move out."

"*Trust* you?" I asked incredulously. "After you arrested me?"

"I followed orders."

I was shocked at how cold he sounded. I had rationalized that maybe there was still some humanity left within him—he *had* promised my mother he'd get me out—but I realized now that his actions were in no way altruistic. They were full of resentment.

The shock burned into rage. Before I thought it through, I clenched my fist and punched him.

He reacted instantly, tilting back so that I missed his jaw and just barely grazed his ear. I lost my balance and pitched forward, but before I fell he grabbed my shoulder hard and jerked me back upright.

"You'll have to be faster than—"

Furiously, I kicked him as hard as I could, stomping my heel into his thigh. The breath whistled out of his clenched teeth as he staggered back a step. One brow quirked, and I felt my heart kick up a notch.

"Better," he commented. As if we were playing some kind of game.

I seethed, hating him in that moment, but when he released my arm I didn't attack again. It didn't seem to get the point across the way I had hoped.

"What is wrong with you?" I shouted.

A shadow flew across his features. "A lot. Now, if you're all done, get in the truck."

He slid in the driver's seat and slammed the door in my face. Gritting my teeth, I rounded the front and propped open the passenger door. I wasn't about to get inside without him telling me what was going on.

"Where is she?" I demanded.

"Get in and I'll tell you."

"How about you tell me and I'll get in." I crossed my arms over my chest.

"You're a pain," he said bitterly. A hand clawed through his neat soldier haircut. I was learning quickly that this meant he was angry with me.

I waited.

"A safe house in South Carolina," he said. "She knew it was too dangerous to go home."

"A safe house?"

"A place off the FBR's radar. People go there to hide."

My throat constricted. I'd known my mother and I would have to hide. But knowing it and doing it were two different things.

"So we're going to meet her in South Carolina?"

"Sort of. The exact location is a secret. You've got to meet someone who'll bring you in. There's a man, a 'carrier,' at a checkpoint in Virginia who'll get us there. We've got until noon tomorrow to meet him."

"Why tomorrow?"

"He only transports on Thursdays."

"Every week?" I asked, thinking of my mother. Maybe she had met him last week. If not, she might be there when we arrived. I might see her tonight!

"We don't have another week!" Chase said, misinterpreting my question to hear that I wasn't in a tremendous hurry. "After a soldier is AWOL forty-eight hours they put him on a list. Each unit gets a copy of it when their tour of duty starts. After noon tomorrow they're coming after me."

I shuddered. "And me."

He nodded. "You've got a little longer before the overnight pass is invalid. But they'll link you to me—"

"I get it," I interrupted. "How did you find out about this?"

If he'd heard about the safe house in the FBR, surely other soldiers had, too. My mother could be walking into a trap.

"Civilians sometimes talk about safe houses during arrests, but this one . . ." he sighed heavily. "My uncle. I ran into him on a training exercise in Chicago a few months after I was drafted. He was going to South Carolina. He told me about the carrier in Virginia. Good enough?"

"That was almost a year ago. How do you know it's still there?" Chase's uncle had ditched Chase during the War. I didn't exactly trust him.

"The FBR never found out about it. My security clearance gave me access to operations. South Carolina hasn't had any movement since they evacuated the coast."

"And you're sure my mother found this carrier?" I pressed.

"No," he answered bluntly.

Which meant she could be anywhere. Still, if she'd been attempting to get to South Carolina, we had to as well. In less than twenty-seven hours, the MM would know we were fugitives. We needed to hop aboard this underground railroad as soon as possible.

For the first time, I truly felt like a criminal. I rolled my still sore shoulders back and, making my decision, scooted into the truck.

Chase jammed the screwdriver into the steering-wheel column, and it released with a soft pop. Then he fiddled around with something under the console until a few fast clicks sent the engine squealing to life. He sat up, revved the gas. There was no key in the ignition.

"Learn that in the MM?" I asked spitefully.

"No," he said. "I learned that during the War."

I reminded myself that it shouldn't matter that the truck was hot-wired. Or that it was stolen. As long as it got to Virginia fast.

I COULDN'T stop looking at him. A month he'd been home from Chicago, and sometimes I still couldn't believe he was really here.

"What?" he asked, a smile in his tone. He didn't have to look over to know I'd been staring. We sat on his back steps, facing the jungle of grass and weeds that had become his back yard.

"Nothing," I said. "I'm just glad you're back. Really glad."

"Really, really glad? Wow, Em." He rocked back, laughing, when I shoved him.

"Don't push it."

He laughed again, and then became quiet. Pensive. "I'm glad I'm back, too. There was a while I wasn't sure it would happen."

"When Chicago was hit, you mean." My voice sounded small under the big, open sky.

"Yeah." Chase frowned, leaning back against the top step. I didn't want to pressure him; I knew some people didn't like to talk about the War. I was just about to change the subject when he continued.

"You know my chemistry teacher tried to tell us the air sirens were just drills? He was still trying to get us to pass in our lab sheets when the quakes started. By the time we all got outside, the smoke was so thick you couldn't see the school's parking lot. " He paused, shook his head. "Anyway, they bussed us all to this old arena on the west side and gave us two minutes each to use the phones and call home, and my uncle told me to meet him at this restaurant in Elgin. So I took off. Hitched there. It was a good thing too: The bombing didn't stop for three days."

"Wait, you hitchhiked there? What were you, fifteen?"

"Sixteen." He shrugged as though this detail was unimportant. "When we met in Elgin, we found out Chicago had been attacked on the southeastern side, all the way up I-90 from Gary. What was left of it was just . . . chaos. We were being displaced to some town in the middle of Indiana, but we only made it as far as South Bend before the busses got called somewhere else. We stayed there for a while; my uncle found some work doing day labor, but they wouldn't hire me because I was too young.

"And then he told me he was sorry, but he couldn't look out for me anymore. He gave me his bike and told me to keep in touch."

My eyes were wide.

"He couldn't . . . what? You must hate him!"

Chase shrugged. "One less person to worry about, one less mouth to feed." At my horrified expression he sat up. "Look, when Baltimore and DC fell, and all those people started packing inland into Chicago, he knew, just knew it was going to get bad. So he taught me to scrap. He and my mom had grown up poor, and he was, well, resourceful." A guilty laugh had him turning his head the opposite direction, making me wonder just what that meant.

"I'd have been scared to death," I said.

He took off his hat and tapped it against his knee.

"Losing your family . . . it puts fear in a different perspective," he said. "Besides, I got by all right. I stayed on the fringe around Chicago, hopped around tent cities and Red Cross camps. Worked for some people who didn't ask questions. Avoided case-workers and foster care. And thought about you."

"Me?" I huffed, completely unsettled. In awe at how vanilla

my life seemed. In awe of what he'd endured. He turned then, meeting my eyes for the first time. When he spoke, his voice was gentle, and unashamed.

"You. The only thing in my life that doesn't change. When everything went to hell, you were all I had." It took me a full beat to realize he was serious. When I did, I had to remind myself to keep breathing.

I SHIFTED in my seat. My life did not seem so vanilla anymore. I knew what he meant about losing family now, and in another day, every soldier in the country would have our photos.

Had we been able to take the highways, we would have crossed the border into Virginia before sunset, when everyone had to be off the roads for curfew. As it was, Chase had stuck to back country roads, which led us east rather than south, cautiously avoiding any potential contact with an MM patrol.

By late afternoon, the sun was heating up through the windshield. Chase removed the navy MM jacket and slung it over the seatback between us. He wore only a thin T-shirt, and beneath it I could see the sculpted muscles in his arms and shoulders. My gaze lingered a little too long, and I rubbed my stomach unconsciously.

"We'll stop soon for supplies," he said, thinking I was hungry.

I didn't like this; we needed to get every mile in that we could before curfew. But as I glanced over Chase's forearm I saw that the gas gauge was nearly empty. It would take us a lot longer to get to Virginia if we had to walk.

We passed two closed gas stations before we found one

that actually claimed to be in business, at least on weekdays. It was a small place called Swifty's, with only two pumps and a note taped over the price board that said PAY INSIDE, CASH ONLY. We were the only ones in the parking lot.

"Wait here," Chase instructed. I had just been getting out of the truck but paused.

"I'm sorry, you must have forgotten. I'm not actually your prisoner."

His jaw twitched. "You're right. You're a wanted runaway. You can be *their* prisoner."

I glowered at him but slammed the door. As much as I hated to admit it, he was right. We shouldn't both be showing our faces if we didn't have to.

Chase removed a worn red flannel shirt from the back of the cab and buttoned it up over his T-shirt. He untucked the bottoms of his pants from his boots, and hid his MM jacket, and it hit me, a furious pang of nostalgia. A vision of him sitting on his front steps, long legs stretched out and crossed casually at the ankles. Eyes, dark and watchful as a wolf's, still piercing even from a distance. His smooth bronze complexion, a reflection of his mother's Chickasaw heritage. His hair was short now, cleanly cut like the other soldiers', but then it had been thick and glossy and black, hanging around his angular face.

He looked like the old Chase, even if he didn't act like him. I swallowed hard.

The change made me suddenly self conscious of my appearance: My gray sweater and pleated navy skirt screamed "reform school." I scanned the parking lot for any bystanders, worried that I might be recognized.

Chase disappeared behind the tinted glass of the mini-mart. As the minutes ticked by, my paranoia intensified. I'd believed his story about leaving the MM without question, but I didn't know what had really happened. He wasn't telling me *anything*, not why he'd arrested us, not why he'd come back. For all I knew, he could be contacting the MM right now. My heels drummed a cadence on the rutted rubber floor mats.

The sun was just above the tree line now. It would be getting dark soon.

What was taking so long?

I was just grabbing the door handle, intent to check for myself on Chase's intentions, when I saw it. A large bulletin board on the far side of the store window. The blood drained from my face. Though I was twenty feet away I knew exactly what it would say.

MISSING! IF SIGHTED, CONTACT THE FEDERAL
BUREAU OF REFORMATION IMMEDIATELY!

I had seen this board before, of course. At the mini-mart near school.

My photo from the reformatory would be posted just as soon as Brock figured out I'd escaped. A desperate need arose in me to see if it was there now, but I couldn't risk being spotted. What if the clerk inside had already caught a glimpse of me when I'd opened the door earlier? How could I have been so careless?

It's too soon. You've only been gone a few hours, I reminded myself.

I envisioned Beth and Ryan scanning through the pictures the way we had looked for Katelyn Meadows. Defending me when people whispered about what I'd done to be arrested. They were true friends, not the kind that would turn their backs. It struck me that they didn't even know Katelyn was dead. I shivered, frightened by the reality that my friends would never know if *I* was dead.

The door lurched open, catching me off guard. I nearly leapt out the window.

"Here," Chase said. The change was sliding off the top of a wrapped flat of plastic water bottles he shoved onto the seat, and I grabbed it before it fell to the floor. The total on the receipt was over three hundred dollars. I hastily shoved the assorted bills into my pocket, uncomfortable with any money sitting out in the open. I was shocked by the amount of cash he'd been carrying.

"I worked for it," he told me snidely before I could ask. "Soldiers collect pay. It's a regular job."

"It's hardly a *regular* job," I grumbled.

I placed the supplies on the floor while Chase filled up the truck. Among the groceries—peanut butter, bread, and other staples—was a chocolate bar with almonds. Had he remembered that this was my favorite kind of candy? Probably not. He didn't do things out of the kindness of his heart anymore. Still, it seemed too frivolous to be anything but a peace offering.

It only took him a few moments of connecting the exposed wires beneath the wheel before the truck *thrummed* to life again. As we pulled onto the street, I stared out the back window at the Missing Persons board, in grim awe of how my life had changed. My freedom from the MM's clutches had come with a stifling loss. I would never be able to walk around in the open again.

CHASE flipped on the MM radio. A man with a cool, flat voice was talking.

"*. . . another FBR vehicle stolen outside Nashville earlier today from the parking lot of a textile plant. The truck contained uniforms to be shipped to bases throughout Tennessee. No eyewitnesses. Rebel activity suspected. Any suspicions should be reported to command.*"

"Who is he?" I whispered to Chase, as though the speaker might hear me.

"A reporter for the FBR. He does a newscast for the region every day. They cycle through it at the top of the hour."

"Are there lots of rebels?" I liked the idea of people striking against the MM. I wondered what they planned to do with the uniforms.

"Occasionally someone gets it in their head to steal a rations truck, but not often," he informed me. "Mostly it's just anarchy. Ripping up the Statutes, attacks on soldiers, mob riots. Things like that. Nothing that can't be managed."

I frowned at his confidence. There had been a time he was much like the people he now denigrated.

"*The overhaul of Kentucky, West Virginia, and Virginia is nearly complete. Oregon, Washington, Montana, and North Dakota will be overhauled beginning June one, with estimated compliance by September. . . .*"

Anticipating my questions, Chase explained that an overhaul was when the MM systematically went through a city's census to weed out Article violators.

"It's what they did to you," he said.

For a fraction of a moment his eyes flickered with pain, and I found myself glad that some part of him felt guilty for what he had done. The mention of the arrest had triggered my hands to fist in anger, and I had been fighting the urge to hit him again.

"It's a tedious process," he continued. "It takes a lot of manpower. All records—medical, employment, anything you can think of—are reviewed. Anyone who's not in compliance with the Statutes is subject to sentencing, or is automatically sequestered."

"Sequestered?" I felt as if I were talking to a stranger rather than someone I'd known my whole life.

"Put into federal custody. Like you were."

"What happened to tickets and fines?" I remembered the night we'd received a citation for an old pre-War fashion magazine my mother had hidden under her mattress. "Lewd Materials," the sheet had said. "Paper Contraband— $50.00".

"They're history. No one can pay them."

I'd complained about this to him when he'd come home from Chicago. I hadn't at the time considered that this would be the alternative, or that Chase would be a part of it.

We listened to a list of missing persons. I held my breath, but my name was not spoken. Chase's forged documents had worked. Brock still believed I was on an overnight pass. When the report ended, Chase flicked off the radio.

Dusk was imminent; the sky had already tapered to a dull gray. I sighed apprehensively. We were going to have to look for a place to stop for the night, which meant the hours we could be traveling would instead be spent hiding somewhere just over the Pennsylvania border. It seemed like an insurmountable waste.

A road sign appeared on the right. The white paint stood out in sharp contrast to the metallic background.

RED ZONE

I could feel Chase tense across the cab.

"What's a Red Zone?" I hadn't heard the term before.

"Evacuated area. Like Baltimore, DC, all the surrounding cities. Yellow Zones house FBR bases. Red Zones are deserted."

It struck me just how small my world at home had been.

"This is new," he added. It was clear from his tone that he hadn't intended to cross into an evacuated zone on our way to the carrier.

As we neared the sign, a car, hidden behind a tangle of brush, was revealed.

A *blue* car. With a flag and a cross on the side.

All at once, every nerve in my body screamed danger. We couldn't stop and turn around, because it was too late. Though Chase was driving the speed limit, the MM highway patrol pulled out onto the road behind us.

A moment later the bar of lights on the cruiser's roof flashed to life and a loud siren pierced the air.

CHAPTER
6

CHASE swore. Loudly.

My mind raced through the possibilities. Brock had figured out what had happened. Chase had underestimated his time before the MM came after him. We'd been seen together at the gas station.

This couldn't be happening. We had to get to South Carolina. My mother was waiting for us.

"Can you outrun them?" My question was met with a withering look. "*Go!*" I shouted.

"Ember, listen. Reach in the bag behind the seat. There's a weapon in the bottom zippered pouch. Give it to me," Chase ordered.

I hesitated.

"*Now!*"

I jerked upright and stuffed my hand as smoothly as I could into the pack.

"Easy," he cued.

"I *know*." Anyone behind us would be able to see through the back window of the cab. My fingers found the zipper. I pulled it aside, feeling something solid and cold rest against my palm.

"Oh . . ." A knot lodged in my throat.

"Hurry up," he said sharply.

Very slowly, I pulled the handgun over the seat, hiding it from the window with my arm. I dropped it on the leather between us, retracting my hand immediately. Without the holster covering it, the exposed gun looked lethally ominous. The way it had looked in the woods, aimed at my chest.

Chase must have removed it at the gas station when he'd changed. He hid it now in his belt, beneath his flannel shirt.

"If I tell you to run, do it," he said. "Go straight into the woods and don't look back. Do not, under any circumstances, let them find you."

I shuddered. I'd suspected that I would be thrown back into rehab if I was found, but Chase's tone scared me. It insinuated something far worse.

My mind was reeling. He wanted me to run. To leave him alone with the soldiers when I was the reason his life was at risk. But I couldn't have Chase's imprisonment on my conscience. Not after what I'd done to Sean and Rebecca.

But I had to get to my mother. That was my only priority. Wasn't it?

"What are you going to do?" I asked as the truck's speed decreased.

He didn't answer.

As much as Chase had changed, as much as the darkness in his eyes unsettled me, it seemed impossible that he would consider killing someone. Still . . .

I snatched the blanket out from behind the seat and covered my skirt. I hoped that the soldier wouldn't know that my sweater was part of a reformatory ensemble. It looked mainstream enough.

Chase pulled onto the side of the road and turned off the vehicle, blocking the wired area below the dash from view with his knees. I glanced at his navy uniform pants and hoped the patrolman didn't look down.

The seconds passed with biting intensity, until finally a soldier stepped out of the passenger side of the cruiser. The sound of the door slamming was as loud as a cannon firing in my ears. In the mirror I saw that another stayed behind in the driver's seat.

The man that approached was older than most of the soldiers I'd seen, with a stark, silver comb-over that topped his weathered face. He sauntered to the front door and motioned for Chase to roll down his window. In my peripheral vision, I watched my companion's every move.

"License and registration," the soldier said, just like the cops used to say before the MM took over. There was a handheld scanner in his right hand.

Chase reached across my lap to open the dash. When his forearm rested on my knee, the warmth from his skin spread up my leg, and my sharp intake of breath smelled of soap and home and safety. The feeling faded as quickly as it had come. He grabbed a thin piece of paper the size of a note card and handed it to the officer.

"Sorry. A soldier took my ID during our last inspection. Said it was part of the census. He said I could still drive."

"Yeah, yeah," nodded the highway patrol, as though this were a commonplace occurrence. I remembered the way

Bateman had tucked my mother's ID into his pocket during her arrest.

The soldier scanned the bar code on the registration and squinted at a tiny screen, presumably checking for outstanding warrants. I was ready to crawl out of my skin.

"Lucky there's a freeze on car payments, Mr. Kandinsky. Your registration's expired. Three years."

Chase nodded. The soldier handed back the registration.

"So, where you headed?" he asked. "Town's cleared. Been empty for months."

My hands squeezed each other with bone-breaking intensity. I flipped them over to hide the bruises.

"I know," Chase lied smoothly. "My aunt's got a place just down a-ways. I told her I'd check in on it. We've got a pass."

"Let's see it."

Chase reached into his pocket. Just beside the gun. I turned to face the opposite window, eyes squeezed shut. My fingers clenched in the blanket as I braced for the gunfire.

He's going to do it, I thought. *He's going to shoot this man.*

"I saw it in your jacket pocket," I blurted. Soldier or not, this man had done nothing to us. Chase shot me a scathing look.

"This your girlfriend?" asked the soldier, finally registering my presence. His eyes were roaming over my hands. I forced them to steady.

"My wife," Chase answered between his teeth.

Yes, of course. An unmarried couple would be issued an Indecency Citation for spending time alone together so close to curfew. It occurred to me the soldier had been looking at my hands for a ring. If we lived through this, I'd have to find some cheap jewelry.

"Good thing," he commented. My stomach twisted.

Chase looked at me. "In my jacket? Really?" He winced. "Damn. I left it at home then. I'm sorry, sir."

"What was the number?" the soldier tested.

"U-fourteen. That was it, wasn't it honey?"

I nodded, trying not to look petrified.

"It was a blue form, about this big." Chase motioned with his hands the size of an index card.

"Yeah, that's the right form." The soldier bounced the scanner in his opposite hand, thinking. "I'm letting you off the hook, but make sure the next time you venture into an evacuated area, you have a pass, got it? You've got twenty-four hours."

"Yes, sir," said Chase. "Thank you, sir."

A few minutes later, the cruiser disappeared behind a turn in the road.

"Oh. Wow." The words were sticky in my throat.

"Old bastard can't even do his job right," Chase said. "The regs clearly state you can't allow a civilian to enter a Red Zone without a U-fourteen. Everyone knows that."

"Thank God he didn't!" I practically shouted.

Chase lifted a brow. "Well. Yes."

A somber fog settled over us. I couldn't help wondering what Chase would have done had I not said anything. I knew by his demeanor now that he hadn't intended to shoot him, but I also knew he hadn't taken the option off the table.

Nothing happened, I reminded myself.

But tomorrow, after we'd been registered missing, this scene would play out very differently.

It was time to get off the road.

WE drove through the empty streets of the Red Zone, hunkering down on an old hunting path beneath the charcoal sky. We hadn't seen any more cruisers, but Chase said that they patrolled Red Zones to manage crime, and after our run-in with the MM, I wasn't eager for a replay.

Still, waiting for dawn wasn't any easier.

I made peanut butter sandwiches to busy my hands, and told myself that it did no good to focus on how we were sitting around while the clock on our safety dwindled down. There was nothing we could do until curfew lifted.

Chase took the sandwiches hesitantly when I shoved three his way.

"I didn't spit in them," I told him, long past feeling offended. His brows, arched in surprise, returned to their normal scowl. He may not have been used to someone taking care of him, but I felt compelled; making dinner was my usual chore at home. The reminder, sharp as a knife, brought on a new wave of desperation.

"I have to show you something," he said, as if to reciprocate for the food I'd made. He went outside, sending a blast of cold air into the cabin of the truck, and reluctantly, I followed with the flashlight.

My breath caught when I saw the silver barrel of the gun emerge from his waistband.

It was too dark, and the woods smelled too heavily of dead leaves and earth. A sick sense of dread emptied my mind of the present and took control of my senses. I could still hear that fateful metal click, hear Randolph's voice, pitched with excitement, accusing me of running.

"Hey," Chase said quietly, startling me when he was closer than I expected. I shoved away from him, gulping a mouthful of frigid air.

"I've already seen it," I told him. My heart was beating like I'd just run a mile, but I stood tall, hoping he hadn't noticed my lapse.

Get it together, I told myself. Chase wasn't a soldier anymore. I wasn't at the reformatory. I shouldn't have to remind myself of that.

His brows drew together as if in pain. For an instant I could have sworn he'd read my mind, but then his expression hardened once again.

"Do you have any idea how to handle a gun?" His voice was low. I knew he was thinking of what had transpired earlier with the highway patrol.

I cast him an acerbic look. "Do you *really* have to ask me that question?"

He gripped the barrel, offered the weapon to me.

"I . . . I don't like guns," I said.

"You and me both."

That was surprising. As a soldier, he would have been used to carrying a firearm. When he didn't give up, I plucked the handle out of his hand as if it were a dead rat and, surprised at its weight, nearly dropped it.

"Watch where you're pointing that," he snapped.

I winced and aimed the barrel toward the ground.

"It's heavy."

"It's a Browning Hi-Power nine millimeter. A pistol."

He swallowed, wiped his palms on his pants. Then he gently placed his hands around mine, forcing me to grip the handle but taking care not to press on my injured knuckles. My skin seared with heat where we connected, betraying the will of my mind, which wanted very much to despise him. It was less confusing after everything he'd done.

"Look. This on the side is called the safety. When it's on you won't be able to pull the trigger. All right so far?"

"Uh-huh."

He guided my hands, showed me how to empty a clip.

"The magazine holds the thirteen rounds. It's a semiautomatic, which means that it's self-loading, but only after you cock back the slide. That chambers the first round. After that, all you need to do is pull the trigger."

"How convenient."

"That's the idea. Now, we're not really going to do this, but here's what happens if you get in trouble: Safety off. Pull back the slide. Point and aim. Squeeze the trigger. Use both hands. Got it?"

"Yes, sir."

"Say it."

"Safety off. Pull back the slide. Point and aim. Squeeze the trigger." A forbidden sense of power seemed to vibrate through my hands as I said the words.

He took back the gun, and my ability to breathe returned. But then he pulled out a knife.

For the next ten minutes I hunched over my knees while Chase sawed off my hair by the fistful. Though I knew we had to do as much as we could to avoid recognition, I couldn't stop the gnawing concern that my mother, Beth, my *friends*, might soon find me unrecognizable. That all the old pieces of me—the pieces I knew—were being cut away just like my hair, leaving something distorted and raw in their stead. But that was stupid of course; I was still me. It was everything else that had changed.

We returned to the truck, where we sat on opposite ends of the seat and stared straight ahead in stubborn, tense silence. As the minutes passed I became acutely aware of his breathing—even, rhythmic—and soon found that my own had matched his tempo. How he could soothe me in a time like this, without even trying, how we connected on this most basic frequency made my heart ache for something impossible. Made me angle my body away so he wouldn't see how much it hurt just to be near him again.

I missed him more now than I had when he'd been gone.

Only when the night grew so dark that I could no longer define his shape beside me did I allow myself to peek his way.

"Would you have left the MM if she hadn't asked you?"

My voice sounded small, barely louder than a breath.

"I don't know," he said honestly.

I drifted to sleep, knees bound tightly to my chest, secretly wishing that his answer had been more certain. At least then I would have known how one of us felt.

"GOOD morning."

He rested his elbows on the windowsill. The same old cap was fitted over his hair; the bill was arched in a permanent half-moon. Tired as I was, when I saw that smile I knew I wouldn't be able to fall back asleep.

I shoved the window the rest of the way up, kneeling on my rumpled comforter in my nightshirt. The sky was as black as it had been when I'd gone to bed last night.

"Why aren't you sleeping?" I nodded toward his bedroom, directly across the space between our houses. He looked back at it, then shrugged.

"Wasn't tired. Your mom and I had a nice walk. She told me to tell you to be good today. And not to do anything she would do." He winked dramatically, like I knew she would have done.

I rolled my eyes, but my heart softened. I liked that Chase had walked her to the soup kitchen. Our town wasn't as safe as it had been, especially in the dark mornings just after curfew lifted. She was never as vigilant as she should be when out alone.

"Thanks," I said, "for looking out for her."

He gave me a funny look, as if I should have expected no different.

I SNUGGLED my cheek deeper into my pillow and . . . it moved.

My eyes shot open.

I was in the cab of the truck. Not at home. Not at the reformatory. I was curled across the seat, my head on Chase's thigh. And things between us were not as they once had been.

I jolted up.

The gray, predawn light cut through the film of condensation covering the window. It was Thursday, the day we'd meet the carrier . . . the day I'd see my mother.

The day that Chase would be reported AWOL.

I pushed back the MM uniform jacket I'd used as a blanket, trying to remember how it had come to be spread over my body. . . .

Chase rubbed his hands over his stubbled face. His eyes grew wide when they landed on me. I ran a hurried hand through my short, uneven hack-job, and covered my mouth.

"Toothpaste," I demanded. I didn't have a toothbrush; my finger would have to do. But when I reached for the bag, he snatched it away and retrieved the item himself. I didn't know why; I'd already seen the gun.

A blast of freezing air shocked me when I opened the truck door. Shivering, I walked far enough from the truck to shake off the dream but not so far as to lose sight of it completely.

It would be warmer farther south at the safe house. Maybe my mother was already there, head on her forearms, grumbling that there wasn't any caffeinated coffee like in the old days. Maybe there were other mothers there, too—people who could support her so she wouldn't worry so much and calm her down when she inevitably tried to launch some knee-jerk rebellion. I could see her leading the charge, a contraband magazine rolled in one raised fist, a trash can of burning Statute circulars to her side. Thinking of this made me smile, a secret smile I would never let her see for fear she'd take it as a sign of encouragement.

"Nice coat," Chase said, breaking me from the trance. I hadn't thought twice about slipping on his enormous jacket when I'd gone outside, but now I was suddenly embarrassed, torn between throwing it at him and nestling deeper into the bulky canvas. I ended up shuffling my weight, as if trying to negotiate a balance beam, until he spoke again.

"We need to find some other clothes," he said, watching my struggle with some interest. "You'll stand out wearing a combination of your uniform and mine."

I forced myself to be still. I didn't know what he had in mind, but I figured it was in the same vein as his procurement of the vehicle. The prospect of stealing didn't bother me as much as I thought it might, as long as it didn't hurt anyone or take too long.

I gathered the extra sleeve lengths in my fists and focused on the fact that by nightfall, my mother and I would be back together.

We were on the highway within a half hour.

JUST after seven, we passed a sign indicating that the Maryland border was nearing. I wanted to go straight to the checkpoint, but we couldn't take the chance of backtracking into the highway patrol. Instead we were forced into a wide arc to go south. I checked a map every few minutes, tracing Chase's proposed path. He'd shown me the exact coordinates where we would meet the carrier: 190 Rudy Lane in Harrisonburg, Virginia.

If we didn't run into any more soldiers, we could still arrive in time.

Though there were no cars, our momentum was stunted. The road was pockmarked by missing chunks of asphalt and man-made debris: a bed comforter, the skeleton of an umbrella. We frightened a deer that had been eating the weathered remains of a Horizons cardboard box.

I took it all in with a mixture of awe and vanquished pride. I'd been nine when the War had taken Baltimore, and the remainder of the state had been evacuated before my tenth birthday. This was the only evidence of human life left.

Chase leaned forward slightly, steering around a rusted motorcycle laid out across the middle of the street. A strange, familiar feeling stirred in my belly.

"COME on. You're not scared, are you?" His grin was fast and wicked, his challenging tone deliberate. He knew full well I hadn't backed down from one of his dares since I'd been six years old, and I wasn't about to now.

I threw a leg over the back of the bike, squeezing the frame with enough force to bend the metal. His dark eyes flickered with amusement as he grabbed the handlebars and released the kickstand. A tilt of his head told me to shove back, and when I did, his long leg slid between me and the front of the bike.

I fumbled with the back of his shirt, needing something to hold on to.

"Try this." He grabbed my hands, sliding them around his waist until they were pressing against his chest. The warmth of his skin soaked through my thin mittens. Then he reached back to grip behind my knees, and pulled me forward until my body was flush against his.

I didn't breathe. We were touching in so many places I couldn't concentrate. His right foot slammed down and the bike roared to life. The seat vibrated beneath me. My heart was pounding. I could already feel the panic begin to trickle through.

"Wait!" I yelled through the helmet. "Don't I need instructions, or directions, or a training course, or . . ."

For just a moment, his fingers interlaced with mine over his chest.

"Lean the way I lean. Don't fight me."

DON'T fight me, Ember.

Absently, I rubbed my right temple with my thumb. I had to stop thinking of the person Chase had been.

"How did Mom look when she was released?" I asked, shaking off the memory.

"What?" His shoulders hunched, and he glanced out the side window.

"How did she look? After the sentencing."

"I never said she'd been sentenced."

My back straightened. "You implied it. You said people either get sentenced or sequestered. And you said they let her go, right? So she fulfilled her sentence?"

"Right."

I groaned. The vague commitment to an explanation was almost worse than the earlier vow of silence.

"How long did you hold her for?"

"Just a day," he said.

"Don't give me too many details, okay? I don't think I'll be able to handle it." I crossed my arms over my chest.

He was quiet, brooding again. *What did I do to you?* I wanted to shout at him. *Why won't you just talk to me?* It would be so much easier to accept this person if I didn't know him before he was guarded and wary and cold. If I couldn't remember that once he'd been an open book and that the days had been too short to hold all our words. It was infuriating, and worse, it made me question if I'd grossly misjudged everything there had been between us.

He stretched his stiff neck from side to side.

"She looked . . ." he hesitated. "I don't know, she looked

like your mom. Short hair, big eyes. Little. What do you want me to say? I only saw her for a little while."

I snorted at this summation. Leave it to a boy to be so literal. "How did she *seem*? Was she scared?"

He considered this, and I could see a slight change in his face. A strain, pulling on the corners of his eyes. I was instantly worried.

"Yes. She was scared." He cleared his throat, and I could tell her fear had pierced that callous shell. "But she was clear-headed, too. Not crazy, like some people get when they're afraid. She was good under pressure, considering everything that had happened. She was absolutely determined we follow this plan."

"Huh." I slouched into the seat.

"What?" he asked earnestly. It crossed my mind that this was the first time he'd been interested in what I was thinking.

"I just never would have described her as clear-headed. I . . . I can't believe I just said that. That's terrible." I cringed, feeling like I'd just betrayed her. "I don't mean that she's not capable of making decisions or anything. It's just, under pressure, she's usually . . . not."

I saw a flash of our kitchen. Of her crying on the floor when I'd made Roy leave. Of all the times she'd brought home contraband, or gotten it in her head that she would tell off a soldier at the next compliance inspection. I was the safe and steady one. Not her. Now he was saying she didn't need me, during the scariest time of our lives? That she could do this on her own? What had I been worrying about?

I pinched my eyes closed. They were burning, hot with tears I wouldn't set loose.

"You'd have been proud of her," he said quietly.

My heart cracked wide open. What was wrong with me? His words should have been a relief. But here I was, feeling inadequate because she could manage on her own. As if I were codependent or something.

Just as the wave rose, it receded, and left in its place was clarity.

I didn't need her to feel strong, because she had *made* me strong. And I had made her strong, too. She was a big girl, like she'd told me countless times when I'd gotten fed up with her rabble-rousing. She'd make it to South Carolina; I just needed to get myself there.

"**SORT** of makes you feel short, doesn't it?" I said as the highway approached an enormous wedge cut into the mountainside. The mustard-colored walls stretched up over three hundred feet on either side, so that only a band of silver sky was visible overhead. Trees and vines, in various states of maturity, reached their crooked fingers toward us, having been long without the care of city maintenance workers. Chase was forced to reduce our speed as we jostled over a mudslide that had spewed out onto the road.

A large sign on my right that read SIDELING HILL VISITOR'S CENTER, NEXT EXIT, had been tampered with: Just below the words, a cross and a flag had been spray-painted with a big neon green X through it. I'd seen symbols like this on the news when we'd had a television, but never in my hometown. It made me feel like a domesticated housecat thrown out into the wild.

"You *are* short," he commented, so late I'd forgotten I'd said anything. I tried to make myself taller in the seat, as if to say *Five four isn't that short,* but the truck bounced so hard over the ground it was impossible to stay rigid.

We passed through the gap of Sideling Hill and continued on toward Hagerstown. Thirty-three more miles, the sign said. It was evacuated so quickly that most stores had been abandoned, full of merchandise. We'd see how intact that merchandise still was, eight years later, then catch the connecting highway south to Harrisonburg.

"Do you think it's safe?" I'd heard about gangs in the empty cities. The original purpose of the MM had been to reduce crime in these places.

"Nowhere is," he said. "It's been cleared by the FBR though."

"That makes me feel so much better," I said.

He connected to Interstate 81, a vigilant eye on the road as we entered Hagerstown. The first houses we came upon were large, surrounded by rolling properties and stout trees. As we drew closer to the heart of town, little neighborhoods sprouted, then lines of track homes and condos. A supermarket. A restaurant. All covered by a gray film of ash, like dirty snow, that had grown impenetrable to weather.

No kids played in the street. No dogs barked in the yards. Not a single car on the road.

The town, preserved by time, was absolutely still.

I noticed a shopping center on the right and pointed to it. Chase took the nearest exit, turning onto a street called Garland Groh Boulevard. Within a minute, he had pulled into an alley beside an old sporting goods store. We'd had one of these at home, but it had closed during the War. The MM had turned it into a uniform distribution center.

I could see the empty highway just beyond the parking lot, a straight shot to the checkpoint. My heart pounded in my chest. It was a little more than five hours before the MM would report Chase AWOL. We'd have to get what we could and get out. *Fast.*

Chase unhooked the wires near his knees, silencing the engine. Before he opened the door he removed a slender black baton with a perpendicular handle from beneath the seat. His face grew dark when he caught me staring at it with wide eyes.

The other weapon was in the front pouch of the bag. In case we ran across people, he didn't want anyone seeing we had a gun. It would have been like hanging a hundred-dollar bill out of your pocket and hoping someone didn't steal it.

"Stay close, just in case," he told me.

I nodded, and we stepped outside the safety of the truck. Our shoes left footprints in the thin layer of gray ash over the asphalt.

I stayed close beside Chase as we rounded the front of the building. The store's tall windows had been shattered, the remaining glass forming icelike stalactites that hung from the green-painted frames. The columnar handles of two French doors were bound together by a thick metal chain and a padlock, but the glass on either side was missing.

I scanned the parking lot behind us as Chase stepped through the doorframe. Apart from a scorched Honda that someone had set fire to years ago, it was deserted.

I breathed in sharply as I followed him inside.

A cash register was dumped on its side directly in my path. Metal racks and tables had been overturned or tossed into the aisles. Much of the clothing was missing, probably stolen, and what was left was strewn about as though a tornado had taken the interior of the building. As I made my way farther inside I spotted exercise machines and weight sets, all tagged by neon spray paint with the same symbol: the MM's insignia X'd out. A rack of sporting equipment spilled onto the weather-stained, laminated floor. Baseballs, footballs, and flat basketballs were peppered all the way to the far wall.

"Try to find some clothes. I'm going to see what else I can pull together."

I nodded. Even though I knew it was ludicrous based on the condition of the place, I checked for security cameras.

"You won't get caught," Chase said, reading my mind. "Anyway, look around; it's not like you're going to do this place any more damage."

He had a point, but the last weeks had made me paranoid, and this place was scary. I worried that somehow the MM might be spying on us. That this was a trap.

I was glad that Chase wanted to go upstairs, because that's where the arrow and sign for WOMEN'S CLOTHING pointed as well. The frozen escalator groaned beneath our weight as we climbed toward the camping section. It seemed surreal that people used to camp recreationally, but I knew Chase and his family had done that a lot when he was little. As he departed toward the steel racks, I felt a twinge of panic.

"You'll just be over there?" I pointed to a mangled tent across the floor.

Something changed in his face when he registered my concern.

"I won't be far," he said quietly.

A central skylight gave the top floor a faint glow. The closer I got to the far wall, the more shadowed the area became, until I had to squint to see the floor. I stepped gingerly over the rubble crowding the aisles and found several racks of clothing in the back that looked relatively untouched. The tops were all fitted, and the pants were bootleg—that had been the style back then—but old as they were, they were new to me. Though the fabric was dusty, these clothes still held the crisp, folded lines and size stickers. I hadn't owned clothing that didn't come from a donation center since my mother had lost her job. Despite the circumstances, the thought had me giggling.

There was a special on women's hiking boots: $59.99. *Free for me!* I thought guiltily, and searched through the shoe boxes strewn across the floor for my size. We never would have been able to afford these, even eight years ago. With inflation, these shoes would be well over $100 now. I was getting $100 shoes! I couldn't wait to tell Beth.

If I ever talked to her again.

I forced the thought from my mind. Behind me was a display of jeans, and I quickly grabbed a pair in my size. A winter coat off the floor had minimal dust covering it, so I took that too. Then a tank top, a fitted tee, a thermal shirt, and a sweatshirt. I grabbed some extra socks, just to be safe, and an unopened package of underwear. It hit me that my mother might not have a change of clothes, either, so I grabbed one of everything for her also.

But as I made my way into the changing area, the laughter died in my throat. The dressing room was the size of a closet, and without the bright overhead lights, it looked like the containment cell I had seen in the shack.

I wasn't about to shut myself inside.

I scanned for Chase but couldn't find him. I was glad he hadn't seen me falter; the last thing I needed was him thinking I was afraid of guns *and* the dark. With a deep breath, I dropped the items right where I was and hurried to change before he came looking for me.

The jeans fit pretty well, though they were loose around the waist from the weight I'd dropped at the reform school. I was midway through pulling down the tank top when I heard rustling behind me.

I spun toward the sound and saw Chase, ten feet away, wearing jeans and a new sweatshirt and carrying a pack over one shoulder. I twisted back away from him, the tank still hiked above my bra.

"Give me a second!" My voice hitched. "Turn around or something!"

He didn't listen. He closed the space between us. I heard him breathing, felt the closeness of his body. I was frozen in place, but inside, every inch of me was taut and live with electricity. How long had he been standing there, watching me?

"What happened to you at the reformatory?" His voice was just above a whisper, hedged with a barely restrained violence.

"What?" As if submerged in a pool of ice water, my fingers finally thawed enough to pull down my shirt. I threw the other pieces over top.

"When I got there, they brought me down to that room, and I *heard* you. I can't get it out of my head."

The shack. He'd interrupted Brock and the soldiers just before my punishment. I'd screamed. The memory of it was enough to make me ill.

"You want to talk about this now?" I asked, incredulous.

He didn't wait for me to turn back around. Suddenly he was in front of me. He leaned down, a breath away, and stared into my face. Both of his hands gripped my shoulders. I bit back a wince at the pressure.

"What did they do to you?"

"What did *they* do to me?" I shook out of his hold. "*You're* the one who sent me there! Now it matters what happens to someone else when you disappear?"

The betrayal, the *resentment*, stormed through me. After he'd been drafted, he hadn't called or returned my letters. He'd sent no word that he was alive, that he was okay. He hadn't checked in on my mother and me. His promise that he would come back was a lie. Because a soldier had come back, not him. And that soldier had ruined everything.

He faltered back as though I'd shoved him. His hands went to his short hair.

"What made you do it?" I rolled on. "I know you . . . *cared* once. About me and Mom. Don't even try to say you didn't." My fists squeezed so tightly the nails bit into my flesh. The angry bruises on my knuckles sent a jolt of pain up my arms. I was laying too much on the line; I could see it in his face, the conflict raging in his eyes. Did I want to know this answer? Or would it crush me when, more than ever, I needed to be strong?

His mouth opened but then shut. His gaze met mine, a kind of wild desperation in it that begged me to read his mind. But as much as I wanted to, I couldn't. I didn't understand. *What is it? What are you afraid to tell me?*

"What happened?" I asked, this time softer.

His eyes hardened, like glossy stones.

"I don't know," he said. "People change, I guess."

He grabbed the backpack, stuffed with supplies, and headed down the stairs.

The shock doused my rant like a frigid bucket of water.

I laced the new boots as quickly as I could with my trembling hands and followed.

"**WHAT** did you find?" I asked Chase at the bottom of the escalator when my breathing had returned to normal. He was gloomy again; I could almost see the storm clouds over his head, which overrode my hurt and rekindled my irritation. *People change?* Not good enough. Obviously he was different, but that didn't explain *why* he'd arrested us or set us free, it just made me want to kick him again. And it made me want to kick myself even more, because despite his secrets, I was worried. I hadn't made up that crazed look in his eyes. Something dark was inside of him. Something cancerous. *That* was what was changing him.

He didn't want to talk about the past? Fine. Probably better anyway. We needed to focus on finding the checkpoint.

"A first-aid kit and a tent. Some dehydrated food that the rats didn't get."

I cringed and shoved the extra folded clothes, along with my reformatory sweater, under the flap. He fastened a bulging sleeping bag around the bottom of the sack without once looking up at me.

"We should go," he said, throwing the backpack over his shoulders.

I didn't have a watch, but I guessed that it was probably about eight. The checkpoint was still almost two hours away.

Outside, the parking lot was still vacant. I didn't know why I thought it might not be. The high clouds from the morning were pressing lower and had grown pewter since we'd entered the store. The air, which smelled faintly of sulfur, had a chilly, electric feel.

I followed Chase around the outside of the building and nearly slammed into him when he stopped abruptly.

My body reeled, sensing the danger from Chase before I saw it for myself.

There were two men outside our truck. One was in his late twenties, with unkempt black hair and a hooked nose. He wore a gray hooded sweatshirt and baggy camo pants. A hunting rifle was cocked over his left shoulder. The other man was halfway into the cab of the truck; I saw the dirty skater shoes sticking out beneath the driver's side door.

"Rick, hey!" hissed the first man. He swung the rifle toward us in a wide, sweeping arc and butted it against his shoulder. I heard the fateful *click* as he chambered a round.

My heart stopped. Guns were contraband for civilians and had been since the War. Only the MM carried them.

Or AWOL soldiers. Which I was pretty sure they weren't.

The man I took to be Rick emerged from the vehicle. He was tall, not as tall as Chase but still a head above me. He was thick, too; even through his capacious clothing I could tell he was muscular. His muddy hair was long to his shoulders, and he tossed it back with a flip of his head. There was an eager expression on his face.

"Morning, brother," Rick called out.

Chase said nothing. His face was as hard as steel.

"Maybe he's deaf," said the other man.

"You deaf?" asked Rick.

"No," Chase answered.

"It's been too long since you were around people then, brother. When someone says 'Good morning,' you're supposed to respond back."

"I don't make small talk when someone's pointing a rifle at my chest." Chase's tone was low, very controlled. "And I'm not your brother."

Rick looked to his friend, then back to us. I noticed that their skin, and even their eyes, held a yellow tint, which clashed against the gray sky and the gray ash.

"Stan, you're not making our friends very comfortable."

Stan chuckled but did not lower the weapon. The hair on the back of my neck prickled.

Rick turned his attention to me. "What's your name, sweetheart?"

My hands squeezed the jacket in my arms. I didn't respond, trying to think fast. I might be able to reach the gun in Chase's bag, but not without drawing the attention of the rifle carrier.

"See, Stan, you scared the poor thing."

Rick stepped forward. Chase shifted deliberately in front of me, and Rick smirked.

"Oh, don't be stingy, brother. Didn't your mama teach you to share?"

Stan was laughing raucously behind him. I couldn't swallow. My throat felt very thick.

Chase took a step toward the truck. I clung to his shirttail.

"Whoa now. Where you going?" Rick swaggered closer.

"We're leaving," Chase said with authority.

"*You're* leaving. But not both of you."

"I'm not going with you!" The words leapt from my throat. Chase stiffened.

"Ooh, she's feisty!" Rick said, as though this was a delicious quality. I remembered how Randolph had groped me and called me "trash."

Chase shifted his weight. Swiftly, Rick's hand shot behind his back, reaching for something tucked within his belt. Chase knew exactly where I was without having to look. Roughly, he shoved me back, shielding me completely with his body.

I saw Rick rip the leather case off of a thick, gleaming knife that hooked into a menacing point.

Danger pulsed in my ears. For some reason, the knife scared me more than the rifle had. I couldn't think why. I couldn't think anything.

"Leave the pack," Rick ordered. "I'll take the keys and the truck."

"Get in the truck," Chase told me quietly.

I didn't know what to do. Chase wouldn't look at me. He couldn't possibly think I would leave him here alone against two armed men. Our best chance was together. If they didn't want me hurt, maybe, *maybe,* they'd spare him.

He shrugged out of his jacket and backpack, and let them slide to the ground.

"Chase," I whispered, "I'm *not* leaving."

I shouldn't have said what I did inside the store. Now he was going to try to protect me, to make up for abandoning me before.

"Get in the truck," he commanded. Stan was approaching us quickly, the gun still pressed against his shoulder. His finger was on the trigger.

"No!" I said forcefully.

"Aw, it's all right. Daddy will take care of you," said Rick. Stan laughed.

"Take it easy," Chase told them, and reached beneath his untucked flannel shirt into his pocket.

"Slowly, brother," warned Rick.

Both men were close now. They watched Chase's hands, as did I.

In a flash of movement, Chase tore the black baton from his belt and swung it upward into the double barrel of Stan's rifle. The metal on metal sandwiched Stan's fingers, eliciting a howl of pain. The gun clattered to the ground.

Chase used the upward momentum of the baton to cut sideways into Rick's jaw. Upon impact, the nightstick flew from his hands and cracked against the side of the building. Rick stumbled, then lurched to his feet, barreling toward us, knife first. A flash of terror slashed through me just before I was roughly shoved out of the way. An instant later I heard a tear and a growl, and watched as a crimson line bloomed from Chase's bicep around the back of his arm. The flannel fabric clung to his damp, bleeding skin.

"Chase!" I screamed, clambering to my feet.

Stan swore, reminding me of his presence. On impulse, I sprinted around him toward the gun, but as quickly as I reached it, he was upon me. His body, heavy and rank with old sweat, arched over my back. I clenched my jaw, and wrapped my fingers around the wooden handle of the rifle. The tender skin of my knuckles scraped against the asphalt.

Stan knotted his fist through my hair and jerked back hard. I cried out as the burn seared across my scalp and ripped away.

When I turned around, I saw that Chase had thrown Stan into the front of the truck. When he fell, Chase kicked him hard in the gut, and Stan collapsed to his knees and forearms, sputtering. I didn't watch. I picked up the rifle and ran to the truck, stuffing it behind the seat without thinking twice.

I spun back just as Rick—face smeared with the blood that ran like a faucet from his nostrils—hurtled himself onto Chase's back. Panic raced through me. I could not see the knife.

In a frenzy, I searched the ground, hoping that the weapon wasn't embedded into Chase's body, and instead found the nightstick near the front tires, where Stan was still laid out, gasping for breath. I picked it up, prepared to run back to aid Chase, but I was intercepted by Rick, wild-eyed and blood-stained and rabid. He grabbed the collar of my shirt, and heaved me around so fast that I lost my balance. I knew he meant to use me as a shield against Chase.

I swung the baton like a baseball bat in all directions. It connected twice, maybe three times with something solid, but I didn't know who or what. My cropped hair was streaming around my face, blinding me. Then suddenly, I was flung to the pavement.

A sound halfway between a gasp and a gurgle overrode

the pulse in my eardrums. I lifted my head and saw, in horror, that Chase had pinned Rick against the side of the store and was using the cement wall as leverage to choke him.

To kill him.

Rick's yellow eyes bulged. He swiped drunkenly at Chase's tightening grip.

"Chase!" I panted, the oxygen having been sucked from the air around me as I realized his intent. "CHASE!"

He registered the sound of my voice as though waking from a dream. Startled, he dropped Rick, who crumpled to the ground, motionless.

I stared at the body in absolute dread. He was still breathing. He was still alive.

Barely.

An instant later I felt a hard pull on my forearm as Chase lifted me almost completely off the ground. Blood was smeared across one cheek, but his face looked otherwise unharmed.

"Truck. *Now*." His eyes were so black I could not see the deep brown irises around them.

I obeyed. I ran on numb legs to the open driver's side door and slid across the seat. My eyes remained on the two men lying on the pavement. Chase moved fast, grabbing our supplies and shoving them inside. Within moments, the truck roared to life. The tires squealed as we flew from the parking lot.

CHAPTER
7

THE truck tore down the empty highway, tires pumping so viciously I thought they would ricochet off.

I was breathing hard, my eyes glued to the back window of the cab for any sign of pursuit, the baton still lifted defensively in my hands like a sword.

"Are you okay?" Chase asked, tearing his eyes away from the curving highway as often as he could spare a glance. His black hair looked gray, the colors of his clothing subdued, all covered by the same thin gray dust that had blanketed the asphalt. But his eyes, dark with concern, were suddenly familiar. They scanned over my body, intent to see if I'd been harmed.

I didn't get it. He'd been a soldier, automatic and emotionless, just moments ago. He'd tried to kill that man. He would have, had I not distracted him.

I tried to speak, but my throat was too constricted.

"Your arm? What about your head?" he said.

My shoulders jerked in a shrug. He made a quick reach for

the nightstick, and I shied away without thinking, leaving a cloud of gray ash in my wake.

He exhaled sharply. "Okay . . . I won't touch you." One hand raised in surrender before returning to the wheel. The lines of his throat twitched.

No, I did not want him to touch me. Not after those hands had curled around another's throat.

"Were you going to kill him?" I asked, scarcely louder than a breath. I knew the answer, but I would have given anything for him to tell me the opposite. That I'd misread the situation. That I was blowing it out of proportion. I wanted desperately to believe he wasn't just as cold-blooded as Morris and Randolph and the other soldiers.

He kept his eyes on the roadway, swerving around the larger pieces of trash that had gathered in slopes against the concrete barriers.

"Chase?" It took great effort to swallow. It didn't seem possible, but somehow my heart was beating even faster than before.

He didn't respond.

I began to tremble in abrupt recognition of the chill that swept through me. The baton felt suddenly hot in my freezing grip and I dropped it on the floor. My knees curled into my chest. The bench seat seemed too short; we were crowded too close together.

"C-can you slow down?" Everything was moving too fast. And yet it needed to go fast, otherwise all the terrible and dangerous things were going to catch up. Still, I felt like I was barely hanging on.

He shook his head.

The silence that settled over us did grant me one comforting illusion. It provided distance. As the miles passed, Chase slipped farther and farther away.

AS we exited the Red Zone, it was Chase's own blood that eventually forced him to pull over. When the sharp twinge of copper permeated the stuffy cab, I remembered that Rick had cut him. The consistent drip of fluid hitting the ribbed upholstery of the seat slowed as the wound on his right shoulder began to clot, but it did not stop completely. I glanced down for only a second, because when I saw how the red smeared on the cracked beige leather, my stomach clamped with worry.

I'd cleared the gravel from the scrapes on my knuckles, but as my fingers kneaded the new jeans that covered my thighs, some of the older wounds reopened, cracking under the pressure I exerted.

My mind kept echoing the same question: *What happened back there?*

The swing of a shotgun barrel. The glint of light off a sickle-shaped knife. *Daddy will take care of you.* Shards of a few petrifying minutes that were as clear as if they were still happening. And then struggle.

Recapping this part of the scenario made my chest squeeze inward on itself and my whole body grow cold and clammy. Sometime during that fight the lines between bad and good had become blurred. Reversed.

Not reversed, I reminded myself. Chase had only been trying to protect us. Rick and Stan were still the bad guys.

But I could still see Chase's detached, furious stare as he'd held Rick's limp body against the building. No matter how much I told myself he'd been protecting us, I couldn't be sure. In that moment, he'd forgotten everything. He'd become a machine.

It wasn't that I was afraid he was going to hurt me; at least I didn't think so. The old Chase never would have. But the soldier . . .

Chase killing someone was something I could not be a part of, no matter how perilous it would be without him, no matter what past we'd shared. Whatever part of him was still *him*, the greater part, the more dangerous part, was always lurking.

By the time we'd passed Winchester, Virginia—a small town still occupied by civilians—I'd made up my mind to leave him.

The semblance of a plan shot through my brain. I still had the change in my sweater pocket from the gas station. I could follow the highway back to Winchester. It was early still, mid-morning. I could still reach the carrier on my own before noon.

I had pretty good intuition about people—I would seek out someone trustworthy to help me find a transport station. If it was anything like home, buses left the station at noon on weekdays. Then it was just a matter of blending into the crowds, like I had in high school. Not popular. Not a loner. Middle of the pack. The MM wouldn't notice me if I kept my head down and didn't linger too long.

I'd give a new name when I bought the ticket. If they asked for ID, I'd tell them an officer took it during the census, like Chase had told the highway patrolman.

My mom and I had been fending for ourselves all my life. I could manage a short trip to South Carolina, wanted or not.

Near Winchester, I'd asked to stop so that I could use the restroom, but Chase had told me to wait. I'd pointed to the blood dripping from his arm, but instead of tending to the wound, he'd just scrubbed away the puddle with his shirt-sleeve.

We crossed into farmland. First rolling fields of fruit-bearing trees, picked clean and nearly camouflaged by the gray dust and the high weeds overtaking them, then corn in equally unattended condition. Abandoned vehicles, red and black with rust and mold, slowed us down. Most were parked off the asphalt, but some had died right in the middle of the lane. Chase eyed them warily as he sped down the highway, looking, I realized, for scavengers hidden in the shadows. Most of the windows in these cars had been broken out and cleared of anything valuable, but that didn't mean that some-one wouldn't still come treasure hunting.

There was an eerie, graveyardlike silence in this place. A deserted stillness that made my skin crawl. This had been one of the evacuation routes when Baltimore had gone down, or maybe DC. I'd seen it on the news once, years ago after the first attacks, from an aerial view. That was when reporters could still use helicopters, before nonmilitary aircraft were banned from the skies.

The mass evacuation. Then, the streets had been packed with cars and frantic pedestrians, who slept on roadside cots at Red Cross stations when an accident or an overheated ve-hicle blocked traffic. I remembered the news capturing fights and victims of heat exhaustion. Kids wandering around looking for their parents.

Some of the cities had started to rebuild, but after eight years, this highway had been forgotten.

Chase eased off the pavement onto the bumpy soil and steered around a broken dining room table. Most of the dull yellow stalks immediately off the road had been trampled by scavengers or vehicles too impatient to wait in line during the evacuation. But beyond those there was heavy cover, enough to hide me when I disappeared.

With a pained grunt, Chase slammed the shifter into park.

My anxiety notched higher. It was almost time.

He'd be angry at first; I remembered his begrudged promise to my mother. Hopefully he wouldn't look too long. After a while he'd probably figure I'd gone to the carrier and be relieved that his burden was lifted. Then he'd go on with his life. Just like he'd done before. He'd lost his military career, but I couldn't feel guilty about that: The old Chase had never wanted to be drafted anyway. The old Chase had hated the MM.

We both stepped outside from our respective doors. I was moving too cautiously, watching him out of the corner of my eye to see if he was watching me. He jerked the bench seat forward with his good arm, muttering something about a first-aid kit.

Just go. Why was I stalling?

Because it's your fault he's this way, a small voice inside of me said. I could rationalize that this was not all true, but the bare fact remained that I could have changed everything.

I could still see him waiting in my driveway beside his motorcycle, the rain dripping from his hair and his chin and his sopping clothes.

Ask me not to go.

His eyes had burned then, so many conflicting emotions, but I'd been only afraid. Afraid that they would come after him and punish him, and that it would be my fault because I couldn't let him go. Afraid that if I wasn't strong enough to say good-bye, my mother would be left there alone.

The letter quaked between my trembling fists. I didn't shelter it from the rain. I wanted those words to wash away, but every reading yielded the same results.

"Chase Jacob Jennings: In accordance with Section One, Article Four of the Moral Statutes of the United States, you are hereby ordered for immediate induction into the Federal Bureau of Reformation. This is your third and final notice."

The look on his face ripped my heart clean in half.

"One word, Em. That's all. Tell me you want me to stay."

If I had, he never would have gone to the draft board. He never would have arrested my mother. I never would've known Rick and Stan, Brock or Randolph, Morris. Or what it was like to ache every day for him.

It had begun to rain, just a drop here and there, a tease of the oncoming storm. In the distance I heard the ominous crack of thunder. While he was distracted I reached into the cab and grabbed the chocolate—sustenance should I not immediately find a local soup kitchen.

I had some money, food, and clothing. It was as good as I was going to get with the circumstances as they were.

I looked at Chase one last time. His hair was streaked with

sweat, likely from the pain he was in. It brought forth a staggering sense of helplessness, something I knew I could not indulge now.

He'd be all right. He was a survivor. And now I had to be one, too.

"Good-bye," I said, knowing that my voice was too soft to hear. I forced myself to ignore the sharp pang of regret as I took a step back, away from the truck.

"I've got to go to the bathroom." My voice cracked.

"Go," he grunted, still consumed with peeling off his shirt. "But stay close."

I nodded then turned quickly and walked through the rows of corn in a straight line away from the road.

MY plan was to get as far away from the truck as possible before turning parallel to the highway. I walked fast, glancing behind me often to see if Chase was following.

The high yellow stalks surrounded me on all sides, the scent of rotted corn permeating my senses. When I could no longer see any traces of the truck, I made a hard left turn, but the rows weren't as even in this direction. I had to loop around clumps of plants and weeds to continue my forward momentum. My line ceased to be straight.

I lost my bearings.

The cornstalks were too high, and I continued to cross curving paths left by vehicles, which threw off my sense of direction even more. I looked up, but the sky was a consistent pewter. Even if I knew how to find my way by the placement of the sun, I was at a loss now.

The rain came, soft at first but then with sudden vigor. It

clattered off the sheaths of dried corn, growing in volume until I could barely hear my own footsteps as I tromped through the weeds.

I wiped the hair from my face and the pouring water from my eyes and tried to control my breathing. I was reluctant to raise my hood for fear that I'd miss some landmark or clearing that would show me the way back to the road. I spun in a circle, but even my tracks became distorted by the rain. There was no turning back. Everything looked exactly the same.

Panic clawed its way up my spine.

"Pull yourself together," I said out loud. But I was acutely aware of each passing second. I had to make it to Winchester soon. To catch a bus and find the carrier. I didn't have time for this.

I could feel my mother slipping away.

Spooked, I began to run, needing to escape from the prison walls that reached two feet above my head. I thrashed my arms to clear the way in front of me, but the plants had sharp edges, which sliced into my exposed skin. Every time I knocked down a stalk, another sprang up in its place.

Slow down, I told myself. *Breathe. Think!*

But my body didn't listen. I couldn't see the highway back to Winchester. I couldn't even find the truck. The fear stabbed deeper into my chest. I ran on, feeling the sweat mingle with the mocking rain from the sky above. Where was the road?

I fell once, slapping into a puddle of mud that splashed onto my face and into my mouth. I spit out what I could, choking, and ran again.

Finally, I spotted a clearing ahead. Without pause I steered toward it. I didn't even care if I'd backtracked to the truck, just so long as I figured out where I was. As I drew closer, I could see more clearly and grasped my knees, gasping for breath but exalted that I was no longer alone.

Ahead was a double-wide trailer, the same dull yellow as Rick and Stan's skin and eyes. It was covered on one corner by a strip of aluminum where the weather had worn down the siding. Below huddled three large plastic drums, transparent enough for me to see the liquid that sloshed within—water, presumably. Several wind chimes swung violently from the front door's awning. I couldn't hear them over the pelting rain.

On the square cement step, a woman sat in a rocking chair watching the storm. The sweatpants she wore bagged around her calves, and a knit shawl the color of plums was wrapped loosely around her shoulders. She looked like she'd been heavyset at one time but had grown suddenly thin and been left with too much extra skin. I could see such a pouch hanging from her chin, and more on the exposed areas of her forearms. A big yellow Lab lay on the ground beneath her feet.

Behind the house was a car, and behind the car was a gravel driveway.

My spirits lifted. The woman looked friendly enough. She could have been any one of my peers' mothers, sitting on the porch, waiting for her children to come home from school. Maybe she could give me a ride into town.

Maybe she could give me a ride all the way to the checkpoint.

190 Rudy Lane. I repeated the address over and over in my head.

The butterflies began beating in my stomach. I heard Chase's voice cautioning me that nowhere was safe. Well, there was only one way to find out.

I emerged from the cornfield into the clearing, fifteen feet away from where the woman sat. She jumped up so quickly she nearly knocked the chair off the step.

"Hello!" I called, walking slowly toward her. I tried to look as nonthreatening as possible. "I'm sorry, I'm a little lost. I was hoping you'd be able to help me."

She had widely spaced eyes and flattened cheeks, which drained of all color as I approached. Her mouth fell open, and she absently went to smooth down her salt-and-pepper hair.

It's probably been a long time since she's had surprise guests, I surmised.

"Oh!" she said suddenly, then motioned for me to come closer. "The rain! You're getting soaked! Come up here!"

I moved cautiously forward toward the front steps. She was smaller than I'd expected, several inches shorter than me. When I was under the awning, she placed a tentative hand on my shoulder and then patted me gently, as though to assure I was real. I became aware of how I must have looked, covered in mud, soaked to the bone. I swiped the back of my hand over my face, hoping I wasn't too dirty.

I could hear the wind chimes now; they were nearly deafening. I jumped at a particularly loud clang that she seemed not to notice.

"You look like you've had a hell of a day," she said.

I laughed, or sobbed, one of the two. At the end of it, we were both smiling.

"Sorry, sorry! Come in. I'll make you some tea."

I hung by the door as she pushed through. The dog, which had ignored my presence up until now, sniffed my hand lethargically with his whitened muzzle, then padded inside.

I tilted my head in, looking from one end of the compartment to the other—and was blasted with a pungent odor that was so strong it made my eyes water. A cloud of flies swarmed through the tepid room, and the buzzing, combined with the clanging of the chimes and the downpour, made my head hurt.

It was a mess. Dirty dishes were stacked in the tiny metal sink and spilled over the countertop. Tissues and cloths of all colors and sizes were strewn across the compact table. On the bed at the far right end there was barely enough room cleared for one person to sleep.

The woman sorted through the dishes, probably searching for a clean cup. Finally she gave up and shrugged, her cheeks glowing with embarrassment.

"Don't worry about it," I told her over the noise. "I'm really not that thirsty. I was wondering if you might be able to give me a ride. I've got family in Harrisonburg," I added. The smell was so strong I had to take a step back.

The woman shuffled over to me and reached for my hand. It was warm and soft against mine, but I started at the contact. I was glad that she didn't appear to sense my unease. I didn't want to appear rude while asking for a favor.

"You can't go now, sweetie. Not with this weather. Please come in."

"Actually, they're expecting me," I tried to smile. "I'm sure they're worried."

Against my better judgment I took one step inside, suddenly aware of all four walls. The room was too small for both of us, the dog, and all this clutter. I could feel the stifling air sticking to my throat as I tried to swallow. Unconsciously, I began to tug my hand back.

"I'm sorry about the mess. Things have been so hard since Dad's been gone." Her lower lip quivered, sending rippling waves through the loose skin connecting her chin to her collarbone.

I couldn't picture this woman living with a full-grown man in such a crowded compartment. I wondered where her father had slept. Hopefully not in bed with her.

"I'm sorry about your loss. . . ." I stopped, eyes growing wide. What had been hidden behind a coatrack when I'd stood outside was now visible. An animal carcass, maybe three feet long, hanging from a hook in the ceiling. The source of the sickening stench. It had been dripping blood onto the floor, which the dog was now slowly licking at. The thing—whatever it was—had been skinned and was turning a bluish white. Flies and maggots covered one side that had gone completely rotten. I tasted the sharp bite of vomit in my mouth and struggled to swallow it down.

"They shut off the water you know. Power, too. I get some supplies from old John's place, but, well . . ." She batted a hand in front of her face, not sensing my discomfort in the least. "None of that matters now that you're here."

"I . . . um . . ." I turned to look at the door, feeling her hand tighten around mine.

"I like your hair that way," the woman said. She moved closer to me, and I automatically stepped back.

"You . . . like . . ." I began, still too distressed by the dead animal hanging in what appeared to be her living room to finish. The dog continued to lick at the spot that had stained the patch of linoleum peeking through the dust.

"Oh, yes. I always told you it would look better short, didn't I?"

Of all the things that had sent alarm bells ringing through my head since my arrival, this was the comment that scared me the most. It took everything I had not to push her down and run out the door.

"Miss . . . I'm sorry, I don't know your name," I started, jerking my hand away and bumping into the coatrack.

"Alice, you know I hate it when you say that. Call me Mother, please."

"Mother . . ."

"That's right, sweetie."

It became explicitly clear that this woman did not intend to let me leave.

"No, I mean, I'm *not* Alice. You don't understand. I'm sorry, I shouldn't have come here." I turned to the exit. The woman moved with surprising dexterity, shoving her body in front of me and latching both fists around the doorframe.

"Let me go," I said, voice trembling. The flies clouded the air between us. The stink was rising as I became more frightened. I could barely stop myself from gagging.

"Sweetie, is this because of Luke? I'm sorry. I'm so sorry about him. But I told you. They shut off the power and the water. The corn's gone dry, and there's not much food that old John doesn't need for his family. I had to kill him, Alice. I know you loved him, but I was starving," she rattled frantically. Her face had gone white again, and all the empty skin quaked.

"That's a *person?*" I screeched, glancing against my better judgment at the carcass hanging from the ceiling. I gagged again.

"Luke? That's your puppy! Don't you remember? Oh, Alice, we'll find you another, I promise." Tears filled her eyes. She was genuinely upset that she had hurt me. Or Alice.

The sound of the dog licking up the spoiled residue on the floor pushed me over the edge. I tried to cover my mouth with my hand, but it was too late. I vomited all over the floor.

The woman stepped cautiously from the door and grabbed a towel. With a mother's kindness, she dabbed my mouth. It smelled as sick as the rest of the room. I weakly pushed her back. My knees were wobbling now, and my head spun. I focused on the open door before me, and the cool, fresh air of freedom.

"I have to go," I told her.

"No, Alice. We're okay now. You came back to me, and we're going to be okay," she crooned. She lifted an arm around my shoulder for comfort. I jerked away from her touch, stepping on the dog's tail. He barked viciously, snarling at me.

"Max!" the woman screamed. He returned to his slow work cleaning the floor.

"My friend is waiting," I tried. My throat burned from the bile, and my eyes were now streaming. The little room was spinning. Shrinking.

"No, dear. Mother's your only friend," she soothed again.

I pushed shakily past her, and in an effort to stop me, she wound her arms around my waist. A snake constricting her prey.

"Now, Alice . . ."

"Let go!" I shouted, and as we began to struggle, my strength returned. Some small part of me knew I didn't want to hurt her, but I was going to if she didn't let me through that door this instant.

"Alice! Please!" the woman begged laboriously between sobs.

Finally, I grasped the doorframe, pulling myself forward. At the first whiff of humid air, I renewed my efforts, gasping in breaths. She only tightened her grip. Something metal clanged as it fell off the countertop. The wind chimes smacked against each other in chaotic cacophony.

Get out! my mind ordered.

I bent my knee and, like a donkey, kicked her as hard as I could in the shin. With a cry she released her hold and fell onto the floor.

I turned, suddenly fearing that I'd hurt her badly. To my horror, she curled up on the dirty linoleum in the tufts of dog hair and trash and began to weep. The Labrador moved from licking the blood to licking her face.

"What's going on?" asked a male voice. One I had never in my life been so happy to hear.

I spun toward Chase, probably appearing crazy myself. His face was grim but otherwise unreadable. Sensing the urgency, he grabbed my arm and jerked me out the door. I tripped over the chair but righted myself and ran, pausing at the edge of the field when he didn't follow. He had hesitated in the doorway, blocking the woman from coming after me.

I swallowed mouthfuls of fresh air, thankful for the rain striking my face. My stomach was still knotted. How could I have been so stupid as to step inside her house? How could I have thought she would have helped me? My plan and my prized intuition were useless. The world outside of my hometown was as foreign as an alien planet.

Thunder cracked, and a white fork of lightning stabbed across the sky.

"Can't you Bureau bastards just leave her alone?" the woman shrieked at Chase. I could see her through the open doorway as Chase jogged away. She was still on the floor, her sagging arms wrapped around her chest.

"Hurry!" I motioned to him. My knees were knocking hard, the stench and the sound of buzzing flies still fresh in my memory.

"Alice!" the woman wailed. "I'm sorry about Luke! *Alice!*"

There was a moment where I was torn between fear, pity, revulsion, and the guilt that my mere presence had upset her fragile mental balance. Then the woman screamed, a bloodcurdling sound that ended in a gargling sob, and I ran blindly into the cornfield.

CHASE led the way, moving fast. It didn't take long for me to realize he'd marked his path by cornstalks bent at right angles. *Clever,* I thought fleetingly.

After several minutes he slammed to a halt, grabbed me hard around the shoulders, and gave me a firm shake.

"Don't do that again!" he reprimanded. "I told you to stay close!"

Then he turned just as unexpectedly and plowed onward. I could hear him tossing indecipherable comments over his shoulder, but he didn't glance back.

I did. I searched our path, panicked, convinced the woman was ready to do whatever it took to retrieve me. I jogged to catch up.

"Crazy lady probably hasn't been off her property in months," he was saying. "Why'd she call you Alice, anyway? And who's Luke?"

It was as if he'd pulled the trigger on a loaded gun. I pitched forward onto my hands and knees and heaved. Black spots appeared before my vision as the spasms raked my body. I could still smell the dead, rotting animal. I could taste it in my mouth.

Chase stopped. The anger he had been directing my way replaced itself with alarm, and he knelt beside me.

"She thought I was her daughter, Alice," I gasped, spitting. "Luke was the dog. She butchered him."

"That explains the smell," he said.

"Come on! She's following us!" I groaned. We were a good distance away from the trailer, but I could feel her presence on me, her arms winding around my body. When I tried to stand, I stumbled again. The rain seemed to bore me straight into the ground.

"No she's not. She's gone," he said in a hushed tone. A gentle hand was placed on my back—a test, I knew, after I'd shied away from him earlier. I didn't shake him off; his touch was oddly reassuring. His dark eyes probed mine, searching for the details of what had transpired in his absence.

"Help me up." I didn't care if he saw me crying, if he could even tell through the rain. I just wanted to get out of there.

Without a word, he slid an arm behind my knees and lifted me, cradling me against his chest like a child. I watched the rain pool on my jacket at the bend of my waist and gave myself, for the moment, to lightness.

"At least this way you won't get lost," he said dryly.

But I *was* lost. The lines between danger and safety were blurring.

A FEW minutes later, the truck appeared through the cornfield. It was a bitter reminder of my failure to escape, but I still felt a flood of relief at the sight of it.

"Put me down," I said, wriggling out of his arms. Though my strength hadn't fully returned, I needed the distance. His presence had too quickly become a comforting shield; one I wasn't sure which side to be on.

He paused, as if he were reluctant to let me go, but then he set me down abruptly. The second I was out of his arms he shoved his hands into his coat pockets. When we were close enough to the car, he reached around me and opened the door. As if I would just get in. As if we could pretend that nothing had happened.

"Are you all right?" he asked, registering the fury that flew across my face.

I had vomit coating my mouth and my hands. I had mud and wet hair plastered to my face. Every inch of me was streaming with cold water. I'd just been accosted by an insane woman while trying to escape a guy who'd nearly killed an armed robber. And that was just since this morning. No, I was definitely not "all right."

I slammed the door shut. His brows rose in surprise.

"I was leaving, you *idiot!*" I shouted over the rattle of the rain hitting the truck's metal hood. "I didn't get lost—not on purpose. I ran away!"

CHAPTER
8

THE seconds passed. I still felt the urgency to fly, but my feet were stuck in the mud. The weight of my words hung between us, and though part of me feared his reaction, I did not regret them. I knew what he was capable of; he needed to know the same about me.

After what seemed like a long time, he shrugged.

"Hope you've got good shoes. It's a long walk to the checkpoint." He lifted his arm toward the road. His eyes mocked me, but there was a hint of something else in them, too. Almost like fear, but that couldn't be. He wasn't afraid of anything.

"I . . . I can catch a bus," I stammered, glancing into the corn for Alice's mother. She'd had a car behind her house. What if she drove to town to look for me? It didn't seem so ludicrous based on the strength of her delusion.

"A *bus*? To a transport station? Great idea. Watch out for the soldiers that search the vehicles, though. And the Missing Persons boards. And the cashier who'll need your U-eleven form. And . . ." His tone became increasingly sharper.

"I'll give a fake name, and I have . . . money," I shot back.

"You have *my* money. Probably only half of what you need, too. Why don't you go back and ask your friend to spot you the rest?"

"I get it, okay!"

I hated him then. For everything he knew. Everything I didn't.

"You *don't* get it!" he said with sudden ferocity. I jumped at the volume of his voice but was surprisingly unafraid. "Other places, they aren't like home! There's no safe side of town out here. There are no doors that lock after curfew. Jesus, they told us girls like you were dangerous, but I didn't believe it until now." He looked very close to pulling his hair out. If he didn't soon, I thought I might do it for him.

I could picture him sitting in a classroom while an MM officer wrote terrible things about "girls like me"—girls with scarlet fives pinned to their shirts—up on a board. The thought of him believing it was infuriating.

"*I'm* dangerous? *Me?* You almost killed that guy! You would have if I didn't stop you!" It flew out of me, the disappointment, the *confusion.* Like waves pummeling a concrete dam. I didn't even care in that moment if he *had* been injured.

I saw the change come over him slowly. The rise in his shoulders. A slight bulge in the veins of his neck. The narrowing of his black eyes, more like a wolf than ever. He moved toward me, large and ominous, blocking the light. I took a step back, bumping into the truck, forced to acknowledge the sudden panic in my chest.

"They were going to hurt you." His voice was low and uncontrolled.

"So that makes it okay?" I countered. No, I didn't want to be hurt—I certainly didn't want to die—but that didn't excuse murdering someone, however foul, based on speculation!

A crack of thunder shattered my concentration, and my eyes shot back into the cornfield. Was the woman coming? Or was she still on the floor, weeping for Alice? Only a few minutes had passed, but it seemed like much longer.

"Yes, that makes it okay," he said between his teeth, eyes flashing with the lightning. "And don't pretend you wouldn't have done the same thing."

"I would never!"

"*Never?* Not even if they'd threatened your mom?"

His words pierced clear through me. If I had been Chase, and my mother had been me, nothing in the world could have peeled me off of Rick.

I realized then with terrible clarity that maybe Chase and I weren't so different after all. Everyone knew that a dog backed into a corner bites. I'd just never actually considered that the dog could be *me*.

At the same time, Chase had just used the love I felt for my mother to justify his actions. Like the two were somehow on the same level. It was a cheap shot, even for him.

He'd watched the transition of my thoughts in silence but could hold back no longer.

"If you think you're safer on your own, stay here. Otherwise, *get in the truck.*"

His knuckles whitened as he gripped the door, but he did not advance any closer. He was not going to force me inside. He was giving me a choice.

I had to go with him. Despite how much I hated it, he was right. I needed to get to the carrier, so I needed him.

He slammed the door after me and rounded the hood, but he paused outside with his hand on the driver's side handle before he joined me in the cab. Maybe he was making the same decision I had: to risk his life to stay with me or to go his own way.

We didn't speak immediately. A puddle of rainwater soaked the seat and pooled on the rubber floor mats. My feet sloshed in wet shoes. My fingers had gone numb with the cold. Chase's hands disappeared beneath the dash, bringing the engine to life. A moment later we were jostling along the path back to the main road, wrapped in prickling, uncomfortable silence.

The clock on the radio said 10:28 A.M.

"Oh no," I whispered miserably. I'd wasted so much time! We would have been nearing the checkpoint by now if I hadn't run away. Soon the MM would be gunning for us, and who knew how late the carrier would wait.

Chase knew all this, too. I'd put us in grave danger, and he would not pretend I hadn't.

We passed a truck flipped on its side with a shredded tarp tied around the top wheel well. It had probably been a lean-to at one time. The material now floated in the static breeze like a flag of surrender. I looked away, fighting back the hopelessness.

I slumped in the seat, stripping off my jacket and wiping my puke-covered hands on the rainwater that had gathered in the hood. There seemed no better place to put it than the floor, as it was still soaked. Without the barrier, the cold air of the cab needled through my sweater. I had dry clothes in Chase's bag, but I wasn't about to ask him to stop so I could change. We had to make up for lost time.

"You need to know something," Chase said abruptly, startling me as I swished water from one of the bottles around in my mouth.

When I glanced over I found him sitting perfectly straight, his eyes boring holes through the windshield.

"I'll get you to the safe house, and then I'll be gone. I won't bother you again. But while we're together, you don't have to be afraid of me. I won't hurt you. I promise I will *never* hurt you."

It wasn't just his proclamation that surprised me but his proposal. I'd seen what soldiers could do—what they'd done to my mom, and Rosa, and Rebecca. So maybe Chase wasn't like that—he *had* taken me from rehab, and despite my discomfort, defended me with his life—but that didn't erase the cold, hard look on his face when he'd taken away my mother. There were plenty of ways to hurt someone without using your fists.

Still, I wanted to believe I was safe with him, despite the soldier that was so easily triggered inside of him. I wanted to trust him again, maybe not like I had in the past but in a different way. Yet here he was, saying he was going away again.

But that's what I had wanted, wasn't it? That's why I'd run away, because I needed to get away from him. Suddenly that decision—despite how much I'd thought it through—seemed very impulsive.

"Okay," I said.

His shoulder jerked, reading my confusion as disbelief.

"When noon comes, the game changes."

"I know."

"I can't get you to South Carolina without your help."

I glanced over at him. It surprised me that he was giving up some control.

"What do I need to do?"

"Don't take off," he said. I crossed my arms, annoyed.

"Is that all?"

He pulled in a deep, steadying breath.

"You have to listen to me," he said authoritatively. "I mean *really* listen. If I tell you to hide, do it. If I say run, you *move*. And you have to let me call the shots. You'll stick out too much as a Statute violator otherwise."

Lean the way I lean, he'd once said. *Don't fight me.*

I remembered all the demeaning lectures on the proper, subservient role of a woman from the reformatory, but couldn't help thinking Chase was going a little overboard.

"I think I know how to blend in, thanks." I had done it my whole life, after all. It was how I'd kept us off the MM's radar. How I'd planned on reaching South Carolina.

He scoffed. "You've never blended in. Even when you were . . . You just can't," he finished, slightly flustered.

"What's that supposed to mean?"

"It means . . ." he stammered. "Look, people lock in on you. That's all."

I felt his eyes on me now. And suddenly I was eight years old, biting back tears after falling off my bike. The neighborhood boys were calling me "crybaby," which hurt more than my skinned knees. Chase, forsaking the consequences of defending a girl, was running them off. My ten-year-old hero.

– 175 –

The déjà vu receded, but the feelings echoed through the space between us. Fear, embarrassment, intimidation. Security.

"I never asked you to protect me," I said quietly. Not then, not now.

I could see from the look on his face that it would be no use arguing with him. Even if he acknowledged that I was completely capable of taking care of myself, on some level he would still be hardwired to look after me. A pressure grew in my chest the longer I watched him. I turned away.

"Anything else you want to tell me?" I asked.

"What?" He sounded startled.

"Rules," I said, scowling. "Any other rules?"

"Oh." He shook his head. "For God's sake, don't trust anyone."

I agreed, but only halfheartedly. Because despite everything, I *had* gotten back in the truck with him. And since I'd made that choice, I hadn't been afraid.

AT eleven thirty, we arrived in Harrisonburg, Virginia.

My eyes were seeing double from staring vigilantly out the windows for the MM. Every few moments I would glance down at the tiny print on the road map to help Chase navigate, but the moment I assured we were on track, I was scanning for soldiers again.

The rain had stopped, and this road was clearer, although we had to swerve around the occasional fallen tree. A few cars had passed, but none for a while.

The outskirts of town were mostly rural. High wooded mountains climbed in the distance to our right. The atmosphere cast a purple hue over the layers until, far against the horizon, the soaring peaks blended completely with the sky.

Most of the homes were deeply set on acres of land, boarded up and tagged with spray paint, like the abandoned buildings in Hagerstown. From the highway I couldn't discern the details, but I had a feeling it was the same symbol: an X over the MM insignia. I began to feel a slight swell of pride wherever I saw it; it was proof there were some people out there that hated the MM as much as I did.

Chase exited onto a street cratered with mud-filled potholes. The truck jostled from right to left like a theme-park ride, until finally the asphalt gave way to gravel, and the grassy hills beside us rolled like waves.

Rudy Lane was nearby, but Chase didn't want to park in front of the checkpoint. We were leaving the truck, and whatever extraneous supplies we couldn't carry—Rick and Stan's shotgun included—behind.

If Chase hadn't insisted we hike off road in the high overgrown tangles, I would have run the whole way there. Even though I knew the chances were slim, I couldn't help but hope that maybe my mother was still at the checkpoint. I might see her in just a few minutes! After everything we'd been through, we were finally close.

The time passed, indifferent to my impatience, and soon we entered a small rural neighborhood. As we edged around a central clump of trees, a narrow, two-story Victorian house appeared. It struck me as a pleasant place: sunshine yellow, with white decorative trim, wooden steps, and a quaint little porch. It might have been welcoming had the two rocking chairs not been chained to the railing, and had the thick boards not been nailed across the front door.

190 Rudy Lane.

"This is it?" I asked, feeling a growing sense of unease. It did not look inhabited, but maybe that was for security.

"I think so." He removed the gun from his belt. It wouldn't be left in the bag after what had happened at the sporting goods store. The precaution sent a quiver of anxiety through my chest.

We followed the circular step-stones around the yellow siding to where the back door gave way to an open brick patio. The edge of the yard was bordered by a broken-down laundry line, and beyond it lurked a dark, dense forest. Chase continued around the perimeter before returning to the entrance.

"Come here," he called after a moment. I followed.

There, posted on the side paneling of the house, was a dented tin sign, marked by black, spray-painted letters. It wasn't crossed out like the MM insignia we'd seen around, but it was clearly FBR propaganda.

One Whole Country, One Whole Family.

Chase had a perplexed look on his face.

"You don't think it's a trap, do you?" An image filled my mind of soldiers meeting here, but then I realized how ridiculous that was. The MM paid for buildings and signs, not abandoned houses tagged with graffiti.

"No," he answered, but could not provide a better answer. He turned back toward the rear of the house.

We knocked on the back door. Nothing.

The concern that had been brewing within me finally boiled to the surface.

"Are you sure it was Thursday?"

Chase's temper flashed. "That's what my uncle said."

Your uncle also abandoned you at the age of sixteen, I wanted to say. I'd foolishly trusted him because Chase trusted him, but I'd forgotten that I barely trusted Chase.

"Do you think we're too late?" It wasn't yet noon, but we didn't know when the carrier left. My mistake was looming just over my head, ready to rain down its punishment.

One shoulder shrugged. I jiggled the doorknob hard, but it was locked.

No answer.

This had to be it. We weren't wrong. We *couldn't* be wrong. Not after everything we'd been through.

I hadn't realized how fragile I was until that moment, when all the fear and anxiety slammed into me with the force of a sledgehammer and I cracked. I beat my hands against the wood. I kicked the door, bruising my feet. I screamed for them to let me in. I barely registered Chase's arm around my waist, yanking me back.

He set me aside with one stern look. Then he backed up slightly and, with a heave, kicked the door, just above the handle. A loud crack split the air. He kicked again, and the wood bowed, dislodging the lock.

"Stay here," he told me as he pushed through into the dark room and disappeared. I was still breathing hard and shaking. A few moments later he returned, beckoning me forward into the glow of his flashlight. Without a thought, I reached for the switch, and to both of our surprise, an overhead light poured brightness into a quaint, rectangular kitchen.

"Huh," said Chase. "We must be close enough to a city to get standardized power."

The space smelled heavily of mildew, but after a short while I no longer noticed. Atop the counter were blankets, a cardboard box of secondhand clothes, and empty cans of non-perishable foods. Canned vegetables. Tuna fish. There was a paper shredder plugged into the wall and a stack of blue forms about the size and shape of index cards.

U-14 forms.

Chase had referenced this when we'd been pulled over. This was what you had to have to cross into a Red Zone.

This certainly seemed like the right place. So where was the carrier?

Down the hallway was a bedroom with not much more space than a double bed and dresser required. A dining room followed. The overhead chandelier blanketed the room with a nostalgic kind of elegance, despite the cobwebs that connected each light. There were fresh footprints in the dust on the floor.

I wandered to the bathroom and found the glass-box shower, immediately remembering how dirty I was from the mud and the ash and the vomit. Linens were stacked in the narrow closet behind it. For some reason the sight of clean towels made me miss home terribly.

Chase searched upstairs, but there was no one home.

"Do you think we missed him?" I asked urgently.

"I doubt it. I think he might just be out for a while. No one would be stupid enough to leave those forms on the counter for a full week."

Unless he didn't have the time to clean up. Neither of us voiced what we both thought.

Maybe Chase was right; he was out just for a little while. Or maybe he was making a run to South Carolina. Worst-case scenario, we'd have to hide out here for the next few days. I tried to think positively, but the prospect of waiting another week to see my mother was a crushing disappointment.

I used an extra pillowcase to wipe down the counters in the kitchen and was somewhat heartened when water gurgled then shot out of the spigot into the sink. The stove worked as well. The moment I turned it on, my stomach began to growl. I hadn't been able to eat anything since I'd thrown up in the cornfield.

Luckily, resourceful Chase had taken a camping pot and a knife-spoon combo from the store earlier. I filled the pot with water and set it on the stove, preparing to make vegetable soup from a packet of dried crumbles.

While I stirred the soup, Chase sat at the table and flipped on the MM radio. The mere sight of it retriggered my apprehension, but I was morbidly curious to hear if we'd made the headlines.

It crackled with static. I was so intently staring at it that Chase's clumsy attempt to remove his jacket caught me off guard. I slid over to assist, glad for the distraction.

"I forgot," I acknowledged guiltily. "Here, let me help."

He lowered his hands, and I tentatively released the zipper, biting my lip as I pulled the jacket off his right shoulder. He'd replaced the flannel shirt for warmth, but the sticky blood had formed an adhesive, binding the shredded fabric to his skin. My empty stomach turned.

I had seen it happen and now remembered just how easily the metal had sliced into his flesh. Chase allowed me to touch his arm, gauging his condition from the expression on my face.

"You need to take off your shirt," I told him, instantly blushing. It wasn't like I'd meant anything intimate by it; I'd seen him hundreds of times without a shirt when we were kids. Maybe not after our friendship had changed into something different—we'd never gotten quite that far—but still. There was no reason to be embarrassed. No reason whatsoever.

He didn't try to lift his injured arm, and I wondered just how much damage had been done in the hours his wound had gone unattended.

When he struggled, I slid between his knees, and tried to act like my fingers freeing each wooden button down his chest had no effect on my drumming pulse. He nodded a curt thanks and then stared out the window.

The same voice from the previous night filled the kitchen, erasing the static over the radio. Though it was stupid, I felt like we'd been caught doing something we shouldn't.

"Colonel David Watts, covering Region Two-thirty-eight. It is Thursday, March tenth. Here begins the daily report."

It had been only a day since I'd been at the reformatory, I realized. It seemed months ago.

I left Chase momentarily to click off the stove and place the pot of soup on the table. Wispy ringlets of steam swirled into the cool kitchen air.

Colonel Watts discussed continuing efforts to secure the Canadian and Mexican borders from the "traitors to the cause," Americans trying to escape, and reported that there was still no information regarding the missing uniform truck in Tennessee. I finished helping Chase out of his flannel. He was wearing a thermal underneath, and when I pulled it over his head, his undershirt came off too, along with the pathetic wrap he'd managed to secure around the wound.

I'd never seen Chase like this before, and what I'd imagined paled in comparison. Hard lines of muscle cut into the copper skin of his shoulders and collided into his broad chest. His abdominals were perfectly sculpted; the slight indention of a V disappeared beneath the denim waistline.

My fingertips tingled. I wondered if his skin felt as smooth as it looked.

"Hand me the pack. There's a first-aid kit in there," he said. I jumped at the sound of his voice, and then flushed so darkly my cheeks must have been purple.

What had gotten into me? We'd just broken into a house, and I was preparing to look at a knife wound. Nothing about our situation spelled romance.

I'm just tired, I told myself, even though I knew I wasn't. When I bent down to retrieve the bag, I flattened my hair against my face, hoping that it would hide my mortification.

He found the first-aid kit and opened it on the counter beside the cooling soup. I laid out the materials I would need: a handful of gauze, a miniature bottle of peroxide, and a damp towel. Then, as gently as I could, I pressed the cloth against the wound, mopping up the blood that had painted his skin. The cut was deep and spiraled from the inside of his bicep around his shoulder.

I knew what I had to do, and I knew he wasn't going to like it. I drenched the gauze in peroxide.

"Sorry," I whispered, just before pressing the gauze over the wound.

He swore furiously, nearly knocking me over. His teeth were bared; I could hear the sharp intake of breath through his mouth.

"I said sorry."

I collected myself, having been flung into the table, and wiped up the new blood bubbling to the surface. I found a clean part of the rag and applied pressure to the cut. The wound was so long I needed both hands. It took me a moment to realize he'd caught me by the elbow with his good arm and was still holding on.

"You probably should have had stitches," I said with some remorse. "I know it stings, but it'll ease up."

"It burns like hell."

"Don't be a baby," I gibed. He shook his head, but his expression was lighter than before.

There was a dark bruise forming on the bottom of his jaw, and an even larger contusion on his side that I hadn't seen before. I touched it gingerly with my fingertip, and he hissed.

"Did he break a rib?" My fear of Rick was burning into anger.

"No," Chase said, still wincing. "But you may have."

"What?"

"Swinging that stick around. You clocked me in the side." My eyes grew round, and my mouth dropped open.

"Relax. You hit *him* at least twice." He chuckled at this.

"Oh. Good. I think. God, I'm sorry."

"Don't be. Just remind me not to meet you in a dark alley."

I half smiled.

When the bleeding had stopped, I closed the wound with several butterfly Band-Aids from the kit, hoping this would be enough. I wrapped clean gauze around his entire arm, securing it in place with heavy white tape.

"Your knuckles look pretty torn up," he acknowledged, his mouth tightening.

I examined my fingers. They were raw from scraping the gun off the asphalt, bruised and wrecked from the reformatory, and achy now that he mentioned them. I had forgotten my pain in place of his.

I cleaned the skin, but he put the Band-Aids on my fingers. Again, he gazed over Brock's damage but said nothing about it.

His hands were very warm under mine, and I realized they were swollen from the fight. He couldn't quite close them, nor could he stretch them all the way open. There were several fingers that didn't even line up quite right, but I suspected these had been broken long before today.

When he finished, he withdrew his touch quickly.

We began alternating turns with the spoon. The soup was too salty but warm. I tried to ignore that his skin sometimes brushed against mine, but it was difficult.

Chase jerked suddenly and turned up the volume on the radio.

". . . *assaulted by a man and woman, late teens or early twenties, outside a sporting goods store in Hagerstown, Maryland. The assailants are armed and should be considered dangerous. They are believed to be driving a late seventies era Ford pickup truck, maroon, Michigan or Minnesota plates. Male subject may have defected from the Federal Bureau of Reformation.*

Victims reported presence of an FBR nightstick used in the beating. A lineup of AWOL soldiers' photos are under review by the victims. If found, perpetrators are to be detained and brought in for questioning. Any information can be forwarded up your chain of command."

I lowered my forehead to the table, everything inside of me frozen. The man on the radio continued.

". . . list of missing persons grows by two today. Ronald Washington, African American, sixteen years old, runaway from the Richmond Youth Detention Facility. Ember Miller, Caucasian, seventeen years old, possibly abducted from the Girls' Reformatory and Rehabilitation Center, Southeast."

My heart stopped.

"Oh," I said in a tiny voice.

I caught a couple of additional lines: *"no leads . . . call the crisis line if apprehended."* But I could barely focus on the man's callous tone.

"Brock figured it out," I said weakly. I had doubled over my stomach. "She must have called to verify the trial."

If they knew I was gone, "possibly abducted," it seemed safe to say they knew Chase was the one that had taken me. Soon the highway patrol that had pulled us over would add to the report. Then Rick and Stan from Hagerstown. The pieces fit together, burned into my brain.

I had a hard time swallowing.

Chase's expression was as gloomy as I'd ever seen it. Not surprised, like mine surely was, but deeply concerned.

"You're worried about something," I prompted.

"That's not enough?" He gestured to the radio, raking a jagged hand over his skull. I could tell he was unnerved but trying to hold it together. Maybe for me. Maybe just for himself.

"It's more than what we just heard. Tell me. You can tell me," I assured.

He rolled his head in a slow circle.

"It's too soon for you to be reported missing. I don't think the headmistress happened to call Chicago to check on the trial. I think that someone may have contacted her first."

CHAPTER
9

"WHAT? Who?" Was it Randolph? Had he suspected something?

My thoughts backtracked to the overhaul, to the blond soldier with the green eyes. And the three marks down his neck from my nails.

"Morris." I guessed. It had seemed like they were friends. *You said you'd be cool,* Morris had said when Chase protected me. He'd obviously known Chase and I had had some sort of connection in the past.

"You know him?"

"How could I forget? He arrested me."

"Tucker Morris is . . ." Chase grimaced, as if unable to find the right word. "He was in my unit. He came back with me after he . . . delivered you to transport." He glanced quickly over and then looked away, his face tightly drawn.

"Why would Tucker have called the reformatory?" I asked, glad that Chase seemed to dislike him as much as I did.

An odd expression crossed his face. He was beyond angry

now. Tortured almost. Clearly Tucker had done something really bad to Chase.

Or Chase had done something really bad to Tucker. Which would explain why Tucker would have turned him in.

"There's . . . sort of a history there."

"What 'sort of a history'?" I asked dubiously.

I could hear Chase's heel tapping the floor. He hesitated so long I thought he wasn't actually going to answer me. Then he sighed heavily, resigned to sharing.

"Tucker enlisted in the Bureau about the time I was drafted. We were in the same training cohort." He was rubbing his eyes with the heels of his hands.

"And you two hit it off?" I prompted dryly. Getting Chase to explain anything was like pulling teeth.

"*No,*" he said. "We had some things in common. Important things for training. We're about the same size, so they put us together for hand-to-hand, and—"

"Hand-to-hand fighting?"

"Yeah. Combat maneuvers. He seemed all right at first, quiet, but decent anyway. We had classes together, just like in school. On the Statutes and all their caveats. Negotiations. And then policies and procedures for management of disruptive civilians."

I snorted, thinking of my mom telling the soldiers to get off our property.

"He got in some trouble. . . ." Chase waved his hand, indicating that this part of the story was inconsequential. "After that he was a real pain. Arguing with everything the instructor said. Refusing to follow orders. Kid couldn't even fill out the correct paperwork for an SV-one."

I frowned. I didn't want Tucker to have rebelled against the MM, because that's what *I* had done, and I didn't want to have anything in common with that blond-haired, green-eyed coward. I motioned impatiently for Chase to continue.

"It wasn't that he couldn't get anything right. It was that he purposefully tried to get things *wrong*. He kept sneaking off base, then getting caught and thrown in the brig. Getting his pay docked, his rank stripped. He was sort of used to calling his own shots, and he had . . . uh . . . ties he couldn't cut at home," he added.

"Have to dedicate your life to the cause, right?" I feigned indifference but remembered with a pang what Rebecca had told me in the reformatory. *How convenient for you,* I thought bitterly, *that your ties were so easy to sever.*

"Yeah," he looked mildly relieved. "It's standard procedure to break off any previous relationships. Women are a distraction, *temptations of the flesh* and all that." He laughed awkwardly.

An acidic taste crept up my throat. It seemed unthinkable that he would follow such a ridiculous rule, but his compliance made the transformation seem even more real. The thought that Chase had changed so quickly after being drafted made me feel like I'd never really known him at all.

I was beginning to think that maybe I'd gotten the wrong impression of Tucker, and that any hope I'd harbored for the return of my old Chase was about as likely as me going back home and finishing high school. But these thoughts felt just as wrong as what Chase was telling me now.

"So my CO—my commanding officer—made Tucker and

me partners. He told me I couldn't make rank until he passed all his courses."

"And that's what you wanted?" I spouted. "To move up?" I tried to picture Chase as MM leadership, calling the shots in an overhaul, charging people for Article violations. He couldn't be that heartless, could he?

"Got to be good at something." The sound of his voice was as foreign as the look on his face when he'd taken my mother away. I shivered.

"He didn't go down without a fight. Fought me a few times at first. Then he started fighting everyone. He fought so much that the other guys harassed him just to see him lose it. Like it was funny."

I tried to ignore the wave of pity I felt for Tucker.

"The officers even got into it. They started setting up matches for him after drills at the boxing ring on the base. Word spread. Lots of guys came to place bets. If they bet on Tucker, they usually won. That's when our CO got it in his head that Tucker would be good leadership material."

"How's that?" I asked, confused. "I thought they hated him."

He shrugged. "Maybe they did at first. But when he fought they started to see the soldier he could be. Vicious. Unstoppable. But still too much of a liability."

Chase cleared his throat then and scowled, and I felt a wash of relief that he seemed to struggle with this concept. There was still some humanity inside of him.

"Our CO offered him a deal. If he would just dedicate himself, work hard, be the damn poster boy for the FBR, then they would stop the fights. They'd put him on the fast track to captain, which normally takes years, but they were going to make it happen in months if he just played nice.

"It was a double bind. The harder he pushed, the more they wanted him. The more he conformed, the more they wanted him. He couldn't win. They started rigging the fights, to try to break him. . . ." He trailed off.

"How?" I asked.

"Nothing terrible," he said, the color in his face rising. "Sometimes they'd make him run before a fight. Or wouldn't let him eat that day. They started setting him up with bigger guys. He got knocked around a lot more and . . . it got worse. He quit trying. He took their deal. After that he didn't really have anything to fight for."

Nothing terrible. Right.

I chewed my lip, quietly making sense of the last few minutes. Feeling a fresh sense of grief for not one, but two good people.

"He's jealous of you."

"What?" Chase's head shot up.

"Tucker's jealous. You got out. You're free. He doesn't want you to have what he can't."

Chase considered this.

"What I don't get," I said slowly, "is why you're jealous of him."

"Why would I be jealous of him?" Chase blinked, taken aback.

"I don't know. Maybe because all you wanted to do was move up, but he was the one chosen."

"He paid for it." Chase's shoulders rose an inch.

"I know, that's the part I don't get," I said. "It's pretty sick to be jealous of someone that was practically tortured. Even if he *did* want to be a soldier. . . ."

"He *didn't*!" Chase said with sudden vehemence, slamming his fist down on the table. My spine straightened.

Silence.

A heavy sigh escaped between my teeth.

"I thought you said Tucker wasn't drafted. That he enlisted."

Chase's eyes were dark and indecipherable. He looked right at me, but he wasn't seeing me.

"Right . . . he enlisted. . . . I only meant that he didn't adjust well."

I lowered my eyes to the fist that had banged the table. I watched the way the gnarled knuckles couldn't quite straighten.

His hands hadn't been like that last year, had they? I would have remembered. They'd been calloused but still soft when he'd touched my face, gentle when they'd run through my hair. They were rough now. Fighter's hands.

And just like that, all the mixed emotions I'd felt for the two soldiers during this story—the pity, shame, and anger— were tossed into the air like bingo balls, jumbled chaotically, and then suddenly reassigned to their rightful places.

Tucker, the career soldier. Chase, the broken rebel.

Once, soon after Roy had left, my mother and I had gotten into a horrible fight; the worst we'd ever had. It was about the same thing. How I'd made him leave after he'd hit her, how I should have minded my own business.

I hadn't known what to do. I'd hated her for saying those things, for blaming me for Roy leaving, even though she was right: I'd made him go. I hated that she couldn't see how terrible he had been and how I'd saved her—us—from more of the same danger. But when I looked at her red, swollen eyes, all of that fury burned into something different. I just felt terribly sorry for her. So I'd gathered her in my arms and squeezed her as tightly as I could and told her that we were both going to be okay. She fell apart, but I was right. We were both okay.

I had the overwhelming urge to do the same for Chase now. To hold him so tightly his ribs hurt. To tell him we'd both be okay. I didn't though. Maybe because I still didn't trust him. Maybe because I didn't trust myself. The truth was, even if I held him now, even if he'd *let* me and he did fall to pieces, I would have no idea how to put him back together. I had no idea if any of us, my mother included, would be okay.

"You were right about the double bind," I said softly.

He stood too quickly, the chair tipping and cracking against the floor behind him.

"No, wait." I didn't want him to leave, but I didn't know what else to say.

And just like that, the gate closed. His eyes dulled, his mouth relaxed, and the connection that had just threatened to build between us disappeared.

Without another word, he grabbed his coat off the chair and was out the door.

"Chase," I called, but my voice had little volume.

I sat down at the kitchen table and clicked off the static hum from the radio. Absently, I traced the thin, raised welts on the backs of my hands and I thought about his hands, and how deeply the wounds beneath some scars ran.

. . .

"DO you miss them?"

I regretted asking when he hesitated.

"Yes."

"It was really awful, wasn't it? The accident I mean. I-I'm sorry, that was a terrible thing to say." I chewed my fingernails.

"No, not terrible. I just . . ." He scratched his head. "I've never actually talked about it."

I remembered the police knocking on our door. Telling my mother what had happened. They had needed someone familiar to wait with Chase until his uncle arrived from Chicago. I remembered the tears that had stained his innocent face.

At fourteen, Chase had lost everything.

"I was so sad for you," I told him. I thought of how his mother would let me braid her thick, black hair. How it stayed in place even without a tie. His father used to pat my head and call me "kiddo."

"My sister was a nightmare," Chase said, and laughed a little. "She was a little better after she went to college. She was on winter break when the accident happened, did you know that? They were going out to get dinner."

I remembered. It had been the first freeze of the season. The other car hadn't been able to stop.

"I was mad at Rachel because she'd taken my bed and I had to sleep on the floor. I stayed home that night because we'd been fighting. It was so stupid." He scowled. "The last things I said to her weren't nice things."

"But if you hadn't fought, you'd have been with them," I pointed out. It hurt, hearing that guilt in his voice.

He sensed my sorrow and turned to face me.

"You know what I remember after the police came?"

"What's that?"

"You sitting on the couch with me. You didn't say anything. You just sat with me."

THAT accident had taken Chase away from me. Had led him to Chicago, where his sorry excuse for an uncle had abandoned him in the wreckage of the War. Three years later Chase had come back home, a sturdier, more intense version of the boy he'd been, and my joy at his survival had led to something different, something deeper than I'd thought was possible. Something I'd only just discovered before he was drafted and had to leave again.

Of all the things he'd lived through, it was becoming a soldier that had torn him apart.

After a while I stood, leaving the pot still half full on the table, and went to rinse off the spoon. Still distracted and confused, I forgot my task as the water ran over my fingers. Slowly, a very different realization crept into my brain.

Hot water. The hot water heater was working.

I looked out the door for Chase again, worried. What if the carrier came while he was gone? What if he didn't intend to come back at all?

He needs to be alone, I told myself. Reluctantly, I left him to his mood and went to check the shower. I'd clean up quickly, just in case we didn't have a chance when it was time to go.

I caught a glimpse of myself in the mirror before starting the water. I'd grown thin in the last month—not starving thin, but lean, and more muscular. All traces of the girl I'd been at home had vanished. I wondered if Chase had noticed. Not that it mattered or anything.

Maybe Rebecca had been right. Maybe the MM had made him break up with me, but that didn't mean he'd been chaste. Had he been with other girls? Sean had found a way, so surely Chase could. I found I detested this thought, and then I detested that I detested it. It was none of my business. In fact, Chase's love life was the *least* of my concerns.

What was wrong with me? Even if some of his actions made a little more sense after an explanation, it didn't mean he wasn't still insufferable. And besides that, who knew if he was even telling the truth. His whole story had been under the guise of Tucker's misadventures, after all. Even if he had seemed genuinely affected back there, it didn't mean he was the same person he'd been a year ago.

I turned on the water and was just about to disrobe when a slam in the kitchen interrupted my thoughts.

Chase was back. And, I soon found, frantic.

He bolted into the room, nearly knocking the door off its hinges, and slammed off the valve. His eyes darted wildly behind me.

"What—"

Without a word of explanation he jammed us both inside the closet and jerked the door closed behind him. I became acutely aware of the sound of his breathing, of the feel of his chest pumping in and out and pulling me with it. Of the truth: We were in imminent danger.

It was a tiny space, barely large enough for us to stand. The shelves holding the towels cut into my knees and hips, but he'd still managed to wrap himself around my body. One hand was firmly latched over my mouth. When I automatically bit down, I could taste the salt from the sweat on his fingers.

The adrenaline was pouring off of him. My own heartbeat accelerated to meet his.

"Hello?" a man's voice called from the kitchen. I went stiff in Chase's grasp. He held me tightly against him, angling his side and back toward our exit.

"Don't answer," he breathed into my ear.

"Hello? Is someone here?"

An instant later I heard a loud *clang* and splatter, likely our soup pot being knocked off the counter. Then the scrambling of footsteps across the wooden floor.

I couldn't get enough oxygen. Desperately, I pried off Chase's hand. He relaxed his grip slightly, only to press my face into his shoulder.

"Got him?" shouted a second male voice.

"Where you gonna go?" said another. There was a loud crash. Maybe the kitchen table.

"You going to arrest me?" the first man called. He sounded willing to bargain.

One of the others laughed. "You know we're past that, old man."

There was another struggle, then the sliding of something heavy across the wooden floor.

"No!" he begged. "Please! I've got a family!"

"Should have thought about that before."

The other snickered. "Think they're compliant?"

At the mention of compliance my body began to quake. These were soldiers.

We couldn't run. We had no escape.

Click. The metallic sound that only a gun could make.

I jerked instinctively. I couldn't stay here. I couldn't die in this closet.

"No one is going to touch you," Chase murmured into my hair.

I wanted to believe him, but as I turned my head, I saw in the crack of light from the doorframe that Chase had raised his own gun and was aiming it at chest height straight out into the bathroom.

I gasped. He continued whispering things I couldn't make out. I wrapped my trembling fists in his shirt and bit down in the fabric covering his chest.

Someone walked into the bedroom down the hall.

"Clear," he reported after a moment.

Don't come in here. Not in here.

The bathroom door creaked open.

Footsteps moved across the tile floor, with just a little squeak. New boots.

With the door open, I could hear the carrier sobbing in the other room. He was begging for his life. He was crying for his little boy. *Andrew.*

"You try to take a shower, old man?" the soldier yelled from the bathroom. I pinched my eyes closed and tried to be absolutely still. Why had I turned on the water? What was I thinking? That we were at home? That mistake was about to get us killed.

The carrier continued bawling, and then grunted when he was struck with something. I smothered a sob into Chase's shoulder.

"I was going to but . . . but t-the water heater . . . it's broken . . . I forgot," the carrier answered.

My stomach twisted.

Chase slowly eased back the slide on his pistol. It made a nearly unperceivable *click*. I prepared myself for the blast. I was ready to run.

The soldier abandoned the bathroom.

A second later, the deafening sound of gunfire split my eardrums.

It took me a moment to realize that Chase's whole body, from the shins up, was cramming mine into the corner of the closet. He'd begun whispering again. I couldn't hear him over my raging pulse, but I felt his lips move against my ear.

"Upstairs," said a soldier. "Cover me. We'll move the body in a minute."

Footsteps ascending. The ceiling groaned under their weight.

I couldn't hear the man anymore. He wasn't crying for his son. I felt the bile scrape my throat.

The FBR was murdering civilians.

Before I could think through the ramifications of this, Chase was dragging me out of the bathroom. My legs didn't feel right. Like they were pulling through water.

He halted unexpectedly at the entrance to the kitchen. I glanced down and saw a man's denim-covered legs emerging from beneath the table. Before I saw anything else, I was again smashed beneath Chase's heavy arm. His hand snaked around my face, blocking my vision.

But I could smell it. The metallic tang of blood. The peppery sting of gun smoke.

And I could hear the carrier gasping for breath.

I took a step, guided by Chase. I slipped on something wet. I tried to swallow, but my throat felt like sandpaper.

There was a change in the man's breathing.

Chase paused. Leaned down. He did not release his grip over my eyes.

"Lewisburg . . . West Vir . . . ginia . . . two . . . o'clock . . . Tuesday . . ."

"Oh, God," I sobbed. Imagining the scene below me was just as terrifying as the real thing must have been. The ceiling creaked again.

"*Clear!*" one of the soldiers called upstairs.

"Look for . . . the sign. . . ."

That was all the carrier said. He sighed, a sound infused with liquid, and then he was gone.

Chase didn't release me until we were outside, and even then, he didn't let go of my hand. He pulled me at a run through the empty backyard, toward the woods. My legs, to my relief, were working again.

"Don't look back," he ordered, breaking the silence of our flight.

Frigid air needled at the drops of sweat lining my brow and neck. The grass crunched, frozen, beneath my rushed steps. I had to sprint to keep up with his breakneck pace as we crossed through the threshold of the woods. Neither of us made any attempt to soften the noise of breaking branches. My eyes stayed fixed on the pack over his shoulders; he must have grabbed it when we'd gone back through the kitchen. My strained hearing picked up only the sounds of the forest, tempered by the rush of my breathing. But my thoughts were loud, loud, loud.

The carrier was dead. Murdered.

My mother would have to find someone else.

Even if she'd already made it to South Carolina, she wasn't safe. She'd never be safe again. *I'd* never be safe again.

I would never see Beth again. Contacting her would only invite soldiers to her doorstep.

And finally: *It's my fault.* I hadn't caused the carrier's death, I hadn't been responsible. But just as I knew this, I knew that he would never have been there if not for people like me.

They told us girls like you were dangerous, Chase had said after I'd run away. I hadn't believed him then, but I did now.

I *was* dangerous. A man, a *stranger,* had just died to save our lives.

A commanding resolve shuddered through me. If I died now, his death would be in vain.

Focus. His last words had been to help us, but this plan was more thinly laid than the last. What sign? Surely checkpoints didn't advertise their purpose. We didn't know where we were going. We didn't know who was safe to ask. We couldn't even go back to the truck, now that the radio report had described it. We only had a time and a date, one that was rapidly approaching.

I kept seeing his legs, spread awkwardly over the kitchen floor. I could hear his sobbing plea to return to his son—to *Andrew.* My brain morphed the faceless soldier who had executed him into the guard Randolph. Then the scene changed from the kitchen to the woods outside the reform school, and I was the one crying out for my mother. It was my legs splayed out across the cold, wet ground.

"Ember!" Chase gave my shoulders a firm shake. I snapped

alert. It was dark now. I didn't know how long we'd been moving. I'd lost track of time.

"If we're caught, that's what will happen," I said, refocusing on the present. He'd begun pulling me along again, and didn't confirm or deny my statement.

I gulped down the frigid air. My heart rate was high from the exertion and the adrenaline.

"What if they catch my mother?"

She'd already been sentenced. And if she'd made it to the base, she'd already served her time. Would that matter if she was caught at a checkpoint?

He slouched but kept moving at a fast walk. The woods were growing denser; the line of houses no longer visible in the distance behind us.

"'Multiple-offense Article violators are subject to trial by a senior jury of the Federal Bureau of Reformation and sentenced appropriately,'" he quoted.

"What does 'sentenced appropriately' mean, Captain Jennings?" I said, exasperation rising above the panic.

"I'm not a captain. I was just a sergeant."

"What does it *mean*?" I growled.

He didn't answer for a full minute.

"The worst thing you can think of." His voice was very low. "It might be worthwhile to consider the . . . reality of the situation."

I slammed on the brakes; the inertia after so long in motion made my head spin.

"Worthwhile?"

He turned back to face me, eyes guarded and unreadable. His jaw twitched ever so slightly.

"*Worthwhile?*" I shouted at him.

"Keep it down," he warned.

"You . . ." My voice shook. My whole body shook. The simmer had jolted back up into an overflowing boil. "I need your help, as much as I hate to admit it. You say jump and I'll jump. You say run and I'll run. Only because you know things I don't have the time to learn right now. But you will *not* tell me what is *worthwhile* to think about when we are talking about my mother! Not a minute goes by that I don't consider the reality of this situation!"

He stepped forward, grabbed my shoulder, and leaned close to my face. When he spoke his voice was grounded by a very controlled fury.

"Good. But does it ever occur to you that I *don't* need you? That if *I'm* caught, I'll be *lucky* to die as fast as that poor bastard back there? Here's my reality: There's no going back. I am risking my life to get you safe, and as long as I live, I'll be hunted for it."

I felt all the remaining blood drain from my face. He released me abruptly, as though he'd just realized he was clutching my arm. I focused on his Adam's apple. It bobbed heavily as he tried to swallow.

The shame suffocated my anger. Hot, ugly, gut-wrenching shame. I could have melted from it, but with his eyes locked on mine, I found myself unable to look away.

"I-I haven't forgotten how dangerous this is for you," I said carefully, trying to control the hitch in my voice.

He shrugged. I wasn't sure whether he was dismissing my apology or the worth of his own life. Either way, it made me feel worse.

As cruel as his tone had been, the earlier appraisal of his fate had been the devastating truth. That I had so much influence over someone else's mortality seemed impossible; I couldn't conceive of it. So, awkwardly, I motioned us back in the direction we had been heading.

Time was ticking.

WE walked all night and then through most of the next day, taking breaks only when we had to. He caught me more than once startling at shadows, and at times I could see his eyes darken as some terrible memory consumed him. We didn't speak of our mutual vigilance. When the pressure got too tense, we moved out.

It was hard hiking. No trails had been carved through these hills, and when we weren't shoving aside swollen brush, we were wading across streams or slopping through the mud. As the adrenaline wore off, our bodies stiffened and slowed like machines without oil.

We didn't talk about what had happened at the house or what we had both said afterward. These things were tucked away in a locked box in the recesses of my mind. Instead I became consumed by thoughts of my mother's safety, thoughts that brought me to the edge of hysteria before the fatigue finally numbed my mind.

As dusk descended, Chase finally forced us to stop. We were both stumbling regularly now, and getting clumsy.

"No one's following. We're making camp here." His tone was so firm and so exhausted I knew I would lose any argument otherwise.

We were in a small clearing, a lopsided circle lined by pine trees. The ground was relatively flat and not too rocky. Chase checked our perimeter for safety and escape routes, then went to work connecting the curved aluminum poles of the tent he had stolen.

When I grabbed the pack to take out the food, he quickly stopped his task to retrieve the supplies himself. I wondered what he was hiding, but was too tired to care. I used the last of the smashed bread to make sandwiches, and inventoried our supplies. We still had two packages of freeze-dried soup and eight FBR-packaged granola bars left, but they wouldn't last long. We were going to have to find some food fast.

"Chase?" I asked after a while. My thoughts had returned to the reformatory.

"Yeah."

"If a guard at rehab was, um . . . *caught* . . . with a resident . . . do you think he'd be executed, too?" I hoped he understood what I meant, because I didn't really want to go into a whole twisted explanation of what had happened.

Chase began stuffing the long pole into the nylon loops with fervor. I thought his face had darkened some, but maybe it was just the low light.

"Probably not. He wasn't committing treason. He'll probably be court-marshaled. Dishonorably discharged. It's not common, but it happens."

My face rose. I felt a little better at this news. Freedom from the FBR was what Sean and Rebecca had wanted.

"It's not a good thing," Chase added, seeing my face. "The civilian sector blacklists dishonorably discharged soldiers from everything. Getting a job, buying a house, applying for public assistance. Anything on the books. He'll be held in contempt if he's caught collecting pay."

"But how's he supposed to live?"

"He's not. That's the point."

My shoulders slumped. Sean would still be a soldier, conflicted as long as he loved his Becca, but safe, if it hadn't been for me.

Chase had stopped and was staring at me. "You seem pretty concerned about him," he blurted.

"Well, yeah. His life is probably ruined because of me," I answered miserably.

Chase went back to building the tent, no less forcefully than before. "If he would have followed the rules, he wouldn't have had a problem."

"And if you followed the rules, you wouldn't have *this* problem! I remember!" I snapped. My head throbbed. His words from after the murder came forward, cutting fresh wounds. He would be hunted for life because of me. I was a liability. I was dangerous. I was his *burden*. I got it already.

We were interrupted by a long, whining cry in the distance. I jumped to my feet, but Chase only cocked an ear toward the sound. After a while, he continued working on the tent, unconcerned.

"Coyote," he informed me.

I rubbed my arms, distracted. "Hungry coyote?"

He stared at me for a moment, ascertaining if I was really afraid.

"Probably. But don't worry. He's more scared of us than we are of him."

I glanced around the campsite, visualizing a pack of rabid coyotes stalking their next meal.

Chase laughed suddenly.

"What?" I asked.

"Nothing. You just . . . Just, after everything that's happened in the last couple days, you're freaking out over a coyote."

I pouted. He laughed again. Soon I was giggling, too. The sound was infectious.

The intensity of all my emotions seemed to make my hilarity that much more acute. Soon, the tears were streaming out of my eyes and I was gripping my stomach. I was happy to see Chase in the same boat. As the silliness died away, he smiled at me.

"That's nice," I said.

"What?"

"Your laugh. I haven't heard it in, well, a year."

His smile melted, and I felt a striking loss at his withdrawal. An uncomfortable silence settled between us. Talking about the past had been a mistake.

He turned around to finish the tent, and it was then that I saw the gun peeking out from beneath his shirt. He must have put it there sometime when I'd been distracted. Apparently he was more concerned about a hungry coyote than he was letting on.

Brushing my teeth made me feel a little better. After I'd splashed some water on my face, I removed the boots from my aching feet and crawled into the tent. Erected, it was no more than three feet high, a tight squeeze for one person and extremely cozy for two—especially when one of them was the size of a small mountain.

Still, when Chase zipped up the entrance behind me and turned, it was a surprise to find ourselves face to face, only inches apart.

A black-and-white photograph seared into my mind. His tousled hair and scruff and thick lashes. The high cheekbones that made the shadows of his face bold and secretive. The soft curve of his bottom lip.

A flash of heat sparked in the pit of my stomach. For a moment, I heard only the sound of my thundering heart. And then he slid away.

I willed my pulse to slow, but it would not listen. He had weakened me, stolen some of my control in one drawn-out look. And that, I knew from previous experience, left me treading on very dangerous ground.

I could not fall back in love with Chase Jennings. Doing so was like falling in love with a thunderstorm. Exciting and powerful, yes. Even beautiful. But violently tempered, unpredictable, and ultimately, short-lived.

You're tired. Just go to sleep, I told myself.

And then I realized that there was only one sleeping bag.

"I guess I leave my clothes on, right?" My head reeled. I pinched my eyes closed.

"If that's what you want," he said, his voice low.

"I only meant in case we have to get out quickly. Like yesterday."

"Makes sense."

Shut up and lay down, I ordered myself. But it wasn't that easy. Nerves danced in my belly. I had no idea how to approach him. I began analyzing every possible movement, where I should put my arm, my leg.

"You're thinking so loudly it's giving me a headache."

I tried to reciprocate his annoyance, and that helped some. It was easier to be around him when he was cruel. It was harder when we weren't fighting. It reminded me too much of how things used to be.

"Are you waiting for an invitation?" he asked.

"It would help," I admitted grouchily.

"Get over here."

I had to smile then. He had such a polite way about him. After a deep breath, I crawled up beside him, and rested my head on my sweater.

Chase exhaled dramatically. His arm slid beneath my head and wrapped gently around my back, then pulled me flush against him. I felt the warmth of his skin through our clothing, his breath in my hair. My pulse scrambled. He zipped the remainder of the sleeping bag up, and on a whim, I slid my knee over his thigh and rested my head on his shoulder. I heard his heart there. Faster than I thought it would be, but strong.

He cleared his throat. Twice.

"Sorry. I'm sort of cramped here. Hope that's okay." I wiggled my leg a little to indicate what I was talking about.

He cleared his throat again. "It's fine."

"Are you feeling all right?" I asked.

"Fine," he said shortly.

His chest felt firm yet inviting against my cheek, and his scent—like soap and wood—relaxed me, made me dizzy. Every muscle ached, my blistered feet cried, but even that faded into white noise. Exhaustion lowered my defenses; I knew I should be cautious being so close to him, but I couldn't help it. I felt safe, finally. Calm. As the minutes passed I even stopped caring if the MM found us, just as long as I could sleep awhile.

Chase breathed in slowly, and the rise and fall of his chest made him feel so much more human than soldier. It stripped away some of the loneliness that had been saddled on my shoulders all day. I found myself longing for him to touch my face, my hair, my hand curled on his chest. Some small, reassuring message that everything was going to be all right. But he did not.

The coyote bellowed one long, lonely cry. I shivered involuntarily.

"What if he . . ."

"He won't. I'll make sure." Chase paused, sighed softly, and then whispered, "Sleep easy, Ember." And though the ground was cold and uneven and my jeans were twisted around my legs, I slipped away.

CHAPTER 10

IT began with a slight jerk in his shoulders. Nothing unusual really, but as my head still rested on his chest, the movement jolted me awake.

A soft groan. Then a stifled gasp. I heard something hit the ground—his fist maybe, or his heel. Half of his body had escaped the sleeping bag; I could tell by the freedom in his movements. The slippery fabric rustled loudly as he twitched again.

I pushed the rest of the bag off us and sat up, breathless when the cold air snaked between our bodies. Chase had gone very still. I thought that my movement had woken him, but then he twisted sharply, his torso turning toward me, his knees drawing up beneath mine.

Moonlight filtered in through the nylon tent, revealing the side of his face, contorted by agony. The vision of such a large person reduced to curling into himself, quaking with fear, was like a fist closing around my heart.

Then he cried out. The sound cut straight to my bones.

Whatever uncertainty I'd harbored about Chase Jennings

dissipated immediately. One hand slid to his shoulder, the other to his cheek.

"Chase," I whispered.

His eyes burst open, wild and disoriented. In a flash, his left fist locked around my throat. The other wound back, ready to strike.

I couldn't breathe to scream. My throat burned. The tears erupted, stinging my skin.

"Ember. Jesus." He swore.

Immediately his grip released. He shot back, slamming into the giving wall of the tent, jostling the entire room. Startled, he tried to stand, but this didn't work, either; he hit his head on the upper rod and was forced back into a crouch. His whole body quivered, like a wild animal locked in a cage. I couldn't see his face, but I heard his breathing, hard and ragged.

My arms were shaking, raised up before me in surrender. I could still feel the band of friction encircling my throat, pulsing there. A reminder of Randolph's baton. Of my self-inflicted vulnerability. I scooted back, bumping into one of the flimsy metal poles. The whole tent shook again.

"I'm sorry," I managed weakly.

"Wait. I didn't . . ." Kneeling, he reached to grasp my shoulders but drew back at the last second, not trusting himself to touch me. I put one hand over my mouth, hugging my elbow with the other. My eyes squeezed shut.

"Did I hurt you?" His voice was strained.

I said nothing, only shook my head quickly. I wouldn't open my eyes. I couldn't stand to see the soldier when I'd allowed myself to lay with someone else.

"I'm so sorry. I . . . I didn't know. It was a dream." The words rushed out, and I could hear in them the precarious balance between fear and self-loathing.

His hands were so close to my body I could feel the heat from them. Very slowly, his fingertips skimmed over my damp cheek. Reflexively, I shrunk from his touch, however gentle it may have been.

He shuddered. Then, without another word, he shoved on his boots, grabbed his jacket, and went outside.

I SPENT the hours staring into the darkness, confused, at times afraid, while Chase paced outside the tent. I thought of running again, but I knew I would certainly end up lost in the forest in the middle of the night.

After a while, I became aware of the quiet that had replaced his footsteps. The sudden fear struck me that *he* had left. I couldn't let that happen. Despite how much I didn't care to admit it, I was now relying on him to help me find my mother. I needed him.

I clambered out of the sleeping bag and crawled to the exit. My frozen fingers fumbled with the zipper before I pulled away the nylon barrier.

The darkness had lifted some, but it wasn't yet dawn. Chase was sitting against a tree, ten feet away, keeping watch. I sat back onto my heels, relieved that he was still there.

The temperature had plummeted; the pine needles on the ground were glimmering with iced dew. By the time I made it outside he was standing. Like an old man, he stretched his back, stiff and half frozen. A rush of irritation inflamed me. Why had he not just come back into the tent? I would have given him space. Our discomfort with one another was a lot better than him dying of hypothermia.

But as I got closer, my irritation warped into concern. Bright red patches of skin lit his cheeks, and his lips were chapped and nearly blue. Though he wore a coat, it had done little to shield him from the elements, and it crinkled loudly with each violent shiver. His breath did not fog in front of his face as mine did. There was no warmth left within him.

I ran back to the tent and returned with the sleeping bag. He didn't object when I threw it over his shoulders, but when he tried to grasp the material, it slipped from his numb fingers. That was when I saw that the knuckles of his right hand were swollen and bruised. A line of blood stained his fingers down around to his palm.

"Your hand!" I exclaimed.

He stared at the ground, intentionally avoiding my scolding glare, like a child who'd been caught stealing.

"I'm f-f-fine. You can g-get some more sleep." Even his throat sounded as if it were glazed with ice.

I crossed my arms over my chest and raised my brows expectantly.

He stretched the fingers with a wince.

"I got in a fight," he said with a small smile. "With a tree," he added when he saw my distress.

My eyes widened. "I guess you lost."

"You sh-should have seen the tree."

I laughed in spite of myself, now feeling the cold penetrate my clothing. How had he managed out here without moving?

He began stomping his feet as his blood warmed. This was mildly reassuring.

"I'm s-sorry, Ember."

I was taken aback by his use of my name. He'd said it when giving me orders, or in anger, even in surprise, since he'd come back. But the broken way he spoke it now made my chest hurt.

"And I'm sorry about yesterday, w-what I said. I didn't-t mean it. And everything else, too. Reform school . . . and everything. I never thought . . . God, look at your hands. And I know worse stuff has happened to you. I can see it. I wish . . . I'm so sorry." He kicked the ground, then winced as though he'd broken a toe.

I'd known he had noticed the scars from Brock's whip, and my unease around his gun, but I was surprised at how they plagued him. He hadn't mentioned anything earlier.

Unable to stand it any longer, I moved closer, not retreating when he backed away. I rubbed his arms, carefully avoiding his wound. I wasn't sure what to say. His apology had caught me completely off guard, and I didn't know if I could trust it.

"Don't." His tone lacked conviction. "You shouldn't . . ."

"Touch you? Don't worry. I won't tell anyone," I said, stung.

"I'm not who I was," he said. "Don't be nice to me."

I wondered what he'd done that had been so terrible that he wouldn't accept even an ounce of kindness from another person. It seemed impossible just then that I could ever hate him more than he hated himself.

Very gently, as though I were made of glass, he pushed me away. I knew he was scared to hurt me again, but all the same, I felt the bite of rejection.

"I would have let you come back inside," I said.

"I know."

I looked up at him. There were dark shadows beneath his eyes.

"So why . . ."

"I promised I'd never hurt you."

I felt my neck. There were no reminders of his grip; he'd detached his hand too quickly. I'd been scared but not hurt.

As if his guilt and embarrassment hadn't been enough, he'd sought punishment by the elements and his own strength, accepting pain with the twisted logic that he deserved it—something I knew he'd picked up in the MM. I found myself wishing I could muster the anger to berate him for it, but found none. What I did feel—sympathy—I could not share, because I knew he would only use it to fuel his shame. So when I felt the renewed desire to wrap my arms around him, I held back. I settled for standing close while he slowly defrosted, hoping he knew by my presence that his penitence was over.

THE day warmed, though not much. The freezing temperatures made our path slippery and the fog obscured our way; it mandated we travel at maybe half of the previous day's pace. Each step took double the concentration and effort.

Two days passed, and in them we ate, slept, and talked little. Time was dwindling down. By the time the sun rose on Monday, a strained urgency had taken us. We had less than a day to find the checkpoint.

That wasn't our only problem. We'd rationed what we had,

but still run out of food in the early morning and hadn't come across a stream to refill the canteens since the previous day. My stomach felt empty.

As we got closer to civilization, the trash littering the ground returned with increasing volume. Chase kicked through the scraps, cans, and faded Horizons-brand refuse for supplies we might use. The prospect of eating garbage didn't seem as revolting as it had in the past.

It was late in the afternoon before we heard it: tires on asphalt. A single car had driven by, somewhere near.

"Did we pass the state line?" I asked, pushing by him in an effort to see evidence of our progress. As much as I hated to reenter the roaming spotlight of the military, I knew we had no choice.

The woods gave way to a thicket of gray-green brush, which crept wildly onto an empty dirt road. Beyond it stretched an open field, surrounded by barbed wire and edged by trees. A cockeyed red mailbox announced a twisting dirt road a half mile down the way. The car, wherever it had come from, was gone.

Chase hauled me back into the bushes and went out to scout the way. From my hiding place I saw him retrieve the map from his pack and look up the road. Then down. Then up at the sky.

This is what my life has come to, I thought, watching him. *Taking cues for survival from a guy who is clearly waiting for some kind of sign from the universe.*

Beth would have found this hilarious. Ryan would have found it highly impractical. It helped a little, thinking of what my friends would do. Their presence in my mind made me feel stronger, even if for a split second I imagined them doubting me. Thinking I must have done something really bad, something they didn't know about, to be in the position I was in now.

No. They would never change.

But Chase had changed.

"We're running southwest, parallel to the highway by a couple miles," he said when he returned. "But we're farther from the checkpoint than I thought. We need to step it up."

A shimmer of anxiety passed through me. My legs were so stiff they could barely bend, and the blisters on my feet were damp with blood, but still we pushed harder. We could not miss this carrier. We had to get away from the MM and find my mother. Again I felt as if our survival would somehow even validate the sacrifice of that poor murdered man in Harrisonburg.

After a while, Chase took out the last bit of food, half of an FBR-issued granola bar, and handed it to me. I broke off the corner and handed it back to him, appreciating the gesture but knowing he had to be just as hungry.

I had just opened my mouth to ask him about his wounded arm when we heard voices filtering through the trees. Instinctively, we both ducked, but it became apparent after a moment that they weren't moving toward us, they were blocking our path.

"From the house?" I asked, remembering the mailbox.

"Maybe. Stay behind me."

We crept forward. Ten yards, and the volume of the voices increased. Men, two at least, shouting at each other. Twenty yards, and the undergrowth thinned.

"Get off my property!" one yelled.

"I'll shoot you if I have to!" countered another. "I don't want to! But I will!"

Shoot you? The words injected fear straight into my bloodstream.

I was close enough now to see three people. My eyes went first to a wiry man, thirty feet away in a cattle field, with dark hair that turned silver at his temples. He was wearing jeans and an old green army sweatshirt and had a baseball bat swung over one shoulder. His movements were awkward; I realized after a moment that he only had one arm. To his right were a bearded drifter with a silver handgun and a smaller figure dressed in rags. As my breathing quieted, I could hear her sobbing. On the ground between all of them was a dead cow.

Poachers.

Chase gripped my arm. He nodded for me to back up. In his hand I saw the glint of his own weapon. He kept it ready, thumb over the safety, but aimed at the ground. I could tell that he did not want to make this our fight.

I was torn. It seemed right that we should help the rancher, clearly trying to defend his livelihood with only a baseball bat. But at what risk to ourselves?

Just then a shot rang out, cracking against the trees and reverberating in my eardrums. The drifter had fired over the rancher's head, but not scared the brave man away. An image of the carrier's legs on the kitchen floor flashed before my mind. Defensively, Chase raised his weapon, pushing me all the way down to the ground.

A cry pierced the air. The closeness of it startled me: I almost thought that I was the one who'd made the noise. I turned my head to the side, straining to hear over my raking breaths. It couldn't have been the woman—she was too far away—and the sound was much too high for a man.

I could hear whimpering now. Nearby. My fingernails scraped the earth, ready to run. I sprang up to my haunches and saw him.

A child. No older than seven.

He had parted brown hair and a sniveling nose that matched his tomato-red sweatshirt. I knew immediately he must be with the rancher; he was too well dressed to belong to the couple. He was hiding, terrified, watching as the thief aimed a gun at his father.

My breath froze its rapid assault to my lungs, and without thinking I jerked out from under Chase's grasp to crawl toward the boy's hiding spot, ten feet to our right.

"*Ember!*" Chase hissed.

The gunman's voice hitched before us. "Yeah, sure, I had a house once, too. A house and a job and a car. *Two* cars! And now I can't even feed my family!" I could hear the thief crying now. His desperation was ramping up. Both Chase and I tensed in response.

The boy sobbed loudly. The thief spun in our direction.

"What's that? You got someone else out there? Who's there?"

"No one!" the rancher said forcefully. "It's just us."

"I heard someone!" He began stomping toward us.

I froze. My knuckles sank into a damp patch of leaves. The boy was still five feet away, but he'd seen me now. He was covering his mouth with both hands. His face sparkled with tears.

I moved one trembling finger to my lips, desperately trying

to shush him. Why hadn't we backed up like Chase had wanted to?

The deliberate crackling of undergrowth snapped me out of my trance. For a brief second I caught Chase's eyes and recognized the soldier's hardened stare. Then, to my shock, he dropped the pack and stood to his full height. He had never looked more formidable.

"Who the hell are *you*?" yelled the thief, aiming the gun right at Chase's chest.

My head reeled. *What is he doing?* I tried to grab Chase's ankle so that I might still pull him back and make him see reason, but it was too late. He was covering for the child, I realized. Showing himself before the gunman started shooting at random into the forest. The prospect of Chase being harmed crushed me with powerlessness.

"Hey, easy. Put the gun down," I heard Chase order calmly. The thief hesitated and backed up several steps.

"Who *are* you?"

"A traveler, just like you. Damn cold, isn't it? That's the worst part, I think. The cold. Listen, I know you're hungry. I've got some extra food I'll share with you tonight, and we'll think of a plan, all right?"

"Back off!"

The rancher's eyes were darting between the two armed men, then toward the woods, where his son was hiding. The evening air bristled with static.

"Please Eddie!" bawled the thief's wife. "Please, let's go!"

The man brought both of his hands to his head. The barrel of the gun pressed lengthwise against his temple.

He's going to shoot himself, I thought, horrified.

"Look, I'm putting my gun down, okay?" said Chase. "You put yours down, too, and we'll get you some food." I watched in shock as Chase bent to lower his gun. Negotiations had been part of his training, but was this right? He was about to be defenseless!

A crack in the bushes a few feet away refocused my attention.

The boy was leaving his hiding place.

"Hey kid!" I whispered. "Get down!"

He didn't listen. He seemed to think that Chase had defused the situation.

"*Dad!*" The boy began running toward the rancher, whose surprised expression lapsed into terror. He dropped the bat.

The thief swore, startled, and jerked the silver handgun toward the boy charging out of the bushes.

"Ember, STOP!" roared Chase.

I hadn't until that moment realized that I'd stood as well, and that my feet were running, too. Toward the boy. I was closer than the father. I could stop him first. Those were my only thoughts.

Crack! The shot was fired the moment the kid and I collided. We tumbled into the grass in a heave of expelled breath and tangled limbs.

"Ronnie!" The rancher flung me to the side as he desperately clutched his young son's body, searching for injury. My eyes ran over him as well. The jeans and sweatshirt were mud stained, and his innocent face was white with shock. Still, he had not been shot, and I felt no pain apart from getting the wind knocked out of me, which only left . . .

"Chase!" I was on my feet at once, sprinting over the

patches of damp grass and puddles toward the two men on the ground. It took me a full second to see that they were both struggling. Neither, at least so far, had been fatally injured.

As I rounded the dead cow it became clear to me that Chase was winning. He outweighed his opponent by fifty pounds and had youth and training to his advantage. The woman had attacked him too, though, and was flung to the side, sobbing miserably. Somehow, both guns were lying on the ground.

My eyes found Chase's first, as it was closest. I scooped it up quickly, forgetting about safeties and chambers, and pointed it at the jumbled mass of blood-stained clothing that rolled frantically over the earth.

My hands trembled. I couldn't shoot one without risk of hitting both.

"Stop!" I shouted.

Chase elbowed the thief savagely in the face. The man clawed at Chase's wounded arm, and Chase hissed in pain.

Something changed inside me then. A bolt, straight down my spine. The blood ran hot and fast through my veins. My vision narrowed into compressed slits, and over it descended a red veil. Suddenly, I didn't care how pitiful this stranger was or how hungry.

This had to stop. *Now.*

I raised the gun upward, toward the sky, and pulled the trigger. A loud *pop* slammed through my eardrums. The metal recoiled, sending a vicious kick through my wrist, down my forearm. I yelped, and the gun fell from my numb hand to the ground. My mind went absurdly but peacefully silent.

Chase lunged to a stand, shoulders heaving. All the calm

negotiating had been stripped from his face to reveal the ferocity beneath. His eyes searched wildly for the source of the shot and came to rest on me.

The woman helped her husband to a stand. His mouth and nose were a mess of blood and dirt. They fled into the woods without another word.

I stared after them, feeling suddenly displaced, like a hammer with no nail. *What do I do now?* Everything had happened so fast and had ended just as abruptly.

When I turned around, Chase was coming toward me. His gait told me that he was furious before he ever opened his mouth.

I couldn't think clearly. My ears were ringing from the shot, and my mind buzzed with the fleeting remnants of rage. Tears blurred my vision. The fear, momentarily paused, returned with full force, and in this frantic, baffled state I ran to him, and leapt into his arms.

He seemed surprised at first but soon was squeezing back.

"It's all right," he soothed. "No one's hurt. You're okay."

His words sliced through me, and for the first time since he'd taken me from school, I knew the truth about us: I could not be okay if he was not okay. Pain, nightmares, fighting— all of it aside—he was a part of me.

"Don't do that again! Not ever again!" I told him.

"I should say the same to you," he said. I could feel his breath, warm on my neck.

"Promise me!" I demanded.

"I . . . I promise."

"I can't lose you."

In that moment, I didn't care about getting to South

Carolina. I meant that I needed *him*. The way he had been. The way he still could be if he never let go. I don't know what made me say it, but in that moment I had no regrets.

He hesitated, then pulled me even closer, so that I could barely breathe. My feet no longer touched the ground. I could feel his hands grasping my coat.

"I know."

My heart rate slowed but pounded harder than ever before. He *did* know. He remembered now what it was like when we were together. I could feel it in the way he let himself go, in the shimmer that connected us when he stopped thinking. Here, returned at last, was my Chase.

Someone cleared his throat.

We detached like the wrong ends of two magnets, and what had felt so solid between us shattered like brittle glass. Having forgotten anyone else was present, we now faced the rancher. The baseball bat was tucked under his amputated arm, and his opposite hand rested on his son's head. The boy was now smiling foolishly. My face heated, despite the falling temperature that came with the evening.

"Sorry to interrupt. My name's Patrick Lofton. And this is my son, Ronnie."

TWENTY minutes later we were following Patrick and Ronnie down to the main house. Much to the rancher's chagrin, we had to leave the cow where it had fallen until morning, when he could bury it properly. They couldn't butcher it; they didn't have a cold room large enough to store the meat, and their buyer, a man named Billings, wasn't due for another week. At the mention of the slaughterhouse, I shuddered; it made me think of the dead dog hanging in the woman's trailer.

Patrick had insisted that we stop in so his wife could thank us properly with a meal. When we told him we had to move on, that we had family waiting in Lewisburg, he offered to drive us there, and we agreed: The unknown tenants of the ranch house had to be safer than the desperate, starving people in the woods.

Besides, we weren't going to be a whole lot better off than the drifters if we didn't eat soon.

Chase had introduced us as Jacob and Elizabeth, and Patrick seemed to accept the pseudonyms, despite the fact that we'd used each others' real names earlier. I didn't like them; I looked nothing like an Elizabeth. The only one I'd known was Beth from home, and she was five inches taller than me with bright red hair. But at least it wasn't Alice.

Chase had then created a flawless story about our displacement to Richmond after the Chicago bombings, which encouraged Patrick to share that he too had borne witness to such atrocities. He'd been a soldier in the U.S. Army, stationed in San Francisco, when it had fallen. It was there that he had lost his arm.

We approached a rickety red barn with white trim and a green tractor outside its oversized doors. A pasture lined the land opposite it, where thirty or so black cows were just barely visible through the failing light.

"Mind dropping your firearm here, Jacob?" Patrick asked, pausing in front of the barn. "Just until we leave. We don't bring guns in the house, what with Ronnie so young."

I nearly said something about the child not being too

young to be shot at, but held back, knowing the request had more to do with Patrick's concerns about us than with his son's youth. I felt Chase straighten, then nod in agreement. He still had his baton and knife, after all.

"Sure. No problem."

Patrick forced open the creaking door of the barn. We were blasted by the musty scent from the hay bales that lined the splintering wooden walls. In an open space before us, a motorcycle with wide silver handlebars leaned on its kickstand. I felt a trickle of nostalgia looking at it.

"Whoa. They stopped making Sportsters before the War," said Chase in awe.

Patrick laughed. "Not bad. You know bikes, huh?"

"I used to have a crossover. It didn't have a customized transmission or—"

"Dad, come *on*. We've gotta get Mom!" Ronnie interrupted.

Patrick's smile from the compliment faded, and he opened a cabinet in the back corner with a key from his pocket. On the top shelf was a hunting rifle. He added the thief's handgun to it. Chase left his there as well, with only a moment of hesitation.

The Loftons' house was warm and spacious. The living room, just past the laundry room, was littered with toy cars and action figures. A fireplace was embedded into the wall, and on its mantle were a dozen family pictures. All smiling faces.

Chase and I scraped off our boots as he removed the backpack. I looked at him, brows raised, and he returned the sentiment.

The Loftons had money.

They weren't rich. In fact, they probably had less than we'd had when my mother still had a job. There wasn't even a television in the living room. But there was a glass vase and a decorative lamp on the end table, toys and books lying around, and extra clothes cluttering the floor that the boy—Ronnie—had shed at some earlier time. These were all things I would have sold when we'd been in a tight spot. The fact that they hadn't needed to meant that they were doing significantly better than most of the country.

The kitchen had a skylight centered above an island. The walls were painted burgundy, and the towels and utensils on the counter were all fashionably black. A delicious salty scent emanated from an oversized slow cooker atop the marble counter. It had been a long time since I'd had meat; the soup kitchens never carried it, and with standardized power we couldn't maintain a fridge. It took everything I had not to stuff my face in the cooker. The familiar hum of a generator outside distracted me.

I couldn't tell if my stomach gripped from hunger or the sudden onslaught of nerves. A *generator?* They were commonplace in businesses, but not in private homes. Who were these people, friends of the president? They obviously made a good living; the price of beef was sky-high.

"Honey!" called Patrick. "Mary Jane! It's all right, come on out!" He placed his keys in a ceramic bowl beside the fridge.

I heard a lock click down the hallway, and a door pushed open over carpet.

"When there's trouble, the family hides in the basement," Patrick explained. Ronnie ran back into the kitchen and slid across the linoleum floor on socked feet. "Well, most of the family," Patrick added under his breath.

"Does this happen a lot?" I asked him.

"More than I'd like," he responded bitterly. "Once every few months, less often when it's freezing out. The pistol, that was new," he added, his expression bleak.

"Ronnie? He's still with you?" A petite woman bounded urgently into the room. She had ginger-colored hair, cut sharply at her chin, and was wearing an argyle sweater and jeans. She was quite stunning, not at all the plain rancher's wife I'd pictured, and made me acutely aware of how dirty Chase and I were from days of tramping through the wilderness. She stopped abruptly when she saw us.

Patrick introduced us, quickly explaining the situation. A blush lit her cheeks. Unconsciously, she began running her hands through her son's hair. He leaned against her leg like a purring cat.

"Welcome . . . Goodness, welcome," she said finally. "And thank you."

"I thought Jacob and Elizabeth might like to stay for dinner." At Patrick's suggestion, my stomach rumbled again. "They've got family in Lewisburg. I've offered them a ride in the morning."

Morning?

"You . . . sure. I mean, absolutely," Mary Jane said, shaking her head.

"I'm sorry," I said, hoping I didn't sound ungrateful. "I was thinking we were going to Lewisburg tonight." I looked out the window. It wasn't completely dark yet.

"My uncle hasn't been well," Chase added.

Patrick frowned.

"It's illegal to travel after curfew. Besides, after all you've done . . ."

The way he said *illegal* made my spine tingle. Patrick clearly followed the rules. I stepped stealthily on Chase's toes, and he nodded once, without looking my way, in silent confirmation.

We had no choice but to stay the night—or at least make them think we were staying the night—unless we wanted to risk them contacting the MM for a curfew violation. They did have a generator, which meant a working phone after dark. Their obedience frightened me.

Mary Jane faked a smile. "Don't you dare argue. You're staying, and in the morning I'll drive you to Lewisburg myself. We wouldn't have it any other way."

They wouldn't. That much was clear.

"That's very nice," I said, hoping my voice didn't sound too grim.

In confirmation of my ragged appearance, Mary Jane hustled me into their bathroom with a tattered old towel that she pulled from the washroom and a bar of soap. Chase followed with our bag. I knew he was getting a layout of the house, the exits.

"They're awfully friendly," I whispered while he washed his hands. "We could be serial killers for all they know."

He made a small sound of agreement in the back of his throat.

"We can't stay until morning," I informed him. But my bloody, blistered feet, and the cramping muscles in my lower back and calves argued otherwise.

He didn't answer, his mood black again, and I found myself resentful that he put on such a happy face for strangers while I got the silent treatment. The moment between us outside had obviously been lost, and that hurt more than I cared to admit.

As he stalked out of the bathroom, I saw his eyes lift to scan their oversized dresser and plush gold comforter with interest. Surely he didn't mean to steal anything. Not while they were in the next room.

The water was warm, thanks to the generator, and soothed my aching body while I scrubbed away the layers of grime. Even so, I couldn't relax. I didn't like not knowing what was happening in the rest of the house.

I changed quickly, making sure my boots were on tight just in case we needed to make a quick exit, and checked my hair in the mirror. The short length of it shocked me; since Chase had cut it I hadn't had the chance to grow accustomed to my reflection. Now wet, I could see the uneven patches where his knife had gone astray. Frowning, I knelt to search the backpack for my hair tie, but my hand stalled on the outer pocket.

Why did Chase never allow me to look through the bag? He'd insisted on getting everything I needed from it himself. There had to be something he was hiding.

I glanced toward the door, now worried that he might come back to check on me. When I strained my ears I only heard the sounds of Ronnie playing with his toy trucks in the living room. I pulled open the thick copper zipper.

The top layer in the pack was clothing, rolled economically to a more compact size. Most of it was damp from when the weather had soaked through the canvas the other day. Beneath, I found my hair tie, which I automatically latched around my wrist, and matches, a flashlight, the dreaded nightstick, a plastic box of soap, and some other toiletries. I came upon a plastic Ziploc bag, filled with cash. My jaw dropped as I flipped through the bills. All twenties. Nearly five thousand dollars. How long had Chase been saving?

My hand bumped into something else. A Statute circular, rubber-banded around something rectangular and hard. The band slid off easily, and the paper unfolded at the creases, revealing a paperback novel, stuffed thick with folded papers.

My heart thudded against my ribs. The worn cover read *Frankenstein*.

"WHAT is it about that book?" His tone was mildly teasing.

I set it on my nightstand and watched him wander around my room. He picked things up carefully. Set them down. Wiped them off if he left a fingerprint. Since the War he'd never really known what to do with possessions.

"I like it. What's wrong with that?"

"It's just an interesting choice," he said, now even more intrigued. "It's just not very . . . girly, I guess." He laughed.

"It was written by a girl."

"A girl who likes monsters."

"Maybe I like monsters." I hid a smile.

"Is that right?" Chase narrowed his eyes my direction. He sat beside me on the bed and bounced a little, unused to a mattress, then grinned like a little kid.

"He's not really a monster, anyway," I said. "It's everyone else that makes him that way because he's different. It's sad, you

know? How people can tear you down like that. How you try to do the right thing but you just can't."

Like telling Roy to stay away from my mother, I almost added, and felt my face heat up.

He tilted his head, eyes peering deep inside of me in a way that made me feel exposed, like I'd never really been seen before, yet at the same time safe, like he'd never tell a soul what he'd found. His fingers laced with mine.

"It sounds lonely," he said.

I OPENED the book and gently unfolded a small bundle of papers, two of them sherbet green. These were legal documents, passing on the deed of his parent's house to the surviving family member, Chase Jennings. It saddened me to think of this weight he carried.

The next papers, and there were thirty or so of them, were pounded thin and creased so severely they could have ripped if I'd opened them too fast. My pulse raced forward. I recognized the paper . . . the penmanship.

These were *my* letters. The ones I'd written to Chase in the MM. I opened a few, knowing I needed to hurry but not able to resist the temptation to verify they were real. I read through my meaningless small talk: what Beth and I were doing, how classes were going, conversations I'd had with my mother. My words produced a flood of nostalgia. The hard feel of the kitchen table and the smell of vanilla candles as I wrote late into the night. The fresh concern for his safety. The longing I'd felt for him.

I'd written about some of this. I'd told him that I missed him. That I was waiting impatiently to hear about his life.

That I thought of him constantly. I'd finished each letter with "Love, Ember," and it had been true. I'd loved Chase Jennings.

I thought of how he'd held me outside and wondered if I didn't love him still.

Acknowledging this made my heart twist with confusion. He was infuriating and inconsistent. Bossy and overprotective and *vague* about everything. No one bothered me as much as him.

Because, I knew, no one meant as much to me. No one except my mother, and the love I had for her felt entirely different. Like needing oxygen and needing water.

Somehow, I was annoyed. Why had he kept these letters? At times it seemed he could barely stand being around me, and yet he'd carried mementos of our relationship through the service and halfway across the country. How separate was the old Chase, *my* Chase, from the soldier, after all?

And what would the hope that he still cared cost me?

I placed the letters back into the novel, careful to leave them just as they'd been found. When I did so, my eyes fell upon a quote, spoken by the narrator, Victor, to his beloved.

"I have one secret, Elizabeth, a dreadful one; when revealed to you, it will chill your frame with horror, and then, far from being surprised at my misery, you will only wonder that I survive what I have endured."

I shivered involuntarily. Apparently my false identity hadn't come out of nowhere.

CHAPTER
11

"HOW come you're so big?" Ronnie said in wonderment from the dining room. He stood on top of his chair to try to measure up to Chase, but still fell drastically short.

"I eat lots of vegetables," Chase lied, eliciting an encouraging thumbs-up from Mary Jane. "You mind if I sit here?" He'd chosen a seat that backed against the wall so that he had a clear view of the room.

"Nope," said the kid.

"Use your manners, Ronnie," said Mary Jane. I was helping her set the table.

"No, *thank you*," said Ronnie.

She laughed nervously. "I mean, sit down please. Over here, by Mom." She clearly wanted her son—the only one who seemed comfortable with the dinner arrangement—between his mother and father. Which left me relegated to the stranger's side of the table with Chase.

I hated that Patrick hadn't taken us straight to Lewisburg. His earlier friendliness had washed away, and he now gave off the distinct impression that he regretted asking us inside.

And to think I'd banked on just such kindness when I'd tried to run away.

We gathered around the table, and Ronnie gave the slowest rendition of Johnny Appleseed I had ever heard. The tension thickened. Finally we were eating, focused on something other than each other. I had hardly swallowed the first bite of pot roast before jamming the loaded fork back into my mouth. I told myself to eat as much as I could; we didn't know when we'd get the chance at another hot meal.

I let Chase do most of the talking: He was more skilled at lying than I was. He embellished on his story about his family relations in Lewisburg, never saying enough to draw suspicion. I was impressed at how much he talked. He hadn't said that much to me in the last week.

While they were focused on him, I snuck a bread roll into my pocket for later.

As the conversation turned to Ronnie, the signs of Chase's exhaustion became more obvious; his eyes seemed to focus on nothing, he hunched over his bowl. How much had he slept in the last few days? Last night, barely any. The night before we'd been on the run. Before that, who knew?

And tonight he wouldn't sleep, either. Our next minute alone would be spent deciding to stay the night or sneak out. Either way, there'd be no relaxing.

The mood remained uneasy for the rest of dinner. Unless Ronnie was telling some story, no one spoke. I began to feel more trapped by the second. The threat of a curfew violation and the morning's ride to Lewisburg were the only things holding me to my seat.

In response to the strain, Mary Jane turned on a countertop

radio, and I joined her in the kitchen while she washed dishes. The crackling sound reminded me of the MM radio in Chase's bag. I hoped for music but was not so lucky.

The newscast had already begun. The reporter, a woman named Felicity Bridewell, clipped the ends of her words with an annoying sense of self-importance. She was talking about an increase of crime in the Red Zones and the FBR's decree to boost their presence at the borders.

I remembered the highway patrolman with a shiver.

The men's voices in the other room paused, and I knew Chase was listening now, too. I stood by in anxious silence, my mouth dry.

"... *investigating the murder of another FBR officer in Virginia earlier today. Authorities have determined this to be the second victim of whom they are now referring to as the Virginia Sniper. No witnesses have yet come forward. ...*"

A sniper killing FBR officers ... was this linked to the stolen uniform truck in Tennessee? I felt an odd tingling in my chest. It wasn't right to wish for violence, but people were fighting back, and that made me feel *hopeful*.

Before my mother was taken, I'd accepted how ingrained the MM was in our lives. I didn't like it, but the truth was that not everything they did was bad. The Reformation Act had instituted soup kitchens and mortgage freezes, things we might have died without. But since the overhaul, my views had begun to refocus. It now seemed blatantly obvious that those programs were just leverage, making us dependent on the very machine that oppressed us. The schism between the government and the people had never felt wider.

The MM had taken away my life. I couldn't go back to school; I couldn't go home. I might never see Beth or Ryan again. For the first time since the War, I envisioned what things would be like with no MM. With no Red Zones and curfews. No reform schools and Statutes. And I realized I could survive, because Chase and I were doing it right now.

I shook my head to clear it. I was the one who held things together, not the person who stirred up trouble. Joining a resistance was crazy. Irresponsible. And it didn't even matter— not when I had to find my mother.

"... *execution-style killing in Harrisonburg, Virginia. The deceased is an unidentified Caucasian male in his mid-forties.*" A pause and the shuffle of paper. "*We're now receiving word that the Federal Bureau of Reformation has linked this death to the Virginia Sniper. Again, this constitutes the third serial murder in a chain throughout the state of Virginia. As always, citizens are strongly encouraged to stay out of evacuated areas and observe the Moral Statutes.*"

I gripped my hands together so that they didn't shake.

The MM was blaming their own kill on the resistance— on this sniper, whoever he was.

Mary Jane was babbling about how dangerous the country was becoming and how thankful she was for the FBR. I wanted to scream the truth at her but knew I couldn't. I froze completely when the radio snagged my attention again.

"... *Jennings, who defected from the FBR earlier this week, should be approached with caution as he may be armed and dangerous. Any information on the whereabouts of this criminal can be called in on the crisis line. That concludes the nightly news. This is Felicity Bridewell.*"

I'd missed the story! What had been said? Mary Jane had talked over most of the report!

I couldn't look at her; she'd see the truth right on my face. And if we ran now, the Loftons would know we were guilty. So I fixed my eyes on the window, staring at the tear tracks down the glass left by the earlier rain, and I nearly screamed when Chase's hand came to rest on the small of my back.

"Dinner was great, wasn't it Elizabeth?" he said with a hollow smile, interrupting my panic. I knew it was for show, but the touch comforted me enough to maintain my role.

"Delicious," I said. The muscles in my legs were already working.

The next minutes seemed to pass in a fog. The next thing I knew, Chase and I were standing in a guest bedroom across the hall from Ronnie's room. An Amish quilt covered one wall; the intricate pattern of colored squares made my eyes cross.

Chase shoved open the window, but it was reinforced by steel bars. Keeping out thieves. Keeping in criminals.

I swallowed a deep breath.

"I don't think they know," I said unsteadily. Chase shook his head, grave now that his acting stint was finished. "Maybe Patrick didn't hear me say your name outside."

"He was a little preoccupied." Chase closed the window delicately, a line furrowed between his brows. He transferred his weight from foot to foot.

"What do we do?" I asked. "I don't want to wait until the morning."

"They've got a van in the front of the house, and there's the bike, but we can't risk the roads after curfew." His tone was heavy. "We'll hike out after they go to sleep."

Which meant we were prisoners until the family went to bed.

WHILE Chase washed up, I tiptoed through the hallway, curious when I didn't hear Mary Jane or Ronnie. Bedtime reading, I guessed. That seemed like a normal thing to do. In fact Patrick, who was still in the living room, was doing the same. His feet were up, and he was wearing glasses now. I swallowed some resentment, remembering home, and how my mother and I used to read on the couch after curfew.

My heart rate slowed. Nothing seemed out of the ordinary. Not that I could tell.

When I slipped back into the guest room I found Chase sitting on the edge of the bed, elbows on his knees, face in his hands. He was so still, I thought he might be asleep.

I watched him just for a moment, unable to draw my eyes away.

He seemed to have become distracted in the midst of changing. He still wore his jeans and his boots, but his clean shirt lay untouched beside him on the bed. The lights worked on account of the generator, but he'd lit a candle to combat the shadows instead, and the hard lines of his jaw and neck were accentuated in the flickering flame. From this angle, I now noticed several raised scars on his back that I hadn't seen in the house on Rudy Lane. They angered me, those scars, cut at a diagonal like the swipe of a claw. I wanted to know who had hurt him like that. I wanted to protect him. If such a thing was even possible. I felt sort of powerful thinking it might be.

Still, his scars, combined with the serpentine wound now

visible without the bandage covering his shoulder, made him all the more dangerous.

He was, to me, terrifyingly beautiful.

All the nerves that had been crackling inside of me seemed to transform and redirect toward Chase. My body trembled with anticipation. What energy remained sparked in the air between us like electricity.

I wanted to move to him, but my feet were nailed to the ground. I opened my mouth to speak, but there were no words. I thought of the letters that he'd kept, of what they could mean if he let me in, and was confused again.

He remained as still as I was, then sighed softly, and my heart clenched. Something was wrong. That had been a noise of pain, not of exhaustion.

"Does your arm hurt a lot?" I asked. He jumped up, not having heard me approach. I'd forgotten that I'd been tiptoeing so as not to disturb Patrick.

He shoved on his shirt, a little too forcefully, I thought. I eased the door shut behind me.

"It's just . . . that kid. He's just a child. He could have been shot." The shame was so thick in his tone that it nearly choked him, and I sagged back against the wall, staggered by how much it affected me. "I didn't even think about him. He's what, six? Seven? I almost walked away and let him die."

I could feel my brows draw together. A shiver went down my spine when I thought of Chase walking out into that field.

"But you didn't."

"Because of you." He looked up then, eyes black and filled with pain. "That guy was swinging a pistol toward a kid, and all I could think of was you. That he was going to hurt you.

That I couldn't let him. Those guys, those *stupid* guys in Hagerstown. And that highway patrol . . . I could have . . . What's wrong with me?"

I swallowed, but it was hard because my throat was so tight. His stare returned to his hands. They didn't look like a fighter's hands now. They looked big and callused and empty.

That same knot twisted inside of me. If I had told him to forget the MM, to stay with me when he'd been drafted, he would not be broken now.

"You look out for people, you always have—" I began, but he shook his head, dismissing my modesty.

"You're the only thing that's tying me down."

"Well, I'm sorry I'm ruining all your fun," I said, appalled.

"Fun?" he said weakly. "You think . . . Ember, you're the only piece of me I have left. Everything else—my family, my home, my *soul*—they're all gone. I don't know who the hell I am anymore. If it weren't for you . . . I don't know."

His voice went thick again and he stared at the floor, bewildered and ashamed. Though my mouth was open, I had no idea what to say. I wished that I could reassure him that he was still Chase, and reassure myself, too, but what if he was right?

"Come here." It was my voice. My request. But it surprised us both.

Nothing happened for several long seconds, but then some magnetic force took over, drawing us slowly to each other. His face was speculative, confused. I could tell he did not want to come closer, that he couldn't understand why he was already so near.

He tore away from my eyes and, to my shock, tentatively nuzzled his face into my hair. I could feel his breath warm my shoulder. He smelled of the woods and faintly of soap. My whole body tingled.

I moved my cheek to brush against his neck, and the feel of his skin sent aching waves through me. No one made me feel the way Chase did. He was my anchor in the hurricane, yet at the same time, the hurricane itself, so that I nearly always felt safe and afraid simultaneously. There was nothing in the world as confusing and powerful as being close to him. Could he feel it? Did he know?

"I saw the letters," I confessed. "The ones I wrote. I saw them in the bag."

His head jerked up, his eyes pinning me in place, irritation instantly coating his raw exposure. They burned into me with an intensity I didn't understand.

And then they went out.

"I'm sorry. I shouldn't have done that," he said.

He took a step back. Then another. He shoved his hands in his pockets and swallowed a shallow breath, as though there weren't enough air in the room.

He was sorry for touching me. He regretted it, even. I felt small and unworthy and *mad* that he could see me as so insignificant when I cared for him so much.

Well, I wasn't insignificant. I was important. Maybe not to him, but to someone.

I didn't immediately know how to respond. My eyes burned with tears, but I wouldn't let them fall. I lifted my chin as proudly as I could and tried to keep my voice steady.

"You should get some sleep, Chase. You look tired. I'll stay up and keep watch. You don't need to worry about that."

I turned away and sat on the bed, still in my clothes. He

didn't move for a long while. Finally, he laid on the floor, his knife in the palm of his hand. He didn't even open the sleeping bag.

I ROSE *up on my elbows, positioning myself on his chest, looking down at his face. His finger grazed my jawline, teasing my hair to the ends.*

"You won't forget me, right?" I tried to play it light so maybe he wouldn't see just how scared I was for tomorrow.

For a second, the corners of his eyes pinched. Then he sat up, and I backed onto my knees. His hands straightened my T-shirt, tugging it down.

"No," he said. His face darkened. "I don't think it's possible to forget you."

The slow, heavy weight of his breath, the seriousness of his tone, made everything too real. I didn't want it to be real. I didn't want him to leave. And if I opened my mouth, I'd ask him to stay. Ask him and ruin his whole life.

My eyes stung. A great lump had formed in my throat. I turned away and held my breath and tried to stop my shoulders from trembling, but he saw, and when he touched my arm I jerked away because it hurt even more that he wasn't angry about leaving. That he was being kind to make it easier for me.

I hated the MM. My mother was right: They took away everything good.

There was too much uncertainty. What if I never saw him again? Everything seemed beyond my control. And then I thought, crazily, maybe if I could just make this part go faster, he'd come home again. It would be like ripping off a Band-Aid, but then he'd be back.

"I want to say good-bye now," I said, my voice finally breaking. "I changed my mind. I don't want to wait until morning." I couldn't look at him. So what if I was a coward.

His touch, this time gently moving aside my hair. His lips, brushing my ear.

"I won't forget," he said again, quietly.

I slumped miserably back against his chest. He pulled me closer. His arms crossed over my body; his knees rose on each side of mine. I felt him breathe in, press his lips against the base of my neck.

"I promise I'll come back. No matter what happens." Though his voice was only a whisper, there was a fierceness behind it. I believed him completely.

"I'll wait for you," I told him.

I turned my head and buried my damp face in his shoulder, and he held me until finally my breathing slowed. After a while, he laid down beside me and said, "Sleep easy, Ember." And when I woke in the morning, he was gone.

CHASE did sleep, silent and dreamless, while I stayed awake with my burning thoughts. The urge to move on was stronger than ever. I began wondering just how likely it would be that an MM cruiser would catch us at night. We could be perfectly fine. We could get all the way to Lewisburg, find the carrier, and be in South Carolina by tomorrow.

If I was being honest with myself, it wasn't just my mom that had me chomping at the bit to get out. What had passed between Chase and me would surely turn to awkwardness, and I was looking for any way to avoid it. He was obviously still planning on leaving when we got to the safe house, and maybe that was better. If I wasn't enough to make him stay, I didn't really want him around anyway.

I chewed my thumbnails and hated that I cared.

After an hour I tiptoed down the hallway, only to find that Patrick's light was still on. I could hear him shift on the couch, hear him turn the pages of that infuriating book. Why wouldn't he just go to bed? I had a feeling he was staying up on purpose now, guarding his house to make sure we didn't steal anything.

I didn't entirely blame him.

I was on my way back to the room when I heard another creak in the floor, this time from the opposite end of the hall-way. I ducked into the guest bathroom and waited. And then I heard the rattle of the basement door.

"Billings here?" I heard Mary Jane whisper. So she was in the basement, probably with the boy. I felt stupid for thinking them so naïve; they'd been down there since dinner. It was where the family went when there was *danger*.

Billings. Who was Billings? The answer came to me slowly. Patrick had said his name earlier. He was their buyer. The person who took the cattle to the slaughterhouse.

"Not yet. Should be soon though. Keep the door locked."

"You'll be careful?" she asked in a small voice. "If he really is that guy on the radio, he's dangerous. I can't believe you brought them inside. And with Ronnie . . ."

"Don't talk to me about Ronnie," Patrick snapped, then sighed heavily. "Look, I don't like it, either, but we got a thousand dollars for the last soldier. This one, he's got to be more, what with the law after him and all. And who knows, maybe they'll kick in a bonus for the girl. That would be enough to keep us here through the summer. We wouldn't have to move to the city, like we talked about."

My stomach felt like I'd swallowed a bag of thumbtacks. Everything became implicitly clear.

The Loftons had placated us with hospitality just to keep us here. I'd known something was off the moment we'd seen the inside of their house. A generator? Toys for the kid? Why hadn't I trusted my intuition? Now we didn't even have the gun.

Billings, whoever he was, was coming. The soreness in my body was forgotten. I had to get Chase, and we had to leave. *Immediately.*

I didn't wait to hear any more. Silently, I hopped across the hallway back into our room and grabbed Chase by the ankle. He sat up quickly, but it was so dark that I could barely see him.

"What's wrong?" he said, instantly alert. "Are you okay?"

"We've gotta go—they called someone. The boy and the mom are downstairs, and Patrick's playing prison warden," I told him in one expelled breath.

Chase was up in flash. He slid the baton into the waistband of his pants and pressed his knife into my hand.

"Here," he said, shoving the backpack toward me.

"How are we getting out?" I asked. "Patrick—"

"Leave him to me. Ember, listen, all right? You go out through the back. Get to the woods and head for the road. I'll be right behind you."

"You're not coming with me?" I'd heard it in his voice. He was going to make sure I wasn't followed, whatever the risk to himself. I felt a little light-headed.

His hands cupped my face, his thumbs grazing along my cheekbones. He was close; I could feel the air move before my mouth when he spoke.

"Stay out of sight. Follow the road to Lewisburg and find the carrier. There's money in the bag, enough to pay him off. Make sure you don't show him all of it until you get to the safe house."

"I won't. . . ." I was frightened now. My hands had covered his and were squeezing his fingers. I couldn't believe he was saying this. I could not imagine leaving him here in such danger.

"Be careful who you talk to; keep your head down. You know what to do. Just don't trust anyone." His words tumbled out so quickly they nearly connected.

"But what about you? I can't leave you here!"

"Yes you can!" he insisted. "Ember, I'm sorry for screwing everything up. I never meant to hurt you. There's so much more . . ,"

And suddenly his lips were on mine. Warm and demanding. Angry and afraid. Filled with everything his words could not say.

He pushed me back but then pulled me in once again, deepening the kiss, thrusting his hands through my hair. My fists knotted in his shirt, torn between shoving him away and refusing his dismissal. My head was spinning.

He ended it too soon, kissing me once more on the temple. Then we were gently pulling open the door, tempering the urge to rip it back off its hinges. I couldn't believe I was preparing to escape without him. He'd have no money, no supplies. Everything within me told me this was wrong.

He'll follow, I told myself. *If he can.*

I crept into the hallway, Chase right behind me. I would have to pass the living room to get out through the back door. Patrick was likely back on the couch, maybe with a weapon, reading. Watching. The lights would be on, damn the generator. He would see everything.

I passed the basement door and wanted suddenly to kick it as hard as I could. Had she been the one to call this Billings? Or was it Patrick? Yes, probably him. He could have done it while Chase and I cleaned up for dinner. All this, after we'd saved their child.

Chase passed me, his thumb grazing over my lips once more in the darkness. His good-bye, I knew, and felt the touch shoot straight through my core.

He walked into the living room, and I heard Patrick scramble up suddenly.

"Don't get up," Chase said in a low voice. "I was just going to grab a glass of water if it's all right."

"Sure. Here, let me," Patrick offered. I caught one more sight of Chase's back as he disappeared into the kitchen, and I prayed that it would not be the last. I snuck through the foyer, back toward the laundry room, but paused once my feet hit the linoleum.

If I opened the door, they'd be able to hear it from the kitchen. Chase knew this. He wasn't going to let Patrick follow me. What that would entail, I didn't know.

I listened briefly to the sound of water in the sink and muffled conversation. Every nerve within me felt live and raw. I gripped the door handle until my knuckles went white and it rattled under my grasp. The next time I heard voices, they were coming from was the living room.

Why isn't he running?

But I knew: He was giving me time. He hadn't heard me open the back door yet. I cursed him under my breath.

I gathered every ounce of courage within me, and raced around the corner, entering the kitchen from the opposite side. The lights were on, blinding my eyes, but the room was empty. I went straight for the fridge, grabbing all the keys from the black ceramic bowl beside it, and returned to the back door.

I opened the door as quietly as I could and bolted outside on numb legs. The freezing air slapped against my face, stealing my breath. I ran for the only thing I thought might help.

The generator. Just outside the kitchen window. Maybe if I could turn off the lights I could give Chase a chance to get out.

I slammed on the brakes in front of the humming metal box, searching desperately through the darkness for the switch. I didn't have time to get the flashlight out. Every second mattered now.

In my silence I heard another sound break through the night and froze. Footsteps. They were far off; I thought for a moment it might even be the cows in the field. My spine went rigid when I heard low human voices, when the footsteps drew closer.

It couldn't be Patrick and Chase: They were inside, as were Mary Jane and Ronnie. This had to be Billings.

I listened as hard as I could, but the noise from the generator blocked me from picking anything up. There were definitely men arriving at the house, but how had they gotten here? I hadn't heard a car approaching.

It didn't matter. Chase was still inside.

I felt down the serrated metal sides of the power source in a panic. Something burned my hand, and I bit back a cry. Finally I found the switch, flipped the protective sheath back, and shut down the machine.

My ears rang in the sudden presence of silence. The kitchen window above me went black.

There was a great deal of commotion from the darkness inside, and with the fear taking over, I ran blindly. I stumbled over the rocks and raised patches of grass. The moonlight cast an ethereal silver glow over the pasture, and I felt the dull eyes of the cows in the field upon me.

I didn't go to the woods. I ran toward the barn. I had the keys. I might be able to get the gun and then find Chase and . . . I couldn't think any farther ahead than that. I was just pulling open the huge wooden door when I heard someone behind me.

No!

I spun toward the house but was unable to see in the darkness. Crouching into the shadows, I held my breath, knowing whoever had followed might not see me in the faint light if I didn't move, but if I ran, they could track the sound.

The steps didn't stop, and a great shadow blocked the moon. Then strong arms lifted me bodily from the ground and hauled me inside the barn. I opened my mouth to scream, and one large hand clamped down over it.

Chase.

I sobbed for joy when I realized it was him. He didn't speak.

He set me down once inside and ran to the back, looking for the rear exit. It was locked and chained. He kicked it, and the wood splintered. He kicked it again, and the chain fell to the ground. *Too much noise!*

"Keys!" I whisper-shouted, and revealed to him everything that I had stuffed into my denim pockets.

He searched through them briefly. I thought he was looking for the key to the gun cabinet, but he wasn't. He let the remaining rings fall to the ground with a clatter and heaved me toward the motorcycle.

An instant later I was mounted behind him. He turned the key and squeezed the clutch with his left hand. The bike hummed softly, but did not yet growl like I knew it would.

I did not hesitate like I had a year ago. I slid close behind him, fit my knees into the backs of his, and wrapped my arms tightly around his body. I couldn't hear anyone following yet.

"Keep your head down," he ordered. "And hold on."

I nodded, my cheek pressed hard into his back.

We pushed out the back door of the barn, which faced the woods. Chase steered right, walking the bike toward the far side of the darkened house. My heart thumped through my chest into Chase's ribs. We were almost there. Almost to the driveway.

Finally, we could see down the gravel path curving toward the main road. Two cars were parked on the street, but both were empty. They'd left them there in order to surprise us.

A knife of fear punctured my lungs, and I could barely breathe. Not just cars. FBR cruisers.

Billings was a soldier. The FBR bought the Loftons' cattle.

The government owned most of the major food-distribution plants now. Horizons had bought out all the big brand names during the War. Of course Patrick would sell beef to them.

Chase grabbed my hand on his chest, squeezed it tightly, and rammed his foot down on the pedal. An explosion of growls filled the air. The sound would definitely be heard within the house.

I gritted my teeth and held on.

We hit the road in a spray of gravel. I don't know if Patrick and the soldiers came outside. I didn't look back.

We didn't stop until we reached the road. It took Chase less than thirty seconds to swing his leg over the front of the bike, jump off, and puncture the tires on both vehicles before we were off again.

WE rode toward a town called Hinton; I saw the name dimly shimmer on a green metallic road sign and felt the crushing blow of defeat as we passed the exit to Lewisburg. We had to. The Loftons would have told the MM they'd planned on taking us there.

We were going to miss the carrier.

As the adrenaline wore off, I began to tremble, though I didn't know if it was from the freezing air clawing through my clothing, or from the fear.

We were out on a road after curfew with only the occasional flash of the headlight to guide us. The rumbling of the motor screamed in my ears, calling out our location to anyone nearby. I could feel Chase concentrating hard, trying to maintain a rushed pace, but swerving to avoid the debris from the woods that popped up in our path.

I pinched my eyes closed. The Loftons had reported us. Even after we'd saved their son. *Don't trust anyone*, Chase had said. He was right.

How long did we have before the MM pursued? They had certainly already called in for backup. If we were lucky, we'd bought ourselves some decent lead time by slashing the tires. If we were really lucky, whoever came next would follow the lead to Lewisburg. Was it worth the hope?

The darkness unsettled me. I imagined eyes all around, watching us from the roadside. Each time Chase twitched, seeing a new obstacle in the road, I jumped.

We drove for the longest half hour of my life, finally passing a sign indicating that Hinton was only eight miles farther. Chase helped me off into a shadowed ditch on the side of the road and drove the bike straight into the bushes. We buried it silently and efficiently beneath the brush and pine needles and covered our tracks. Then we disappeared once again into the woods. I couldn't help but feel fortunate we'd survived this long. Then again, there was still time before sunup.

Chase had taken the backpack and was creeping ahead of me, parallel to the road. The sickle moon barely provided enough light to guide our way.

And then I heard the sirens.

CHAPTER
12

MY hand was in Chase's, and he was pulling, then I was pulling, and we were running, dragging each other farther away from the road, where the woods became so thick that even the moonlight couldn't reach us. The dry leaves crackled beneath our boots; branches clawed against our clothing and scratched burning lines into our exposed skin. I tripped, but before I had the chance to pick myself up, Chase had already righted me.

They were getting closer.

My heart was pounding, and even in the cold March air, a line of sweat dewed at my hairline. The throbbing *whir* of the sirens penetrated the barrier of trees and pierced through the breath that crashed in my eardrums. Blue lights flashed in streaks through the tall, black shadows.

Closer.

"Stop!" I yanked Chase down behind an enormous tree trunk, broken by some long-ago storm and now covered with ivy and brambles. He crouched beside me, still and silent, immediately camouflaged by darkness.

They came speeding up the road, silencing the insects and animals with their sirens. I was too petrified to move.

Don't stop don't stop don't stop.

They blared past. One. Two. Three cruisers. Heading toward the Loftons'.

And then we were alone in the woods.

Chase released an unsteady breath, reminding me that I hadn't done so in some time.

On trembling legs, we hiked again, all the way until we reached the edge of Hinton. It was a slow grind: Neither of us was willing to get any closer to the road, but the path we carved thirty yards inland was pitch black on account of the thick woods. My body became gradually more exhausted—a combination of an adrenaline crash and a sleepless night—but my mind was wound as tightly as a copper coil.

Finally, still well before dawn, we reached the edge of a parking lot, dusted with the trash that overflowed the scattered cans. Across the way I could vaguely make out a stucco strip mall. It was deserted; most of the glass shop fronts were covered with graffiti, but otherwise it seemed safe. No FBR patrol cars. No gangs.

There were four cars in the lot. All of them looked abandoned.

"Can you hotwire any of those?" I asked immediately.

Chase snorted. "We'll wait until closer to dawn. We can't drive now, and I don't want to be pinned out in the open if the MM show up."

I nodded in grudging agreement. There were still several hours until sunrise.

Far to our left was a great hulking shadow. An old, rusted

semitruck bed without the cab. I didn't like how it blocked the woods behind it. It made me feel too exposed, which reminded me that we shouldn't have still been out in the open. That we should have been with my mother by now. I twisted my heel into the soil.

"Hey, forget about Lewisburg," Chase said, not unkindly. "I said I'd get you to the safe house, and I will. I promise."

Tears I didn't know had gathered spilled down my cheeks. *How?* I wanted to scream. *How will we get there? How can you promise that? You don't even know the way!* But I knew he didn't have answers, and asking him would only make us both feel worse. I grabbed for the bag, searching through the darkness for the zipper, and covertly wiped my eyes.

The other clothes we'd stolen from the sporting goods store were near the top. They were still damp from the weather and would be bitingly uncomfortable in the low temperature, but it didn't matter. We had to change. I handed Chase another flannel, wishing we could ditch our jackets, but it was too cold.

"What happened back at the house?" I asked, after the knot in my throat had gone down. As quickly as I could, I stripped down to my thermal and replaced my sweater with the pink fleece I'd picked up for my mother. The instant the coat was back on, my chin was tucked inside the neck, stifling the cold air that had been needling my face.

"Patrick rode my heels like a lapdog," answered Chase. "I was trying to pull him away from the back of the house, maybe get him down in the basement with his wife. That's when the guys he called busted through the front door. Billings, I guess, and three others. I got one good hit in before—"

"You *hit* a soldier?" I squeaked. This could mean terrible consequences if we were caught.

"Didn't see too many other options," he said. I heard him change shirts and grunt as the fabric scraped the wound on his arm. "One of them said, 'It's him,' and reached for his weapon. That bastard and his wife must have known it was us before the news report."

I nodded but then realized he couldn't see me. "They thought they'd get a reward," I said aloud. *We got a thousand dollars for the last soldier,* Patrick had said. *Who knows? Maybe they'll kick in a bonus for the girl.* Knowing our lives had a price tag, one that could keep a family housed and fed, made me nauseous.

Chase swore softly, and I could feel this fact settle on him, sink into his pores. When he continued, his tone was bleak.

"One of them shut the lights off. It didn't work out like they hoped. I took off out the back, and that's when I found you."

"I shut the lights off," I confessed.

"You what?"

"I cut the power to the generator."

"You . . ." A long beat passed before he slowly approached and placed his hands on my shoulders. The confusion reflecting from his dark eyes made me uncomfortable. Here he was again, touching me while his mind disagreed with his actions.

"You're shivering," he said anxiously. I shook out of his grip, but it was too late. All the feelings I'd been trying to stuff away since his good-bye kiss came pouring back. The longing and the hope. The rejection. All magnified by the fact that we were now barred from Lewisburg and, it felt, my mother, too. He seemed to sense something was off and lowered his face to mine.

"Hey, are you —"

I slapped him.

We sat in stunned silence for a full three seconds before he spoke.

"Damn. That was fast."

"That's all you've got to say for yourself?" I nearly shouted at him. My hand stung just enough to tell me it hadn't shattered in the cold.

He floundered. "I . . . I guess. What exactly was that for?"

"You know what it's for," I accused furiously. "How dare you do . . . *that* . . . after . . . you know!"

"I *don't* know," he said bluntly. "I have no idea what you're talking about."

"You kissed me!"

He faltered back a step, and I heard the breath whistle through his teeth.

"You didn't seem to mind so much at the time."

I growled at him and then grabbed the bag and violently zipped it shut. "I was thinking you were someone else." *The old you.*

He snatched the bag out of my hands and shoved it onto his back. Then he shook it off, remembering we weren't going anywhere, and slammed it down on the ground.

"I told you," he said in a low voice. "He's gone. That's over."

I fought back the tears and spun away from him. Chase's acknowledgment of the two separate entities within himself should have made me feel better, but it only made me feel worse. I couldn't stand being near him any longer. Dawn couldn't come fast enough.

"Ember, wait," Chase called. He snagged my arm and held fast. Reluctantly, I turned, but I refused to look up and meet his eyes.

"Look . . .. I know you're torn up about him. He's probably fine," he said, frustrated.

He's probably fine?

"What do you . . . who are you talking about?" I thought he'd understood that we were talking about the Chase who cared for me and the Chase who didn't, but he was referring to someone else entirely. I felt the slow burn of oncoming humiliation.

"The guard from reform school. Isn't that who you're talking about?"

"*Sean?*" I asked, baffled. And then I remembered. Randolph, in the shack, had insinuated that I'd messed around with a guard when Chase had inquired, and then later I'd reinforced that fallacy when I'd asked Chase what would happen to a soldier caught with a resident. With everything that had happened, he remembered *that?*

I felt only a breath of embarrassment, because immediately after that came my awareness of the insult.

"You think I would have let you kiss me if I was with somebody else?"

"It's not like you had much of a choice," he said indignantly.

"I'm not some three-dollar hooker!" I blurted. "I don't know who you're used to spending your time with, but—"

"Hold on—"

"*You!* You kissed me thinking I was with someone else! What kind of person does that make *you*, huh?"

"Hold *on!*" he interrupted. I had encroached on his personal space in my anger, and now we were only inches apart. "First, I know you're not easy; you're actually the most difficult person I've ever met. Second, I never claimed to be a good person. And third, if you weren't talking about *Sean*, who the hell were you talking about?"

"That's . . ." I stammered. "That's none of your business," I said evasively.

"If you're thinking of another guy while I'm kissing you, I'm pretty sure it is my business," he said heatedly.

"Not anymore it's not! Why do you care anyway?"

He straightened, making me look up nearly a foot to see his eyes.

"I don't."

"Doesn't sound like it."

He kicked the ground. Seconds passed. They felt like hours.

"You're right. It doesn't matter," he said coldly.

My stomach plummeted, but he was right. It was better this way. He was leaving when we got to the safe house, and caring about him only complicated things.

He blew out a long breath, and we both faced the parking lot, stamping our feet impatiently. He attempted to turn on the radio, but it didn't even hiss; the battery had gotten wet in the rain or had simply died. If he could pick up a local frequency, we might be able to track the MM's movement. As it was, we were flying blind.

The anxiety settled my temper. The cold numbed my nerves. And when I glanced his way, I was surprised to see that he was already watching me. Just the outline of his face was visible in the moonlight.

"Thanks. For saving my life tonight."

He didn't add anything to it, and I didn't press. Instead I sat, and he sat beside me. I pulled my knees to my chest, tucked the jacket hood over my head, and waited for the dawn.

CHASE roused me an hour later. He'd placed the sleeping bag around us when I'd drifted off, but he had stayed up to keep watch. I rubbed my eyes, instantly alert.

Though the sun was coming, it was still dark. The crickets had ceased their chirping, giving way to the second shift of outdoor musicians: a woodpecker tapping away and the high train-whistle buzz of some likely enormous insect. When I felt something crawling on my hand, I jumped up in a flurry of unnecessary movement.

There was nothing crawling on my hand. There was, however, a thin gold band around my left ring finger.

"Where did . . ."

"They were right to think we were thieves," Chase said, referring to the ranchers.

I thought of how he'd scoped out their house right after we'd arrived, but I didn't feel even a little bad after what they had done.

"You married me while I was sleeping?" I asked in amazement. The sky was beginning to bruise with the purple haze, and in it, I could see Chase's face glow a little deeper copper.

"You hit me for kissing you. It seemed in my best interest to marry you while you were passed out."

A short laugh caught me by surprise. I wondered when I'd

last heard Chase make a joke. I supposed that meant we weren't fighting anymore. I admired the ring. The Loftons had so much, they probably wouldn't even notice it was gone.

"My mom will be so surprised."

His head dropped a little.

"It's just a cover. It's nothing serious," he said, with a twinge of annoyance. Apparently the joking was over. I was just about to bite back about him not having to be so rude, when he stiffened and pointed across the lot.

"Look!"

The dawn brought clarity. There, on the semitruck was a tin sign, nailed askew to the metal siding.

ONE WHOLE COUNTRY, ONE WHOLE FAMILY.

"Do you think . . ." I began, but he knew what I was going to say before I finished. The corners of his mouth had risen deviously.

The carrier had said to look for the sign. I felt certain that this was what he'd meant.

We scanned the parking lot for any signs of danger, and then ran for the semitruck, a hundred yards away. I couldn't help but think of the last empty parking lot we'd been in, at the sporting goods store, and I felt the hair on the back of my neck rise up. My wary gaze circled our position.

Just as we approached the eighteen-wheeler, a scuffle came from within.

I snapped back against the metal siding and froze. Though I expected help here, my body was now trained to react. Chase swooped in front of me and removed the baton from his belt. I wished we had the gun and ignored the fleeting awareness that I wouldn't have thought that two days ago.

It could be an animal. But then we heard the distinct and steady groaning of footfalls on metal.

Chase glanced over his shoulder, making sure I was behind him.

I squatted to look under the truck, past the flattened tires, and saw a person's legs as they jumped down. Then another, and finally a third, though this one more slowly, waiting for a hand from the other two.

Three of them. Two of us. They must have been sleeping when we arrived. Either that or the truck's compartment had muted out voices. We wouldn't be so lucky now. We didn't know what weapons they had, and it was fifty yards back to the trees. If we made a run for it, they would certainly hear us.

Please let them be friendly.

A moment later, a boy about my age came around the corner—and froze.

He wore an old suit jacket, torn and patched by various fabrics on the stress points, and several layered T-shirts beneath it. His cargo pants were tied on by a length of red twine. He said something we couldn't hear, and then two girls revealed themselves. One was about his height, wearing a torn long-sleeved thermal. The other was short, with pretty mocha skin and rounded, candy-apple cheeks.

She was at least six months pregnant.

I felt my blood buzzing with the same suspicion these strangers surely felt. They turned their heads to confer with each other quietly. Chase returned the baton to his belt and raised his empty hands in peace. He took a few slow steps forward.

We were twenty feet away, and the trio still had not moved. I saw the male pull back his jacket, revealing a black tire iron tucked into his waistband. My breath caught, but I was somehow relieved that there was neither a gun nor a knife visible. Yet.

Chase scoffed.

"Hold up," the boy called. We stopped.

"We don't want trouble," Chase told him, clearly not intimidated. The tall girl turned to the boy and whispered something in his ear. Closer now, it became obvious that these two were twins. They had the same androgynous face: straight brows, flat cheekbones etched by the shadows of malnourishment, dark hair coming to a widow's peak in the center of their foreheads.

"Got a trade?" the female twin asked.

"We're looking for a carrier," I said.

I felt Chase brace before me and wondered if I'd been too bold. But it wasn't like these people were going to turn us in to the MM, at least not immediately. Scalping anything that the MM had profit rights to was illegal.

"We're car salesmen, not drivers," said the female twin. The boy elbowed her.

I didn't like her tone. Or the way she was staring at Chase.

"Do you know a carrier or not?" I asked.

"There's one in Lewisburg that goes to Georgia and South—"

"Can't go to Lewisburg," Chase interrupted.

"Then Harrisonburg, but that's farther."

"Can't go there, either," Chase said flatly. I felt my jaw tighten.

"Bad boy," clucked the girl. She grinned flirtatiously at Chase. I narrowed my eyes at her, and though it was cold out, I rolled up my sleeve to show off the ring on my left hand.

The small girl was whispering something to her boyfriend. When she turned to the side, she placed a hand on her distended abdomen. I felt suddenly sorry for them. She was only fifteen or sixteen—too young to be married—and certainly in violation of the Moral Statutes. That was probably why they were living in a truck.

"MM following you?" she asked.

Neither Chase nor I answered.

"You need Knoxville," she continued. "Tennessee. You know it?"

My attention perked at this.

"What's in Knoxville?" Chase asked.

"A carrier?" I clarified, feeling my breath begin to come faster.

"A whole underground system," said the girl twin. "Lots of people have been heading there. That's where half our cars have gone. Total liquidation." She laughed.

"Knoxville," I repeated. I felt Chase release a slow breath beside me.

We were back on track.

IT was a long day.

The new Red Zones, those cities evacuated from the War, and Yellow Zones, those areas entirely comprised of MM, were marked in bold corresponding colors on highway signs and called for multiple detours throughout Virginia and Northern Tennessee. For brief patches I dozed, never falling fully asleep. I lingered on edge, my heart always beating a little too fast, my mind filled with worries.

The girl twin occasionally popped up in my mind, and I found myself bitter when I thought of her. She'd insisted on a trade for the car, and since we had nothing they wanted, we'd had to pay them. One thousand dollars. *Cash*. For an item that wasn't even theirs to begin with. But since they'd siphoned all the gasoline, our hands were tied.

Still, I didn't regret the interaction.

A *whole underground system*, the girl had said. A whole resistance movement. My mind couldn't wrap around what this might look like. People like us. On the run. Scheming against the MM. My fantasies seemed too unrealistic. All that mattered was that someone would take us to South Carolina.

As the day wound on, my chest began to squeeze with that familiar anxiety. My mother was just beyond our grasp, but now when I focused hard on her, I only saw fragmented images. Her short, accessorized hair. Her socked feet on the kitchen floor. I needed to find her soon, or I was afraid even more of her would disappear.

Finally, we came in range. As we closed in on the city of Knoxville, the MM presence on the highway increased. There were other cars as well. Not many, but enough for us to blend in. This fact didn't ease our minds as the FBR cruisers began flying by with regularity.

Then we saw the sign. YELLOW ZONE. The western half of Knoxville had recently been closed to civilians to make way for an MM base.

"Think they lied?" I asked Chase nervously. "Do you think they sent us here because we didn't give them enough money?"

"No," Chase answered, though he didn't sound very convincing. "I think the safest place is right in the enemy's shadow. There's resistance here."

And so we went to hide beneath the belly of a monster.

He took a busy exit after crossing over the gray waters of the Holston River, and parked in a dark lot behind an outcropping of sandstone medical buildings that belonged to the city hospital. Outside we were flooded by the sounds and scents of a working city during rush hour. Even after just a couple days in the country, being around so many human bodies made me feel crowded and paranoid, like everyone was watching us. I could smell the sewers, the sweat, the smog filling the stagnant air. It did nothing but add to my sense of unease.

It was cool, but not cold. The sky hung low with humidity. Rain was coming. Chase grabbed the bag and rounded the car. He didn't have to tell me not to leave anything. I already knew we wouldn't be coming back.

We entered the street and were immediately surrounded by pedestrians. Some rushing, fortunate enough to be wearing their work clothes and therefore employed. Some homeless, begging off to the side with their cardboard signs. Some twitching, scratching, talking to unseen hallucinations. High or mentally ill. The Reformation Act had eliminated treatment programs to fund the FBR.

There was hardly enough room to walk here. Chase came close, and though his expression was dark, I knew he was more comfortable than me. After Chicago had been bombed, he'd survived in places like this. Places where people had congregated after being displaced from the major cities.

"Watch your back," he warned me. "And mine, while you're at it," he added, tightening the straps of the pack. He'd moved the money to his front pocket.

"Where do we start?" I asked. This was the biggest city I'd ever seen. No matter how large the resistance here, we were searching for a needle in a haystack.

"Follow people in dirty clothes," he said. "They'll lead us to food, and where there's food, there's people talking."

He was right. We walked for several city blocks, finding ourselves part of a massive stream of hungry people. Every telephone pole, fence, or door displayed a prominent posting of the Moral Statutes. We crossed the train tracks and came to a place called Market Square, a long cement strip lined by flat-faced brick buildings that might once have been shops but were now hostels, medical stations, and abandoned buildings.

The crowd grew denser toward the back of the square. Thousands of people were here for food or shelter. Sisters, too, in their navy skirts and knotted handkerchiefs, bustling around the temporary cots of the Red Cross camp. I swallowed thickly, realizing this could have been me.

A dose of adrenaline shot into my veins when I caught a uniform from the corner of my eye. The clean, neatly pressed blue stuck out amid a sea of shabby garments.

Soldiers.

My eyes lingered, and I saw two more, standing behind an unmarked moving truck, unloading wooden crates of food. Their setup was positioned on the right side of a bottleneck, leading to the open space of the square. They didn't try to hide their weapons; they were all armed and ready to fire upon anyone who might try to steal.

Chase had seen them, too. He lowered his head, trying not to look so tall. I scanned the crowd. Too many people were shuffling into the square; no one was going out. If we ran now, we'd cause a commotion and our way would be impeded by bodies. Besides, if the MM wanted to pursue us, they had guns. People would get out of their way a lot faster than they'd get out of ours.

We needed to get to the kitchen. Chase thought we'd be safe asking some discreet questions about the carrier there, and the only way to get there was to walk by the soldiers. We wouldn't be locked in once we passed—there were exits in the back of the square that I could see from my vantage point—but it would be a tremendous risk. The soldiers would only be ten feet away.

I reached for Chase's hand, and a quick squeeze asked the question I didn't dare speak aloud. With only the briefest of hesitations, he squeezed mine back. We were going to pass them.

"Pull your collar up," Chase commanded. I did so quickly. We shuffled forward, bodies bumping against us on all sides as we entered the bottleneck.

Please don't look this way. I concentrated all my energy on the two soldiers.

"Eyes forward." Chase's voice was low enough that only I could hear. "Don't stop."

Sweat rained down my face, so contrary to the firm gust of cool evening air that blasted over the crowded square. A vice squeezed my temples.

Keep walking, I told myself.

I saw the soldiers in my peripheral vision, only ten feet away.

One of the guards turned quickly, a radio glued to his ear. From the back I caught a glimpse of his light brown hair and narrow build, and an odd sense of familiarity crept over me.

Keep walking.

We passed by the crates of food and the soldiers and headed toward the open area of the square.

I fought the urge to turn around. Chase strode faster, pulling me around the corner on the damp sidewalk, out of the stream of pedestrians. It was quieter here, and I breathed for what felt like the first time in minutes.

"What are they doing here?" I asked. The MM provided the food for the soup kitchens at home but relied on volunteers to deliver it to the sites. I always thought this was because it was below them to mingle with poor people they didn't have reason to arrest.

"The city must be on a supply crunch."

"That explains the guns," I commented wryly. The sooner we could get out of here the better.

As we resumed our path, I became acutely aware of how clean, how *well fed*, we looked. Single floaters loitering near the sidewalk stared resentfully at us like we were royalty. From their famished condition, I guessed that Chase was right about the supply crunch: There clearly wasn't enough food to go around in this large city.

We passed a homeless man leaning against a loud generator outside a community restroom with a sign that read "anything helps." He was emaciated. Ragged, stained clothing hung from his bony frame. Paper-thin skin lidded his deeply set eyes, and his face was masked by the olive-colored blotches of starvation.

Chase paused in front of this man, and for a moment I thought that he was going to give him some money. His generosity scared me. If Chase took out his wallet, these starving people would be on us like a pack of wolves.

An instant later Chase straightened and reached for my hand again, pulling me beside him.

"Stay close," he said.

I jumped when I heard the scuffle behind us, and turned back, expecting to have to defend myself. My mouth dropped open. The pack of wolves had indeed descended, but they weren't coming after us, they were closing in upon the man. The starving, *homeless* man. My anxiety rebounded, ten times more intensely than before, when I realized they intended to rob him. The palms of my hands dewed with sweat, but Chase's grip held fast.

A man and a woman with sunken cheeks stole the man's change cup and his cardboard sign. Another took his shoes. Another his soiled sweatshirt. When it was jerked off his body, folded Statute circulars fluttered into the air. He'd been lining his clothing with paper to keep warm.

The crumpled victim's bare, ashen chest was revealed. His sticklike limbs were bent at awkward, contorted angles, but he remained as supple as a rag doll. Someone had probably knocked him unconscious, or he had been simply too weak to fight back.

"We have to help!" My voice was high with distress. This crime was intolerable. How would the man survive without the warmth of his clothing?

"There's nothing we can do. If we stay, we'll be next." He urged me forward.

"Chase!" I yelped. I dug my heels in but could not pull him to a stop.

"It's too late," he said in a hard voice. At once, I knew what he meant.

The man was dead.

How long had he sat there, with no one checking on him, no one noticing how many days had passed since his last meal? A day? Two? A *week*? How cold and foreign this city seemed, that even death could pass unnoticed.

And where were the soldiers now? Weren't they meant to stop this?

The answer was all too clear. *No*. The MM would do nothing. They wanted the poor and unfortunate to kill themselves off. Less work for them that way.

An image of Katelyn Meadows filled my mind. What had the guards at the reformatory done to her body? Had she been taken back to her parents? Were her parents even still alive? I suddenly felt old, far beyond my years.

Chase pulled me through the skirmish. I felt as if I were floating. Like my feet barely touched the ground. I wanted to go to sleep and wake up in my bedroom at home, with my mother singing in the other room. I wanted to go over to Beth's house to do homework and talk about anything and everything and nothing important. I wanted things that were impossible.

Someone shoved into us, knocked undoubtedly by someone else. Chase's hand was ripped from mine and I was tossed to the side. I didn't fall. There were too many people buffering my stumble.

But Chase was gone. Swallowed by the crowd.

My ears rang. The blood pumped through my veins.

"Ch— Jacob!" I screamed, hoping he would respond to his middle name. People were shouting, shoving, pushing now. Were they still moving toward the dead man? Or something else? Chase did not respond.

"Jacob!" It was like shouting under water. No one heard me. A hard slap to my back had me jolting forward, toward the concrete, but I bounced off a body in my path. Someone grasped my arm hard and nearly jerked it out of the socket trying to hold himself up. A sea of chaos took me, flinging my upper half one way while my legs went the other, and then the crunch, the sick, soft feel of flesh and bones beneath my boots.

"Food!" I heard someone yell. "Over there!"

They couldn't be talking about the soup kitchen: That was at the other end of the square. And the dead man only had so much to steal. It had to be the truck we'd passed earlier. What I couldn't imagine was how these people expected to break through the barrier of armed soldiers.

Just as I regained my footing, a hand latched hard around my elbow.

"Oh, thank God!" I cried, and turned to see the back of a man with clean-cut brown hair and a navy blue collar. He was dragging me out of the riot.

Not Chase. A soldier.

"No! Wait, please!" I tried, planting my feet and jerking back. "There's been a mistake."

"Keep moving, Miller," I heard him call over his shoulder.

Dread punched through me. This soldier knew who I was. They'd found me. Chase had to run. He was in more danger than I was if he was caught. He could still get to my mother.

It took all my power not to shout Chase's name at the top of my lungs. But I knew that if I did, and if he came, he was as good as dead.

"I'm not . . . I don't know who Miller is!" I said, pulling back with both hands now. No one noticed me. There was too much commotion. Too much chaos.

"Help!" I yelled finally. *"Help!"*

But even if they heard, they didn't react. I clutched a man's coat as the soldier yanked me toward a black alleyway. He shrugged me off. I grabbed a woman's hair. She punched my shoulder, and my fist returned with loose strands.

The world became suddenly silent. It was as though we'd stepped through some invisible force field. The roar of the crowd remained in the square, but the alley was absolutely still, apart from a few rats scurrying behind an overflowing Dumpster. I saw one or two people glance after us as I was dragged inside, but though their eyes widened, they looked away in fright.

I was alone with the soldier.

CHAPTER
13

PANIC seized me.

I struggled, my hair a curtain blocking my vision. I refused to stand, forcing the soldier to carry me. I saw flashes of his uniform. The bloused navy pants over black boots. The belt. The *gun*. A gold name badge—WAGNER. Dusk had come, and back here in the shadows I couldn't get a clear view of his face.

"Stop!" the soldier demanded. I swallowed my fear and swung my fist at his head, well aware that such an action was either going to land me in prison or get me killed.

"*Stop!*" he yelled again. "Look at me!"

In a heave, he rammed my body against the alley wall. My head smacked hard against the brick. All of my organs reverberated inside of me, and I gasped, seeing stars.

But I stopped, and that was when I saw his face. Strong, handsome features. Blue eyes, no longer vacant. Sandy brown hair. This was the soldier I had glimpsed by the truck guarding the food. The one who had given me a funny feeling.

"*Sean?*" I said, shocked. Sean Banks. Not Wagner. Who was Wagner?

I didn't have time to ask. A second later we were thrown to the ground as some large object was propelled from the side and slammed into Sean.

Not an object. Chase.

I scrambled to clear the fray. There was a thudding sound, then a grunt as the air expelled from someone's lungs. They wrestled for just a few seconds before Chase pinned Sean, facedown in the cement, holding his arm awkwardly behind his back. He ripped away the gun and thrust it none too gently into the back of Sean's head.

"Ember." Chase was too distraught to use my alias. He was asking if I was injured, and I knew immediately that my answer would determine how he would punish my assailant.

"Chase, that's Sean! I know him!" I said. "It's okay! *I'm* okay!"

"What I saw didn't look okay," he answered.

"Man, let me up!" Sean's voice was muffled by the filthy alley floor. He cried out as his shoulder popped. "I'm not FBR!"

"I know," said Chase. "Your weapon isn't standard issue." He turned the gun to look at it. I looked at it too. It was black, whereas Chase's had been silver.

I realized what Chase must have thought when he'd seen me pressed against the wall. It was the same thing he'd feared when Rick and Stan had told me to get in the car with them.

"Chase, let him up." I was shaking.

"I was just trying to tell her it was me!" Sean pleaded. "She almost knocked my head off!"

"That's what happened," I agreed quickly.

Chase looked my way, reading my eyes for truth. After a moment he nodded, but he didn't look happy about releasing his captive.

"Don't touch her," he warned Sean. His fury did not immediately abate, and he did not release the gun. "Why'd you start the riot?"

Sean had started the riot? *Intentionally?* When I thought about it, it did make sense. That was why he hadn't been torn apart by the crowd. That's why he was wearing a stolen uniform with the name badge WAGNER.

Sean stood indignantly, wiping off his face with his shirtsleeve.

"Because that was today's mission. Steal from the rich, give to the poor. Now later, when the real FBR shows up and doesn't give away extra rations, the people get pissed off enough to take them down."

Sean had joined the resistance. The thoughts began racing through my mind. The uniform truck, stolen here, in Tennessee. The sniper. Were his people responsible for that too? Maybe Sean was who we had been looking for! Maybe he would even know the carrier.

Chase helped me up, placing his thumb on my chin and gently turning my face from side to side to check for damage.

Sean watched us curiously. "I saw you in the square. I followed you and—"

"—and waited until she was alone," Chase growled. Sean took a step back.

"Yeah," said Sean. "Can you blame me?" He waved his arms at Chase.

"Be nice, both of you," I said.

Chase took a step toward him. Sean balked.

"They discharged me after that night I helped you," Sean said quickly. "I came here to find Becca."

"What?" I tried to get closer, but Chase stopped me. "She's here? With you?"

"She's inside. In the base. Where they hold all the prisoners awaiting trial. Or didn't you know?" he said between his teeth, blue eyes flashing.

"I didn't know," I swallowed, reliving the last moments I had seen Rebecca Lansing. "They took her away. I didn't know where."

Sean watched me speculatively. I knew he wanted to believe me, but he was wary to trust. I wondered how he'd found out Rebecca had been taken here. Did the resistance know? Did they have access to MM records? Would they know about my mother?

"We don't have time for this," Chase said. "The safe house—the one in South Carolina—how do we get there?"

Sean looked from Chase to me and then out into the square, where the people still rioted.

"It's almost curfew." He shoved his arms across his chest and shook his head. "You'd better come with me. I know the guy who makes that run. He's leaving in a couple days. I'll take you to him just as soon as you tell me about Becca." He snorted cynically. "You help me, and I'll get you out. Just like old times, right, Miller?"

I avoided Sean's accusing stare, and then Chase's as well. It occurred to me Chase had no idea what was going on, what I'd done. My stomach curdled with guilt.

"I'd just as soon leave you, but I have a feeling that's not going to fly, is it?" he said to Chase.

Chase cast him a hard look and turned to me. "It's your call."

I realized this was the first time he'd left the decision solely in my hands. My eyes turned to the ex-soldier in the stolen uniform. Going with Sean seemed more dangerous, but it was a risk we needed to take in order to find the carrier. Besides, I owed him information about Rebecca. It was the least I could do for the trouble I'd caused them.

I nodded reluctantly.

SEAN shed the uniform behind the Dumpster, revealing the shabby civilian clothes beneath, and stuffed it into a black trash bag, which he threw over his shoulder like the other transients who carried their worldly possessions on their backs. We followed him down the alleyway in silence. After several blocks of turns and obvious backpedaling, we came to an old brick motel called the Wayland Inn.

It was a downtrodden place—somewhere I would have avoided even if it hadn't been deserted. Overgrown ivy snaked up the side of the building, and every other window was boarded up, but there was no evidence of graffiti here, as there was on the other abandoned buildings around. This place had been left alone.

The light was fading, twilight bringing a pearly hue to the gathering clouds. We crossed the open street hastily, scanning for patrol cars, and ducked in through a single glass door.

Clouds of white dispersed in the room as the evening air blew in after us. The room stank of nicotine, which emanated from a drooping cigarette in the mouth of an orange-haired man behind the counter. Cigarettes were luxuries most people couldn't afford. I wondered if he was part of the resistance, too.

As if to answer my question, Sean dug in his pocket, removed a pack of unfiltered Horizons brand cigarettes, and placed them on the counter. The clerk's ruddy brows rose, and a smug look slid over his face. He offered a slight tilt of his head, which was enough to indicate he wouldn't ask questions, and we crossed over the stained red carpet without another word.

Lying across the floor in front of the stairway was a man in tattered rags. Long dreadlocks hung like dead snakes over his shoulders. His eyes were heavily lidded. As we approached, he clambered up and gave us a suspicious glare. I could smell the sweat and alcohol wafting off of him.

I skirted around him into the stairwell, where Sean had stopped.

"Is this where we meet the carrier?"

Sean shook his head.

A moment later, the drunk from the hallway slithered in, straightening to his full height once the exit door shut completely. As he neared us, I could tell that he wasn't drunk at all; the lights in his eyes were too focused, and his movements were unhindered.

"Wallace know they're coming?" he asked Sean in a gruff voice.

"Yeah. Of course," Sean responded. Then he gave Chase a sidelong glance. "He's going to frisk your girlfriend. Try not to beat the hell out of him."

I felt my face heat up at the title, but no one, including Chase, seemed to notice.

Whoever Wallace was, he couldn't have known we were here; my presence in the square had taken Sean by surprise. I didn't want to maintain a lie I knew nothing about, but I stayed silent.

The bouncer patted down Chase first, then me. It was done quickly and efficiently, but I still felt violated when his hands stroked my legs and waist. When he reached into my pocket to take Chase's six-inch pocket knife, I jerked back sharply.

"You can collect this later if Wallace says so," he informed me. He searched the bag and removed the baton and the MM radio. "These too," he added, shoving the items into his jacket and slinking back into the hallway to resume his watch.

"Who's Wallace?" I asked as we climbed the metal stairs. They made a bright *ting* with every step we took.

"He runs the operation here. He's not the carrier, before you ask. That guy goes by Tubman. And it's too late to drag you across town to his checkpoint."

"So what is this place then?" I asked, deflated, but still edgy.

Sean pushed through the door into the hallway on the fourth floor. The lights were out here, and the dim corridor made me feel claustrophobic. A man and a woman, dressed in street clothes, loitered in front of one of the scuffed wooden doors. They had been playing cards and stood abruptly when we came into view.

"This is the resistance," Sean said.

. . .

"WHO are you?" asked the man, sizing us up. He was not much taller than me but built like a tree trunk. Even his head was shaped like a can. He seemed impressed by Chase, but he frowned my way. He probably thought Chase would be more useful to the rebellion—an assumption that irritated me.

"I know her from the girls' school," Sean said. "She's Miller, and he's . . ."

"Jennings," the girl finished. She knotted her long black hair back in a ponytail. I could tell it wasn't her natural color: Her eyebrows were nearly transparent, and her skin was very light. I wondered where she'd gotten the dye; that was contraband now. *Indecent*, the MM called it.

"We've been following you on the nightly report," she explained.

My eyes widened. People knew who we were, just from my name. This couldn't be good. If they knew, the MM was still tracking our flight. Waiting for us to screw up. I couldn't tell by her neutral tone if she objected to our presence.

"They haven't been cleared," the guy said irritably. "You know the rules, Banks."

"I know the exceptions, too. Miller's got information."

For *him*. Information for Sean about Rebecca. I didn't know anything else. I sincerely hoped Sean wasn't setting me up for trouble by bringing us here.

Can-Head narrowed his eyes at me. "Yeah, I bet she does."

Chase shifted.

"I'll take responsibility for them." Sean gave Chase a stern look as if to say *Don't make me regret it*, and knocked twice on the door they guarded.

"What's his problem?" I asked Sean under my breath.

"A carrier was murdered at the Harrisonburg checkpoint a couple days back. They found evidence that points to a female."

"What kind of evidence?" I said quickly. Chase had gone very still beside me.

"Footprints, I think."

I had to remind myself to keep breathing.

I'd slipped on the floor when Chase had dragged me outside. Slipped on something wet. Blood. My bootprints were all the way out the door. It took everything I had not to rip them off right there.

"I think Riggins thinks it was you." Sean didn't try to keep our conversation a secret.

"Well, it wasn't!" I said, aghast, turning to Can-Head.

Riggins looked unabashed and unconvinced.

I clasped my hands together to keep them from fidgeting. The danger was stacking up. People recognized our names. I was being pinned to a murder. We were now hiding out with a large body of resistance. It was going to take a hope and a prayer to reach the safe house alive at this point.

My eyes darted to Chase. He looked like a wolf ready to attack. I felt the energy radiating off of him and knew to be prepared for anything.

The door cracked open and then pulled inward as Sean was recognized.

We entered a narrow room that smelled stale. The walls were bare and yellowing. In the back were a few crates of food and nearly thirty cardboard boxes marked by sizes: M, L, XL. Uniforms. The *missing* uniforms.

A gray wool sofa, the only piece of furniture present,

sagged against the side wall. Above it hung a blueprint of the building. The exits were marked by bright red circles. A man in his mid-thirties stood from his seat on the couch. He had long greasy hair, too gray for his youthful face, and a mustache.

The guy holding the door was younger. Fourteen or fifteen maybe. A mousy mop of hair hung over bright green eyes. He held a rifle, lowered but still lethal.

"Who are they?" interrogated the man with the graying hair.

"A girl I knew on duty. She came here to find me," Sean lied. "They need shelter."

"They need—"

"Before you blow a gasket, Wallace, remember I'm only here because of—"

"You're risking the entire operation for a girl?" he exploded. "This isn't a damn game, Banks!"

I was already on edge, tired, hungry, and hedging on desperation. On some level I understood the need for caution, but the rest of me was furious that this man was treating us like children who had run away from the babysitter.

"Does it look like we're playing?" I said hotly. I felt Chase's hand on my arm. The boy still held the gun. The tension in the room was palpable.

Wallace turned on me.

"There are induction procedures in place."

I felt a flash of anger, and without thinking, displayed the discolored welts running across the backs of my hands.

"I know about *induction procedures*," I spat. "So we can go ahead and skip the initiation."

A cynical smirk lifted Wallace's face but faded away into understanding.

"I can see that. This is merely a safety precaution, I assure you," he said, calmer.

Sean cleared his throat. "Wallace tries to make sure recruits aren't followed or working for the FBR."

"You cleared me," I said stubbornly. "Sean can vouch for me. We weren't followed, and we sure as hell don't work for the MM."

"Sean hasn't been with me long enough for that responsibility," answered Wallace flatly.

Sean's jaw was set. "So what are you going to do, discharge me?"

Wallace groaned. "Maybe it would sink in the second time."

He stared at both Chase and I for several seconds. Seeming to have made up his mind about our threat, he motioned for the boy at the door to put down the shotgun. I sighed audibly. Chase did not.

"I'd apologize for the reception, but I'm sure you understand why we can't send out open-house invitations." He dipped his head toward me. "I'm Wallace. That over there is Billy. And you are?"

When I introduced us, recognition dawned on Wallace's face.

"Jennings. Interesting. Been a while since we've had celebrities." His curiosity was quickly snuffed. "I don't suppose Sean stressed the importance of discretion?"

"We won't say anything," I promised.

"Certainly *he* won't," said Wallace, eyeing Chase.

He was right. Chase was uncharacteristically silent. He

was rarely loquacious, but neither was he usually so deadpan. Something was weighing heavily on him. I could feel it.

"I suppose you're here for work," Wallace said. I felt Chase stiffen beside me, and wondered what he was thinking. It would make sense for him to want to join the resistance. That way he could strike back at the MM for everything they'd taken away.

I felt the same pull inside my own self but stuffed it down. I couldn't allow myself to project past finding my mother. One step at a time.

"We're looking for Mr. Tubman," I said, when Chase hadn't answered. His silence was starting to make me uncomfortable. It appeared he was more tempted by the resistance than I had thought. If he joined here and now, he might not even come with me for the rest of the journey. I shifted my weight from foot to foot, faced with the sudden reality of his upcoming good-bye.

"A safe house." Wallace clicked his tongue inside his cheek. "Waste of your talents." He was talking to both of us, not just Chase, when he said this. I didn't know what talents of mine he could possibly mean, but then I realized that the radio reports had probably insinuated that I was far craftier than I was. That I had escaped reform school and the MM. That we'd accosted thieves in Hagerstown and stolen vehicles. All of this was true of course, but much less impressive in reality than it was when relayed secondhand.

"It's no waste," said Chase firmly. It made me feel a little more confident that we were still making the right choice.

We were about to say more when there was a commotion

outside and three more men charged through the door. Two must have been brothers. One was in his late twenties, the other older. They had dark hair and dark eyes, but the younger had recently broken his nose, and the other now had a bruise below his right eye. The third was a wiry redhead, about Chase's age. Dry blood had crusted over his cheek. I didn't recognize them from the square, but I knew it must be the other soldiers Sean had been with, because they all held the same trash bags filled with their uniforms.

There was an eruption of voices and movement. Everyone was trying to speak at once.

"Get them out of here, Banks. Then come back for debriefing," ordered Wallace. "Tomorrow, take them to Tubman yourself."

I wanted to stay but was glad Wallace had approved our departure.

Sean led us down the hallway in the opposite direction from the stairs. A few heads popped out of the doors, interested in what had transpired in the square. I realized with some amazement that the entire floor must have been filled with resistance fighters.

The single room we entered was more tightly confined than Wallace's had been. A moth-eaten velvet chair crowded the corner, bumping into a bare queen-sized mattress. On a small nightstand were boxes of cereal and Horizons bottled water.

"Is this someone's room?" I asked, staring longingly at the food. I hadn't eaten since a rest stop mid-morning in eastern Kentucky, and I was famished.

"It was," he said grimly. My spirits crashed as I realized the previous occupant was either captured or dead. "Talk, Miller. Quick."

I promptly told him everything I knew, beginning with the night I'd blackmailed them and ending with my abduction from the shack. I didn't dare look at Chase. It wasn't as though he hadn't done bad things, but the secret of how I'd hurt these people had festered inside of me, and I was more ashamed than ever.

Chase prowled like a trapped animal while I talked, opening a window, which revealed the wrought-iron fire escape just outside. This seemed to settle him, but he remained quiet. The weight of his judgment hung over me. Maybe I deserved it.

"Was she hurt?" Sean looked far away. Broken.

"I don't know." I closed my eyes. I remembered the crack of the baton on her little body. Yes, she had been hurt. But the frantic gleam in his eyes stopped me from telling the truth. It seemed cruel to tell him when there was nothing he could do about it.

"And you never told Brock about me and Becca." He still sounded a little leery.

"No. Rebecca was . . ." I paused. "Rebecca was my friend. Maybe not at first. And she probably doesn't think so now. But I'll always remember her. I know it doesn't matter what I say, but I wish things had been different."

Sean was quiet for a moment.

"How did you know she was here?" Chase asked Sean finally. I wondered if it was curiosity or some other purpose that had caused him to break his silence.

In a rush, Sean told us how he'd been discharged from the

base in Cincinnati, where he'd been sent after the incident at reform school, and met Billy and Riggins, who had been in town collecting stray soldiers for the resistance. Billy's other talents included breaking into MM cruisers and accessing prisoner lists via their scanning device. That was how Sean had found out about Rebecca's transfer.

I remembered the scanner the highway patrol had used when he'd pulled us over. A miniature computer. Billy was quite clever, it seemed.

Since there was no way to break into the base without getting killed himself, Sean had settled on working for the resistance until Billy could get him more information about Rebecca.

Before Sean could say more, Wallace summoned him from down the hall.

"I'll take you to the carrier tomorrow," he said.

"Sean, wait," I said as he was leaving. "I just . . . I'm so sorry."

He looked at me for a long time through tired eyes. They were not resentful, not mistrusting anymore. He didn't blame me. And somehow that made me feel worse.

"It's them, Miller. Not us. It's the FBR that should be sorry."

AFTER a while I went to the window, comforted by the cold air on my face. It was dark now. Through the bars of the fire escape I could see headlights snaking through the city intersections in the distance, and the goose bumps rose on my skin. Curfew was on. The MM was just below. All around. Everywhere.

It's the FBR that should be sorry, Sean had said.

He was right. They'd taken Rebecca. They'd taken my

mother. They'd nearly broken Chase. Now we could never go home. We would have to live in hiding forever.

I tried to force my thoughts elsewhere but was bombarded by images from the day. The throngs of starving people. The dead man by the generator. Sean—when I hadn't known it was Sean—yanking me through the crowd. The acceptance that Chase could still make it, even if I didn't.

He was stronger. A fighter. He could survive in this world.

"We need a new plan. New rules," I began, trying to sound strong. Chase had been listening down the hall, but at the sound of my voice he stepped away from the doorway and waited for me to continue. I hoped he wouldn't try to be difficult; it was hard enough acknowledging what I was about to say myself.

"If the MM finds one of us, the other needs to go on. The other needs to get to the safe house and find my mom and make sure she's okay."

My words sounded hollow. He didn't say anything.

"You can't come after me if I get taken, do you understand?"

Still nothing.

"Chase!" I slammed a fist down on the windowsill and the pane rattled. "Are you listening to me?"

"Yes." He was standing right behind me. I spun into him.

"Yes, you'll do it?" I knew I should be relieved, but I didn't feel it.

"Yes, I'm listening. No. I won't do it."

The same fear iced my spine that I'd felt earlier today in the square. The fear that my mother would be on her own. The fear that Chase would be caught and condemned to death. The tears were coming now; there was no use trying to hide them.

"Why not? If something happens to me . . ."

"Nothing is going to happen to you!" He grabbed me by the elbows, making me stand on my tiptoes. His eyes burned with the anger I knew he only reached through fear. How did I know that about him? I thought fleetingly. How could I read that, when I hardly knew what I was feeling?

"What if something does?" I threw back. "I can die, just like Katelyn Meadows! I can starve like that man in the square! I can be taken by the MM, or shot—"

"STOP!" he shouted. My mouth fell open. He breathed out unsteadily, his face pale in the dark room, and tried to compose himself. He was only mildly successful.

"Ember, I swear on my life, I will not let anything like that happen."

I crumpled in his arms, crying freely now because I was afraid. Because I didn't want to die. Because if I did, I had secured no future for my mother or Chase. For the people I loved.

I hadn't ever cried before him like this. Everything I'd been holding back crashed over me. Losing my mother. Missing my friends. Hurting Sean and Rebecca. The carrier on Rudy Lane begging for his son. The man in the square. Chase pulled me in tightly, sheltering me with his body, hiding me from the fears that lashed both of us.

"Why did you come after me?" I sobbed. "If Sean had been a real soldier, you could have been killed."

"I don't care."

"I do!"

"I won't leave you."

I shoved back. He was averse to letting me.

"Isn't that what you're doing anyway? Leaving? Just as soon as we get to the safe house?"

He opened his mouth, closed it.

"I . . . I was going to leave that up to you."

What did that mean? I could just kick him away from his own safety because I didn't want him around? As if we hadn't lived five yards apart for most of our lives? Who was I to make that call? No, that wasn't the reason. He was deflecting to me because it was easier for him if I was the one that pushed him away. That way he wouldn't have to hurt feelings. That way he could run back here and join the resistance.

"Let go of me," I said unsteadily. I tried to breathe, but my lungs felt constricted. "I know you want to keep your promise, so go ahead. Protect me. But when we get there, your obligation's over. You don't owe me a thing. I survived you leaving before, Chase. I'll do it again."

He stared at me, shocked. I could hardly believe what I had just said.

"I'm tired now," I said. "There are more than enough people taking watch." I reminded myself to keep my chin lifted as I opened the door. "I'll be fine alone."

"I won't."

Before I could turn toward him, he placed his hand over mine and closed the door softly. I became aware of every one of his movements. The tightening of the muscles in his shoulders. The difference in his breathing. Each one of his warm fingers over mine. And the changes in myself, also. The tingling of my skin. The doubt, like a stone in my belly.

"I'm not fine," he said. "Not without you."

My whole body felt like I'd just missed a step going down

the stairs. What he was saying didn't make sense, but the emotion soaking through his words affected me.

"Don't mess with me, Chase. It's not funny."

"No, it's not," he agreed, somber and conflicted.

"What are you saying?"

He put a hand on his throat, as though trying to stop the words, but they came anyway.

"You're home. To me."

My first thought was one of self-preservation. *He's going to take it back.* Just like at the Loftons'. Like in the woods again afterward. I wanted to tell him to stop, just so it didn't hurt when he did, but I couldn't. I wanted it to be real.

I sat on the bed.

"I remind you of home," I clarified, feeling the memories of the past conjured.

He kneeled before me. "No. You *are* my home."

I was too surprised to speak.

I thought of home, what it meant to me. Safety and love. Happiness. I could only guess what it meant to someone like Chase, who'd had no center holding him, no stability or consistency since his parents had died.

And all this after he'd heard what I'd done to Sean and Rebecca.

He was watching me, trying hard to read my reaction to his words. I wanted to tell him just how much they moved me, but nothing could touch what I felt.

Tentatively, I reached for his hand, and when he gave it willingly, cradled my cheek within it. I could see him swallowing, see his big brown wolf eyes go dark, as they always did when harboring some deep emotion. He leaned closer.

"Think about me," he whispered. And then his lips touched mine.

His kiss was so soft it felt the way my memories did when I imagined his touch a year ago. When he was only a ghost reminding me I was alone. I needed more. I needed him to be here now, not just an echo of the past.

I pulled him closer. His kiss deepened at the invitation, making my whole body feel alive and electric. Then his hands drifted to my shoulders, and down, around my back, leaving streaks of heat in their wake.

"It was you," I said softly. "It's always you I think about."

The intensity in his gaze took my breath away.

I could feel him. Every part of him. His soul was sewn to mine. His heated blood flowed through my veins. I'd thought that I had been close to my mother, and I was, but not like this. Chase and I barely touched—our hands, mouths, knees—but there was no part of me that was not his.

I couldn't speak, but if I could, I would have told him I'd missed him. That I accepted who he had become, with his guilt and his fears. That I would stay beside him as he healed.

"Thank you," he whispered. Could he hear my thoughts? It did not seem unreasonable. Whatever his motivation for thanking me, I felt grateful too.

He held me as our heartbeats slowed and joined into one single pulse. And my mind went completely and blissfully silent.

I WAS woken by a racket in the hallway. I didn't know how long I'd slept, but I was now lying on the sleeping bag alone.

Had I dreamed what had happened earlier? Everything had felt so surreal these past few days; Chase's confession was really right in line. Still, my lips remembered the pressure of his, and my heart hurt with his absence.

I sat up, pulling on my boots, and ventured into the hallway. It was dimly lit and empty. The sound seemed to be centering from Wallace's room, and I snuck toward it. From the outside I heard the man's voice, speaking in low tones.

"You sure you won't change your mind?" he asked.

"Not now," said Chase. "Maybe someday."

I stuck my head around the door. Chase was leaning back against the kitchenette counter with Billy, while Wallace and Sean stood opposite.

His eyes found mine, and for a moment everything around him wavered. I knew then that I hadn't dreamed up what had happened between us. That it had been real and that he'd felt it too. I blushed.

Chase came over to me, ending the conversation with the others. He held out his hand, and I took it. I couldn't hide the shy smile that blossomed at the gesture.

"Wait a minute." Wallace grinned, and I knew what was coming before he continued. "You'd be welcome in our family, Miller."

I saw the MM's credo then, as it had been painted on the outside of the van that had taken my mother. Then on the wall of the house on Rudy Lane, and on the semitruck in Hinton. One Whole Country. One Whole Family. Wallace believed you could choose your family. If the country's stepchildren all joined together, we might really be whole after all.

A crack of thunder outside. And then the rain began to beat against the covered windows. Sean lit another candle and placed it on the counter behind us.

"I told you no, Wallace," said Chase. I could feel him tense.

He was right. I couldn't join the resistance. Not now. But I didn't like Chase answering for me. My brows drew together.

What had they been talking about? Chase hadn't said a word to these people earlier, but they'd held a secret meeting when I'd been asleep? My shoulders began to rise. I tried to meet his eyes, but he was staring at Wallace.

"Why did they throw you into custody?" Wallace asked me. There was curiosity in his voice, but I knew he was asking to make a point. Exploiting the injustice of my capture would give me reason to fight.

"Not important," Chase answered for me.

"Article 5," said Sean. "That's why half the girls in reform school are there."

"Let's go," Chase said suddenly. Was he trying to protect me? It didn't feel right.

"Sick, all that business. That's why I got out. Stuff like that." Wallace scratched his arm, and I saw the end of a black braid of wire sneaking out at the wrist beneath his long sleeve.

"You left the MM because they send girls to reform school?" I asked slowly. That seemed an odd thing to do.

The energy of the room had changed completely. It was strained now, grievous.

Chase was pulling me into the hallway.

"Wait," I told him. The rain was coming in pattering waves.

"He left because of the executions," Billy said helpfully. I remembered the carrier in Harrisonburg. I knew what the MM was capable of. The blood drained from my face.

"Who?" I asked.

"Shut your mouth," Chase said harshly to Billy.

"The Article violators." Billy looked mutinous.

My heart stopped.

"That's enough, Billy!" snapped Wallace. He passed Chase a hard, judging stare.

"You don't know?" Sean's eyes darted to Chase, too. "I thought you told her."

"Don't say another word," Chase threatened. Billy stuck his chin out defiantly. Sean jumped between the two of them.

"No, do. *Please* do," I said.

"Ember, come on," Chase had a hard grip on my arm and was pulling me away.

"Stop it!" I shouted. "Someone tell me what's going on!"

Rain. Waves of it. Pelting the motel.

"The Article violators, the AWOL soldiers. They're executed, like Billy said," Sean spoke quietly. Chase took a step back. "She has a right to know," he finished.

"They're going to execute me?" I asked weakly.

"Not you," said Billy. "The people charged. Your mom."

CHAPTER
14

THE room began to spin. I braced myself against the counter, vaguely aware that Billy and Wallace had left.

"Ember," Chase said slowly. He did not approach me.

"Why would they do that?" I asked weakly. But even as I asked I knew it was possible. I'd been in the checkpoint on Rudy Lane when the MM had found the carrier.

"We don't exactly fit the bill for a new, *moral* country," said Sean grimly.

I rounded on him.

"You knew. At the reformatory. You knew when I was trying to escape and you didn't tell me."

He shifted uncomfortably. "I'd heard rumors. You have to understand, I thought you were going to tell Brock about Becca and me. I thought if you didn't have a reason to leave, you wouldn't have a reason to keep the secret."

"Get away from me."

He backed up.

"Ember." Chase cradled my name as though it was an injured bird.

He'd known this all along. He'd hidden the truth. Why hadn't he told me?

"We have to leave." I shoved past him, sprinting to our room. People were out in the hallway watching me, but I barely noticed them. The fear was so thick in my body that I could hardly swallow. My knees felt very weak, but I knew I had to be strong. Yes, now I had to be especially strong.

I threw the backpack over my shoulders too quickly and had to grasp the wall to steady myself.

"Damn it, Ember. Hang on." Chase tried to pry the pack off. His face was pallid in the candlelight.

"Don't. We're going. We don't have time!" I yelled at him. "What's wrong with you? We have to go!"

"Ember, take off the pack."

"Chase! She's in danger! They're probably looking for her right now! We have to find her!" Hot tears, full of confusion and terror, ripped from my eyes. I wasn't angry with him. I was too frightened to be angry.

"We can't go. Not now."

"She's scared! I know her. No one takes care of her like I do!"

He backed away from me into the wall. His eyes were enormous, glassy, and just as terrified. I thought for a moment that he finally understood. But I was wrong.

"Ember, I'm sorry."

"Don't be sorry! Let's just go!"

"Ember!" He punched his own leg. The move was so violent it stopped me cold. "She's dead."

What a horrible thing to say. That was my first coherent thought. *What a cruel, hideous thing to say.*

The bag seemed very heavy now. It was pulling me backward. It slid to the floor with a thump.

"What?" That voice sounded distant to my ears.

He moved his hands over his mouth, as though to heat them with his breath.

"I'm so sorry. She's gone, Em."

"Don't call me that," I snapped. "Why are you saying that?"

"She's dead."

"Stop!" I screamed. The tears released in full force. I could barely breathe.

"I'm sorry."

"You're wrong. You're *wrong*!"

He shook his head.

"I was there." His voice cracked. I felt the wall support my weight.

"You . . . were there? What are you talking about? We have to go." This time my voice had no volume. No conviction.

Somehow we were both on the floor. He grabbed me, pulling me hard against him. I was too shocked to struggle.

"I thought if I told you, you wouldn't come with me. Or that you'd run away. I know it was wrong, Ember, I'm so sorry. I needed to get you safe first. I was going to tell you once we got there."

He wasn't deceiving me. His tortured face spoke the truth. My mother was dead.

I became aware of a screaming pain at two points. The front of my head and the center of my gut. Icy knives of reality stabbed into those places. Stabbed at me until I bled. Until my body was turned inside out.

I could hear her. I could hear her voice. *Ember.* She called my name. How could she be dead when I heard her so clearly?

"I'm so sorry," he repeated over and over. "I didn't want to hurt you. I just wanted you safe. I'm so sorry."

He was too close to me. Crowding me. I pushed him away.

"Get back," I groaned.

"What do I do?" he asked me desperately. "I don't know what to do."

"What happened to my mother?" I asked him.

He hesitated. He wasn't going to say.

"Tell me!" I insisted. "Why is everyone hiding everything from me? Tell me!"

"Ember, she died. That's all you need to know."

"Don't be a coward!"

"Okay. All right."

He kneeled in front of me, his arms now crossed over his midsection. His shoulders were shaking. A line of sweat poured down his temple.

"Fighting didn't turn me, so my command needed something else. Tucker showed them letters. Ones I had written back to you. I thought they'd been mailed but . . . he'd been hoarding them. They learned who you were. That I didn't end it with you like I was supposed to. They told me I had to buy in or . . . *Jesus.* Or you'd be hurt. So I cut a deal. No more fights. No more *you.* And they'd promote me to show the others that the system always wins. I did whatever they said. I thought it would work, that they'd leave you alone, but it didn't matter.

"It was the final test. Your extraction. They used *you* to break me.

"We took your mom to a base in Lexington, with all the other Article 5s in the state. She was put in a detention cell. My unit leader, Bateman—he was pissed off by what happened at your house. That I didn't follow orders and stay in the car. He said I was out of line. I was a failure as a soldier. He reported me to command."

He stopped there and leaned over his knees like he might vomit.

"Finish," I demanded. I could barely hear him over the screaming in my brain.

"They brought me in front of the board for discipline. My CO was there. He told me that it was time to put my training into effect. That I could still make captain someday. He told me I could *redeem* myself by . . . by executing the detainees, starting with your mother. I told him no. I'm just a driver. I just transport. I told him to kick me out. Give me a dishonorable discharge."

Chase punched his thigh again. I wept softly.

"He told me to follow orders. That if I didn't do what he said, someone else would. That they'd pull you from school and do the same. I didn't know what to do. The next thing I knew, Tucker was escorting me to her detention cell, and I had a gun in my hand."

I wanted to scream at Chase to stop. But I had to hear. I had to know. The tears ran from his eyes freely now.

"Your mom. God. She had been crying. Her shirt was all wet. She saw me and she smiled, and she ran over to me and grabbed my jacket in her hands and said, 'Thank God you're here, Chase.' And I was there to kill her.

"I held the gun up, and she backed into a chair and sat there, watching me. Just watching me. I thought for a second I was going to do it. That I had to. But nothing happened. My CO was behind us. He told me to pull the damn trigger or I'd watch them murder you. Your mom heard him. She grabbed the gun in my hand, and she leaned in close and told me to find you, wherever you were, and take care of you. 'My baby,' she called you. She told me not to be scared. *She* told *me* not to be scared.

"And then he shot her. And . . . she died. A foot away from me. I don't even know what happened afterward. I ended up in a holding cell for a week."

Silence. Long, suffocating silence.

I felt my brain twisting, trying to understand, even as it was trying to erase the last thirty minutes.

"Maybe if you would have talked to your officer. Maybe if you had tried to tell him that she didn't deserve this. . . ." My voice sounded small.

"It wouldn't have made a difference."

"You don't know that! You didn't even try! You could have talked to them and . . . and . . . you could have never come home. . . . In training you could have not been so . . . *you!* You could have told us to run!"

I felt as crazy as I sounded.

"I know." He had no conclusion to this statement.

A frozen hammer against my skull. I knew the truth, even if I didn't want to.

"She's dead," I realized.

He nodded. "Yes."

"You lied to me. You let me believe she was alive. In some safe house!" I screamed suddenly. Now there was anger. Hot and vicious and poisonous within me.

"I know."

"Were you ever going to tell me?"

"I would have, once you were away from all this. Maybe not all of it. I didn't want you to know all of it. No one should have to hear all that."

"So you can take it but I can't? She's *my* mother, Chase!"

"I didn't mean you can't handle it. I just mean . . . I don't know. I didn't want to hurt you."

"You'd rather me believe a lie than be hurt? Who the *hell* gave you that authority?"

"I don't know." He was honest. He didn't know what he was doing. His hands lay open on his knees before him, begging for some shred of direction to which he could cling.

I was rolling now. A snowball plunging down a hill. Knowing that at the bottom there was a brick wall that would smash me. That would break me into a million pieces.

"You knew all this from the very beginning. From the day you got me at school. You knew she was dead. You'd seen her dead. And you kept that from me."

"Yes."

Faster, I rolled on.

"How could you do that?"

He shook his head.

Twisting inside of me. *Nothing is real.*

"You said . . . you said all those things . . . and . . . I believed you."

"Wait. Please. That was the truth," he was pleading now.

I shook my head. There was no truth.

"Ember, I love you."

His words hacked a bright new pain into me. I stared at him for a full second, horrified, recognizing that this was the first time he'd said these words. Thinking maybe the opposite was true. That Chase might actually *hate* me. That was why he lied about everything. That was why he kept hurting me. How could someone be so cruel?

His eyes were filled with what I'd once thought was honesty.

"I shouldn't have said that now. It's too much. I'm putting too much on you. But . . . Christ. I mean it, I—"

"*No!* I trusted you, and I thought it was right and it wasn't right. It was a lie." I felt ill then, disgusted by my own self. I wanted to crawl out of my skin, to leave it in this dirty room with its ugly truths.

"It wasn't like that. You know. *Please* know."

His reached out to touch my hand.

"No!" I bawled. "Don't touch me. Don't you *dare* touch me. Not ever again."

I struck the wall. My world was crashing down. Everything I believed was scattered. False.

I didn't think. I couldn't. I rocked forward and hit him as hard as I could. My hand seized with pain from where it had connected to his jaw. I hit him again. Again. He didn't try to stop me. He placed his hand beneath my elbow, giving me the strength to hit him harder.

When I had no punches left, I folded over my reeling stomach. I was no better than Roy, hitting my mother. I wanted violence to resolve my anguish. To show Chase how wrong he was. The parallel made my reality infinitely more devastating.

"It's okay. Hit me. I deserve it."

As though that would make it better. As though that would fix anything.

"No more," I moaned.

He lifted his hands in surrender. "Ember, I'll do whatever you want. Just please let me get you somewhere safe. That was the whole point in this. I knew that once you found out, you'd want to get as far away from me as possible, and if you believed your mom was in South Carolina, you'd let me take you there. I told you in the beginning, if you want me gone after that, I'm gone."

"I'm not going anywhere with you."

"Please. Just let me get you somewhere safe."

All the slashes of pain inside. All the losses. My mother. Chase. Beth. Rebecca. Trust. Love. I had nothing left but the skeleton of integrity.

"No."

"If you won't listen to me, do it for her. Lori wanted you away from all this."

"Don't!" I cried out. I could not bear to hear her name.

He hung his head. "I've messed everything up. From the beginning. I've done nothing right by you. By your mother. She loved you so much, Ember."

"She's dead because of you!"

And what was worse was that she was dead because of me, too. Because if I'd never told Chase to leave, he wouldn't have gone into the military. They never would have targeted him. They never would have used us to break him. Through some twist of fate, I had killed my own mother. The shame was so thick I could not speak it.

He rocked back onto his heels and then stood. I knew I had wounded him. I had done so deliberately. I wanted to injure him. To make him hurt as deeply as I did. But how could he?

"Yes," he said simply. "She's dead because of me."

"Get out. Get away from me."

Minutes passed. But he did leave. I heard the door close softly behind him.

I SOBBED for hours huddled in a clenched ball. I cried until the tears dried up. And when they did, my body cried without them.

Every image that entered my mind pained me. Every thought led me to the same conclusion.

I was alone. Absolutely alone.

When I could breathe again, I forced myself up and stumbled toward the window. I could hear other people in the hallway asking Chase what had happened. He didn't answer. It didn't matter.

My arms were heavy. My head felt heavy. Bloated.

Air. *That feels nice,* I thought absently.

I slid over the ledge and out onto the fire escape, needing the cold to stop the fever. The balcony was too small. I could climb down the ladder. I could get to the street. It looked like a black hole from up here. Maybe I could disappear inside it.

The rain was soothing. The first soothing feeling I'd felt in what seemed like an eternity. It soaked through my clothing, my hair. It washed away the salt on my face. It entered my eyes by way of my matted lashes and cleansed them.

I walked. And walked. Unable to focus on anything. Remembering nothing.

The lights didn't surprise me. They barely roused my curiosity. But soon the car had stopped alongside the sidewalk where I stood. Men got out. They spoke to me in harsh tones I didn't understand. They grabbed my arms. They dragged me into the backseat, where the rain no longer reached me.

A CLANG on the metal door. My eyes blinked open, unfocused. A fluorescent light directly above my head buzzed and flickered. The ceiling was pocked with dried peels of white paint. Mildew and body odor soiled the mattress I laid upon. I had no pillow. No blankets.

Where was I? How long had I been here? It didn't matter. Nothing mattered.

"She won't eat." Someone's voice came muffled through the door.

"I don't give a damn." Another male.

"Me neither," the first scoffed, "but she'll be dead before her trial if she keeps this up."

"Then she'll be dead. Wouldn't be the first time."

I closed my ears to their callous disregard. I closed my mind to all consciousness.

A HAND was shaking my shoulder. Then a hard pinch to the sensitive skin on the underside of my arm. The pain snapped my eyes open. Apparently I could still feel some things.

"You need to get up. Get up!" A woman's voice now, warped with annoyance. I moaned and rolled away. My face pressed against the cool, cement wall.

"If you don't knock this off, *I'll* get in trouble for it."

"Leave me alone," I managed weakly.

"You've had three days of that already. Now you've got to get moving."

She shook my shoulder again. When I rolled onto my back, she grabbed my arms and pulled me into a seated position. My head went very fuzzy and dim.

"Hey." She slapped my cheek lightly. "Are you going to throw up?"

"No," I said feebly.

"Hmph. You've got nothing to throw up anyway."

She shoved a plastic bowl onto my lap. It was filled with something that resembled soupy oatmeal. I stared at it blankly.

"Unbelievable," the woman said. She picked up a spoonful and shoved it into my mouth.

I sputtered and choked. But the tasteless, lukewarm mush slid down my throat and entered my starved stomach. Soon my mouth was watering for more.

I ate, focusing for the first time on the woman. She had gnarled, arthritic bumps on her hands and deeply etched creases beside her mouth. Her face held a look of concern it seemed would never fully dissipate, and her eyes were almost translucently blue. It wouldn't have surprised me if she were blind, but her movements dictated otherwise.

Her hair was gray and wavy, and she wore a navy pleated skirt and button-up blouse. The uniform covered her sagging body the way a burlap sack covers potatoes.

Haven't you ever seen the Sisters of Salvation? I heard Rosa say in my mind. *They're the MM's answer to women's liberation.*

It was like I'd never left the reformatory.

In the tiny cell, the narrow bed reached out from the wall and nearly collided with a metal toilet at its foot. There was barely enough room for the woman to remain standing in front of me without our knees touching.

"Where am I?" I asked her. My voice cracked. It had not been used in some time.

"Knoxville Detention Facility."

So I had been captured after all.

It won't be long until they kill me, too, I thought, in a completely detached way.

"Finish up, Miller." She slapped the side of my bowl, and some sloshed onto a paper gown, like the kind people wear in hospitals. Somewhere along the line someone had taken my clothes.

"You know my name." My haircut hadn't disguised me in the end. Oh well.

She huffed. "Put the dress on. You can't stay in that."

With no notions of modesty, I stripped down to my undergarments and slid into the oversized Sisters of Salvation uniform, forgoing the handkerchief. My appearance now matched the clear-eyed woman.

"Now what?" I asked.

"You wait until someone comes and gets you." She knocked twice on the door. It opened from the outside, and she slid out of view.

I stared at the wall across from me, my mind blank.

SOMETIME later I heard keys jangle against the door, then a metallic squeal, and the barricade was removed, revealing a lean soldier with a broad chest. He had a slight face. Piercing green eyes. Golden hair slicked to one side. One large hand held a clipboard and a pen. His other arm was casted from the elbow down.

He had a gun holstered beside the nightstick on his hip. I wondered if he was here to shoot me, the way Chase's commanding officer had shot my mother. I was surprised that I didn't much care. At least this nightmare would be over.

There was a dreamlike quality about him. I felt like I recognized him from somewhere. Pieces began to pull together, one at a time.

"Your knuckles look like hell. What have you been doing, cage fighting?"

I glanced down, thinking that my hands actually looked pretty good. The scabs had peeled, leaving behind thin, white scars. Most of the darker bruising had faded. I wiggled my fingers. Just a dull ache.

"You have no idea who I am," he said, stealing a look back toward the door.

I saw three discolored lines on his neck. Fingernail scratches. My scratches.

"Tucker Morris."

"Yeah," he said slowly. As if this were the most obvious thing in the world.

Silence.

"Aren't you even curious why I'm here?"

"Does it matter? I'm sure I'll be executed either way." My voice was flat. Emotionless.

"That's morbid."

"Am I wrong?"

He smirked. "Where is he?"

"I don't know who you mean," I said with my jaw locked.

"Withholding information won't help your case."

"What *will* help my case?" I asked sourly.

"Being nice to me might." There was a buoyancy in his tone. Almost as if he were flirting. I nearly gagged.

"I will not be *nice* to someone who participates in the murders of innocent people." The words burned my tongue but did nothing to my dead heart.

"So he told you? I thought he'd chicken out. Just like he did with her."

There was a flash of anger. I wanted to claw at him again, like I had when he'd taken my mother. But then the desire was gone. All that remained was bitterness.

"You're a bastard, Tucker."

"I should say the same." He grinned at his own cleverness. "But watch your mouth. You can't talk to a soldier that way."

I scoffed. What was he going to do? Kill me? Get in line.

He hesitated. "Jennings already has abduction of a minor, assault with a deadly weapon, theft of federal property, and at least ten other petty charges tacked onto his AWOL. This isn't someone you want to protect. He obviously wouldn't return the favor."

I hadn't given him the chance to protect me—I'd left when he'd been guarding my door. By the time he realized I was gone, I'd probably already been thrown into this cell.

I wondered what my charges were. Something about running from the reformatory. Theft and assault. What else? Fraud for our non-government-approved marriage? For some reason, I found the tally mildly amusing. I didn't even care if they pegged me as the sniper now.

"Why are you even here? I thought you were in a transport unit or something."

"I made rank. I'm on a fast track. I'll probably be an officer soon."

"Congratulations." I said. My tone didn't faze him.

"Your trial's been moved to the end of the week."

"Damn. You couldn't fit me in today, huh?"

"I bought you three more days to ponder your fate. I'd like to make sure you get the full experience of incarceration. That's as a favor to our mutual friend." His jaw twitched as he spoke.

Tucker was flat-out evil. He was even more despicable than Chase.

"I'm detailing you to cleanup until your sentencing."

He opened my door and motioned for me to step outside into the hall. My legs were weak from days of not walking, and my head spun for a few seconds. I was surprised Tucker let me out without handcuffs.

The woman who had woken me earlier in the day was busying herself scrubbing floors. She had a sudsy bucket beside her and wore elbow-length rubber gloves.

"Delilah, this is Ember Miller," said Tucker from the doorway.

She glanced up and then hoisted herself to her feet.

"Yes, sir."

"She'll help you until her trial."

Delilah nodded submissively. Tucker pulled me aside before turning to go.

"I'll be down the hall at that office. Come see me when she's done with you."

"I can't wait."

He chuckled as he walked away.

"Grab a brush. We're scrubbing floors. And then it's cleanup of another kind." Delilah wasn't much for small talk.

We went room by room, cleaning the floors, making the beds, scrubbing the toilets. Only two of the rooms were occupied, and those we did not enter immediately.

While I was working, a handcuffed man with sallow skin and bruises on one cheek slumped down the hall. He was accompanied by four guards, one of whom carried a silver briefcase. They pushed him roughly into an empty room. A few minutes later, all four guards disappeared the way they had come.

"Just gone to trial," commented Delilah. I wondered morbidly what the outcome had been.

When we were finished, I followed Delilah downstairs to the cafeteria, where we picked up two trays of gray mush from a soldier wearing a hairnet. I watched as several soldiers were cleared in and out of the building's main entrance by a guard behind a thick plate of glass. Every time the door opened, a spine-curdling buzz spiked my eardrums.

Back upstairs, Delilah used a key hanging on a thin metal chain around her neck to open the door.

The man inside was curled into a ball on the back side of his bed. He wore a canary yellow jumpsuit and rocked back and forth pitifully, muttering something to himself.

"Food," Delilah said, laying the tray on the opposite side of his bed.

She shut the door, and marked the checkbox beside MEAL on the clipboard hanging from the handle.

In the next room, a man with olive skin leaned against the wall, biting his nails.

"You got a blanket or something?" he said quickly. "Oh. Hey there," he added when he saw me. I stared back at him curiously.

"Food," Delilah said again, leaving the tray on his bed.

A guard passed by, heading down the stairs.

"Where's he going?" I asked Delilah.

"Rounds. They walk the halls every thirty minutes."

"It seems like there should be more security for a jail."

She shook her head. "This is a small detention center. Only holding cells. Temporary stays. It's minimum security. The prison's in Charlotte."

Delilah was very matter-of-fact.

"Hope you have a tough stomach," she said.

"Why?"

"Now it's time for the real cleanup."

I followed her to a storage room, which held supplies. Bleach. Gloves. Prisoner uniforms. Towels. Blankets. I thought she would grab one for the man in the cell, but she did not. Instead, she retrieved a deep laundry cart with a metal cover. Then we headed toward the third occupied room, the one holding the soldier who had just completed trial.

I looked at his clipboard. In large letters was written one word: COMPLETE.

There was a fleeting moment where I remembered a conversation between Rebecca and me at the reformatory. Sean had told her that he had heard the term *complete* used for the Article violators. That was when I'd naïvely thought my mother had been sent to rehab.

I knew when the door swung open why Delilah had asked me about my stomach.

The man before us was lying twisted on the narrow bed. His knees were stacked on the mattress while his shoulders faced the ceiling. His brown hair was still tangled, and a bruise still blackened his pasty cheek.

But he was now dead.

My mind conjured an image of the man who had starved in the square. How thin and fragile his body had looked. How I assumed he had fallen asleep, when really he had wasted away.

This was different. This man looked dead. Not peaceful. Not sleeping. But ashy and cold and tortured, as though his mind had been taken by death before his body was ready. I knew then why people close the eyes of the dead. Those life-less globes tracked me like the eyes of the *Mona Lisa*.

I took a step back before my knees began knocking. Within seconds, my whole body was shaking. I couldn't stop staring at the dead man. My brain morphed his face into Chase's face. His dark, probing eyes gone dim. If caught, this would be his fate.

Even now, I didn't want Chase to die. I hoped he was far away. That he'd run once he'd found me gone.

Delilah heaved the body into a seated position. I felt the bile scratch up my throat. Deliberately, I swallowed. She rolled the body sideways into the laundry cart, and it thudded against the metal base.

I felt ill. I forced my mind to focus. To magnetize some semblance of strength.

"You still upright?" Delilah asked as she pushed the cart down the hall, the opposite direction of the stairs.

She wasn't looking at me, but I nodded, trailing behind her slightly. I watched my feet, one after another. It was the only thing I could focus on without vomiting.

"It helps if you don't think of them as people."

Yes. I imagined that would help.

At the end of the hallway was a freight elevator. It was black and greasy and had poor lighting. She pushed the cart inside, and I tried to tell myself that there wasn't a body within it.

We got off at the bottom floor and exited through an un-guarded door, which Delilah unlocked with the same key from around her neck. She pushed the cart down a narrow back alley until we reached a high fence with rolls of barbed wire cresting its ridge. There was a gate there, manned by two soldiers in a guard station. They saw the cart and let us pass without a second glance.

"I guess they know what we're doing," I observed.

"You gonna help?" Delilah asked as she began to labor. I slid beside her, checking my nausea, and grabbed one side of the slick metal handle. Together, we pushed the cart up a steep asphalt embankment lined by flat-topped hedges that curved around the back side of the station. I was sweating by the time we reached the top.

A single cement building, flat and square, came into view. It was surrounded by lovely drooping trees, a contrast to the black factory smoke puffing from the chimney. The air reeked of sulfur. The driveway arched into a teardrop before the entrance.

"Just over to that door there." Delilah pointed. I helped her push the weighted cart to a side exit with a canvas shade awning. She rang a buzzer. Then, without waiting, she walked away.

"We just leave him—it—here?" I asked.

She nodded. "The crematorium."

My stomach churned.

They took my mother somewhere like this. I was flooded with so much horror I could barely stumble behind her.

The sickness numbed, and I was able to follow Delilah weakly back to the highest crest of the hill. Here she paused. I tracked her gaze, feeling my feet stabilize under me for the first time since we had entered that third room.

Before us stretched the FBR base. The buildings all matched, gray and drab, some with stout additions, others slender. All variations on the same deathly theme. Little manicured lawns cropped up between them, and white walkways bounced from entrance to entrance. It reached on for miles, surrounded by the high steel fence that we had passed through below. In the distance I could see the river and the hospital where we'd left the car. The square would be nearby, as would the Wayland Inn, where the resistance plotted.

Oh, the information I could offer Wallace. The layout of the detention center. How many guards roamed the halls. The geography of the base. I'd doubted my use to the resistance before. I didn't now.

I felt a flame flicker inside of me. A feeling, almost unrecognizable.

Hope.

What if I *could* find a way to tell Wallace? Even if I was doomed to die, the information I had might save others. Innocent people like my mother. It physically hurt to think that the information I now had might have helped someone save her.

I turned around and saw the remains of an abandoned town. Probably some residential offshoot of Knoxville. Twisting asphalt avenues were lined by crowded duplexes and condos. From the distance, their tiny yards did not look overgrown or weed eaten. The tagged walls and broken windows were too far away to see clearly.

An old sign posting fuel prices reached up atop the horizon, drawing my attention. A main street ran down the left side of my view; a straight line away from me.

"Is that all part of the base, too?" I asked.

"No. The base is just over there. This side of the city is evacuated. A Red Zone."

I felt my brows draw together.

"Do you mean that we're not currently on the base?"

"You're a bright one," she mocked.

Anxiety shimmered through me.

"How often do you come out here?" I asked.

"Every time I have to take out the trash."

I grimaced at her analogy. "And you've never thought to just keep walking?"

"I think it all the time."

"Why don't you?"

She looked at me, her face tired.

"If there was anything for me out there, I'd be gone."

She looked at me in judgment, sizing up my intentions. Apparently, my thoughts were as transparent as her eyes.

Beth was still out there. Rebecca was in danger. Wallace and the resistance could use me, and after my mother's murder, how could I not help them? There were too many people like me who didn't know just how lethal the MM was. Too many people dead, while their loved ones remained hopeful for a reunion.

I had to do something, no matter how small. *Something.* For my mother.

If I ran now, Delilah didn't have to go more than ten feet to flag down the guard at the watch station. But Tucker had said I still had three days before my trial. If I could earn enough trust to make it outside on my own, I might be able to escape.

"You want a bullet in your back, don't you?" She wasn't looking for an answer.

She trudged down the hill. And I followed, scheming.

CHAPTER
15

DELILAH didn't speak to me for the remainder of the afternoon. As the day shift dwindled on, she tasked me to fold towels in the supply room, not bothering to conceal her annoyance that I hadn't been returned to a cell.

At curfew, a buzzer sounded, and the power switched to a generator. Not many were there to hear it; apart from the stairway guard, the hallway was already empty.

Tucker was finishing some paperwork when I finally dragged myself to his office. "What do you want?" I asked.

He slid his gun out of the holster, and I thought, *This is it. He's going to kill me.* I braced for the pain that was sure to come. But instead, he deposited the weapon within a safe in the back corner, locked it, and placed the key inside his desk drawer. The breath reentered my lungs in one hard *whoosh.* He waited a beat, eyeing me with a strange expression.

"You aren't *married*, are you?" He said it as if he were a ten-year-old talking about broccoli.

I felt a light flush creep over my skin, a subtle reminder that I was still a living, breathing human.

"No."

"What's with that ring?"

I was almost surprised to see it still on my finger.

"Nothing. It's just something I found."

It was the ring Chase had stolen for me from the Loftons'. When we'd been pretending to be married. A lot of things had been pretend with him.

Because Tucker was watching, I didn't take it off, but it suddenly felt much too tight. His expression returned to the normal haughtiness.

"I talked to my commanding officer. You're sleeping up here until your trial."

I'd figured as much but still shuddered. Who would still be alive in the morning?

"I saw the result of one of your trials today," I said accusingly.

I remembered how the soldier's face had become Chase's face, right before my eyes. I wondered, for a fraction of a moment, if Chase felt that same sick terror whenever I'd mentioned my mother. If the fear cut fresh with each recall. But then the feeling was gone, clouded by betrayal.

"And?" Tucker said. As though an execution were nothing. "The quickest way to stomp insubordination is to strike fast and sure."

No doubt an officer had fed him that line. The hint of pride in his voice sickened me so much I almost walked out, but then I thought of Wallace and the resistance. Of Rebecca, maybe still here, in this building, and I knew I needed to stay.

"You give them a pill or something?"

"A shot. Strychnine. They can't breathe. Their muscles seize up and go into convulsions. And then they die. It's quick." I almost thought he was trying to comfort me with his last words, but there was no inflection in his voice.

"You do that to the girls, too? The strychnine?" I tried to look frightened, but I wasn't. I was less averse to dying than before, and Tucker Morris didn't scare me. He was weak. He needed the MM. He needed something to believe in, since it was probably too depressing to believe in himself.

"Sometimes." I knew he was thinking of my mother. I hated him for having her in his mind in any capacity.

"Do you know if they executed a girl named Rebecca Lansing? She would have come from the West Virginia reformatory. Blond hair, cute . . ."

"Great rack."

"I guess." My spirits rose.

"Nope."

"You just said—"

"I can't give you that kind of information." His eyes glimmered with power. "Unless . . ."

"Unless what?"

"Well, I'd trade it to you."

"For what?" I asked skeptically. I became very aware of how small the office was.

"How about a kiss? We'll see where that takes us." He leaned back against the wall, hips jutting forward, his cast-free arm hanging loosely at his side. His face glowed with arrogance. I couldn't believe he would want to kiss someone he knew would be dead in less than a week.

"Don't be ridiculous."

He laughed. "I bet he liked that. You playing hard to get."

My face burned. That was too close. Too personal.

When I turned to leave the office, his free hand grabbed both of my wrists, twisting them above my head so that a jolt of pain zinged up my arms. He was fast, just as he'd been at the overhaul. I shouldn't have underestimated him just because he'd broken his arm. He shoved me against the cabinet and pressed his body against mine. He wore superiority as if it were expensive cologne.

Rage filled me. Nobody touched me without my permission. Not anymore.

I wanted to fight him.

Sure, he was bigger and stronger than I was. He'd probably win in the end. But I could at least get a couple good shots in. Especially if I let a good mad build up.

I couldn't believe I was thinking like this. Like Chase. I *was* losing my mind.

His face was close to mine. So close I could feel his breath on my lips. His green eyes blazed with desire; such a different look than I'd known before. Chase had studied me, reading my feelings. Tucker was only trying to see his own reflection.

Disturbing on several levels.

"Back off or I'll scream."

I knew for a fact Tucker could not risk being seen with an inmate, one who was more or less reform-school trash. And I wasn't about to go any further with him until I was sure he was going to make good on his end of the deal.

"Ooh," he groaned quietly. "I didn't think you'd talk dirty."

"Sir?" Delilah stuck her head into the office. "Oh!" Her

face reddened, and her eyes shot to the floor. In a snap, Tucker released my arms.

"What do you want?" he snarled.

"I'm sorry sir. Just going home for the night. I wasn't sure if you wanted me on the same detail tomorrow with Ms. Miller." She said this all in one breath, obviously ruffled. I couldn't help feeling a little embarrassed myself. I certainly did not want anyone thinking that his advance had been invited.

"Yes. Tomorrow, same thing," Tucker said. Then he smiled slowly. "And Delilah? A little discretion if you will. I'd hate to lose you after all your hard work."

Delilah seemed to shrink into the floor. We both knew when Tucker said *lose*, he didn't mean fire.

I didn't have any more time to waste. I all but shoved past Delilah in an attempt to get out into the hallway as the guard on rotation walked by. He gave Tucker a curt nod. Tucker returned the gesture and closed the office door behind him.

Without another word, he locked me in my cell.

I COULDN'T sleep that night. I stared into the darkness and shivered. Tucker, in all his kindness, had given me a ratty old towel and a blanket. It was a power play, showing me he could permit me comfort even in this house of death. What a benevolent captor.

I'd ripped the thin towel to shreds and left the blanket untouched.

Standing on my bed I could see out the high, barred window onto the base. It was absolutely still, apart from the single security guards cutting their paths over the cement walkways.

I assumed there were more civilians like Delilah working here, but they obviously still had to observe curfew. Even if I could get out now, it was suicide to try to escape at night.

I slid down the wall and pulled my knees into my chest. I blew on my wrists, which still bore red blossoms from Tucker's earlier grip.

Without prompting, my eyes filled with tears.

"No," I said out loud. If I let one tear come, another would join it. Another and another after that. I couldn't afford to be weak. I had to help the resistance. I couldn't honor my mother's murder by meeting the same exact fate.

So I lingered on the knife's edge, balancing between recklessness and despair.

I tried to stop the pictures, but they came anyway. The darkness set the scene, and like a movie, Chase's memories played before my vision.

My mother in the cell. Alone, like I was now, but scared. Chase coming in, backed by Tucker Morris and other soldiers. Chase's raised gun. Had she fought? I bet she had. Then fear, followed by compassion, and her whispered plea to protect me. His twisted understanding that he was trying to do just that by killing her. But he couldn't kill her. His faceless CO did that. While he was forced to watch.

I had blamed Chase for her death. The facts had seemed so clear to me. But when I reviewed the scenario, they became distorted, out of focus. He'd been the scapegoat of the MM's wrath just for being himself. Blaming him no longer made sense.

I could not stop the tears now. They flooded me, as did my

grief, my sorrow, my hatred. So much deeper was my self-loathing than what I had seen reflected in Chase's eyes. And so much more justified.

I had made a horrible mistake.

Chase had come back after the War to find me. He had reported for the draft because I had told him to. He had *always* tried to protect me, even when it included the possibility of losing his life or taking another. His lies were meant to be a shield. That was wrong, but I couldn't entirely fault him for hiding the truth once I thought about what he'd faced.

He had wanted me safe all along. I had expelled that, shoved it back in his face. I had tried to hurt him more than he was already hurting. And I had succeeded.

It was Sean's words that slid through my torment.

It's them Miller. Not us. It's the FBR that should be sorry.

I understood this now, more than ever before. What had happened was not Chase's fault. It wasn't mine; it wasn't even really Tucker's. It was the FBR. The president. They were making everyone suffer, and those who didn't feel the pain had been brainwashed.

I twisted the little gold ring around my finger vigorously.

By morning I had my plan.

I was leaving this base. I was going to the resistance and then to find Chase, wherever he was. I had to try to make things right. For him. For my mother. For Rebecca.

And if I couldn't, then I would die trying.

TO my horror, a second soldier was "completed" in the morning. A man I had fed less than a day before lay stretched across the floor, half beneath the bed. His lips were white, his face gray. His eyes were open and dead.

I was just as revolted. I couldn't help but wonder if I could have stopped it. If I could have saved him. I would never get used to this, as Delilah clearly had.

We followed the same protocol from the day before. Only this time, I swallowed down the bile creeping up my throat to focus on the intricacies of the task. Which way Delilah exited the elevator. The dark hallway downstairs that no one seemed to occupy. Every instance she used her key. Where exactly she left the cart at the crematorium.

I had to get it perfect. The next time I made this trip, I'd be alone.

We had more mash from the cafeteria for lunch. It did little to calm my stomach, but I needed the fuel for what was to come.

At the end of the day, I followed Delilah into the storage room. I was wearing the blanket over my shoulders, even though the unit was warm during working hours. I needed Tucker to think I was grateful for his compassion, and he did. When I'd seen him earlier, he'd been the only guard not to balk at my appearance.

My acceptance of the gift made him feel like he was in control. Like I wasn't a threat. He lowered his guard around me, which was exactly what I needed.

I watched Delilah as I had all day. I needed the master key hanging around her neck. She wouldn't give it up; she was far too institutionalized. I was going to have to steal it. And to assure she wouldn't sabotage the plan, I needed to gain the upper hand.

That was where Tucker came in.

Delilah was emptying her bucket of bleach and water into the utility sink as I approached.

"I've got to go talk to Morris," I told her.

She waved her hand at me without looking up, but the color rose in her drooping cheeks. We both remembered the scene she had walked in on last night.

"I'll come get you in the morning," she said.

I nodded.

I forced myself to walk nonchalantly across the hall to Tucker's office. The adrenaline coursed through my body as I anticipated what I had to do. Fighting the urge to glance nervously toward the door, I hugged the blanket tighter around my shoulders.

He was finishing paperwork, as he had been yesterday. He said nothing, only cocked an eyebrow up at me.

"I want to know about Rebecca Lansing."

"You know the price for that."

"I do."

He put down the paperwork with a self-righteous smirk and rounded the desk.

"Then pay up."

"Wait. I'm . . . afraid the guard is going to walk past." I tried to sound nervous. I thought Tucker would like that. I played with the tips of my hair for effect.

"He just rotated through five minutes ago."

"Just go check," I said. "I don't want any interruptions like last night."

A glow spread across his face. "All right. Stay here."

Pathetic.

He was gone for only a few minutes. Long enough for me to do what needed to be done. To set the wheels in motion for tomorrow's escape.

I was sitting on a hip-high cabinet above the safe when he returned. The discarded blanket was piled beside me. I swung my heels against the wood impatiently and made myself think about freedom, rather than what was to come.

"We're clear," he told me, sauntering over.

He didn't hesitate. He shoved himself between my knees, jerking my hips to the edge of the tabletop. Then his face lowered to mine.

He smelled wrong. Tasted wrong. His mouth was too hard. His hands were selfish. I tried to back away, but he wrapped his casted arm unyieldingly against my back. His other hand slid up my stomach. It rose higher, over the itchy fabric covering my ribs. Higher, to where I would not allow those fingers to roam.

"That's enough." Every nerve inside of me flatlined. I shoved him away, appalled with myself.

"Not yet." Tucker leaned in again, but I pushed his shoulders back hard and then lifted my knee between us. The next time he tried to advance, my foot was pressed against his crotch. Ready to kick.

"Just try it," I dared him.

He chuckled, lifting his hands in surrender.

"God, I wish Jennings could have seen that. We wouldn't even have to kill him. He'd off himself."

My temper spiked. "You sure talk about him a lot. If I didn't know better, I'd say you were heartbroken, Tucker."

I'd said too much.

His grin vanished. Then it returned, with a vindictive light in his green eyes. His fingers skimmed my throat, feeling the jugular vein. His touch was too delicate, and I could feel the power thrumming beneath it. I breathed out unsteadily, hands clenching into fists. Tucker was jealous of Chase, of all the attention he had received. He could hurt me just to get back at his old partner.

"Are you scared?" he whispered. "Do you know what I could do to you?"

"Rebecca Lansing," I prompted, working hard to swallow.

To my relief he released my throat.

"Rehab center in Chicago."

My stomach dropped. Chicago. Where Chase had lived with his uncle. Where he had been drafted. It wouldn't be easy to find her in a war-torn city that housed one of the biggest bases in the country.

"They didn't kill her?"

"She got lucky. Who knows, maybe you will, too."

It was time to go. I pushed off the cabinet.

"Wait, wait, wait." He blocked my exit. "We were just getting started. A guy can't just shut down like that."

I tried not to gag. But then my ear perked. "Here comes the guard. Still want to fool around? Maybe he'd like to watch."

Tucker listened, and winced when he recognized the footsteps. While he was distracted, I grabbed my blanket and slid by him out into the hall. Once the guard saw me, Tucker would not be able to hide that we'd been together.

"Well played," he said, clapping his hands lightly. "You *are* a tease, aren't you?"

My face burned and my teeth ground together, but I forced

myself to saunter down the hallway, knowing he watched my every step. I waited for him to open the door and let me into my cell. A few moments later he exchanged muffled words with the guard. I heard them walk all the way down the stairway.

And then I unrolled the crumpled blanket to reveal the handgun—the one I had stolen while Tucker had been checking the halls—and smiled.

AWAKE, I plotted my escape. Step by step.

Delilah would come get me just after curfew lifted. We'd go to the supply room, and I'd force her to give me the key. Hopefully she wouldn't make a fuss when I locked her in. I'd push a cart past the office to the freight elevator, take it down to the first floor. The guards at the back gate wouldn't stop me; they'd assume I was headed up to the crematorium, and they'd be right. I'd deposit the cart at the side door, beneath the awning. And then I would run.

I didn't allow myself to consider any deviation from this plan. I already knew what I would do should something go wrong.

I held the pistol in my hand, turning it, warming the handle with my palm. Inoculating myself to its presence. It was the same kind of gun Chase had been issued: sleek, silver, with a thick barrel. I flicked the safety on and off to become accustomed to the sound and feel.

I wondered what Beth and Ryan would think if they saw me now. I wasn't the frightened little girl being dragged away to rehab anymore. Something had changed inside of me, whittled away and made me hard. I doubted I even looked the same.

Losing your family . . . it puts fear in a different perspective, Chase had once told me. Yes. I understood now. It didn't remove the fear, but made it tangible, like a sharp blade you had to carry.

Muffled voices down the hallway grabbed my attention. It was too late to transport a prisoner; it had to be close to midnight. Curious, I stuffed the gun beneath the mattress and pressed my ear against the door.

"He's a mean SOB, that's for sure. Those two on watch will be in sick bay for a week."

"Got you twice between the eyes, didn't he?"

"Shut up, Garrison. You should talk. Least I wasn't pissing myself in the corner."

A chuckle. Then a grunt. The sliding of fabric over the linoleum. The jangling of keys. A door whined softly as it was opened.

They were quieter now. Maybe inside a cell. Then I heard a thump against the wall over my bed. They were leaving the victim next door. I felt a wave of pity. My heart pounded painfully for my new neighbor. If he'd attacked soldiers, his prognosis was not good.

"His chart is finished." A third voice. The soldier on rotation maybe. "Is one of you standing guard?"

"Look at him, man. He's barely breathing. What makes you think he needs a door guard?"

"Just checking orders, that's all."

"Command said dump him here until morning. He's slated to see the Board first thing. I'm sure they've got something sweet worked out for him."

Laughter. The compression of the door closing. And fading footsteps.

There wasn't another sound until morning. I wondered if maybe my new neighbor was already dead. Even as the lights buzzed on, signifying the end of curfew, I found my mind drifting to him. I was proud that he'd fought the soldiers. I needed to be brave like that if I was going to live through the day.

I jolted up when I heard the key turn in my lock. The gun was tucked in my bra, and I was using the blanket again to cover the added bulk. I had to take several deep breaths to focus myself before I felt calm enough to face the door. Even so, I nearly pulled the gun on Delilah the moment I saw her.

She glanced over me once with a speculative look on her face. I could only guess what she thought had happened between Tucker and me last night.

"Morning." I tried to sound like I was dreading the day, which, in a way, I was.

"Come on. Be quick about it," she snapped, and turned toward the supply room. A guard hustled by, making my skin crawl. I felt like he was watching me. Like he knew what I was about to do.

I needed to calm down.

Once we were in the supply room, Delilah began tearing towels off the wall. She handed me a bucket to fill with water. I took a deep breath and set it on the ground.

It was now or never.

I turned my back on her, and very slowly, reached for the gun.

"Delilah, I need—"

"Delilah! I thought I told you to hurry!" shouted a guard from the end of the hallway.

No! Someone had already given her orders, which meant they would come looking for her if she didn't arrive.

"Hurry, hurry, hurry," she muttered, her voice stressed. "Didn't I tell you to fill up that bucket?"

"Ye-yes," I stuttered, and did as she told. The plan was going to have to wait until these soldiers weren't demanding her assistance.

"An officer is coming in an hour to speak with the inmate in cell four," she said. "They brought him in last night, and he's a mess. Still unconscious. Get him up so they can interview him."

What's the point? I thought. I remembered how Delilah had done this for me, before I'd seen Tucker.

"What are you doing?" I asked. I hadn't been assigned any tasks on my own.

"Cell two cut his wrists last night. Someone's got to mop up and take the body to the crematorium."

I shuddered, unable to stop the image of the soldier's face from entering my mind. Thick eyebrows and freckled cheeks. A dazed, lost expression. I'd brought him dinner last night.

"I can do it," I volunteered weakly. "I'll take the body. You take care of cell four."

She scoffed. The soldier down the hall yelled for her again.

"They want it taken care of fast," she emphasized, as though I would be inept at the task. I bit back the disgust. It sounded as though she was pleased to be needed. I felt sorry for her then; there was not much of her soul left.

"I can do it. I know your back's bothering you," I tried. I'd seen her stretch it yesterday, and hoped that this wasn't a shot in the dark.

"You'd do wise to obey orders," she said simply.

I followed her into the hallway, swallowing the defeat. I told myself there would be another chance today to follow my plan. There had to be, because tomorrow I went to trial.

As Delilah opened the door to cell four, the room just beside mine, I readied myself to get this soldier up fast. If he was alert enough to talk to the officer before Delilah had finished with the cleanup, I could still help her take the body to the crematorium.

She sped down the hall to cell two, where three soldiers had now gathered to ogle at the show. I wanted to scream at them to leave the poor guy alone. I was surprised Tucker wasn't there, but it was still early.

Inside the cell before me a crumpled figure lay strewn across the floor, facedown. His head was a foot away from the metal toilet at the end of the room. His long legs stretched toward the door. He wore jeans. Like the murdered carrier in the checkpoint on Rudy Lane.

I lowered, bending at the waist to cautiously move closer. The blinking lights overhead highlighted his socked feet. A torn T-shirt glimmered with droplets of fresh blood. I leaned closer, my heart pounding hard now.

Broad shoulders. Black, messy hair.

"Oh, God!" I cried, dropping the bucket and towels unceremoniously on the linoleum floor. Vaguely, I registered the door suction shut behind me, locking me in.

And then I was on my knees, my hands feeling up the

backs of his calves, toward his waist. All the muted emotions inside of me exploded in bright, blinding colors.

When I could finally speak, my voice was high and trembling.

"Chase?"

CHAPTER
16

SILENCE.

I tried to check his pulse. I didn't know what I was doing.

There was little room to move in the cramped cell. I rolled Chase gently to his back while he remained unanimated, a rag doll. Like the man from the square. Frantically, I wedged myself against the wall, wrapping his heavy arm around my shoulders.

"Come on, Chase," I prompted, frightened.

With all my strength, I hoisted him up onto the mattress. His upper torso and his hips made it, but his legs still hung over the edge. I laid him down as gently as I could and then pulled his knees up.

He groaned.

"Chase," I said anxiously. His eyes were closed.

The consequent survey had my eyes blinking out of focus. A sharp breath raked my throat.

His face and neck were coated with dark black blood. The front of his shirt was drenched with it. My trembling hand reached for his cheek, stroking it gently. The heat from swelling mixed with the cool sticky residue on his skin.

"Chase, wake up. Please."

Panic twisted inside of me. I thought about the little silver briefcase. The laundry carts. The execution that would surely ensue.

Everything had come together just to fall apart. I couldn't escape with Chase in this condition, and I would not leave him this way.

"Why did you get caught?" I didn't expect an answer.

I lifted his shirt. Several boot-sized contusions had begun to form over his ribs.

"It's okay. This is okay. We just need to clean you up, that's all." It sounded like a different person's voice coming out of my mouth. Someone calm, rational. Not me.

But that voice was right. I needed a task. I needed to focus on something.

I soaked a rag and ever so gently touched it to his face, mopping up the blood beside his nose. When it was soiled I shoved it beneath the bed and grabbed another. His raw lips, his ears, his neck. I whispered to him the whole time. Mostly gibberish.

I heard a rolling cart sliding down the hallway. Delilah was taking the soldier to the crematorium. My last chance at freedom was slipping out of the building. I couldn't even feel regret. All I had room for was concern for Chase.

He didn't stir until I moved to his forehead, where several cuts crossed over his scalp. When I reached a particularly nasty laceration, his eyes jolted open, irises dragging down into a sea of white. He blinked in confusion. His teeth bore down hard.

"Chase?"

I drew back and let him find my voice. I had learned from his nightmares that my hands on him while he roused would be too disorienting.

He swallowed before he was able to speak. His body shivered as if he were cold.

"Em?"

"Yes," I cried, letting my tears rain down on his face. A tidal wave of relief crashed over me.

"I found you." Though his voice crackled, he sounded satisfied.

A memory filtered back from long ago. *I promise I'll come back. No matter what happens.* His words just before he'd been drafted. Yes, he had come back. Despite the costs.

"I'm sorry. I should have told you from the beginning," he said.

I shushed him. "Not important."

"Yes it is." He coughed, and when he did so, his whole body ripped into a spasm that had him curling around his stomach.

"Breathe. It's okay," I soothed, stroking his back. But knowing he was hurting ripped my heart wide open.

It took him a full minute to breathe evenly. When he finally lay back, his eyes were dazed with pain.

"Don't talk," I whispered. It took a minute, but he shoved himself up.

"I can fix this. I'm going to get you out."

I froze, my hand still on his cheek.

"You . . . turned yourself in?" My voice hitched. "Why did you do that?"

"I promised I wouldn't let anything happen to you," he said.

I knew what a promise meant to him. It was tearing him apart that he'd let my mother and me down.

"Sean's waiting for you at a gas station in the Red Zone behind the base. He'll help you."

I knew the place. I'd seen its decrepit sign the first day I'd helped Delilah transport a body to the crematorium.

"Sean . . ." I looked at him quizzically. Sean and Chase had not been particularly fond of each other when I'd last seen them together.

"It's on the western side. There's an exit there. I'll clear the gate for you and . . ."

"No." I saw what he had envisioned: him fighting whomever it took to get me outside these gates. I could hardly breathe. He'd come here to rescue me knowing he was going to die.

My hands covered my mouth, and I collapsed on my knees beside the bed. So many feelings, all slamming together, all tearing through me. If I didn't say it now, I wouldn't be able to. My throat was already choking off.

"What happened . . . it's not your fault," I said, shaking.

I wanted to tell him I was sorry. That I forgave him. That I knew he loved me and that I loved him, too. I couldn't. I fell apart, sobbing into my sleeves. His hands slipped around me, pulling me into his bruised body.

"You scared the hell out of me. I thought . . ." he sighed. "It doesn't matter. You're alive."

A sound in the hallway extinguished my tears.

Cla-click, cla-click. Cla-click, cla-click.

The guard on rotation. Or Delilah, back from her gruesome task.

We froze, listening to the footsteps. They grew louder, then paused, just outside of Chase's cell. I held my breath and watched the door.

A clatter against the outside wall. His chart. Someone was going to come in.

No!

Chase pushed me aside. In a laborious heave he stood, bracing against the wall for support. I jumped up behind him, wrapping my arms around his chest, half certain he was about to fall over, half ready to make the guards tear us apart.

"Lay down!" I whispered.

He didn't listen. It was a good thing he was injured. I was stronger than him in his current condition. I shoved him back to the bed and pushed his head down. He looked like he might throw up. Somewhere in the back of my mind I registered this as a symptom of concussion.

A key fit into the lock, turned.

"Keep your eyes closed!" I said quietly.

Chase complied, but his hands curled into fists.

Delilah entered the room.

"He's not up yet?" I could see the little red dots that had splattered across her blouse and the damp stains on her collar from where she'd been sweating. I tried not to picture what she'd seen in cell two.

"He was a second ago," I said, feeling the solid shape of the gun against my skin. "Come look at his face," I added, gently running my finger over a split on the bridge of his nose.

Chase stirred, ever so slightly. I willed him to be still.

She took another step forward, one hand still on the door. "What's wrong with it?"

"He got hit pretty hard."

"Obviously," she snorted. One more step inside.

I sprung, throwing the blanket off my shoulders and shoving her away from the door. A second later I'd pulled the gun from my dress and aimed it directly at her. I pushed the door back toward the jamb, careful not to let it lock.

"What the hell are you doing?" she cried.

"Shut up!" I ordered, praying no one had heard us. Chase was sitting up now, blinking rapidly. He still looked ill—and more shocked than Delilah.

"Here." I shoved the gun into his hand. He aimed it at Delilah. She bared her teeth at him. I saw his hand tremble slightly but knew it wasn't from physical pain. The last woman he'd held a gun to had been my mother.

"Sorry, Delilah," I told her as I shoved a clean rag into her mouth. "But there *is* something out there for me."

As quickly as I could, I tore the tattered rags to strips and fastened her wrists around the metal bed frame. She didn't struggle, clear eyes glued on Chase. I slipped the key over her head and pressed it firmly in my fist. My heart felt as if it were going to explode in my chest. If it did, I hoped it killed me before the MM did.

Then I eased Chase back to the bed, away from Delilah, and returned the gun to its hiding place in my dress.

"I must have gotten hit harder than I thought," Chase said, with the confusion of someone waking from a coma. "How did you get in here? Who is she? And where did that gun come from?" The heels of his hands were pressed against his temples.

"I'll explain later. For right now, stay here."

"I'm going with you," he said.

I shook my head. His jaw tightened.

Don't fight me, Chase.

I knew he felt as I had so many times on this journey. Completely out of control. Completely reliant. Maybe he realized how I felt now, too, because he didn't argue, he didn't fight. He just looked up at me and whispered, "Please be careful."

A moment later the door locked behind me.

The hallway was eerily quiet, without even the shuffle of the guard around the far corner at the stairs. He was there, I knew, just silent. The guard on rotation would be coming around any second.

Nerves chewed my insides and made my skin tingle. Every step I took felt like walking on a bed of nails. I figured I was losing my mind. It was the only reasonable explanation for my actions.

Before anything else, I grabbed the clipboard outside Chase's cell. I ripped the pen from its hanging cord and in large letters scribbled what had been written on the other soldiers' charts.

COMPLETE.

One steadying breath, to find that emotionless calm from before Chase had come, and I returned to my task.

I used Delilah's key to open the storage room and rolled a cart into the hallway. One of the wheels rattled and flicked awkwardly to the side. I stared furiously at the defective piece, as though this would somehow silence it.

I had just reached Chase's cell when I heard the clicking of footsteps again.

My body became paralyzed.

A guard with dark skin and a permanent frown came around the corner.

"Good morning," I said too cheerily.

"What are you doing out?" He looked down the empty hallway.

"Delilah . . . she came early," I stammered.

"Where is she?"

"Still cleaning up the suicide in cell two. She told me to wait here."

"Why here?"

Several swear words tore through my brain.

"To take out the trash," I answered, quoting Delilah.

The soldier looked at Chase's chart. His furrowed brows smoothed.

"I guess they blew off the trial. Figures. He didn't deserve one."

"Oh no?" *Please just leave!*

"No. There are bad people in the world. He's one of them." He said this as though he were a father talking to his daughter about stranger danger. I thought about where I would shoot him if I pulled the gun.

I tried to look frightened. "Well, I'd better get to it."

He turned on his heels without another word and did not look back.

Only thirty minutes until the next rotation.

My hands shook so hard I could barely fit the key in the lock. The doubt clawed at me, but I shoved it aside. I would not let Chase down.

I reopened his cell. He was standing inside, the stress still evident through his swollen features. I was careful to make sure the lock did not click behind me. Delilah's cheeks were stained red with fury.

"Who was that?" Chase whispered.

"Just a guard." I positioned the cart against the wall. "Get in."

As I explained the plan, his countenance grew grim.

"And if you get caught? I can't live with that."

"You won't have to for long," I said morosely, glancing at Delilah, still bound and gagged. The guilt made my stomach burn. "It's both of us or neither of us."

His hand scratched through his hair.

"Don't you see?" I argued. "We have to do something! So this doesn't happen to anyone else!" He knew what I meant by *this*. What had happened to my mother. To us.

He swallowed. And very slowly nodded.

We were going to try to escape an MM base.

I didn't think about it too long. If I did, the impossibility of it would overwhelm me.

I had to help Chase. He had difficulty bending; I suspected a few ribs may have been broken. He sat on the bottom of the cart, his knees pulled to his chest, his head locked down.

"If I hear things go south, I won't stay hidden."

I didn't say anything and closed the lid over his head. One final nod to Delilah was all the time we could afford.

I shoved my shoulder into the cart, rocking it with effort

until it rolled into the empty hallway. Every sense vigilant, I made for the elevator. I could hear my heart slamming in my eardrums and the screaming rattle of that stupid wheel as my trembling finger pressed the button. The freight elevator doors made a loud clanging noise as they opened. *Did they always do that?* I scanned the hallway. Still nothing.

Leaning into the cart, I pushed Chase inside.

The gears of the metal box squealed, then ground us inch by inch to the bottom floor. It took several steadying breaths to regain my focus.

The doors pulled open, revealing the dark, floor-level corridor where I had originally planned on leaving Delilah. Since this part of the building was not often used, the standardized power did not automatically kick on the lights here. I didn't, either. I held my breath in the darkness, ignoring the frightening sounds and shapes I created in my mind, and took an immediate right. The utility door unlocked easily with my key. When the first breath of fresh air hit me, I felt renewed.

Yes. I could do this. I *was* doing this.

I had to plant my heels into the asphalt to push the cart down the narrow alley. Twenty more yards to the gate station. Fifteen. Ten.

The guard at post stuck his head outside.

No! Ignore me! That's what you did yesterday!

"Where's the old lady?" he asked. He had a chubby face and a dimple in the center of his chin.

"Sick, I think," I responded. I prayed no one had found her yet.

"That old bat's never sick."

I shrugged.

"Early this morning for that, isn't it?"

"They did it last night." *Please let me pass. Please let me pass.*

He pressed the button, and the gate buzzed before dragging open.

We passed through. My heart was racing. I rounded the corner and began straining up the hill. I had to keep my arms locked straight on the handlebar so that I wouldn't topple backward.

"We did it," I whispered giddily between labored breaths. I knew he couldn't hear me. That was okay. He would know soon enough.

Step after step I pushed him up the hill.

Finally we reached the top. I pulled the cart off into a hidden area beside the awning and checked the driveway and hilltop for movement. We were alone.

The metal cover fell open with a clang, and Chase lifted his head.

"We did it!" I stifled a scream this time.

He didn't smile until he'd seen for himself that the driveway was clear. After he was out, we pushed the cart over to the drop-off area at the crematorium. Behind the building was a wooded slope, which led to the subdivision and the gas station. This was where we would disappear.

"Come on." Chase grabbed my hand.

But the skin on my neck prickled. Boots clacked across the pavement.

I spun around, my heart already leaping into my throat.

Tucker Morris was jogging up the hill, alone. It was too late to run, he had already seen us. He stopped three yards away, hands on his belt. His eyes were focused behind me, on Chase.

"So it's true." His voice was filled with both trepidation and disgust. "A soldier in sick bay told me you turned yourself in last night. I had to see for myself." He laughed wryly. "The chart on the door said 'Jennings,' but she sure didn't look like you."

Delilah. "Did anyone else see her?" I asked, flattening the apprehension in my voice.

"Not yet," he threatened.

It struck me as odd that Tucker hadn't alerted the entire base to our escape, but then I realized he would likely get in trouble for it. He was trying to fix a mistake on his shift before his command found out what had happened.

Chase was still silent. Somehow, he'd placed himself between Tucker and me.

"You look surprised," Tucker said to him. "You didn't tell him I was here, Ember?" He used my first name just to get under Chase's skin. He'd never called me that before.

"Don't talk to her," Chase growled. "Don't even look at her."

"Or what?"

"Or I'll finish what I started and break your other arm."

My pulse quickened.

"You can barely stand," scoffed Tucker. But there was a cautious light in his eye.

"So it'll be an even fight."

"We're leaving," I told Tucker flatly.

"The hell you are."

I felt my eyes twitch. Chase took a step forward, intending to make good on his threat. I grabbed his arm.

Tucker's tone turned from vehemence to conceit.

"Have you told him yet? About how you gave it up in my office last night?" Tucker began walking purposefully toward us.

"Nothing happened."

He grinned. "If I'd known you were that wild I'd have busted you out of reform school, too."

"Go," Chase told me under his breath.

"Not a chance," I told him fiercely.

Tucker was still approaching. I knew if we turned our backs to him he'd reach for the radio at his belt and call for assistance. I couldn't let that happen.

Chase was leaning forward, ready to pounce. Before I took another step, Tucker whipped the baton from his hip and lunged at us. Chase moved to intercept, but there was no need: Tucker's advance had been cut short. He was frozen, the nightstick suspended over his shoulder. Surprised by the interruption, Chase glanced back at me. His eyes changed slightly when he registered the gun in my hands.

"*You* stole my weapon?" He seemed genuinely surprised for a brief moment—but then his bravado returned. "You've really screwed yourself now."

The gun was light as a feather in my hands. The rush was kicking through my system. I'd aimed the gun at Delilah but never considered actually shooting her. I thought if Tucker took another step forward I might just pull the trigger.

"Tucker, please let us go." My words were icy.

"Begging?" He spat on the ground. "You sound like your mother did. Right before I shot her."

My world stopped.

Tucker's words sliced through my brain. Again and again.

—352—

Right before I shot her.

"You?" I asked weakly. I had assumed it was the CO that had killed her, but I was wrong. It was Tucker. That was why Chase had broken his arm. That was why Tucker had been promoted. I felt like I was going to be ill.

My blood was running cold. My mother's killer was faceless no longer. I could see him holding the gun up, just behind Chase. See him shooting her.

"I thought you told her," Tucker said to Chase. Chase said nothing.

"You killed her," I said softly. My hands were wobbling.

"Ember." I barely registered Chase saying my name.

"How could you?" Tucker was an inconceivable monster.

"I'm a damn good soldier. I did what needed to be done."

His words hit me like a freight train.

"What needed to be done?" I repeated. The murder of an innocent woman was now necessary?

I focused on the gun. I would show him what needed to be done.

"Like you even know what to do with that," mocked Tucker.

I glanced down, flicking the safety off.

"It's a nine millimeter, isn't it? I just pull back the slide, aim, and fire."

With a steady hand I chambered the first round. *Click.*

Tucker faltered, his face blotching with crimson, his mouth hard and set. I couldn't stop the images. Tucker lifting the weapon. The sound the gun must have made when it fired. The fear in her eyes. The *death* in her eyes.

"Em," Chase whispered. I barely heard him.

I saw her. I saw her mischievous smile. The clips in her hair. She sang songs from back before the War, and we danced in the living room. She made me hot chocolate. She gave away her space in line at the soup kitchen.

She'd forgiven Chase for the overhaul. *Thank God you're here,* she'd said to him in the cell. She'd forgiven Roy for hurting her. Me for making him leave. She would blame the MM for Tucker's corruption.

She would be ashamed of me if I killed him. Because of that single fact, I knew I could not take his life.

But I wanted to.

Chase was still watching me. His eyes were filled with understanding. I knew he would have supported me, regardless of my decision.

"Get the gun from her, man," said Tucker to Chase. He was trying to revive their old friendship. His words jolted me back.

"If I do, I'm shooting you myself," Chase responded darkly. I knew that if I asked him to, Chase would kill Tucker. Part of me wanted him to, *needed* him to. But I focused on my mother's face. She had loved Chase, too. She wouldn't want his soul any more compromised than it had already been.

Tucker shifted. "Think about what this will mean for you. You'll never be able to stop running." Fear laced through his voice.

"I've thought about it." *Last chance,* I told myself. But my mind was made up. "We're leaving, Tucker. Walk away. Or I *will* shoot you."

I ignored the hammering of my pulse against my temple. I felt no fear, no anger. The grief, too, was gone. My whole body focused on the completion of this single task: securing our safety.

How like Chase I had become.

"What am I supposed to tell my command?" Tucker's voice cracked.

"You tell them that Chase is dead. He didn't make it to his trial. His chart is 'completed.' You tell them that he was taken to the crematorium. You tell them that I stole the key from Delilah by force, and when she confessed, you had me 'completed' too."

Yesterday, I'd thought it pitiful that Tucker had threatened Delilah into silence. Now I was banking on it. I hoped this would save the sad old woman from the same fate as my mother.

"And if I say no?"

"You can always tell them that two criminals escaped on your shift, right in front of you. Though I doubt that would bode well for that career plan of yours."

Several long beats of silence.

Tucker swore.

"All right. *All right!*"

Something cracked inside of me. I knew I was on the verge of breaking now.

Hold it together!

"Give me my gun back. I'll be busted down for that." Tucker held his hand out.

"I'm not that stupid. You walk back down to the check station. Once I see you there, I'm going to throw it down the hill into those bushes. I hope you can find it."

"And what's to stop me from shooting you when I do?"

"There won't be any bullets. You can ask the guards at the post, but that will mean a whole messy explanation. I recommend you come back later for it."

He kicked the ground and finally nodded. "Get out of here."

I swallowed a deep breath.

"Don't shoot me in the back," he added with repugnance.

"I'm not making any promises."

Tucker turned and strode down the hill.

The gun grew heavier in my hands, as if I were holding a bucket filling with water. By the time Tucker had disappeared around the curve of the hill, I could barely lift my arms.

Chase gently placed his hand on my shoulder, sliding it down my bicep to my wrist. He pried the gun from my grasp. My ears were ringing.

I watched as he removed the magazine from the handle and stuffed it in his pocket. Then he tossed the handgun into a neat hedge wall, close enough so that Tucker would have to climb back up the hill to find it. If indeed he could find it at all.

"We need to go," Chase said.

I led him back behind the crematorium, to where the asphalt met the woods. The brush thickened immediately, grabbing onto the fabric of my skirt and ripping little holes in it. Some of the branches nicked at my legs, too. I noticed this objectively, as though I were an outsider watching my body from above.

My mind was still reeling with the events of the last five minutes. I could think of nothing but my mother's killer.

Should I have killed Tucker? Should Chase have? Tucker could hurt so many others now. There was no right answer.

The trail declined, leading us into the subdivision. We would have to be careful going between the houses; it was important to stay out of view from the hilltop behind the base.

We rested in a tight alleyway. Chase was struggling to breathe and squeezing his head between the heels of his hands. I wished I could take his pain away.

I searched for soldiers but found no evidence we were being followed.

"We need to keep moving." I slid under his arm for support. He didn't object, which worried me. The concussion seemed severe. We needed to find a doctor.

It was midmorning when we reached our destination. The parking lot was empty but for a thin, ex-reform-school guard roaming around near the Dumpster.

Sean stared at us, mouth open.

"You actually pulled it off," he said in awe.

Chase squeezed my hand. "She pulled it off. I did nothing—"

"—but get your butt kicked," Sean finished.

To my surprise, Chase smirked.

It appeared they were friends now. I thought maybe Sean and I could be friends one day, too. I didn't blame him anymore for not telling me about my mother; people would do almost anything to protect someone they loved. If anyone knew that, it was us.

I walked straight up to Sean and gave him a hug.

"Thanks for waiting," I told him.

"I've gotta say, Miller, I didn't think I'd see you again." His shocked expression morphed into one of concern.

"They moved Rebecca," I said, before he could ask.

His eyes widened. "Where?"

"A rehabilitation center in Chicago."

"A . . . what? How do you—"

"Doesn't matter. That's where she is," I said. Chase glanced over at me but didn't ask any questions.

Later, when we were safe, I would tell him what had happened with Tucker in his office, and how, now that I knew what Tucker had done, my actions revolted me even more. There would be time to talk about how I'd orchestrated our escape, and what I had seen in the MM base. But for now, we had to hide.

"Make the call," Chase told Sean. I glanced at him, confused.

Sean took a step back. After a moment, he shook his head, focusing on the present, and removed a radio from his belt. It was like the one Chase had in the MM but smaller, and it clicked rapidly when he turned it on.

"Package ready for pickup," Sean said. He had to clear his throat. An array of emotions was flying across his face.

Nearly a minute passed with no response from the radio.

While we waited, I caught Chase watching me. His gaze held no more secrets but was clear and honest and deep as a lake. I traced my fingertips over his high cheekbones and saw how the lines between his brows melted as the pounding in his head subsided. Finally finding peace, he closed his eyes.

"One hour," came the response, making me jump. I recog-

nized the voice. It belonged to a wiry man with greasy, peppered hair and a mustache.

Chase nodded his approval. He'd asked Wallace to help us.
We were going back to the Wayland Inn.

We were going back to the resistance.

CHAPTER
17

IT was nearly dawn when I finished with Wallace. A deep exhaustion filled me, one that soaked into my bones until they were soft and pliable and barely able to sustain my weight. In this condition I dragged myself up the stairs of the Wayland Inn, out the exit onto the roof, and into the cool, dark air.

Wallace himself had attended to Chase's injuries when we'd returned. Once a medic in the FBR, the resistance leader taught me how to check Chase's pupils for dilation and how to manage the other symptoms of concussion. I'd led Chase to an empty room, to a bed with a moth-eaten comforter, and waited only minutes for him to fall asleep. Sean told me later that this was the first time Chase had rested since I'd been found missing.

Then Wallace and I had talked. I'd told him everything I remembered from the base: the layout, the personnel, and the horrors within. It was terrifying to relive, but ultimately purging. After hours of his soft but persistent interrogation, I felt empty.

Later we would talk strategy. The time to fight was coming, but until then we'd been granted a moment of peace; a deep breath before the plunge.

There was one thing I had to do before I slept. I had to see the sky.

I sat on an old wooden bench, positioned around the corner of the exit door. My body bowed into the weathered planks, rejoicing in the freedom coating my limbs. I tilted my head back and closed my eyes and felt the last bit of claustrophobia from the holding cells slip away.

My mother was gone, and with her, the child I had been. She'd been taken with violence, as had my youth, and in their place a new me had awakened, a girl I didn't yet know. I felt achingly unfamiliar.

The sky had turned peach and raspberry when the rooftop door burst open with enough force to kick my heart straight into my windpipe. In an instant I was on my feet.

Chase's hair was messy, his eyes wide and wild and tinged with pain. My heart throbbed as it did for him alone, with equal parts love and fear. Only when the sun brightened the bruises on his jaw did I remember to breathe.

"Is everything all right?" I asked.

He took a tentative step forward. Several beats passed. His gaze roamed over my face in a tender, familiar way, and for a moment I forgot that I felt lost and empty. I was the same girl I'd always been. The girl he loved.

"Everything's fine. Sorry," he apologized. "I just couldn't find you and . . ." he shrugged forcefully, looking unbearably vulnerable for such a big person.

He'd thought I'd run away again. I let my hair fall forward, hoping it would hide the guilt heating my cheeks.

I sat again and he sat beside me. We didn't touch, and I felt a severing as he turned to watch the sun stream over the horizon.

You know what I remember after the police came? he said in my mind. *You sitting on the couch with me. You didn't say anything. You just sat with me.* His tone had been softer, less serious than it was now. It struck me how much the years had changed us, and yet here we were, sitting together in silence, watching the same sun rise.

For a long time we were very still, until I noticed Chase's hand resting, palm unfurled, on his thigh.

I wondered how long he had been sitting like that. Unassuming. Possibly not meaning anything by it. I took a deep breath, feeling the nerves tingle down my spine, and placed my hand in his. With our wrists in alignment, my fingers only reached to the first joint of his knuckles.

I studied the blunt, raised scars on his hands from too many fights. His fingers traced the white latticed pattern from a whip on mine. Soft skin trailed over calloused patches and the cool metal of a stolen gold ring. His thumb teased slowly down the side of my first finger, and my whole arm prickled with heat. Then our fingers intertwined. He squeezed and I squeezed back.

I leaned my head on his shoulder, feeling a sudden wave of fatigue. The fear and anger had been left to simmer until a later time when they might actually make sense, and though I knew it was temporary, I was relieved. We were safe and together, and that was all that mattered now.

ACKNOWLEDGMENTS

Growing a book is no solitary venture. It is a process touched by many, and I will never be able to truly convey how grateful I am to the following people for changing the trajectory of my life.

First to my agent, Joanna MacKenzie, who took a huge chance but never made me feel like a risk, who donated so many hours not just to the manuscript but to my therapy, and who is both the best champion and best cheerleader in the entire world. There would be no *Article 5* if not for Joanna. Additionally, without Danielle Egan-Miller's and Lauren Olson's thoughtful comments, guidance, and advocating for *Article 5* on all fronts, I would be lost.

A huge high-five to Melissa Frain, my fabulous editor. I hope everyone has a chance to know someone like Mel — she is funny and kind, and her positivity is simply infectious. She even makes statements like "we need to cut these fifty pages" seem not so nauseating. Also, a big thanks to Tor Teen's publisher, Kathleen Doherty; my publicist, Alexis Saarela; and *Article 5*'s art director, Seth Lerner. I am so grateful for all their hard work.

None of this would have been possible without my family. My husband, Jason, who has been my best friend since a lucky assigned seating chart stuck us together in biology when I was fourteen. My mom, who taught me the joy of reading, and my dad, who doesn't just say I can be anything I want, but believes it, too. My deepest thanks to the whole Simmons family, who made me their own without a second thought. To Dee, Craig, and the boys for bacon nights, handyman work, and answering ridiculous questions on everything from motorcycles to (gulp) firearms—yes, you are with family for a reason. And to Rudy, my precious greyhound, who provided much inspiration and yet did not demand coauthorship.

I am privileged to have some of the best friends in the world. Thank you to the girls from home, the friends who shake it with me at Jazzercise, and the therapists who make me a better therapist *and* a better person.

And finally, thank you to the people who, in the face of hardship, fight. Who turn surviving into thriving. Because of you I now live stronger and wiser, with the knowledge that hope is working through us all, even in our darkest moments.

TURN THE PAGE FOR A SNEAK PEEK AT
KRISTEN SIMMONS'S NEW NOVEL

BREAKING POINT

AVAILABLE FEBRUARY 2013

CHAPTER
1

THE Wayland Inn was behind the slums, on the west end of Knoxville. It was a place that had festered since the War, buzzing with flies that bred in the clogged sewers, stinking of dirty river water brought in on the afternoon breeze. A place that attracted those who thrived in the shadows. People you had to seek to find.

The motel's brick exterior, veined with dead ivy and pockmarked by black mold, blended with every other boarded-up office building on the street. The water was ice-cold when it ran at all, the baseboards were cracked with mouse holes, and there was only one bathroom on each floor. Sometimes it even worked.

It was the perfect location for the resistance: hidden in plain sight, on a block so rotten even the soldiers stayed in their patrol cars.

We met outside the supply room before dawn, when the standardized power resumed, for Wallace's orders. The night patrols were still out guarding our perimeter and those with stationary posts—the stairway door, the roof, and radio surveillance—were awaiting relief from the day shift. Curfew would be up soon, and they were hungry.

I stayed back against the wall, letting those who had been here longer settle to the front row. The rest of the hallway filled in quickly; if you were late, Wallace assigned you extra duties, the kind no one wanted. The supply room door was open, and though I couldn't see our hardnosed leader from my angle, the candlelight threw a thin, distorted shadow against the inside wall.

He was talking to someone on the radio; a soft crackling filled the space while he waited for a response. I thought it might be the team he'd put on special assignment two days ago: Cara, the only other girl at the Wayland Inn, and three big guys that had been kicked out of the Federal Bureau of Reformation—or, as we'd called the soldiers who'd taken over after the War, the Moral Militia. Curiosity had me leaning toward the sound, but I didn't get too close. The more you knew, the more the MM could take from you.

"Be safe." I recognized Wallace's voice, but not the concern in it. Never had I heard him soften in the presence of others.

Sean Banks, my old guard from the Girls' Reformatory and Rehabilitation Center, staggered out of his room, pulling his shirt down over his ribs. *Too thin*, I thought, but at least he'd slept a little—his deep blue eyes were calmer than before, not so strained. He found a place on the wall beside me, rubbing at the pillow marks still on his face.

"*Always am, handsome,*" came Cara's muffled response, and then the radio went dead.

"Handsome?" parroted an AWOL named Houston. His red hair was growing out and flipped in the back like the tail feathers of a chicken. "*Handsome?*" he said again. The volume in the hall had increased; several of the guys were snickering.

"You called?" Lincoln, whose freckles always looked like someone had splashed black paint across his hollow cheeks, appeared beside Houston. They'd joined together last year, and in my time here I'd yet to see one without the other.

The chatter faded as Wallace came around the corner. He needed a shower; his shoulder-length peppered hair was greasy in clumps, and the skin of his face was tight with fatigue, but even in the muted yellow glow of the flashlights it was obvious his ears had gone pink. One pointed glare, and Houston melted back toward Lincoln.

My brows rose. Wallace seemed too old for Cara; she was twenty-two while he might have been twice that age. Besides, he was married to the cause. Everything else, everyone else, would always come second.

Not my business, I reminded myself.

The narrow corridor had crowded with eleven guys awaiting instruction. Not all of them had served; some were just noncompliant with the Statutes, like me. We all had our reasons for being here.

My heart tripped in my chest when Houston moved aside to reveal Chase Jennings, leaning against the opposite wall ten feet down. His hands were wrist-deep in the pockets of his jeans, and a white undershirt peeked through the holes of a gray, threadbare sweater. Only remnants of his incarceration in the MM base remained, a dark half-moon painted beneath one eye and a thin band of scar tissue across the bridge of his nose. He'd just gotten off the night shift securing the building's perimeter; I hadn't seen him come in.

As he watched me, the corner of his mouth lifted ever so slightly.

I looked down when I realized my lips had done the same.

"All right, quiet down," began Wallace, voice gruff once again. He hesitated, tapping the handheld radio, now silent, against his leg. I caught a glimpse of the black tattoo on his forearm that twisted beneath his frayed sleeve.

"What happened?" said Riggins, suspicious only when not outright paranoid. His fingers wove over the top of his buzzed, can-shaped head as though he expected the ceiling might suddenly cave in on us.

"Last night half the Square went without rations." Wallace's frown deepened. "Seems our blue friends are withholding."

Pity was a hard sell. Most of us went straight to anger. We all knew the MM had the food; our scouts had counted two extra Horizons trucks—the only government-sanctioned food distributers—entering the base just yesterday.

Houston balked. "If they're hoping to clear town, they're outta luck. Tent City'll starve to death first. People got nowhere else to go."

He was right. When the major cities had been destroyed or evacuated in the War, people had migrated inland, to places like Knoxville, or my home, Louisville, in search of food and shelter. They'd found only the bare minimum—soup kitchens and communities of vagrants, like the city of tents that had taken over the lot on the northern side of the city square.

"Thank you, Houston," said Wallace. "I think that's the point."

I shivered. Chase and I hadn't left the Wayland Inn since we'd pledged to the resistance, almost a month ago. If possible, the city seemed even bleaker than when we had last seen it.

"Now," continued Wallace. "Billy caught a radio thread yesterday on an upcoming draft in the Square. We don't know when, but my guess is it'll be soon, and they'll be offering signing bonuses."

"I didn't get a bonus," someone whispered.

"Rations, jackass," muttered Sean.

A collective groan filled the hallway. Soldiers using the promise of food to recruit more soldiers. They'd have a whole new army in a week.

"And forgiveness of Statute violations, of course." Wallace smiled cynically. More groans followed.

Work was slim these days. The only businesses still running required background checks, which meant applicants had better be compliant with the Moral Statutes—a list of regulations that took away women's rights, mandated a "whole" family, and prohibited things like divorce, speaking out against the government, and, of course, being born out of wedlock, like me. This had always been one of the MM's prime recruiting strategies. Men who couldn't get a job because of their record could still serve their country. And even if it meant selling their souls, soldiers got paid.

"What're we going to do about it?" Lincoln asked.

"Nothing," said Riggins. "We hit something like that, they'll smoke out this whole town till they find us."

I straightened, envisioning the MM coming here, raiding the Wayland Inn. As far as they knew, Chase and I were dead, "completed" in the holding cells at the base. I'd made certain of it before our escape. We didn't want to give them reason to believe otherwise.

Without looking over, Sean elbowed me in the ribs. I deflated, a shallow breath expelling from between my teeth.

"Quiet," said Wallace when several people objected. He shook his head. "Riggins is right. They plugged up the soup kitchen for seventy-two hours after last month's riot. Soon they'll be compensating anyone willing to sell us out. We've got to be smart. Think." He tapped his temple. "In the meantime, Banks has a report to make."

I glanced over, surprised, as Sean shoved off the wall beside me. He and I had been up late together scanning the mainframe for facilities in Chicago, searching for Rebecca—my roommate and his girlfriend—who had been beaten and arrested the night I'd tried to escape reform school. He hadn't mentioned that anything out of the ordinary had happened during his earlier shift in the Square.

"Yesterday on my way back from Tent City, I ran into a guy looking for trouble over by the Red Cross Station," said Sean.

"What kind of trouble?" Chase's dark gaze flicked to mine.

Sean scratched his jaw. "The kind that makes me think he was looking to join us. He was trying to convince a group of guys to take out the guards posted at the soup kitchen. Talking loud—*too* loud. Said he'd been in the base lately, that he knew things about it. I very politely told him to keep it down, and he called me a—"

"What did he know?" I interrupted.

"A lot," said Sean. "He was just discharged last week. *Dishonorably.* He didn't seem too pleased about it either."

I could feel Chase's tension from across the hall. A recently discharged soldier could have important information about the Knoxville base, he might even know how to break back in, but what if he recognized us? We'd only been there four weeks ago. He could have been one of those who had beaten Chase or even killed another prisoner.

"It's a con," said Riggins. "Banks is getting played. The FBR's sending in a mole."

Wallace, who'd been silent while Sean had spoken, cleared his throat. "That's why we're going to tail him. If he gets within ten feet of a uniform, cut him loose. I don't want to take any chances with this one."

"Then don't," I said before I could stop myself. "Maybe Riggins is right." Riggins snorted as if to say he didn't want my help.

"You think he didn't say the same about you when you came here?" Wallace asked.

I felt myself shrink under our leader's stare. Sean had

– 373 –

brought Chase and me to the Wayland Inn with no more than his word that we weren't going to spill its secrets.

"Besides," he continued, patting the radio against his leg again. "If this guy can get us access into the base, imagine the damage we could do."

The following silence was filled with consideration. The MM was stockpiling food—we'd seen the delivery trucks go in—and there were weapons, not to mention the innocent people being executed in the holding cells.

I shivered, remembering how I'd nearly been one of them.

Lincoln and Houston shoved each other excitedly, but several of the others didn't seem so convinced. Clusters of arguments broke out, which Wallace silenced by assigning a detail to keep tabs on the new recruit. He tasked Sean with bringing him in.

Sean fell back beside me, grumbling something indecipherable. The more time he spent away, the less we had to focus on breaking Rebecca out of rehab in Chicago. Still, Sean was smart enough to know that in order to use the resistance's resources, the resistance had to use *him* as a resource, so he did what he was told.

Over the next several minutes Wallace began assigning people to daily duties: patrol, motel security, and finally, distribution of rations. I paused when he gave this duty to the two brothers who bunked across the hall from the bathroom. For the last few weeks it had belonged to me. I'd just gotten used to the routine, and now Wallace was changing things up.

"We've got supplies coming in from a raid last night,"

Wallace said, and I realized this must have been what Cara and the others were doing. "The truck's parked at the checkpoint and needs to be unloaded. And there's a package in Tent City waiting for delivery."

I still hadn't gotten used to people being *packages*. Fugitives were moved for their safety to a checkpoint, a secret location where they could hide until a driver for the resistance, called a carrier, could transport them across the evacuated Red Zone lines to a safe house on the coast. Once we helped Sean rescue Rebecca, Chase and I would be going there, too.

My breath quickened. The checkpoint was across town, past the Square.

Two eager hands rose.

"Good. Inventory?"

On impulse, I raised my hand. Inventory kept me here, and kept everything on the outside, lurking just beyond the rain-stained windows.

"Miller," said Wallace slowly. "Right. Miller on supplies."

Chase's brows lifted.

I dropped my hand and picked at the peeling yellow wallpaper behind my lower back. Houston whispered something to Riggins, who shot a mocking glance at me over his shoulder.

"What about next door?" Fourteen-year-old Billy spoke up from behind Chase. "You said you'd post me there today." He shoved a mop of mousy brown hair out of his eyes.

Wallace's thin mouth drew into a smirk—an expression reserved for the youngest here.

"Billy, so nice of you to join us."

"I been here!" His claim was cheerfully denied by those closest.

"You been here?" Wallace mocked. "You *been* sleeping late, I think. You're on the latrines, kid, and Jennings and Banks will clear the abandoned buildings next door."

Jennings? Chase was leaving the building? He hadn't even slept yet. I tried to glance back over to him, but now other people were blocking the way.

Billy's chin shot out indignantly. "But—"

"How about tomorrow, too?"

Billy threw his head back and groaned.

A buzz, one that made my spine tingle, and the overhead globes flickered with light. Curfew was over. The day had begun.

The hall began to clear. I looked for Chase, but found my path blocked.

"Inventory, huh?" Riggins smirked. He had a sorry excuse for a moustache, which landed directly in my line of sight.

I planted my feet, not about to let him get to me. The guys here were rough, they had to be, and living with them meant having a thick skin sometimes.

"That's what Wallace said," I responded.

"Let's get some food." Sean tried to move between us but Riggins stopped him with one solid hand.

"Watch out in the supply room. There's *rats*, you know." He grinned, the plucky hairs on his upper lip thinning.

I wasn't sure if he was serious or just trying to make me squirm. "I've seen rats," I told him.

"Not rats this big," he said, stepping close enough to force me back again. "These rats hide in the uniform crates. You can hear 'em sometimes. They squeal, real loud."

Two hands closed around my waist from behind and pinched my ribs. A short scream burst from my throat. When I spun around Houston was cackling. He took off after Lincoln, toward the radio room.

Before any coherent words filled my mind Chase was there, his fist twisted in Riggins's collar as he shoved him into the wall. Because Chase was several inches taller, Riggins was forced to lift his dimpled chin to return a hard glare.

"Temper, temper," Riggins rasped.

"What's going on?" Wallace's voice broke through my surprise. He had rules about fighting. We were family here, that's what he always said. All Chase and I needed was to get kicked out, to be out there again running from the MM.

I squeezed Chase's bicep, feeling the muscles flex beneath my fingers. His grip eased, and finally released.

Riggins smiled before sending Wallace a no-problem-here wave.

"Come on," said Sean. He grabbed my elbow, towing me down the hall toward where the brothers were distributing dry cereal for breakfast.

Riggins leaned close as I passed. "You actually gonna do something useful today? Or just disappear again?" When I turned around he was sauntering toward the west exit, chuckling to himself.

My whole body burned.

It was no secret that Chase and I hadn't left the motel

since we'd escaped the base, but I didn't know anyone had noticed that sometimes, when the fourth floor grew too confined, I'd escape to the roof to clear my head. It wasn't like I was hurting anyone, and we pulled our weight where we could. We passed out rations, and Chase took shifts securing the building, but it wasn't the same as pounding the pavement, holding up supply trucks or helping those in danger. Riggins and I both knew it.

It wasn't like I didn't want to do more. I did. I wanted to make a difference, to help someone, the way no one had been able to help my mother. The MM may have thought we were dead, but I remembered too well what it felt like to be wanted. First as a Statute violator when my mother had been charged with an Article 5, then as a reform school runaway. Chase had been charged with everything from his AWOL as a soldier to assault. Sometimes I could still feel the MM breathing down our necks.

But those things didn't matter to people like Riggins. He hadn't trusted me since Sean had brought us here for shelter. And hiding while he and the others risked their lives did nothing to prove my dedication to the cause.

Fury stoked through me, sudden and sharp. I'd survived the MM's unforgiving rules, escaped execution, and come here, to the resistance, where we were all supposed to be on the same side. I didn't need Riggins making me feel weak, or anyone else doubting me.

I shook out of Sean's grasp and spun around—right into Chase, half a foot taller and broader even with his shoulders hunched forward. Quite a pair they were, like my own personal bodyguards. I should have been grateful for their help, but instead felt small, too in need of their protection.

"I'll talk to Riggins," said Chase. "He doesn't know when to quit."

"It's fine. He's just messing around." My voice was too thin to be believable, though, and I could feel the terror and the emptiness pushing back from behind my thin veil of control. It had been this way since I'd learned of my mother's murder. Sometimes the wall felt thicker, sometimes I felt stronger, but it was all an illusion. It could break through at a moment's notice, just as it was threatening to now.

Chase took a step forward. "Look," he said, leaning down so that our eyes were level. "We don't have to stay here. We can catch the next transport to the safe house. Put all this behind us." His voice was filled with hope.

"Not yet. You know that." We had to find Rebecca first; if I hadn't blackmailed her and Sean into helping me run away, they would still be together, and she wouldn't have been hurt. I could still hear the baton coming down on her back as the soldiers dragged her away.

"You guys go on. I'll catch up later." I cleared my throat. My walls were cracking. Chase sighed, and after Sean's prompting followed him down to breakfast.

Before the despair could take over, I fled down the corridor toward the supply room. It didn't matter if I skipped rations; the hollowness inside had nothing to do with hunger. It wasn't until the hallway was quiet that I remembered that Wallace had assigned Chase to clear the empty office building next door, that he was leaving the Wayland Inn without me. Even if he would be off the main streets, the thought of him out there alone made me sick.